RAMSEY CAMPBELL

THE WAY OF
THE WORM

The Third Book of the
Three Births of Daoloth Trilogy

This is a **FLAME TREE PRESS** book

FLAME TREE PRESS
6 Melbray Mews, London, SW6 3NS, UK
flametreepress.com

US sales, distribution and warehouse:
Simon & Schuster
simonandschuster.biz

UK distribution and warehouse:
Marston Book Services Ltd
marston.co.uk

Thanks to the Flame Tree Press team, including:
Taylor Bentley, Frances Bodiam, Federica Ciaravella, Don D'Auria,
Chris Herbert, Josie Karani, Mike Spender, Cat Taylor,
Maria Tissot, Nick Wells, Gillian Whitaker.

The cover is created by Flame Tree Studio with
thanks to Nik Keevil and Shutterstock.com.
The font families used are Avenir and Bembo.

Flame Tree Press is an imprint of Flame Tree Publishing Ltd

flametreepublishing.com

A copy of the CIP data for this book is available from the British Library
and the Library of Congress.

HB ISBN: 978-1-78758-568-3
US PB ISBN: 978-1-78758-566-9
UK PB ISBN: 978-1-78758-567-6
ebook ISBN: 978-1-78758-569-0

Printed and bound in Great Britain by Clays Ltd, Elcograf S.p.A

RAMSEY CAMPBELL

THE WAY OF
THE WORM

The Third Book of the
Three Births of Daoloth Trilogy

FLAME TREE PRESS
London & New York

for Ice
(Incheol Shin – 신인철)
and Gin –
(Jungjin Lee – 이정진)
our family encircles the world…

"What is humanity except an invocation? Man and his history shall invoke the powers beyond all space and time..."
Revelations of Glaaki, volume 7,
Of the Symbols the Universe Shows (Matterhorn Press, 1863?)

For months I would waken in the depths of the night to find myself back in the house where I'd spent my childhood. Sometimes I lay in the dark, smelling a stale redolence of age while I tried to hear what had robbed me of sleep. I might catch the sound of a car receding slowly as a hearse – police on the prowl if not a taxi searching for an address. There could be a murmur of voices, lowered as though out of respect and sinking into the dark, or shouts more feral than the dogs they roused, which carried on barking long after the culprits were gone. Often I would hear a nightbird and wonder if its song was meant to celebrate the night or fend it off. In time even birds hushed or flew beyond earshot, leaving the house as quiet as an absence of breath. Now I couldn't ignore how empty the bed felt, as extravagantly wide as it had seemed in my early childhood. But it wasn't that bed, and I wasn't in that house. The impression had been just a dream to which I'd clung so as to postpone the return of awareness, and the sour smell of age was all mine.

Sometimes I tried staying where I was. Even if I had no chance of recapturing the dream, perhaps exhaustion might lend me unconsciousness. This very seldom worked, since the empty space beside me felt as though it was gaping within me as well, in my guts and my mind. Before long it would send me out of the room, desperate for some activity that could distract me from my thoughts and from the implacable dark, which I fancied had dimmed all the lights in the house, unless my aching eyes had. Now and then I tried to read, but the words might as well have been in an unknown language, and lay lifeless on the pages of whichever book or magazine I picked up. Films didn't reach me either, though perhaps one reason why they seemed not just remote but muffled was that I kept the volume down for fear of waking neighbours. Besides, every disc I chose reminded me of Lesley: either she'd loved it or detested it or we'd never seen it together, and the idea of watching one that she wouldn't have wanted to see felt far worse than disloyal. Thoughts like these beset me if I tried listening to music, while the headphones made me feel even more enclosed in my skull. Once I sought company in an old photograph album, but I'd looked at just a double page of Lesley with our infant son before I had to shut the album tight and my eyes as well. I blinked them into focus when I'd finished rubbing them, and then I stumbled upstairs to get dressed. I was going for a walk or at any rate a limp, and trying not to feel driven out of the house.

As I lowered the latch of the gate with a shaky clatter I saw weeds among Lesley's flowers beside the path. The unsympathetic light of a streetlamp lay on the flowerbeds, an amber glare that put me in mind of a halfway state, as if the house and its garden were arrested between a dead stop and receiving a green signal to come to life. No doubt they felt this way because I did, trapped in a limbo of the mind.

The suburb was steeped in the light. It stained the broad white housefronts and lent houses of red brick a smouldering glow. It tinted white flowers orange in the front gardens and darkened all the colours of spring. Some of the streetlamps lit trees from beneath, transforming new leaves into paralysed flames. Even the shadows were tinged with the colour. The dilution made my shadow look less present than it should as it shrank back to me at each lamp, venturing forward again once the lamp was behind us. The sight left me feeling there was nowhere I wanted to be and yet desperate to be somewhere else.

Apart from my dull dogged footsteps, the suburb was as silent as a dream. Fog must have gathered on the river miles away, where I heard the lowing of a ship. A howling ambulance sped along the main road, and as the sound dwindled towards inaudibility a pair of cats set about performing a variation on the theme. I was trying to stay amused by the coincidence, despite immediately yearning to share it, when a house ahead flared white. An intruder had triggered a security light under the roof.

The cats weren't responsible. Their yodelling contest was well at my back. It rose to a confrontation and faded to a prolonged parting snarl as I approached the house. By the time I reached the spiky metal gate the night was still again. Or did I glimpse movement behind a car parked at the side of the house? Surely a trespasser had peered out at me before crouching further back.

I used both hands to lift the latch, muffling the hint of a squeak, and eased the gate open. I couldn't help welcoming the excuse to investigate – welcoming any distraction at all. I might almost have been representing the Tremendous Three, a thought that felt like wishing away too much of my life. As I took a step onto the drive the intruder darted out of hiding to scramble over the fence beside the house, but I couldn't identify it until I heard the dismal screech of a fox beyond the fence. The mystery was solved, and no longer any respite from my thoughts. I stepped back to close the gate and saw a police car creeping along the road.

I didn't immediately know how to react, and was afraid my hesitation looked suspicious. I made do with a vague wave as I shut the gate. I was continuing on my way, trying not to appear hasty or betray that I was trying, when the police car coasted to a halt beside me. "Are you lost, sir?" the driver said.

She and her colleague looked wiry enough to have trained in gyms, though perhaps their artificial tan came from the streetlamps. They were no older than my son, but I sensed both thin scrubbed faces had sternness at the ready if it was required in lieu of age. "Not at all," I said, though without risking a laugh. "I live round here."

"That's your house, is it, sir?"

"No, I'm up the road. Just being a good neighbour."

She glanced at the house, where every window was dark. "Rather late to be visiting."

"Not that kind of visit. I thought I heard somebody up to no good, but it was a fox. I expect you both heard it yourselves."

Now that I'd involved her companion he ducked his head to meet my eyes. "Can you tell us who lives there, sir?"

"I'm afraid I wouldn't know. As I say, I was passing and made a mistake." My head felt brittle, unequal to containing my emotions, and I was hardly aware of turning homewards. "I'm sure you can't think I'm a suspicious character," I said, "so if you'll excuse me I'll be off."

"Would you mind saying where you're going, sir?"

"Home. I've had my walk."

"That isn't the way you were going before," the driver said.

"Precisely. I'm going home now, having walked enough." I was afraid that saying the wrong words or even too many neutral ones would let my feelings spill forth. "Look, my name's Dominic Sheldrake," I said. "I taught at the university until I retired. You can certainly check if you want to. Now I'm just a pensioner out for a stroll."

"It's rather late for one of those." Her voice was hinting at sympathy, and I tried to fight off the effects by thinking she sounded too much like a worker in a care home. "I needed it, that's all," I said before I could prevent myself. "I thought it might help."

"Help with what, sir?" To confirm she meant it kindly she added "If you'd like to say."

"No." I was hoping terseness would head off any more words, but felt ashamed of my response. "Lost her," I mumbled, but holding my voice down didn't do the same for my emotions. "Lost my wife."

No doubt my indistinctness was why her colleague said "Did you say your wife is missing, Mr Sheldrake?"

"No, she's gone." In a final bid to rein my words in I said "Gone for good."

I held back from saying I hoped so. I couldn't have told them what I dreaded otherwise. After a brief respectful silence the driver said "Would you like us to take you home?"

While I supposed this was an act of kindness, perhaps it was a way of checking up on me as well. I felt too exhausted to argue, and only just managed to keep my thanks unemotional as I climbed into the back of the car. A combined smell of aftershave and air freshener caught in my throat like a sob. The car swung back and forth across the road, and I wondered if anyone had seen me carried off like a suspect if not a criminal. We were proceeding at the speed of a funeral procession when the driver found me in the mirror. "Have you any family, Mr Sheldrake?"

"Right here." The car halted at once, requiring me to say "No,

I mean turn right." Once she had she gazed at my reflection, and I found as few words as I could. "A son."

"Will he live with you?"

Was she enquiring or suggesting that he should? "He's married," I said, which apparently wasn't enough of an answer. "No," I should have said in the first place.

"He's there when you need him, though."

Since it was easiest to say yes, I did, and was able to remain silent except for directing her to turn left, not in so many words. I felt as if the amber glow of the streetlamps were more solid than light, slowing the car to a submarine pace. "Right," I said at last, only to have to clarify that we'd reached my house.

"Please see someone if you need to, Mr Sheldrake," the driver said, and I remembered Lesley's exhortation when I'd tried to persuade her of the truth about Safe To Sleep. The police car stayed at my gate until I let myself into the house. When I switched on the light in the hall it felt as dim as the gaps between the streetlamps. I sent the police away with a wave, and wondered if they thought they'd done me any good. In a sense they had. I shut the front door and tramped upstairs through the stagnant light for another dogged attempt to sleep. If I couldn't do that, and despite the dormant storm of my emotions – a cloudburst waiting for release – perhaps at least I could begin to think ahead. The driver had reminded me who I ought to see and what I should have done long since.

RECENTLY

CHAPTER ONE

Insufficient Words

"We could have spent all that time together."

"Say what happened, mum," Toby said like a youngster asking for a favourite tale.

"We said we'd see each other at the Shakespeare. They were putting on two weeks of plays, and that night it was *Macbeth*."

"Only they were showing films as well as putting plays on."

"Let me tell it, Dominic." When Lesley squeezed my hand I couldn't tell whether she meant to be gentle or was using all her strength. "So it was *Macbeth*," she said and closed her eyes as if she might be dreaming of the memory. "And I thought your father would have wanted me to see the film, so that's where I waited for him."

"And meanwhile dad was waiting at the theatre because he thought that was where you'd be."

I saw Lesley do her best to grip our son's hand, possibly to hush him. "Mobile phones weren't around then," she said, "and anyway we couldn't have afforded them. So we never met that evening. Sometimes I dream we did."

This made me realise "I've had a dream like that myself."

"I'm glad," Lesley said and clasped my hand a shade more firmly. "I hope it means we're there together."

Returning the pressure left me all the more aware how frail her hand was. Her high forehead bore a life's worth of lines, and her rounded face had grown thinner, while her generous lips appeared to feel their weight whenever she produced a smile. I couldn't avoid seeing how her eyes were faded, both their colour and the light in them. Somehow the childhood dent in her small slightly upturned nose reminded me most vividly of how she used to be, and my answer came out fierce to hide my feelings. "We're together now."

"I know, Dominic. All three of us."

I met our son's eyes across the hospital bed and saw acceptance. This was hardly the place to revive our differences, and I sent him a silent nod. I had to fend off the notion that by holding Lesley's hands we were keeping her from leaving us. However much the heart attack might have taken out of her, we'd been assured that she was stable after the operation. All at once she looked more concerned than I was trying not to look. "Macy hasn't seen me like this, has she?"

"Just Claudine has, mum. We didn't think they'd want young children in the ward."

"Tell Macy I'm getting better, won't you? And when I am, don't you think it would be lovely if we all went away together?"

"I'm sure it would. Aren't you, dad?"

Lesley gave my hand a determined squeeze. "When we're certain you're up to it, Lesley," I said.

Her eyes turned away to find Toby. "Do you remember the first time we took you abroad?"

"Disney World? Of course I do. The best ghost train ever and a whole lot more. I told them about it at school for weeks."

I wished I weren't reminded of other tales he'd told there. Lesley gave my hand a tug so faint it was close to imperceptible. "We'll forget what happened afterwards," she said.

I felt as though I'd spent decades in forgetting it and ignoring much more. Perhaps Lesley sensed my resistance, because she turned her gaze on me. "Just in case I'm not doing as well as we think, will you both make me a promise?"

"Don't say that kind of thing, Lesley. Don't think it either. It won't help you get better."

"You're saying you won't promise."

"No, I'm saying we know you'll be fine, because the surgeon told us."

Though her gaze didn't falter, her lips did, and I could only capitulate. "You haven't said what you want."

"Just be there for each other."

For a disoriented moment I imagined she was echoing the vow I'd shared with Jim and Bobby, but she couldn't know we had. "Of course we will," I said.

"You as well, mum."

"After I've gone, I mean."

"Like dad says, don't say that. It's like wishing yourself away, and you aren't going anywhere."

I wanted to believe he meant this as unambiguously as he should. I was striving to hide my thoughts when Lesley said "And please forget that old obsession of yours, Dominic."

"I think he's come to terms with it by now," Toby said.

I searched for a response I could safely make. "You could put it that way."

I was afraid Lesley might realise how devious this was — I could see Toby did — but she said "Just be the family we should have been."

"Then that has to include you as well," I said.

"It will if you promise."

"Then of course I will."

"And I do," Toby said.

Lesley gave our hands a final squeeze before resting hers together on the sheet, and I tried not to be reminded of the occasion of another promise — the last time I'd spoken to my father. Lesley closed her eyes, and I thought she'd fallen into a doze until she murmured "You never wrote a book, Dominic."

"Neither of us did. You should, and put in everything you used to tell your students."

Did she hear this? Her smile was so faint and fleeting that it could have been the product of a dream. I sat back from crouching towards the bed, and pain flared the length of my spine, impaling my hipbones as well. It had for years whenever I couldn't avoid sitting forward, and I could only walk it off. "I'm going to have to move," I said through my teeth before I managed to relax my jaw. "Won't be long."

Lesley gave no sign of having heard. "We'll be here," Toby said.

I supposed he had his wife in mind. I hobbled painfully into the corridor to find her reading Roberta Parkin's book *The Jargon of Concern*. In it Bobby argued that the fashion for defining vulnerability often worsened the conditions and created too many of them. I couldn't help recalling that Claudine had met my friend at Safe To Sleep when I'd sent Bobby to investigate, and her having Bobby's book seemed indefinably ominous. "How is that, Claudine?" I said.

"She knows people." As Claudine raised her small face her habitual look of deceptively languid alertness gave way to sympathy. "How's Lesley?" she said.

"I think she may be sleeping. Go in by all means. I'll be a few minutes."

A passing male nurse gave her slim long-legged figure an appreciative glance and then another. She made me feel like a decrepit soft toy stuffed too full, not to mention leached of colour and supplied with spots to compensate. My lopsided hobbling took me to Men, where the water from the tap proved to be as hot as a notice warned, after which a ferocious hand dryer crumpled my skin. Moments later my hands grew as sweaty as the rest of me. The hospital felt oppressively concerned to fend off a winter chill, and I limped to the entrance in search of relief.

I had to go a good deal further for fresh air. An ambulance was reciting its movements as it backed towards the hospital, emitting a sharp smell of diesel. Patients with cigarettes clustered near a drain so that they could drop butts through the grid, while other smokers flourished metal substitutes. A prodigious pink-faced man in a frayed white bathrobe barely large enough for him stood eating curried chips with a plywood fork out of a plastic carton, a meal his partner – a dumpy morose woman in a pink track suit – had presumably brought him. As I moved away from the invasive smell the ambulance fell silent, isolating the voice of a woman with her back to me at one corner of the hospital.

Nobody was near her except a girl well short of teenage. Given the woman's angular gestures and many of her words, I took her to be suffering from Tourette's. I was about to retreat when the girl stared at me, and the woman swung around, revealing that she was on a phone. Her broad flattish face was highlighted with makeup, which emphasised her scowl. "What the fuck you looking at?" she demanded.

"I've no idea. Why don't you tell me?" Rather than this I said "I couldn't say."

I should have left it there, but my saddened gaze lingered. "Fucking what?" she cried.

"You might like to restrain your language when a child can hear."

"Don't you fucking tell me how to talk in front of my own fucking kid. What are you creeping round here for?"

"My wife's in hospital."

"Hope they treat her better than my dad." I mistook this for sympathy until her rage became plain. "The cunts are doing fucking shit for him."

As I grasped she'd been saying as much on her phone, my heart jerked, or something near it did. I was afraid I might be having an attack, if nowhere near as serious as Lesley's, until I realised what I'd felt. I snatched out my own mobile to see I'd inadvertently muted the sound. A message from Toby said **Come back**.

I stumbled as I ran or at any rate limped as fast as I could to the entrance. I had to dodge around several paramedics and their patients waiting on trolleys on my way to the ward. More than one of the hospital staff outdistanced me in the corridor, and in a sudden acute hope of seeing them pass Lesley's ward I managed to put on more ungainly speed. I was in time to watch them disappear into the ward. More ominously still, my son and his wife were outside. "What's—" I croaked and had to clear my throat to revive my withered voice. "What's happened?" I said too loud.

Toby looked as if he thought I might blame him and Claudine, and I was dismayed to wonder what they could have said to Lesley in my absence. Their silence alarmed me even once I realised they were waiting for me to come close enough to let them keep their voices low. "It wasn't long after you went out," Toby said. "She had a pain."

"What kind of pain?" When neither of them answered I said so urgently that it left my throat raw "What did she say?"

I saw Claudine willing Toby to respond. With visible reluctance he said "She couldn't speak."

I lurched past him, but he closed a hand around my arm. "Dad, they said we're to stay outside till someone comes."

More like a child than I wanted to sound I protested "Did they say me?"

"They meant any visitors, Dominic. Our whole family, that is."

No doubt Claudine wanted her second comment to placate me, but I couldn't welcome it just now. I stared at the doors of the ward in the hope they would open to show I'd no need to experience the panic that was turning my hands clammy and speeding up my heart until it ached while my cranium seemed to grow as fragile as a shell. Too much time crawled by before I turned away in case willing the wait to be over was prolonging it somehow – my perception of it, at any rate. I felt isolated and afraid, and meeting my son's eyes offered no reassurance. I saw he was keeping some thought to himself, and I suspected Claudine shared it, especially when she said "Dominic, I'm sure it won't be—"

"We don't know if it's the end or not," I said so as to cut her off. "I just hope we all mean the same thing."

I felt ashamed at once, not so much of my outburst as of having flinched from being too precise, but this wasn't the occasion to attack their faith, however much it disturbed me. I didn't realise anyone had come out of the ward until a man said "Mr Sheldrake."

"Yes."

It was Toby who answered before I swung around. "I believe he means me," I said.

"She's mine as well."

I wanted to believe that Toby just meant Lesley was his mother – that he had no more than that in mind, let alone worse. I could only appeal to the plump ruddy doctor who might have been advertising health if not the sort of shape that undermined it. "Who are you looking for?"

"Mr Sheldrake?" Since we hadn't previously met, he seemed anxious for the confirmation. When I nodded he said more quietly still "I'm sorry, Mr Sheldrake."

"For what?"

"I don't know if you should have left when you did. I'm afraid your wife suffered a relapse."

The staff who'd passed me in the corridor were emerging very quietly from the ward. I hadn't time to decide whether the doctor was expressing regret at my absence or convicting me of thoughtlessness. "How bad?" I pleaded.

"Mr Sheldrake, your wife is no longer in distress."

"You're telling me she'll recover." Now I couldn't mistake his regret, and despite the relentless heat I began to shiver. "No," I found it necessary to say out loud, "you're saying she never will."

"Please be aware the end was peaceful."

I fought to keep my voice steady, because if I lost control of it the rest of me felt poised to follow. "Did she say anything?"

"She was beyond that, Mr Sheldrake."

Before my words could grow unsafe to pronounce I said "Can I go to her?"

The doctor stood aside and motioned me into the ward without speaking. When Toby made to follow, Claudine took his arm to detain him. A screen concealed Lesley's bed, and nobody was talking in the ward; I couldn't even hear any breaths apart from my own uneven attempts. As I paced between the beds, feeling as if I were venturing into a funeral home, a nurse beckoned to me and wheeled back a corner of the screen. He closed me in as soon as I reached the bed.

Lesley was lying on her back. Her eyes were shut, her hands were clasped together on her breast, and I felt as if the last time I'd seen her in that position had been an omen I'd failed to read. I laid a hand on hers, only to find they were already colder than the hospital. Lines had been subtracted from her forehead, and her face looked as calm as a dreamless sleep. When I kissed her brow it felt as empty as I did. "Be somewhere beautiful," I whispered for only her to hear, if anybody heard at all.

CHAPTER TWO

Ready or Not

Lesley used to believe that great art could help prepare you for the loss of the people you loved. When her parents died within months of each other she found solace in the requiems of Fauré and Duruflé, both of which she thought epitomised peace without end. For her Nicolay Levin's protracted deathbed scenes in *Anna Karenina* were among the most truthful passages in literature, not least in conveying how long death could take to reach its end. In my case some films had conveyed that experience – *La Gueule Ouverte* did, for instance – while others touched me with the grief of loss: *Pather Panchali, Tokyo Story, Letter from an Unknown Woman.* Yet none of this equipped me for losing the person with whom I'd chosen to spend my life. Not even the deaths of my parents had.

By the morning of Lesley's funeral I felt drained of tears and sleep, not much more than a walking husk of myself. Even the shower I took, having managed to rouse myself from reliving memories that led inexorably to regrets, seemed muted and remote, not quite able to engage my senses. My thoughts were so sluggish, unless they were painfully guarded, that I set about selecting a sombre outfit from my wardrobe before I recalled that Lesley hadn't wanted anyone to dress that way at her funeral – that she'd told me and Toby years ago to make it colourful. At least I'd remembered to advise all the mourners, but now I found that since she wouldn't see the result, acceding to her wishes only underlined her absence.

As I tried to choose clothes that wouldn't make me feel offensively flamboyant, the doorbell rang. A pain like an omen of worse stabbed my heart while I stumbled to the window. I peered around the curtain to see my son and his wife on the garden path. Having fumbled my keys out of the heap of yesterday's and indeed several days' clothes on the floor next to the dressing-table faintly redolent of cosmetics – I kept thinking the array of jars and jewellery made it look like a memorial to Lesley – I rubbed my eyes with the back of a hand before opening the window. "Someone catch the keys," I called.

Toby did with a deftness that made me feel clumsy with age. "Shall I make everyone breakfast?" Claudine said. "We waited in case."

She sounded as bright as her outfit and Toby's, and I had to tell myself that they were making the effort Lesley had requested – that they and their beliefs weren't dismissing her death. "You may not find much," I said. "Use whatever you like."

By the time I decided on clothes I didn't think too garish or too contrary to Lesley's wishes, Toby and Claudine had laid out breakfast – toast, scrambled eggs, coffee, orange juice. I did my best to appreciate the gesture rather than see it as a substitute for how Lesley and I used to make it for each other. Toby gave me a prolonged hug, and Claudine's came with a dry kiss. "We'll be with you now, dad," Toby said.

"As much and as long as you want," Claudine said.

I had no idea how much that was or even any means of knowing. "Thank you both," I said and transferred a sample of breakfast to my plate before either of them could undertake to load it on my behalf. "I'm fine," I said when I was offered more, having succeeded in clearing the plate despite scarcely tasting the food my dogged jaws worked on. "That's it for me just now."

"Maybe you'll be hungry later," Toby said. "We'll see you through the day. Whatever you need, we'll be close."

"And then you can start to let go, Dominic."

Although Claudine's mother Judith had died last year, I found the advice at the very least presumptuous. Toby gave a supportive nod, and the unspecific emphasis was more than I could stand. "You'll be doing that, will you? You'll be letting Lesley go."

"That's part of what today's for, dad."

"I know all about today." This made me realise that I knew considerably less, and it dismayed me to hear myself blurt "You won't be using her for whatever you get up to now."

"We've gone beyond that, Dominic," Claudine said. "We only use ourselves."

I had an appalled notion that she fancied I would find this comforting. "Will you both promise you'll never try to bring her back?" I said as though she hadn't spoken.

"There's no need." When I stared at this Toby added "We promise."

"We do," Claudine said.

I might have ended the discussion out of respect for Lesley's memory, but her death had given me the chance if not the responsibility to ask questions I'd avoided voicing while she was alive. "Just what do you do at this church of yours?"

"It isn't really what you'd call a church, dad. It's more a place for meditation."

"Then why is it called the Church of the Eternal Three?"

"That started in America," Claudine said. "Churches don't pay tax."

"What sort of meditation are we talking about? What is it meant to achieve?"

She glanced at Toby, and I saw them share an understanding. Toby parted his lips, but he hadn't spoken when Claudine said "Here's someone else."

I wondered if she was anxious to interrupt, having had second thoughts about letting me into a secret, until I heard footsteps on the front path. When the doorbell rang, so tersely it sounded imperious or else apologetic, Toby said "I'll see who it is, dad."

"I'll go," I said, standing up so fast I had to grab the table for support. "You two clear up."

In the hall I passed the vase Lesley used to replenish with flowers from the garden. I'd put in fresh ones yesterday – the contents had withered days ago – but now the sight recalled a floral tribute. Answering the doorbell was no distraction from my thoughts after all. I blinked my eyes clear as I opened the door and saw Bobby and Jim.

They'd grown even greyer than me. Jim had developed a stoop that brought his head nearly level with mine, while age had pared down Bobby's face, rendering her chin more indomitable still. I couldn't help regretting that whoever had rung the bell hadn't used our old code – two longish bursts – but perhaps they were afraid of sounding disrespectful, if the code had even occurred to them. Bobby gave me a hug so fierce I almost couldn't feel how thin her arms were. "Dom," she said.

Jim embraced me for the first time in his life. "I'm sorry it's been so long, Dom."

"I'm sorry it had to be now," Bobby said. "I only wish I'd met your wife."

"You'd have liked her," Jim said.

Both of them immediately looked worried that they'd said too much, but I was reminded how seldom the Baileys had met my wife. She'd never had them round for dinner, perhaps because Jim reminded her too much of Safe To Sleep. As I shut the door Claudine looked out of the kitchen. "We'll be with you in a minute. Would anybody like a drink?"

I tried not to feel she meant in any way to occupy the house. Nobody took up her offer, and we trooped into the front room, where I found it indefinably disconcerting to see Bobby sit in my wife's favourite armchair. She and Jim were sharing a wistful silence with me when Toby and Claudine joined us, and I made the introductions. "We've been reading your books," Claudine told Bobby. "We thought you saw things pretty clear."

As I wondered if she and my son recalled meeting Bobby at Safe To Sleep, Toby said to Jim "You were the policeman. Assistant chief con."

"I was till I retired." With a hint of an official tone Jim said "I haven't retired from upholding the law."

"You're another kind of lawman now, you mean."

"I could be if it's called for. So what do you do with your life?"

"We're in research, both of us. Human behaviour and the patterns people act out." With a smile too faint for interpretation Toby said "It's some fun."

"It's as your books say, Roberta," Claudine said. "People are compelled to do things because they can't stand back far enough to see them clear. Nearly everyone's incapable of seeing deep into themselves."

"I don't think I ever quite wrote that," Bobby said.

I saw Jim decide he should speak. "Are you saying you're different from nearly everyone, Claudine?"

"I was saying Roberta might be."

"Call me Bob. No, call me Bobby. These two always have, and Toby can as well." After a pause that suggested she might have liked to stop there Bobby said "What are you saying makes me different?"

"We believe you've made a start," Toby said.

I couldn't stay quiet any longer. "You're talking about when you first met."

"When and where." With a look that scarcely bothered to be challenging Toby said "Safe To Sleep."

"That's all past now," Bobby said, glancing at Jim and me as if she was glad of our presence. "It was a long time ago."

"Less than half a lifetime," Toby said. "Most of mine and Claudine's. Not too long at all."

I felt provoked to retort on Bobby's behalf and my own. "Safe To Sleep may have gone, but do we really think its effects have?"

Nearly everyone seemed to have some reason not to answer. "Are you thinking of anything in particular?" Jim said.

"What do you know about the Church of the Eternal Three?"

"It's another of these operations that have come over from the States. Don't they claim they can put you in touch with your past? Maybe they're taking people for a ride, but I shouldn't think they can be hiding much when they've got celebrities and politicians saying they belong. Or are you saying there's more to it, Dom?"

"Doesn't the name sound a bit too familiar?"

"You mean that place where we all played detectives, the Trinity Church." Before I could protest at his dismissiveness, Jim said "There are real churches with that kind of name as well, you know. I don't suppose for a moment this is one, but a name isn't evidence of anything."

I could have reminded him how the Nobles had played with their names, but Bobby said "Are you sure you want us to talk about this just now, Dom?"

"It's occupying my mind." A surge of grief left me desperate to keep on. "They're all connected," I declared. "Noble's church and Safe To Sleep and now this church."

Jim and Bobby gave me a look altogether too reminiscent of the kind I might have had from Lesley, while my son and his wife withheld their expressions, unless I glimpsed a hint of a secret smile. "Is there any evidence of that?" Jim said.

"Toby can tell us, can't you, Toby? And Claudine can. They're both in the church."

"Not sure what you want us to say, dad."

"For a start, are there any other people in it who were at Safe To Sleep?"

"Nearly all of us."

He and Claudine looked surprised that I'd taken so long to enquire, and I knew I'd kept quiet for the sake of my marriage. "Would that include Toph Noble?"

"There's nobody called that there, dad."

"You know who I mean. Christopher Noble."

"Not that either," Claudine said.

"Bloan. Of course, yes, Bloan."

"No," Toby and Claudine said in chorus.

I was taking a fierce breath while I thought what to ask next when Bobby said "Dom, don't upset yourself."

"I'll be upset," I said wildly, "if I don't find out what I want to know."

"Then let me try," Jim said, turning to Toby and Claudine. "What exactly goes on at your, let's call it a church?"

"We were telling Dominic when you arrived. We meditate."

"On what? For what?"

"It shows you everything within yourself," Toby said.

"If that's all it doesn't sound so bad, Dom."

"Of course it isn't all." I didn't know if Jim had abandoned his investigative skills since his retirement or was trying to avoid conflict because of the occasion. "What has that to do with the Eternal Three?" I demanded. "What is that supposed to mean?"

"I can tell you." To my dismay, it was Bobby who responded.

"Someone from their London chapel was on the radio when they were discussing new religions. She was saying the Eternal Three are the past and the present and the future."

"They're within us all," Claudine said. "What has been and what shall be."

"That's what you meditate about, is it?" I persisted as if this might drive the truth out of hiding. "That's all you do."

"What's to come has always been," Toby said.

To me this sounded like a ritual response, but I saw Jim and Bobby take it to confirm my words. I was searching for questions that wouldn't embarrass my friends any further when Jim left the subject behind. "Dom says your daughter's a real delight."

"She's at school today," Claudine said.

"I know I went to grandad's funeral when I was her age, dad," Toby said. "I hope you aren't upset because she won't be with us."

"We couldn't be sure what will be said at the funeral," Claudine said, "and we'd rather her beliefs weren't confused."

This provoked another question I'd suppressed far too long. "Does Macy go to your church?"

"Of course she does, Dominic. Why would we keep her away?"

"And joins in the meditation?"

"All the children do. I'm sure people who belong to what Jim calls real churches make their children worship."

"Laura and I showed ours the right way," Jim said with some force. "We'd be failures as parents if we'd done less."

"If your church is so legitimate," I said to Toby and Claudine, "how is it I didn't know Macy was involved?"

"Dominic, you never asked."

"Dad, mum knew and she didn't have a problem."

This felt as if I'd lost her even more completely than I feared – as if I'd been robbed of an aspect of her I thought I could trust. "Nobody told me," I muttered and heard how pathetic I sounded.

"Maybe she thought you'd make an issue out of it," Claudine said, "the way you did over Safe To Sleep."

I looked at Jim and Bobby for support, but they didn't look at me. Even if they wanted to avoid further argument, I felt they'd let me down. I was trying to think how to continue, not least because in several ways I felt utterly alone, when Toby stood up. "I think mum's here."

I could easily have feared he was saying Lesley had returned in the sense the Nobles would have meant it, but two long black cars were outside, and the foremost contained a large white box. I'd already seen it unlidded – I'd seen the work of art into which my wife had been transformed, a perfect waxwork so cold and unresponsive that leaving a kiss on its forehead felt like mouthing at emptiness rendered solid – but its arrival brought home how much awareness I was trying to fend off. Panic at the prospect of the day and of the life to follow seized me somewhere in the guts, and I fled to the bathroom.

I didn't throw up despite feeling close to it. I drained myself as best I could, a prolonged and intermittent process, and stumbled downstairs to find everyone bereft of conversation in the hall. The front door was open, admitting an insistent chill. Drops of melted frost glittered on Lesley's flowers beside the path, and some of the tiny globes enshrined rainbows. I tried to imagine they were signs from Lesley rather than think they were among the countless experiences I wouldn't share with her. I almost forgot to turn the key in the mortise lock before setting off along the frosty path.

The limousine held a discreet scent of flowers or air freshener, which caught in my throat like grief. Once Toby had joined me and Claudine on the back seat, the small procession moved off with Bobby's Golf at the rear. Stretches of the roads were black with ice, and despite the measured pace of the little parade I thought the wheels came near to skidding more than once. Most of the traffic on the main road stayed behind us out of respect or so as not to take a risk, but the occasional impatient driver overtook all three vehicles, veering dangerously close to the elongated grove of trees that divided the wide road. Some pedestrians stood still while we passed, and an old man with a stick reached up to lift a hat he wasn't wearing, but most of the folk on the pavements were too intent on their phones to notice the procession. I reflected that the man with the stick might have been no more than my age, and that Lesley never would be. I had to take a deep breath, struggling to hold it steady and silent, as the hearse led the way through the gates of the crematorium.

Outside the chapel groups of mourners – friends of Lesley's, colleagues from her tenure, students she'd taught – turned to face us. The limousine driver opened the door as another of the undertaker's men raised the hatchback of the hearse. I was hauling myself out of the limousine when the celebrant came over – Dophie Lembert, a slim coppery young woman whose loose multicoloured headscarf could have gone with a variety of occasions and beliefs. I thought she meant to offer motivation of the kind she'd lent me last time we'd met, but she murmured "The crematorium has asked me to apologise. The heating's broken down."

I strove not to acknowledge how this sounded like a grisly joke, and still felt obliged to say "You don't mean the, the mechanics of the place."

"Just the heating for yourselves and the other service users, Mr Sheldrake."

I heard shuffling footsteps and equally muffled conversations on the far side of the chapel. The previous funeral was over, and it was time for me to perform the task I ached to do justice as much as I dreaded it. Two undertaker's men eased out the coffin, which looked white as an absence, not just of colour. They waited for me to grasp the left front handle while Toby took the opposite, and the four of us lifted the coffin together. I felt no less dismayed by how relatively easy this was than I would have been if I'd proved unequal to the effort. As we fell into a tortoise's march towards the chapel I noticed frost on the path and grew terrified of stumbling. I had to refrain from hitching up the casket on my shoulder in case that might aid my balance.

More slowed-down hobbled paces than I cared to count took us to the chapel, by which time the edge of the casket was digging into my shoulder. Half the pews were occupied by mourners, who rose to their feet in rather less than unison as we plodded down the aisle. Dwarfish speakers high on the walls were murmuring the adagio from Schubert's string quintet, which Lesley used to find one of the most consoling passages in music. Just now it threatened to blur my vision, and failed to ease the weight on my aching shoulder. I felt the gazes of the congregation gather on my back like a threat that everyone was about to watch me buckle under my burden, or rather the quarter that I presumed to be able to manage. I kept glimpsing my pale breaths, which made me feel as if shivering might rob me of control. I had the awful notion that the only way I would be able not to drop the coffin was to put on speed – to trot or, worse still, run past the front pews and the deserted lectern to dump the casket on a stand in the middle of a stage flanked by curtains, and I would have to trust my fellow bearers to keep up. No, they were dragging me back, and so was my sense of how shameful the spectacle would be. I clutched at the handle with both hands as best I could and trudged onwards, clenching my teeth until I felt a creak. Now I was past the front pews and Claudine's encouraging gaze, and then the lectern was behind, and as my arms began to throb with as much pain as my shoulder I managed to join in lowering the coffin onto the stand. "I did it for you, Lesley," I whispered almost too low to hear myself, and tried not to massage my shoulder as I made for my place.

Claudine gave it a rub as I sidled along the pew. Her hand was soft but firm, and I lingered until the ache grew dull. As it shrank to a blunt pang I couldn't help feeling that Claudine had erased a trace of Lesley, however painful. Dophie Lembert had moved to the lectern, and once I took my seat she spoke. "We are here today to honour Lesley Sheldrake, wife and teacher and good friend," she said as though she might be claiming one of those relationships. "Nobody's life can be summed up in just the few minutes we have, and I know you'll all have memories I hope you'll share when we gather afterwards, but I think these occasions can be like a poem, distilling the essence of a life…"

Her summary was deft and true enough – she'd obtained the details from Toby and me – and felt almost unbearably prolonged yet far too brief, since it was the prelude to my own oration. I barely took in her words for mutely rehearsing my own, and didn't realise she'd finished until I heard my name. Lesley's husband Dominic of many years wobbled to his feet and had to shrug off a resurrected ache while limping to the lectern. When I saw members of the congregation willing me not to break down in front of them, I almost did. I'd practiced my speech for days, persisting doggedly even when my tears grew indistinguishable from the downpour of the bathroom shower, until I hoped I'd exhausted the physical signs of my grief. Of course I hadn't – that reservoir seemed bottomless – and I found myself remembering how Lesley had brought about her end by scrambling up a stationary escalator from the underground station at Lime Street in the rush hour.

We could have used the lift if she hadn't insisted on leaving it for the disabled, and she was as resolved not to hinder anybody on the escalator as the crowd was determined not to be delayed. "I'll be all right," she'd told me before I realised she mightn't be. "Let me get out of everyone's way," she'd gasped as she dragged herself upwards, and I'd seen how the hand that wasn't clutching at her chest was digging its nails into the rubber banister. When I'd clambered up beside her to support her, someone had tried to shove past, and I'd come close to delivering a vicious backwards kick. "Hold on, this lady's ill," I'd cried, making Lesley protest "Just get me to the top, Dominic." Even once we'd struggled to the summit, where she leaned against the white-tiled wall and then sagged into a sitting position, the crowd flooded onwards without hesitating, and more than one commuter stepped over her legs. Perhaps people took her for yet another beggar, but it felt as if the future was streaming onwards without us. Eventually a member of the station staff approached to offer help, by which time I was already phoning for an ambulance.

"I think that's all I can say for now," I said, having described none of this, and stepped back from the lectern. I had a sense that the self who'd enunciated memories had been speaking at some distance from me while I relived the endless minutes at the station. Perhaps that had been the only way I could cope with speaking. As I returned to the pew Toby clasped my arm, whether supporting me or in appreciation I couldn't tell, and then Claudine did. "Thank you for gifting us that, Dominic," Dophie Lembert said from beside the lectern, "and now Toby Sheldrake has words for us."

As Toby left the pew a shiver caught up with me, and I saw my breath. I would never see Lesley's again or feel it on my skin or hear it beside me in bed, and I tried to ignore the sight by watching my son step up to the lectern. "I've got too much to say," he said.

He told us how his mother had been someone he could always confide in. "And dad was," he added, gazing over my head. She'd given up years of her career to look after him at the start of his life, and I saw him share a silent thought with Claudine that I couldn't interpret. If there was a disagreement his mother had always resolved it, and he hoped I didn't mind if he said she'd held the family together. He would always remember how childlike with wonder she'd grown when we'd all spent a week at the theme parks in Orlando – "you'd have thought she was younger than me." He recalled how proud she'd been at his graduation, as if she was responsible for it – "and the way she brought me up was, her and dad." I shivered several times in the course of his tribute, a reaction that kept other feelings at bay until he said "She liked me to read to her when I was little. I remember reading *Peter Pan* to her and Peter saying if he ever went ahead it would be an awfully big adventure. I hope she's having one right now."

I remembered the copy of the book Jim and I had found in the room next to Phoebe Sweet's office at Safe To Sleep – the images of airborne children with their eyes enlarged and filled in with a void. As Toby came back to the pew, Dophie Lembert returned to the lectern. "Thank you for adding to our picture of your mother, Toby," she said, "and now let's all stand for one of her favourite songs."

It was *All Together Now*, a Beatles singalong, which Lesley had said more than once she would like at her funeral. I'd thought she'd chosen it because it was a cheery ditty with which people could join in, as the congregation gradually did, but now I kept hearing three words as if another voice were singing them, like a message she'd left for me: "I love you." I managed to steady my own voice by not much less than roaring the phrase and then the rest of the song. Once everyone was seated again Dophie Lembert said "And now we have a reading that I believe meant a lot to Mrs Sheldrake."

It was from Henry Scott-Holland's celebrated sermon, the thoughts of a professor of divinity at Oxford, not to mention Canon of Christchurch.

"Death is nothing at all…" Lesley had liked the vision of the afterlife, the idea that it resembled entering another room. "Call me by the old familiar name," and I almost did under my breath. "Life means all that it ever meant," and I caught a glance that Toby and Claudine sent each other, which they repeated when we heard "There is absolute and unbroken continuity." I hoped this signified the same to them as I would have liked to be true, along with "I am but waiting for you somewhere near, just around the corner." Surely Toby and his wife could never think of Lesley in the way the Nobles would.

"Now we'll take a few minutes to reflect on the lives we each shared with Lesley Sheldrake," Dophie Lembert announced, bowing her head in a gesture to fit most beliefs. I lowered mine, only to discover that when I searched for Lesley in my mind I couldn't immediately see her. The best I could summon up was a sketchy image of her at an indeterminate age, and I hadn't managed to restore it to any kind of life by the time Dophie Lembert spoke again. "Now if we can all please stand…"

As I wavered to my feet the curtains set about creeping together across the stage. They might have been ending a show more austere than Lesley and I had ever seen in the theatre. To compensate we heard her final choice of music, Sousa's *Liberty Bell* march. She meant it to send everyone out with a smile, but it reminded me how I'd never told her about Monty Bison. I wanted to believe that in some way she knew about the misunderstanding now – that she would know about everything that might still happen in my life.

The march saw everyone to the side door, beyond which I had to wait with Toby to accept the ritual parade of condolences. Hugs and handshakes quickly grew familiar, and quite a few phrases did. At least this helped prevent the sympathy from stealing my control. When a one-time lecturer's moist infirm handshake finally ended the rite, I limped to the limousine, where the wipers gave a solitary muted screech as they scraped frost from the windscreen. "You both did well," Claudine said as Toby sat beside her, and I thought she sounded as if she was talking about an occasion far less distressing than I for one had had to face.

The car took us at a discreet speed to the Chimneys, a pub so close to the crematorium that Lesley and I used to think the name was a macabre joke. The large barroom was portly with upholstery on booths and chairs, all printed with autumnal foliage. While the buffet in a side room looked tempting, I didn't feel enticed to much. I sat in a booth with Toby and Claudine and Bobby and Jim, and was glad that nobody approached except to take their leave. Though I didn't want to drink too much, too little seemed equally unwise. I'd seen off most of a bottle of claret, which none of my companions would let me pay for, by the time everyone but them had bid farewell. "I'd better be heading for my train," Bobby said. "I can drop you off on the way, Jim."

Jim was lingering over shaking my hand when she grasped both of us by an arm. "Just remember what we used to say, the three of us."

"I do," Jim said, and I told them "I always have."

Claudine seemed eager to learn the secret but didn't speak. As my friends made for the door Toby said "Dad, will you let us do something for you?"

"You've done plenty. You both have."

"Then let us do what you need now. Not necessarily just yet, not till you feel you're ready, but will you come to meditation with us?"

Claudine abandoned her unasked question. "It helped me when mum died last year."

"We'll see," I said, which left me with an absurdly inappropriate sense of equivocating over a treat children were wishing for. Perhaps Toby and Claudine viewed it as some kind of treat for me. I didn't want to ask what kind just now, especially when I seemed to glimpse an unreadable thought in his eyes and hers. I would have liked Bobby and Jim to be there to hear, and wondered if my son and his wife had delayed the proposal until we were alone. "We won't talk about it any more now," I said, and although the room was close to overheated, I had to fight off a shiver.

CHAPTER THREE

Stepping Back

After the police brought me home I sat in the garden behind the dark house to await the dawn. In Lesley's last years we'd often dined out here, not least in spring and autumn as the climate changed. Now the picnic table gave me an uninterrupted view all the way across the deserted lawn to the empty house, but I was most aware of the space on the bench that faced me – the aching absence that seemed airless, robbed of breath. All around me the night felt forsaken by my wife: the faint nocturnal scent of flowers, a hint of rising daylight in a gap between two houses, the gathering clamour of birds in the trees, the screech of a fox, more distant than ever. I was desperate to believe that Lesley could somehow share these experiences, but couldn't I content myself with knowing she was present in a sense? I'd scattered her ashes over the lawn and on the flowerbeds as she'd wished, and if I gazed at them I could fancy that the grass and the somnolent blossoms were sending me a gentle secret glow. Perhaps in time this would feel like a token of peace, but for the moment it was more important to remember what the policewoman had reminded me I ought to do. Now that Lesley had gone, there was nothing to hold me back from investigating the new church.

I mustn't blame her. Thoughts of Toph Noble had inhibited me too – of the threat he'd left after stealing me out of my body and transporting me to the site of Safe To Sleep, to the depths of the land infested by the visitor the Nobles had inadvertently attracted to the world. "You're ours when we want…" His grandfather and mother were daunting enough, but the thought of being at the mercy of such an unnatural child seemed more fearful still. For years after that night, whenever I'd wakened in bed I'd felt insufficiently contained, in danger of straying helplessly into the dark, drawn out of my body on a vindictive childish whim. Far too belatedly I concluded that he'd simply lost interest in me; after all, the Nobles thought few people were significant besides themselves. Might I attract their attention again if I looked into the church that seemed to be related to Safe To Sleep? That mustn't matter now that I had nothing to lose, and I'd promised Lesley that I would look after our son.

The entire gap between the houses was touched by light now, and I made the mistake of glancing up at the sky. Night still massed overhead. A few stars relieved the vast blackness, and then more pinpoints began to glimmer across increasingly unimaginable distances of space and time. I couldn't look away while I recalled the voyage I'd taken from Safe To Sleep, past galaxies so remote from the earth that my mind shrank from grasping the kind of life that inhabited the abyss between the stars – the colossal gelatinous globe swarming with eyes and mouths, hungry to drain stars that it left dead and blackened. I felt too close to reliving the expedition, a dread I often felt on seeing the night sky. I clutched at the table to drag my attention back to earth, and then I shoved myself to my feet and stumbled across the cold moist lawn into the house.

It was too early to phone my son. I made myself coffee and drank it down, ignoring a faint sour taste like a tang of neglect and age. Lesley had drunk more milk than I did, and since I'd halved the delivery it tended to start turning before I'd emptied the bottle. I spent time distributing my daily medication among the compartments of my pill organiser, and once I'd downed the morning's five varieties I headed for the bathroom. The speckled shaving mirror magnified my face, as if it weren't already sufficiently mottled and swollen. I had to concentrate to judge how hot the shower was, having chilled and then nearly scalded myself. Once I was dressed I plodded downstairs to watch the latest news: wars, terrorism, lunatics in power, the disintegration of Europe, the depletion of a world well on the way to reverting or otherwise approaching some primitive state… Why did this make my task feel more urgent? I switched off the television and fumbled for my phone to bring up Toby's number.

"Dad."

I gathered this was an announcement as well as a greeting when Claudine said "Love."

"Claude sends her love, dad. Wait, I'll put us on speaker," he said, and then "We haven't seen you yet this week."

"You did on Sunday. Most people would say Sunday starts the week."

"Because it's meant to bring the sun up," Claudine said, "even if they don't know that's what they're thinking. That's how nearly everybody works."

"The old beliefs are always there," Toby said, "and now they're rising up."

Before I could comment Claudine said "What did you want to say, Macy?"

"I wanted to give grandad my love as well."

"And you've got mine, Macy." I was relieved she hadn't joined in the discussion, but how careful would I need to be while she could hear? "Toby," I said, "I was calling about your offer."

I was aware how grotesquely impersonal this sounded, and Toby seemed bemused. "Which was that, dad?"

"Meditation."

"Do you mean you'd like to try?"

"You were both saying I should."

"That's good. It's better than. We're very glad you'll be with us at last. When would you like to start?"

Now that I'd made the move I felt anxious to leave my nervousness behind. "As soon as it's convenient," I said.

"We're here whenever you need us."

I might have taken this to signify no more than willingness, but I couldn't help asking "Where?"

"Starview Tower."

Toby made it sound as if I should have known, and perhaps I secretly had. So they were in the building that housed the Church of the Eternal Three, and their little daughter was. "You aren't there all the time," I hoped aloud.

"Most of it."

"You manage to do all your research from there."

"Easily," Claudine said. "Online."

I envisioned her and Toby looking down on the world from the skyscraper, and it was partly to dislodge the image that I said "Could I come to you today?"

"We're as eager as you are. As soon as you possibly can."

I wasn't quite that eager. "Can you give me an idea what's involved?"

"You are, dad. The whole of you will be."

"All the secrets deep inside you."

I hardly grasped the answers, because the last one dismayed me – not the words but the fact that they came from Macy. "And who'll be doing whatever you do?" I had to learn.

"Just us," Toby said.

I was distressed by needing to establish "Just you and Claudine."

"If you like. Will you be driving?"

"I still can, yes. I haven't lost the skill."

"I only meant we have parking under us. Remind me of your registration number and I'll enter you in the system."

The seconds I took to recall it made me feel as incompetent as I'd just denied being. "Drive straight down when you get here," Toby said, "and the car park will let you in."

"Then go up to the ground," Macy said, "and Mr Joe will send you to see us."

Lesley had always relished her precociousness, and I told myself that the little girl was nothing like Toph Noble, at least in any bad sense. "I'll be with you shortly," I said, making for my car ahead of second thoughts.

Trees were blossoming throughout the suburb, yet another sight my wife had left behind. Soon I came to Toxteth, where Hope Street linked a brace of cathedrals, a thorny concrete Catholic and a solemn sandstone Anglican. By the crossroads at the midpoint of the street the Philharmonic Hall advertised a concert performance of *Pontius*, an opera best known for the aria "What is truth?" As I drove downhill on Hardman Street, a name Lesley always thought should belong to a district run by gangsters, I saw posters for the Chortle Club, a venue in a converted warehouse near the docks. *I'm Disabled So I Must Be Funny* was this week's comedy event, preceded by *Muslim* and *Black* with *Transgender* yet to come. Meanwhile the venerable Empire Theatre was provoking controversy with a show in which a paternity squabble on Jack Brittan's television programme involved Mary and Joseph and God, who couldn't be tested for DNA. Not long ago the theatre had been picketed for staging *Seven Brides for Seven Brothers*, which the protesters condemned for trivialising rape.

Downtown was crowded with pedestrians avoiding the homeless. My car and many others stuttered through a succession of traffic lights to the Strand, the main road closest to the river. Starview Tower was among the skyscrapers that had multiplied within and around the famed riverside skyline of Liverpool. It was a broad white building stacked with ranks of windows, variously curtained except for the top floor, where they seemed to consist of one-way glass. That floor – the thirty-third – and the one below it spread outwards like a bloom, lending the rest of the tower the appearance of an unnaturally broad stalk. When I turned down a ramp that sloped under the building from the Strand, the entrance barrier saluted me at once.

The ramp descended to a car park considerably wider than the tower, and I tried not to be reminded how extensive the cellar beneath Safe To Sleep had been. Cars had gathered around a bank of lifts in the middle of the concrete bunker. I parked close, wondering why so many spaces were unoccupied. Slamming the car door sent echoes scurrying into the corners, where darkness massed like cobwebs. I poked a button between a pair of lifts and tried to fend off an impression that despite all the fluorescent slabs set in the ceiling, there was an unreasonable amount of darkness overhead. An insectoid ticking must be the noise of a vehicle – my own, of course. A lift big enough to contain more than a dozen people gaped at me, and as I dodged in I heard a version of the clatter of my footsteps flee across the car park.

As I reached for the ground-floor button – like the button for the basement it was green, while those above were red – the lift shut me in. The upper half of each grey wall was covered with a mirror, and a sideways look showed a multitude turning to meet my eyes while their companions presented the backs of their heads. I had to fight off an irrational compulsion to count all the manifestations of myself, which receded into darkness the light couldn't reach. I jabbed the button a second time and stared at the door to encourage it to open. I felt hemmed in by innumerable extensions of myself by the time it did.

The lobby was a large high almost entirely white space, deserted apart from a man encircled by a counter. Beyond glass doors traffic sped along the Strand in untroubled silence. The lobby walls were decorated with clumps of concrete stalks or branches, which I imagined expanding into flowers or treetops somewhere up above. As I stepped out of the lift the man said "Help you, sir?"

He was as stocky as a guard's job might require. His smooth pale skin appeared to be entirely hairless, which gave his head the look of an egg. His expression was innocently neutral, and his greeting revealed small unusually regular teeth. "Will you be Mr Joe?" I said.

"That's what she calls me, Mr Sheldrake."

"How do you know my—" I might have seemed even more paranoid if I hadn't realised "They told you I was coming."

"Your son did." Joe bared his teeth in what I assumed must be intended as a smile. "I'll let you up," he said and clicked a detail on a computer screen. "Take the lift you just took, all the way to the top. You'll be thankful you did."

I couldn't let his last words pass unremarked. "Are you involved with them?"

His gaze retreated into innocence. "I've been."

"Can you tell me what to expect?"

"Nobody can tell anyone. You have to be there for yourself."

THE WAY OF THE WORM • 33

"Where?"

"Where just you can go," he said like a direction.

It was plain he had no more to say. "Then I will," I said.

The triple multitude that wore my face crowded forward to meet me as I stepped into the lift, and they grew restless as it crept upwards. They were miming my unease, because I had a sense of rising towards darkness. No doubt the shaft was unlit, not to mention empty, which could explain why I fancied that the lift was bearing me towards a void. An office building shouldn't feel that way, and I thought of stopping the lift so that I could see the floors were tenanted. Or would it only stop where I'd been sent? The idea left me nervous of finding out, and I urged the lift onwards – all its countless occupants did.

It opened on a nondescript lobby across which I was faced by several office doors. The upper panels were composed of frosted glass, and featureless. I'd barely stepped out when the lift crept shut, and I heard its dwindling murmur. I was making for the nearest door when its left-hand neighbour opened, though the glass panel had stayed blank, which unnerved me until Macy stuck her head out level with the handle. "I said it was grandad," she cried.

She had Claudine's roundish face and small features, and Lesley's wide dark eyes, which brightened as she ran to take my hand. She was tugging me across the lobby when her mother looked out of the office. "Are you guiding grandad?" she said.

I imagined families where the question could only be innocuous, and wished fervently that ours were one. As I let myself be ushered, Toby emerged from the next room. "Dad," he said. "True to your word."

I was near to demanding why this should be unexpected when I realised he was saying I'd arrived in good time. He followed me and Macy into Claudine's office, a disconcertingly austere room with unadorned white walls and a single chair behind a desk occupied by a phone and a computer. A child's desk stood under a wide window that looked out to the river's mouth. Macy kept hold of my hand as she returned to the desk, where she was drawing a spectacularly toothy tyrannosaurus. "That's what those look like, grandad."

A copy of Conan Doyle's *Lost World* lay beside the drawing, but I wondered "Have you seen them in films too?"

"She's no need," Claudine said.

"It's good that she's reading books."

"She may as well," Toby said, "while we still have them."

I felt as if I'd missed the significance of his answer and his wife's, but before I could ponder them Claudine said "So what changed your mind about us, Dominic?"

"You said you could help with my loss. I'm not coping as well as I'd hoped." While this was true, it wasn't the reason I was there, and my deceit held back my grief. "I know it has to take time," I said.

"You won't look at it that way much longer."

"Claude means you won't think about time."

"Not like you're doing now, grandad."

Macy's contribution perturbed me so much that I turned away from her. "That's what your meditation does, is it?" I said, but not to her.

"That's some of what it brings you," Toby said. "You have to discover yourself."

I was trying to prepare as best I could. My memories of voyaging at Safe To Sleep were all too vivid. "Shall we, then?" Claudine said. "We'll be there if it gets too much."

"The most dreadful experience of my life," Macy said.

More disconcertingly still, her mother laughed. "She does that, Dominic."

"Does what?" I almost couldn't ask.

"She's just noting in her mind the last sentence she read. It's her sort of bookmark."

As I recalled the scene from my own reading — the narrator's encounter in the prehistoric forest — Macy shut the book. "Are we taking grandad in the room?"

"That's where it starts," Toby said.

She and Claudine stood up as he did, though at least not quite in unison. As I followed everyone into the lobby I said "Who else is in the building?"

"Property companies and financiers and lawyers for three. People you'd say matter, dad."

I didn't know whether I would, and had a sense that he mightn't. Macy ran to open a door off the lobby. "Here you are, grandad."

I overtook her parents, not from eagerness but because I was unsettled by the sight she'd revealed. Beyond the door was blackness, as if the doorway led into a void. I didn't like to see her on that threshold, let alone crossing it. "What's in there?" I said not far from panic.

"Not much," Toby said and strode in. "It's what's beyond."

I heard a click, and half a dozen muted lights came on overhead. Whereas Claudine's office was equipped with one-way windows, this considerably larger room was windowless. More than a hundred leather chairs as black as an absence of light faced away from the door. "You can come in, grandad," Macy urged. "There's only us."

"Sometimes it's full," Claudine said.

"Even if there's only you."

"Don't confuse grandad," Claudine said, though with an indulgent smile. "Sit wherever you'll feel comfortable, Dominic."

I felt as if that might be nowhere in the room. As I advanced to the nearest chair I remembered staying by the door at Safe To Sleep. Though I didn't want to think that might be necessary here, I was reluctant to venture further. I'd hardly sat down when the padded leather set about adjusting itself to my shape. "Sit however helps you relax," Claudine said. "The chairs go back."

I suspected that reclining would leave me feeling helpless. "I'll stay how I am."

"Some do at first," Claudine said and sat next to me, while on my left side Toby did. "Macy, you're in charge of the lights again. Wait till I say."

The five-year-old ran to shut the door and then stood by the switch. "Does it need to be dark?" I protested.

"You'll find it helps," Toby said. "Don't worry, we'll have hold of you. We'll know when you ought to finish."

He took my hand as Claudine found the other. I was put in mind of a séance, except that the ring of us was incomplete. It would need Macy to make it up, and I had to be grateful she was out of reach. "What am I meant to do?" I said.

"Close your eyes, Dominic." Once I had, overcoming my reluctance fast enough to hope it hadn't been apparent, Claudine said "We'll do the rest. Just settle back."

"Join in when you feel like it, dad."

"Join in what?"

"You'll know, but don't worry if you want to leave it all to us this time."

I had no idea what Toby meant. I was preoccupied not just with keeping my eyes closed but with trying to judge how dark it was. I hadn't heard Macy switch off the lights, and the inside of my eyelids was only dim. Even if relaxing was supposed to help the meditation work, I couldn't help straining my senses, which seemed to draw a sound towards me from both sides, barely a murmur. It consisted of three repeated syllables, and I knew them all too well. No, they weren't just repeated, I grasped as they grew fractionally louder or my mind took a firmer hold on them; the slow mesmeric almost liquid syllables were reversed every second time. The insistent repetition felt like a pulse that was lending its rhythm to my own, perhaps because Toby and Claudine kept squeezing my hands at its pace, so gently that I wasn't sure of feeling the sensation. I was even more uncertain how dark the room might be, but at least as far as I could tell, Macy wasn't joining in the whispered chant. Although I didn't mean to, my mind had begun mutely to participate, and I searched for thoughts that would let me feel in control – any thought at all. A memory might do, and one overwhelmed me, catching at my breath. I was struggling to help Lesley climb the lifeless escalator.

I could feel the crawling banister yield as I clutched at it with my free hand. I felt an ache gathering in my right arm as it supported

Lesley, and sweat prickling my armpits, and my breaths growing shorter and harsher while my heart gave jerk after painful jerk. I heard Lesley say "I'll be fine if I can just stand for a minute" in a depleted voice, and I wondered belatedly if she might have been pleading to rest on the steps rather than beyond them – whether she would have survived if I hadn't forced us onwards. On the last few steps she seemed to grow practically weightless, as though preparing to take her leave of me. Someone behind us had started to push, but I never knew if they were simply impatient or meant to help. Lesley and I stumbled off the escalator in a clumsy version of an embrace, and then she let go, covering her heart with both hands as if to hold it steady while she leaned against the wall and slid gradually downwards. When I stooped shakily to lift her she could only gasp two words. "Phone, Dominic."

The memory was too vivid and too poignant, and I couldn't help retreating. By now I was unaware of any chant or even where I was. The recollection seemed to lead directly to another, of being back at university, though not as a lecturer. I was wandering into the students' union when I heard laughter, a sound so musical despite its unselfconscious helplessness that it felt quite separate from the mass of conversations in the bar. When I located the young woman I saw that she was reading the student magazine. At once I hoped my contribution was the cause of her amusement, but could I have known I wanted us to spend our lives together? The thought was inseparable from the memory. I loitered near her chair outside the bar, and when she looked up, wiping her eyes so as to focus on me, I saw she had indeed been reading my couplets. "That's what comes of being brought up a Catholic," I said.

Lesley took time over reducing her mirth to a faint expectant grin. "Do you know the poet?"

"As well as anybody in the world does."

"Are you saying it's you?"

I couldn't tell whether this was as reproving as she made it sound. "Guilty," I admitted.

"I think it's the most reprehensible thing," Lesley said before her grin got the better of her, "I've ever read in my life."

"If it affected you that badly then perhaps you need a drink," I said, and soon I was standing in the haphazard crowd at the bar. Attracting the barmaid's attention took so long that I grew nervous in case my new friend, whose name I had yet to learn, decided I wasn't worth waiting for. In fact we'd never let each other down like that except on the night of our Shakespeare mistake. I didn't want to relive that just now – it summed up my loss too much – and I was rescued by the memory of composing all the verses, most of them in the incontinent stuttering virtually uncontrollable shower in the shabby house I shared with three fellow students. I could smell the redolence we brought to it – a mixture of perfumes and aftershave and four different soaps in the bathroom, curry in the kitchen, cannabis in the lounge even though we blew the smoke up the chimney of the disused hearth for fear of being found out by the landlord. As I struggled yet again to moderate the temperature of the shower I came up with a verse I'd forgotten to include in my submission to the magazine:

Before you down your Sunday roast
Ensure your starter is the host.

This took me back me to another unpublished item – *Three's No Crowd*, the novel I'd attempted in my final year at school, when I still thought I could write a book. I'd tried to imagine an adult version of the tremendous trio, Jack the priest and Tommy (short for Thomasina) the socialist figurehead and Don, their best-selling chronicler. I'd abandoned it when Don discovered Jack and Tommy were having an affair, a situation that embarrassed me so much even though I depicted it in very little detail that I tore the whole book up for fear that my parents might read it. I could still recall the act of writing it: the sense that my mind was flaring with ideas, the way that if I paused too long the next word I put down would grow dark with gathered ink, the odd sweetish taste of the blue stains on my fingers as I tried to lick them clean. This instantly led to an earlier memory – although I'd been writing and drawing for years by the time I started school, the teacher shamed me by announcing Dominic didn't know how to hold his pencil right – and then another taste returned, of the crayon I was sucking while I drew an infant picture of the sun, a yellow ball sprouting squiggles jagged with energy. Could I go back even further? Yes, I was emerging into sunlight or some artificial brightness, but I seemed unable to define the situation, not least because I had no words. Now I had some, which helped to fix how I was looking down at a newborn child in his mother's arms. I felt unsteady with relief that the baby wasn't stillborn, an event so common that it was noted just as SB on the death certificates, and then I was shaken by a wave of affection for mother and child. Despite its intensity, I experienced the emotion at some remove, perhaps because I was anxious to determine why the woman looked familiar, like an old photograph bestowed with life. In a moment she addressed me, and I knew. "Desmond, it's a boy," she said, "so he'll be Dominic."

Recognising that the tiny crumpled suffused face was mine felt worse than any vertigo. It felt like plunging out of time and space with no means of rescuing myself, nothing to catch hold of, not least my own vanished identity. My body didn't help even once I grew aware of it, because I wasn't properly aligned with it and couldn't make it work. Then the darkness within my inoperative eyelids blazed with light, and I felt hands clasping mine, exerting an irregular unsynchronised pressure that might have been designed to interrupt my trance. There was silence until Toby said "Take it easy as long as you need, dad. You're back with us."

The pressure on my hands fed me back into them as if they were gloves composed of my flesh. Once the rest of me returned to alignment I managed to blink. "Where did you go, grandad?" Macy cried. "Were you born?"

Realising she might have had a similar experience disconcerted me even more than mine. "Were you?" I said, hoping for the opposite.

"Yes, and I saw me. I've been you as well."

Her parents were watching me with some concern. No doubt they wanted to establish that the trance and its effects hadn't harmed me, but I was appalled by how unconcerned they were for their daughter. "What does she mean?" I demanded.

"She's been back too," Claudine said. "Our genes remember, Dominic. It's all stored inside us. People used to mistake it for reincarnation."

"You saw your birth, dad, yes? That's nearly always the first step."

The idea that it would lead to more almost stole my words, but I complained "I could have done with being warned in advance."

"We don't want anybody to feel prompted. It's your voyage and yours alone."

"Don't try it by yourself just yet, though," Claudine said. "Wait till you're more used to how far you can go."

I had no intention of achieving that state, but Macy said "Are we going to give grandad a worm?"

My voice came out harsh and infuriatingly tremulous. "What's she talking about now?"

"Just an aid to meditation, Dominic. We'll save that till grandad's settled in." As if to make the situation appear even more mundane Claudine asked me "What would you like now? A drink or just to sit?"

"Neither, thank you. I'll be off home to think over what I saw."

"Are you sure you're all right to drive, dad?"

"How are you saying your meditation might affect me?"

"You may feel a bit out of it for a while, especially the first time. You may need to concentrate."

"Then I will." Far too much like a peevish oldster I protested "Nobody told me I wasn't meant to drive."

I stood up steadily enough and headed for the lifts. I was keeping my thumb on the button between them when Macy called "Be back again soon, grandad." As I turned to respond, however noncommittally, a man came to the door of the office beyond Toby's and Claudine's. He was tall and thin with a long oval face, and some years younger than my son. "Let me welcome you to the Church of the Eternal Three," he said, and was advancing at a measured pace when a phone rang in his office.

He seemed to forget me at once. Darting back into his room, he shut the door. Through the frosted glass I saw him stoop to pick up the receiver, an action very much akin to the salute he'd offered me, and entirely too familiar. I had to swallow an unpleasant taste so as to speak, though I scarcely needed to ask "Who was that?"

"He's Mr Christopher," Macy said.

"He leads this chapel," Toby said.

I swallowed again, because my throat had grown dry as ash. "Christopher what?"

"Le Bon," Claudine said as if there was no reason for me not to know, and I might have confronted her and my son except for Macy's presence. I dodged into the lift and didn't glance back, but couldn't tell whether my myriad selves looked distressed or determined or both. I knew only that I would be returning to the Church of the Eternal Three after all.

CHAPTER FOUR

The Cold Past

"Was it everything you hoped for, Mr Sheldrake?"

"Why are you saying I came, Mr Joe?"

"No need to call me mister, Mr Sheldrake. That's just what your little one does."

"She's hardly mine. Well, she's my granddaughter."

"Close enough, some would say."

A grin presumably intended to be personable displayed his small dauntingly regular teeth, but I didn't mean to be distracted. "You haven't told me what you thought I was hoping for."

"Mr Sheldrake said your wife left us the other week."

I couldn't tell whether Joe meant his bluffness to be bracing, but it angered me enough that I retorted "So why would that bring me here?"

"Mr Sheldrake lost his mother, and it helped him."

"How?"

"It gives us some perspective. That's what meditating's all about."

"That's been your experience."

"Never felt so close to my family."

This reminded me of witnessing my own birth with my father's mind, and I almost grabbed the edge of the counter to steady myself. "Your parents, you mean."

"Them to start with." He opened his mouth further before apparently deciding to withhold a remark. "Has Mr Sheldrake told you what comes then?" he asked instead.

"All I was told was not to try it by myself yet." Rather less truthfully I said "That's why I've come back."

"It's something else when there's a lot of us." As if he'd realised the comment was premature Joe said "Anyway, I'm keeping you. You go up and your family will look after you."

He might have been addressing someone a good deal older and more infirm than I meant to be. "They do their best," I said and made for the lifts, hoping Joe couldn't see beyond my words. My multiple selves swarmed out of the walls of the cage, a spectacle that might have been parodying the way I'd become somebody additional in the meditation room. Last night I hadn't slept much, for fear not just of drifting into someone else's memories but of discovering I couldn't return without help. I'd clung to my own recollections to hold myself in place, and for greater safety only recent ones – the hospital, the funeral, the wake. Even grief had felt reassuring, since it was mine alone, at least until I wondered if my granddaughter could have experienced it by proxy. Ought I to have sensed her somewhere inside my mind? Might Toby have been in there at some point too? Surely this wasn't how the process worked, but this was among the questions I was determined to raise. I would rather Macy didn't hear, though it distressed me to wonder how much she already knew. If she was here I planned to ask Claudine to keep her away while I questioned my son.

As soon as the lift reached the top floor I stepped forward – a great many of me did. My army stayed behind while I crossed the lobby, but I hadn't reached Toby's office when another door swung wide. The occupant of the room leaned out as if he was repeating the bow he'd given me last time or else mocking the gesture. "I missed my chance for a word with you yesterday, Mr Sheldrake."

"You can have a lot more than a word," I said, having taken a deep breath that helped me stand up absolutely straight. "Don't you remember the rest of my name, by the way?"

"Do come in and sit down, Mr Sheldrake."

The invitation seemed to hint at a reprimand, as if I were proposing to cause a scene in public. Might he prefer Toby and Claudine and anybody else who was nearby not to hear? I could have made sure they did, but suppose this endangered them? I was here to achieve the opposite if I could. My host was holding the door open like a mime of patience or a suggestion of its finitude, and I sidled past him into the room.

It was much like Toby's office next door, with unadorned white walls and an equally colourless almost skeletal desk that bore a phone and a computer. Between them lay an object that roused unwelcome memories – a figurine carved out of material so black I had difficulty in making out the details of its shape. It portrayed a worm-like creature with its tail in its mouth and protruding a tongue split in three at the tip. Members resembling rudimentary hands with too many fingers sprouted at irregular intervals and in a variety of sizes from the coiled trunk. I had to force my gaze away from it as my host closed the door and sat at the desk with his back to the window, beyond which a moon like a chewed wafer invoked the night in the otherwise empty blue sky above the mouth of the river. "You were asking for your name," he said. "Will it be Dominic?"

I lowered myself into the chubby leather chair across from his before retorting "You remember that much, then."

"We're all about memory here, Mr Sheldrake."

"So what am I supposed to call you now?"

"If we're going by first names, it's Christopher."

"What's the alternative, just so I know?"

"It should be on my door for all to see, do you think?" When I didn't respond he said "Le Bon's the family name."

"That's not how I remember it."

"It's always been Le Bon. That's where we come from."

I looked away, having glimpsed more than reminiscence in his eyes, a darkness so deep that I feared it could draw me in. I saw fragments of the moon fall towards the bay – no, a scattered flock of seagulls – as I remembered the field in France. In a bid to put my thoughts in order I said "The last time we met you were Toph."

"We all have our pet names, don't we, Dominic?"

Though I couldn't be sure that he almost imperceptibly emphasised the first syllable of my name, it felt like a sly indefinable threat to Bobby and Jim. "So is that what your family calls you?" I suggested.

"Not at all. We've moved on. I'm Christopher to everyone who knows me."

Presumably this authorised me to use the name, but I kept it out of my mouth. "And where's your family now?"

He traced a line across his forehead with a fingertip, and I could have fancied he was describing a religious sign if not an occult one. "Opening more eyes in Europe and America," he said. "They'll be here before you know and pleased to see you."

"Why should they be?"

"We like anyone who knows our secrets to be part of us."

Rather than ask how much he thought I knew I said "What else do you remember about me?"

"You tried to stop Christian, didn't you? You never realised it wasn't us you had to stop, not that anyone can stop it or could have even then." In a forgiving tone I found worse than grotesque he said "Still, you were only young."

"I wasn't so young when I met you."

His lips let me glimpse amusement. "You were pretty well daunted, though."

"That was your aim, was it?" With growing rage I said "And you tried after all of you abandoned Safe To Sleep."

"I think I more than tried, and I wasn't even Macy's age."

I didn't know if he was offering this as an excuse or boasting of his powers, but I was most dismayed by the mention of my granddaughter. "That night's stayed with you, has it?" he said.

If this was designed to revive his infantile threat, it only angered me. "Should it have? I thought you'd lost interest, the way babies do."

"You've attracted our interest, Dominic. You can always count on that."

According to his mother Christian Noble was indifferent to me and to humanity in general, but rather than argue I said "I wonder what exactly drove you out of Safe To Sleep."

"Call it an infestation. Just an inconvenience."

"That's what you sent me to that night, an inconvenience."

"You were one, and so it seemed appropriate."

"More than that." My rage gave me no time to specify whether I meant the subterranean presence or myself. "I don't think any of you realised what you were inviting," I said. "It was more than you could cope with."

"I promise you we've dealt with greater powers."

"That's why you had to shield yourselves with children, is it?" In the confusion I'd forgotten he had been one at the time. "Don't tell me it didn't get to you, that thing under Safe To Sleep," I said. "You started writing about how it happened and you couldn't even finish."

His dark gaze rested on my face, and too late I realised how I'd loosed the truth. "You read that," he said. "You went back to our house."

"Yes, and not by myself either."

At once I regretted having said this, but Toph appeared to think it wasn't worth pursuing. "So you saw it off," he said.

"We saw what happened to it. Perhaps you can tell me—"

"I'm saying you roused what was underneath. You could say you fed it if you like."

"I'd say nothing of the kind. We didn't bring it there." Finding the argument absurdly disproportionate – a petty squabble over a monstrous invasion – I said "What's become of it since?"

"It's still there. It's just gone deeper for a time. Few people realise how much is lying low in the world." Less dismissively he said "Did you rescue your books?"

"The ones your grandfather made my son steal from me, you mean? Yes, I took them back."

"I take it you still have them."

"Why, are you going to try and steal them again?"

"As far as I'm concerned you're welcome to them. I knew them by heart the first time we met." As I hoped he was exaggerating if not simply lying he said "I doubt the rest of us will care about them either. You keep them if they give you any insight, but we've progressed a lot further since then."

"Progressed how?"

"I believe your son introduced you to it. He'll be guiding you onwards, and soon we'll be giving a sermon. I do hope you'll attend."

"You're suggesting I should come to one of your services."

"That wouldn't be our word for it, but a communal occasion of the chapel, yes. The more of us there are the better."

"You don't think I could be inconvenient."

"Your family will all be there." Before I could decide if he meant this should inhibit my behaviour he said "Now you'll be wanting to do what you came for."

I found this ominously ambiguous, and didn't answer. I watched him lift the phone and press a key with a movement so fluid it looked close to boneless. "Toby," he said, "your father's here with me."

Rising to my feet revived a selection of aches, and Toph reached the door well ahead of me. He held it open and delivered the old reptilian bow as I hobbled into the lobby, to find my son emerging from his room. "Everything all right?" he said, a question I thought he was keeping carefully neutral.

"Certainly as far as I'm concerned, and I trust Dominic will say as much."

"I'll say it," I said.

"We didn't realise you were here, dad."

"I had security advise me when your father arrived."

Once Toby shut his office door behind us he said "What happened in there, dad?"

"Just a conversation with your leader."

"You weren't arguing with him."

"Why do you think I should have done that?"

"I know you had some doubts about our church. If you've none now, I'm glad."

"I've no doubts about him." I gazed at Toby, and when his eyes grew not just blank but darker I said "I think you know what he used to call himself."

If the look Toby gave me was a plea, it was beyond interpretation. "I wasn't sure, dad."

"You told me Toph wasn't involved." As if this made it worse I said "You told me just before your mother's funeral."

"We didn't want to upset you, especially then."

"That's right, you and Claudine said there was nobody here called Noble or Bloan."

"There isn't, dad."

For a moment I was too furious to speak, and then my rage collapsed. "You've inherited this from me, haven't you? I used to fool my parents like that, and it was all about the Nobles then too."

"I wasn't lying when I said we tried not to upset you any more."

"I don't suppose you were about that." Having conceded this much, I had to make an effort to bring us back together. "Let's agree not to lie," I said. "Let's tell each other nothing but the truth in future."

"That'll be the future," Toby said and gripped my hand. "The truth."

I remembered past vows – the one I'd made with Bobby and Jim, and assuring my father I would care for my son, and promising Lesley that our family would look after one another. As I closed my other hand around his, Toby said "Did Christopher know who you were?"

"I suspect he may have known for quite a while, and he says he wants me to be here."

"We all do," Toby said, renewing his grip, and the office door swung wide to confirm his assurance as Macy ran in ahead of her mother. "Is grandad going to be born again?" Macy cried.

The prospect felt more intimidating than I'd anticipated. "Do I have to go through that every time?"

"It's just a gateway, Dominic," Claudine said. "We'll teach you another way to make your journey."

"Fix on a memory that's yours and see where it leads to," Toby said. "Make sure it's a strong one so you can use it to find your way back here."

"My one is going on the big wheel with mum and dad and you and grandma," Macy said. "It's like looking out of here."

I glanced towards the window to see shards of bone fly up from the bay – a flock of seagulls. Macy was dancing with impatience in the doorway, and as soon as I stood up she ran to switch on the lights in the meditation room. I was belatedly afraid Toph Noble might propose to guide me, but only Toby and Claudine followed me in. "Have you settled on a memory, dad?" Toby said as I sat close to the door he'd just shut. "Tell us which one if you like."

"Then we can use it to call you back if you need us to," Claudine said.

Macy was singing to herself as she waited by the light switch. "Fly away Peter, fly away Paul..." The names referred to the apostles, though the rhyme hadn't originally included them. The change put me in mind of Christian Noble's interpretation of the Bible, not a welcome memory, and then the sound of a child's song led me elsewhere. "Carol singers coming to the house," I said. "Long before your time, but I miss them."

"Start from that," Toby said. "We won't hold your hands today, but remember we're here."

He and Claudine flanked me as I sat resolutely upright. I hadn't shut my eyes when the chant began, so softly that I could have fancied I was hearing it just inside my head. Despite its insubstantiality, I imagined it gathering on my eyelids, which began to sink. Almost instantly I saw the hall of my childhood home, where multicoloured streamers linked the walls, and heard several children of about my age singing *Away In A Manger* more or less in key and unison. They delivered several verses before someone rapped the knocker.

I recalled how carollers had subsequently offered less and less, until they'd knocked or rung the bell before starting to perform and then sung the minimum that might gain them some cash, and that had been the end of carolling. Rather than advance towards the present, I was tempted to adventure further back. My parents sent me to plant coins in the chilly hand of the foremost singer on our doorstep, but I'd never gone carolling myself, yet now I remembered standing in a slow gentle fall of fat snow, singing in a high voice about royal David's city. My companions and I carried lanterns on poles, lending snowflakes an intermittent yellowish glow, and a muffler wrapped around my head clung moistly to my cheeks. The memory had to belong not to my father but, I suspected, to somebody I'd never known. I couldn't identify them, nor whoever would have recollected skating on a frozen river, though I felt the blades cut into the dazzling sunlit ice and heard their chill metallic screech. The sensations led to a memory that I recognised was yet another person's, of digging a hole in frozen earth. My hands ached and shivered as I slammed the spade down yet again, but the black soil veined with ice barely yielded. My foggy breaths obscured the sight of the tiny makeshift coffin that lay tilted on a mound sprouting a few shrivelled weeds, unless my eyes were blurred by tears that felt like ice. Perhaps I recoiled from sharing more of this experience, which gave way to an even colder one, of struggling through a blizzard on a mountain in the hope of reaching land more fertile than the territory the tribe had left. The windborne ice that slashed my face felt close to piercing my eyeballs, and when I turned my head I could scarcely distinguish the figures trudging with bent heads behind me – my mate and our young son. I had no words for them, just raw feelings, and the paucity of language threatened to draw me back to an earlier state. That condition felt capable of dissolving my mind, of exploding it to merge with shapeless darkness or to shape it into some form alien beyond description and yet seductively familiar. I shrank back into my own mind, or would have done if I'd been able to recapture my personality. The tribe in the blizzard, the blows of the spade that sent pain throbbing through my frozen hands, a mistake with the skates that left me sprawling on the harsh ice, a gust of wind that flattened the flames in the lanterns and pasted snowflakes to my cheeks, the carol singers staring at me as if I were playing the householder when I should be patrolling the night with them...

"Are you back with us, dad?" Toby said in my ear.

I didn't think I was. The remotest memory seemed capable of keeping hold of me to drag me back into the primal dark. The childhood reminiscence of the carol singers was too distant to fix me in the present – and then I remembered what my encounter with Toph Noble and his new identity should prompt me to do. "I am," I said.

CHAPTER FIVE

A Souvenir of France

"Lesley, I'm keeping my promise."

There was no response, but I expected none. I'd spoken only because I was so close to her abandoned desk, where her computer was as silent and inactive as a stone – a memorial. I could have imagined the computer felt secretive, since I didn't know the password. I needn't suspect Lesley of having hidden secrets simply because I'd kept so many of my own, but she had never told me that she knew our granddaughter was attending the Church of the Eternal Three. Might she have known more that she hadn't shared with me? I was unlikely ever to learn, and surely my suspicions were no more than an attempt to exonerate myself from having failed to wonder if the Nobles were involved – from avoiding any thoughts of them for fear of a reprisal. I'd lost too much that I valued to be afraid now, and I switched on my computer.

I shouldn't have looked at my emails. Among the invitations to make links with people who were presented as professional but whom I'd never heard of, I was faced with condolences from an old colleague of Lesley's who had moved to the far side of the world, and a belated offer of a discounted ceremony from an undertaker's, and an exhortation from an insurance firm to start monthly payments that would cover my own funeral. I deleted them in a rage, including the condolences by mistake. At least I'd progressed beyond grief, though I had no doubt that it was lying in wait for me. I brought up the world on the screen and entered **Somme** in the search box.

The viewpoint sailed down like a meteor towards the globular map, and French names rose out of the expanding simplified landscape. Several were places Jim and our schoolmates had passed through or stayed in during the trip that Christian Noble had organised. I magnified the area until it yielded up the name I recalled as closest to the field that Noble had visited after dark. In which direction was the field itself? I'd begun to range about the cartoon territory in the hope that some aspect of it would grow more familiar when I saw what I ought to have done. I typed Le Bon in the search box, and a reference appeared in a sidebar. It was the name of a hotel.

When I clicked on the reference the map sprouted a marker. Once I'd enlarged the image sufficiently to see that the hotel was by the road the bus had followed to the hostel more than sixty years ago, I brought the viewpoint down to ground level by dragging an icon like a chess piece in rudimentary human form across the map. The front of the hotel – an extensive concrete building that made a stark bid for elegance – lurched erect to occupy the screen, and the computer mouse jerked sideways as my hand twitched. The photograph showed sections of the grounds on each side of the hotel, and every tree visible along the edge was leaning if not straining away from the field.

I felt as though I was attempting to retain some hold on the mundane when I clicked on a link to TripAdvisor. The consensus awarded the hotel three stars out of five, and in general the reviews were tepid: "decent but pricey", "okay for one night", "average accommodation, basic food", "service without a smile", "run of the moulin". Photographs showed clinically pallid rooms with beds as flat as sheeted slabs, bathrooms where bidets squatted next to snaky showers, a dining-room dominated by chandeliers with translucent filaments. Exterior shots displayed just the building, not the grounds. One reviewer mentioned that the staff gave the impression of wanting to be elsewhere, but I couldn't tell if this simply meant they were unhelpful. Another commentator found the food too earthy for her taste, but was she saying it was overly coarse for her palate? I'd begun to feel that the reviews were deliberately ambiguous – that some hindrance was preventing me from grasping them, at any rate – when I recognised the man who'd made the joke about the mill.

In the miniature photograph he was years older than last time I'd seen him, as a colleague of Lesley's and mine. He'd worked in Modern Languages, which helped explain why his screen name was Phil O'Logical instead of Philip Trask. His profile placed him on Merseyside, and his phone number was easily located. As soon as I'd thought how to word my approach I rang him, but it was a woman who said "Trask?"

"Is that—" To my chagrin I found her name was out of reach, and I could hardly just call her his wife. "Might I speak to Philip?" I said. "I expect he may remember me. Dominic Sheldrake."

"Dominic, of course we do. How are you and Lesley now? We haven't seen you since we all retired."

"I'm afraid Lesley died last month."

"Dominic, I'm sorry," Mrs Trask said but wasn't quite able to contain a reproof. "You should have let us know. Have you had the funeral?"

"Yes, last month."

"We would certainly have been there if we'd known." With an attempt at gentleness she said "I hope that's not why you're phoning."

The reason I'd concocted seemed rather less persuasive now. "I wanted to ask about a hotel Philip reviewed online."

"Perhaps going away for a few days will help you." This sounded like indulgence if not closer to permission. "Do ignore that awful name he's adopted," she said. "He will have his little jokes."

"It made me smile, don't worry. Did you stay at the hotel too? It's the Hotel Le Bon. If you did, let me ask—"

"I'll put him on," she said as if she hadn't heard, though I suspected she had. "Philip, it's Dominic Sheldrake."

She was plainly calling to somewhere else in the house, so that I didn't expect him to respond at once. "Dominic, what's the occasion? Now that we're back in touch we should all get together."

"I'm afraid it would just be me."

"Excuse my thoughtlessness. We heard you and Lesley had your differences, but we understood they'd been resolved."

"Philip, no," his wife said just as close to me, "he's saying she's passed on."

"Did he tell you that? Kathryn, you should have said."

"Kathryn, of course." In case this sounded like agreeing with his reprimand, I added at some speed "We didn't give her time, did we? I just wanted to consult you about a hotel you wrote up."

"So my thoughts are worth the labour after all." I suspected the comment was aimed at his wife. "Which of my critiques inspired you, Dominic?"

"The place near Bonchamp. Hotel Le Bon."

"Ah." This sounded ominously like reluctance to say more. "Do excuse my deplorable attempt at wit," he said.

"Sorry, which part of the piece was that?"

"If you've expunged it from your memory, so much the better. Run of the mill, but ending up in French."

"It amused me," I said despite feeling as if I'd needed an explanation of a joke.

"Hear that, Kathryn? Whatever you say, I've an audience. So what has it prompted, Dominic?"

"I was wondering if there was anything special about the hotel."

"I shouldn't say so. That was rather the point of my pun."

"How about the staff?"

"On the whole morose, but that can be the French."

"Or the food?"

"Edible enough, would you say, Kathryn?" Having roused a noncommittal murmur, he said "But unmemorable."

My frustration was edging towards nervousness. "Did anything at all unusual happen while you were there?"

"I don't think I can pretend it did. Why do you ask?"

I was trying to devise a reason I could give when Kathryn said "Unless you count my dream."

"Good heavens, I'd have thought you would have forgotten that by now. In any case I hardly think it can be relevant to Dominic's enquiry."

I heard a restless sound suggesting Kathryn was about to leave the conversation. "I'd like to hear about it all the same," I urged.

"It was just a dream I had the first night we stayed. I don't remember all the details now." Kathryn fell silent for so long that I was about to speak when she said "Parts of someone were scattered all over the grounds, and they were still alive. It was so vivid I got up to look."

"And you were rather less than quite awake," Philip said, "because at first you insisted you saw them."

"I did, didn't I? No," Kathryn said with belated vigour, "I said I saw fragments of statues. But of course those weren't there either when you woke me up."

"Evidence of how we can think we're being rational when we're the other thing," Philip said.

I was afraid he might have antagonised his wife enough to end her reminiscences until she said "There was one other odd development."

"Then I'm unaware of it," Philip objected.

"That's because I didn't think it was worth mentioning. It was just that I had the same dream the second night, and I felt as if it wanted me to get up."

"I don't understand what you mean by that, Kathryn."

"I don't really understand myself. I didn't want to disturb you again, so I stayed in bed and made it go away."

"How did you manage that?" I said.

"With ease, I imagine," Philip said. "We're talking about a dream."

"It wasn't so simple." Less defiantly Kathryn said "It isn't now."

I might have asked what she meant if Philip hadn't intervened, perhaps on her behalf. "Well, Dominic, I hope we've helped you plan."

"I think you may have." Rather than try to grasp how, I said "Did you find out why the hotel had that name?"

"After Bonchamp, I should think."

"Wouldn't they have called it Le Bon Champ?"

"I really couldn't say. That's somewhat outside my area of expertise." With less of a hint of defensiveness he said "Perhaps you can find the information online. What's the basis of your interest?"

"I was there once on a school trip as a child."

"We understood the hotel was built more recently. We tend to avoid revisiting memories ourselves. They're too liable to let one down."

"Not the hotel, the area."

"By definition that has changed as well. I shouldn't expect anything out of the ordinary."

"Except the trees around the place. Did anyone explain what was wrong with them?"

"We gathered they were trained to grow in that fashion as a feature."

"That's a lie. I can tell you—"

"There's no call for you to speak to Philip like that, Dominic."

"I mean you were lied to. The trees were like that more than sixty years ago, and I suspect a great deal longer."

"Then I assume we misunderstood." Philip scarcely paused before saying "Good luck with your research if you haven't finished. We'll put our heads together over meeting up and give you a tinkle in due course."

I could tell his enthusiasm had lessened since the start of the conversation. I thanked him and Kathryn and brought up the hotel's website. It showed the photographs I'd already seen and reproduced a few favourable reviews – typical French hospitality, modern with a touch of Gallic charm, ideal base for touring the area. An extensive description of the hotel and its facilities didn't refer to the name, let alone explain it. Perhaps Trask had given me an idea worth pursuing, and I found the website for the town of Bonchamp.

The official photographs looked much as I remembered: narrow winding streets through which the bus had made its dogged way, open spaces too irregular to be called squares, small parks hemmed in by smaller shops, stone bridges arching over a stream scattered with waterfowl, churches that appeared to be contending for the longest name... I tried searching the site for Le Bon, but the couple of examples this produced were adjectival. In growing frustration I scrolled through the tourist reviews. Quaint, unspoilt, needs more parking spaces, authentic regional cuisine... I was close to leaving the site when a street name in a reviewer's photograph caught my eye. Rue Gahariet, the sign said.

Perhaps it wasn't just the plaque that had snagged my attention. The crumbling letters on the rusty white rectangle were elaborated by graffiti, efflorescing in patterns so intricate that I had to overcome a compulsion to grasp them. The multicoloured tendrils might have been transforming the sign into an unknown or at any rate occult language. Above the plaque an irregular stone block much older than the surrounding bricks protruded from the wall. It bore a carved figure, presumably a man, though the face and hands had been chipped or scraped away so thoroughly that the patches of lichen that ended the arms, and the greyish blob that surmounted the neck, looked as though they were searching for shapes to take. For some reason the survival of the block reminded me how Christian Noble's father had been afraid to destroy his son's journal, instead concealing it as best he could.

I zoomed in on the photograph and stared at it until I began to fancy that the filaments burgeoning from the letters of the sign were related to the threads composing the lichenous wads that had taken the place of a head and hands – that all of them were reaching for my mind. I banished the site from the screen and searched for Gahariet, which proved to be an old French name. Without expecting to find much if anything, I typed Gahariet Le Bon in the search box. It brought me a single reference, to a book on witchcraft by Montague Summers, a Catholic clergyman fascinated by the occult, a friend of Aleister Crowley. The book was older than me, and somebody had scanned the whole of it online. A click opened up the reference.

Worse still than the infamous Tanchelin, if we are to judge by the malefactor's fate, was his fellow heretic Gahariet Le Bon, native of the region that today bears the name Bonchamp. Unlike the errant Tanchelin, Le Bon chose to pollute with his vile beliefs the very soil which had borne and supported him. He caused an abomination to be raised in stone on a field close to his place of birth; a field, one chronicler maintains, where his unhappy mother delivered him into the world. There the deluded citizens would attend his foul sermons and practice acts of irreligious worship. Le Bon proclaimed himself a prophet of "the one true faith," which he declared to be the fount of Christianity rather than an infernal parody thereof. Those of the townsfolk who yet embraced the one True God petitioned S. Norbert to intervene, and the Saint was instrumental in purging their countryside of the blight it had spawned. Le Bon was nailed to the door of his abhorrent chapel, together with the single written copy of the prophecies with which he sought to infect the world. The chapel was put to the torch while the wretch yet lived, and at the end of three days the edifice was pulverised by mighty hammers. The remains of both the building and its miserable instigator were buried deep in the field, which continues unnamed to this day. Unlike the sacred architecture which aspires to touch the glory of the Creator, Le Bon's Satanic temple took the form of an obscene flower, spreading wide the topmost segment of its spire in order to communicate with the Stygian darkness to which God brought His light and His Word. The blasphemer was said to have drawn his abominable inspiration from a place of pagan worship which used to occupy the field, but since no remnant of this primitive shrine had survived into his lifetime, the vision was indisputably diabolical.

The book had nothing more to say about Le Bon, but I felt it had told me enough. One point seemed clear: whatever presence had remained in the field near Bonchamp, most of its influence had been transferred elsewhere. While the hotel bore no resemblance to the destroyed church, Starview Tower was far too reminiscent of Summers' description, however overstated that was. I was trying to decide how to use the information – just now it filled me with dismay bordering on dread – when my phone buzzed like a torpid insect on the desk. When I saw the caller's name I could almost have thought my research had roused him. "Toby," I said.

"Dad, I thought you should know we'll be having a sermon here this month."

"You think I ought to be there."

"I'm not sure." Only just before I could ask why, he said "It won't be Christopher on his own. It's his whole family this time."

At once I felt fiercely purposeful. "You couldn't keep me away," I said, hoping this sounded like commitment to their church.

CHAPTER SIX

Tracing the Worm

"They're all on the next floor down, Mr Sheldrake."

While I'd done my best to be ready for whatever the day brought, this threw me. "Nobody's down there, Joe. Just a lot of cars."

He gave me a grin unsettlingly reminiscent of an infant's simper. "Not the basement. The floor next to the top."

"Does anybody have a name for what's up there?"

"That's our chapel, Mr Sheldrake. Everyone knows that."

"I mean the architecture."

"Mr Adlington calls it the bloom."

"That's Roy Adlington, the architect."

"He's up there now. I hope I can be for the sermon." As I thought of asking what he expected Joe said "You go to them. Don't wait for me."

He activated the lifts as I made for them. My army of reflections strode to meet me as the door shut us in, and I tried to think they didn't look remotely apprehensive. We kept up the pretence as the muffled voices of a crowd grew louder, and I was preparing to encounter some kind of congregation when the lift sailed past the sounds. As I lurched to jab the button for that floor again my selves swarmed in various directions like a massive mime of panic. The lift halted on the top floor with an unsteady shudder, and the doors crept open to reveal who was waiting for me.

Despite the effects of several decades, all three still presented versions of the same face. Toph's was fleshiest, while Tina's had begun to sag around the chin. Her father's was the thinnest and his lanky body too, as if he'd been reduced to his essence, most intensely in his eyes, which were practically black. Every face bore the same expression, looking secretly amused. As I hesitated on the threshold of the lift the Nobles gave me a simultaneous bow from the waist while they kept their faces aimed at me, a posture I tried and failed to think was designed to avoid showing how bald Christian Noble had grown, with just a cobweb of grey hairs across his whitish scalp. "Mr Sheldrake," he said and even more enthusiastically "Dominic."

"Dominic," Tina said in the same tone almost before he'd finished.

"Dominic," Toph supplied just as instantly, and I thought they were making my name sound less like a welcome than an element in a ritual. It seemed to hold me where I was, even when Christian Noble darted forward to prod the button between the lifts with a long thin finger. Far from slowing him down, age had increased his similarity to a snake. "Do venture forth, Dominic," he said, "and we'll have a word before we all go down."

I'd been alone with the three of them at Safe To Sleep, but I couldn't help hoping that Toby and Claudine might be up here too, though not their little girl. As soon as I set foot in the lobby Noble released the button. "We'll use your office, Christopher," he said. "I expect our visitor wants to sit down."

Apart from their quick footsteps and my uneven tread, the top floor was so silent that I knew I was on my own. Toph led the way into his impersonal room, where the window was displaying a cloud like a misplaced spotless snowfield above the bay. As I took the chair that faced it across the desk Toph said "The first of us can have mine."

It seemed an oddly strained way to refer to his grandfather. Noble sat opposite me with a movement so effortlessly sinuous that I had to remind myself how old he was. He planted his hands on the desk, widening the digits until I wondered how it couldn't pain him. Tina and her son stood on either side of him, leaning forward slightly as though poised to execute the Noble trait. "So, Dominic," he said, "how long would you say it has been?"

"Pretty well as long as your grandson's been with us."

"I can see why you might put it that way." He nodded, and the versions of his face that flanked him did. "And what do you suppose has brought us back together?" he said.

"My son's here, so I am."

"I believe he set out to convert you. I hope that hasn't made you suspect him. He has your best interests at heart, Dominic."

"I think I know my son."

"You'll get to know him better by belonging to our church."

I was growing too angry not to demand "That's why you think I've joined, is it?"

"No," Tina said, though her father's lips hadn't stopped moving. "We'd say it was what some people call fate."

"You've been ours since we last met," her father said.

I didn't want to know what he meant, and tried to quiet my fears by blurting "Why are you going to say my son joined?"

"He was at university," Toph said, "and thinking for himself."

"Who engaged him? Was it you, Christopher?"

I was distracted by glimpsing his mother's lips shift and her father's too before Toph said "I was catching up with people I'd known at Safe To Sleep."

My rage almost didn't let me speak. "Renewing your hold over them, you mean."

"No need to put it like that," Tina said. "Say returning them to the path."

I had a grotesque notion that she wanted me to speak the words. Instead I retorted "What's brought you and your father back to town?"

"Ask rather what we've brought," her father said. "The ancient word."

I couldn't help feeling childishly facetious for asking "Which one is that?"

"The primal truth. That's what you'll hear."

"The kind of thing I heard you saying at your other church, you mean."

Too late I saw I'd just admitted having eavesdropped. Three pairs of eyes fastened on me, and despite the shining cloud above the bay the room seemed to darken. "Which sermon did you hear?" Toph said.

I wondered why he should speak, since it had been decades before he was born. With an effort I fixed my attention on the central figure of the triptych. "I heard you talking to Eric Wharton."

"You were hiding," Toph said, "and we guess you weren't alone."

"We won't ask where," his mother said. "We'll just say there's no reason to pretend any more."

I couldn't judge if this angered me or made me nervous, but felt provoked to say "Then why is your son calling himself Le Bon?"

"We all are. It's who we always have been."

"The source of our truths," her father said.

"If you're talking about Gahariet Le Bon," I said in what felt like some kind of triumph, "I understood all his thoughts were burned with him."

"You disappoint us, Dominic. We've shown you memories don't die just because the bodies do." With a faint secretive grin identical to those beside him Christian Noble said "Do you still have my thoughts?"

"Why, do you want to take them back again?"

"Not at all. I built upon them long since. I was just about to mention that they came from the source you named."

"In that case I'd have expected them to be in French."

It was a feeble retort, but I could think of no other. "You might wonder if they helped bring you to us," Christian Noble said.

"I think I'd have known if they had."

"You place too much faith in language, Dominic. It's just another veil over the truth," he said and in a moment was on his feet, keeping his hands spread flat and wide on the desk, even once his arms were vertical. "All the same, it's time we addressed our congregation."

I limped fast to the door and across the lobby as well. A lift opened to display the multitude of me, hemmed in on every side by variations on another face, which darted forward at my back. I kept the button depressed while the lift descended, and had a sense that I was surrounded by lurking mirth at my behaviour. A mass of voices rose towards me, and the door opened to let it flood in. "Make your way to your family, Dominic," Christian Noble said.

The lobby was teeming with people. The crowd parted like a biblical body of water as the Nobles headed for the nearest office. The leader of a local council greeted them by holding up an object, and then a member of parliament elevated an identical article, and the owner of a football team did. Their faces and many more in the crowd had appeared in the media, and I recognised the item each of them was flourishing – a copy of the reptilian figure I'd seen on Toph's desk, the serpentine icon swallowing its tail. As I watched other dignitaries and celebrities make sure their icons were noticed, I heard a cry of "Grandad."

Macy wriggled through the crowd and grabbed my hand as her parents came to find me. "Dominic," Claudine murmured, "we thought something had gone wrong. We were just about to phone."

"It's important to you that I should be here, then."

"It's important to you, dad." As more of a reproof Toby said "Where were you?"

"Conversing with our hosts. Christian and Christina and Christopher."

While Macy looked impressed, indeed wide-eyed, her parents weren't so easily won over. "What did you say to them?" Toby was anxious to hear.

"We've reached an understanding. You needn't be concerned any more than they are," I said, only to be distracted by the sight of them. Each of them had reappeared in a doorway to beckon to the crowd.

The doors led not to offices but to a single room furnished with hundreds of folding chairs. They resembled skeletons of the leather seats they faced, a trio at the far end of the room, beyond which the bank of cloud above the bay was growing visibly thinner. The Nobles were leaning forward to talk to people on the front row, and I took a seat near the back, though further from the exits than my instincts prompted, since I had to find space for my companions. As Toby and Claudine sat on either side of me while Macy perched next to her mother, the Nobles moved to face the congregation. They waited for stragglers to sit down, and I found I was grateful they weren't watching me. Then Christian said "Is there anybody here without an effigy?"

I felt singled out even before my nearby neighbours glanced at me. "What's an effigy?" Macy whispered.

"A little image like yours," her mother said as low as someone speaking in a church.

Macy jumped up, and I was dismayed to see her hugging an icon. "My grandad hasn't got one."

"Here's a present for you to give him," Tina Noble said.

When Toph stooped past the leather seats I realised that the blackness on the floor behind them was more solid than a shadow. Icons were nestling together like a brood that had just hatched or was about to hatch, and I couldn't judge how numerous they were. As Toph picked one up, holding it like a proud father, Macy planted hers on her chair and ran to him at least as eagerly as she had ever run to me. "Take care while you're bringing it to him," Toph said.

I supposed he was advising her not to drop it, and wondered if he was recalling the broken icon his family had left at Safe To Sleep. I couldn't help wishing Jim were with me now, and Bobby too. I was distressed to see my granddaughter pacing carefully towards me, cradling the icon as though playing at motherhood. No doubt she was simply following Toph's instructions, but her approach looked ritualistic. When she leaned forward to entrust the icon to my hands she might have been copying the Nobles' snaky motion. "Take care of it, grandad," she said.

I mumbled something disguised as acceptance and closed my hands around the image. It seemed to hint at the chill of the void whose blackness it evoked, and I could have thought the wide thin disconcertingly human smile and the enormous eyes that glistened like globes of black sap were greeting me. The sinuous trident of a tongue protruded from one corner of the mouth while the tip of the tail wormed its way into the other. I found the face so disagreeably fascinating that I almost forgot to mute my phone, having let the icon rest on my lap like a quiescent pet. I cared not at all for the intimate weight, and was lifting the image – clamping it between my hands in case exerting force lent me some sense of power – when Christian Noble said "Let us reflect on our times."

Tina and her son took their seats as he did. The blackness of the leather chairs had camouflaged the icons they picked up, so that the Nobles might almost have been producing them out of empty space, an illusion I did my best to regard as a cheap trick. As Christian Noble gazed at the audience, he and the companions on either side of him began to finger the icons, tracing the circular outlines while they turned the objects in their hands. "Chaos," he said. "Even the unenlightened have started to suspect that is where the world is bound."

His dark eyes seemed to deepen as a smile spread across his lips, a satisfied expression that grew on Tina's face and Toph's as well. I was further unnerved to notice that everyone around me had set about tracing the shapes of the icons they held – Toby and Claudine too, and worst of all their little daughter. I told myself that quite a few religions involved similar activities – prayer wheels, rosaries and other beads – and did my best to concentrate on the sermon.

"Alliances are breaking up across the world," Christian Noble said, and I was disturbed to see Tina and Toph mouthing his words in unison with him. "Continents are separating into countries, and countries are splitting apart too. There are wars and rumours of more wars, and unseen armies fighting for no country are at large all around us. Religions are reverting to their primitive states, and madness is loose on the streets, and ruling country after country. The climate is returning to its birth. Gender grows more fluid, and the minds of the masses are gathering in the space their computers and electronic devices create. The brain is becoming less dependent on the physical, and nobody need feel constrained by the body they were born with. Science is approaching a view of the universe that those of us versed in the occult have known was the truth since before the birth of science. We know that the processes commonly regarded as chaos are no more than a step towards reviving the truth in the world…"

All this sounded prophetic, and I wondered if Noble had somehow retrieved it from his medieval ancestor. Had he used memories as stepping stones through time? The idea made me feel threatened by memories other than mine, and I searched for something on which to fix my mind – not Noble and his family mouthing the words he spoke. I tried concentrating on the view beyond the window, where the bank of cloud was fraying at the edges, so that the attenuated tendrils looked desperate to cling to the sky as their expansive body dissipated. Perhaps deciphering the shape of the item in my hands would help to keep me in the moment, since its blackness made it so hard to distinguish, and I began to follow the reptilian outline with a finger.

"Chaos is a name for mutability," Tina Noble said while her father and son joined in without a sound. "It's the name religion and men's laws try to impose on it. Some religions call it original sin, the memory that's buried deep in us all of when we and the universe were infinitely fluid. Religions try to shape their gods to fit the minds of men, but our church means to extend your minds through time and space so that you can grasp the truths some have called gods. Religions try to fix the thoughts of their followers in the form the faith approves of, to fix the world and the universe too, but it's our mission to revive the infinite potential within you all...."

However much I strained my eyes I was unsure how the icon looked, because I was increasingly uncertain what it felt like. I saw the gleeful face with its entire body for a second tongue, and irregular bunches of digits sprouting like buds here and there on the circular shaft, but my fingertips suggested that it had fewer dimensions than I was seeing, like that marvel of my childhood, the Mobius strip. Or perhaps the opposite was the case: perhaps it had more dimensions than were visible, if only I could distinguish them. My sensations had grown so ambiguous that it felt like trying to mould the body out of a void rather than from any recognisable substance.

"The universe has always been a ghost of itself." When had Toph become the speaker? "Look up at the night sky and you will see the shining dead," he declared, and Macy gave a delighted laugh.

"The stars annihilate time, and you will all learn to see it no more. Generation speaks to generation around the great circle, and soon all will see through the eyes of the unveiled…"

I no longer understood the sermon, but this hardly seemed to matter, though I could have thought the words were reaching me even if I didn't grasp them. I had no idea which of the Nobles was proclaiming that the truth behind the Eden myth was the identity of the three – Adam and Eve and the serpent, who was the essence of their mutability and begetter of the primal race. One name for the serpent was Ouroboros, the personification of eternal renewal, which the Bible tried to reduce to the form of a common snake, but the truth veiled by these symbols was called Daoloth. Norse myth acknowledged it as the Midgard Serpent, which will encircle the globe until it takes its tail out of its mouth to cause the destruction and rebirth of the world. I was tracing the form of the icon, an endless process during which it seemed not merely to grow concave but to suggest a hollowness far deeper than the object could contain, when the Nobles said aloud in unison "In the time of the third birth all shall become one in Daoloth." They elevated the icons above their heads in their cupped hands, and every member of the congregation followed suit, even Macy and a dismaying number of other children. I didn't realise I'd responded until I sensed the icon hovering like a harbinger of night above my skull.

I lowered it so hastily that the wide smile brushed my forehead, and I could have fancied the splayed tongue dealt me a thin lick, which felt cold and sinuous. All around me objects like a flock of solidified darkness were descending to the earth. I was pressing the icon between my hands as if I could squeeze it smaller, a reaction that only made them ache, when Christian Noble passed his gaze across the congregation. "We shall meet again soon," he said.

"In your future," Tina said.

She and her family smiled for no reason I could think of, and Toph said "Not the ones you know."

I heard muted sounds of amusement or appreciation all over

the room, and felt as if everybody else was party to a joke I had no chance of understanding. It seemed more important to observe that the Nobles had sent everybody on their way while themselves staying in the room. I kept my seat until all the worshippers in front of me had made for the lobby, bearing their icons like relics from a shrine, and then I followed my family. I glanced back from the door, but the Nobles were too involved in a conversation to notice.

It was plain that the lifts would take some time to clear the lobby, and I stayed well away from them. I was hoping my behaviour didn't look suspicious when Macy said "Do you like your figure, grandad?"

I did my best to misinterpret the question. "There's a bit too much of me at my age."

She laughed, not unlike an adult indulging a child. "Not you, grandad. The one the church gives us."

I was averse to answering her question but reluctant to ask "What do you think of yours?"

"It looks after us. I keep mine by my bed at night."

Even more unwillingly I said "Looks after you how?"

"It lets me go where I want in my sleep, because I know it'll bring me back."

This led to more questions I was even less anxious to ask, but I was taking a prefatory breath when a voice I hadn't heard for many years said "So you've seen the light, Mr Sheldrake."

I turned to see not only Farr but Black. They looked withered but potentially as forceful as last time I'd encountered them, when they'd scared off the vice-chancellor. Farr's large moist pinkish nostrils seemed in danger of collapsing outwards, while Black's round mouth had shrivelled so much it put me in mind of a navel. The sight of the policemen provoked me to speak before taking time to think. "You're still partners, then."

Black parted his lips with a desiccated hollow pop and lubricated them with a generous length of his porous greyish tongue. "We're mates, if that's what you're getting at."

"I meant whether you're still on the force."

"Retired, us. Doesn't mean we're not involved with the law."

"I thought one of the speakers was saying she hadn't much time for men's laws."

"You'll come to understand as you progress," Farr said. "Our laws are eternal."

"You didn't run into any conflict when you were police."

"There's plenty of those that are members," Black said. "Lawyers and judges as well."

I held back from arguing further. Almost any other excuse to loiter outside the room would have been more welcome than they were. Soon they might wonder why I was lingering, and I was trying to think how to divert their attention when Toby said "I didn't realise you knew my dad."

"We had occasion to speak to Mr Sheldrake when you were your daughter's age. It was just a routine matter."

"It didn't come to much," Black said and stared at me, puckering his lips almost colourless.

I recalled how they'd thwarted Jim's investigation. "To nothing worth remembering," Farr said with a sniff that rendered his nostrils cavernous, and I was restraining any answer when Christian Noble darted out of the room.

The doors on either side had opened too, letting out Tina and Toph. All the Nobles gazed at me, which seemed to add weight to the icon in my hands and intensify its chill. "Were you waiting for us, Dominic?" Christian said.

"Just talking to some" – I did my best not to pause – "some old acquaintances until the lifts weren't so crowded."

"They aren't now," he said as Toph crossed the lobby to push the button. "Are you following us up?"

I wished Farr and Black weren't close enough to hear me lie. "I don't know what there would be to follow up."

Tina made a noise distantly related to a laugh. "We mean are you coming upstairs."

"No," I said and tried to rescind some of my urgency. "I don't think I've any reason."

"Then here's a lift to take you down," Toph said.

I moved towards it, but only in order to falter. "I just feel I've forgotten something."

"You have your avatar," Christian said, and all three of them leaned forward to nod at the item in my hands.

"Shall we go and look for you, grandad?"

Macy's parents were watching me as well, and so were Farr and Black. My palms had grown sweaty, so that the icon almost slipped out of my grasp. I clutched it to my chest while I patted my pockets with my free hand. Once I'd mimed searching I had to say "I must have dropped my phone."

"Have you any idea where?" Christian Noble said.

I was afraid he was setting a trap. "Let me go and see," I said.

He moved aside just enough to let me pass. As I limped between the folding chairs, he and Tina and Toph occupied the doorways. Their scrutiny unnerved me, and I retrieved the phone from my chair at once, only to fear I'd betrayed that I'd known all the time where it was. "It must have fallen out of my pocket after I turned off the sound," I said and had to swallow halfway through.

The Nobles watched me head for the lobby, not as steadily as I would have liked. Farr and Black were at the lifts, and Black was holding the left-hand door wide with a fist. "Will you be coming with us, Toby?" Christian said.

I could have thought he was testing my son's loyalty, and Toby looked apologetic. "We'll see you on Sunday as usual, dad."

"Don't go any further than you feel comfortable with," Claudine said. "We'll guide you again next time you're here."

"But you could have the worm by your bed," Macy suggested.

I had the daunting notion that they thought all their remarks were equally domestic and mundane. They trooped with the Nobles into the lift, and Macy hugged her icon while she waved her other hand – many of them. As the lift shut, its neighbour opened, and Black tramped in while Farr indicated it with one pallid puffy upturned hand. "We'll see you down, Mr Sheldrake."

As I ventured in, a face protruding a divided tongue flocked to welcome me – to surround me, at any rate. Many of its duplications were pretending not to watch me, but far more of the huge black eyes than I could count made no secret of observing. When Farr followed me the exultant faces multiplied as if another brood of them had hatched, and the walls swarmed with darkness. The lift set about crawling downwards, and Black turned to me. "Let's have a look at your phone."

I felt trapped, hemmed in not just by the nighted faces but his and Farr's too everywhere I might look. "What's the issue?" I protested.

"I'll be finding out."

"I thought you weren't with the police any longer."

I was instantly concerned that I'd betrayed he had good cause to be suspicious. His stare hid his thoughts as he held out a hand, a forest of which sprouted all around me. "Don't have to be," he said.

He put me in mind of bullies from my childhood, but surely I needn't feel intimidated at my age. "What does he want?" I appealed to Farr.

"What he says, I should think, Mr Sheldrake." With a dismissive grimace that made his nostrils gape Farr said "Have you some reason not to comply?"

Surely he was sounding more official than he had any right to sound. I wanted to find the sight of Black's expectantly rounded mouth absurd, even comical, but my sense that every wide-eyed reptilian shape was intent on the confrontation didn't help. I held the icon against my chest while I groped for the phone and brandished it. "There it is," I said. "Not even the latest model. Out of date like its owner."

Black's stare didn't let me know if my nervousness was apparent. His hand stayed outstretched as he said "Give us a proper look."

He didn't know my password, and I wouldn't tell him. Surely that would hide my secret, but I'd barely handed him the phone when I wondered if the home screen might somehow let him deduce what I'd done upstairs. I felt my heart thump hard under cover of the icon while

Black frowned at the phone he was weighing in his hand. "Heavier than ours," he said.

"I told you it was getting on like me."

When he turned his stare on me I saw I'd been too eager to feel safe. "Don't see how you wouldn't know you'd dropped it," he said.

"It's age," I said, hoping my panic wasn't evident. "It does that to you."

"Not to us, Mr Sheldrake, nor to Christian."

I couldn't tell how much Farr disbelieved me, and Black's stare was unreadable too. It returned to my phone before he said "You want to watch out what you're doing."

"I hope I do." I would have preferred not to have to ask "Anything in particular?"

"Forgetting where you've left your stuff." His stare had grown as unblinkingly insistent as the eyes of the multitude of icons, and it was close to forcing me to respond when he handed the phone back. "Too much of a weight," he said. "I'll stick with mine."

I wasn't quite persuaded that he'd simply wanted to compare phones or to exert authority over me once again, if not both. Perhaps he'd decided against demanding my password now that he had no official status, and was pretending the idea had never occurred to him. I pocketed the mobile before he could change his mind, and faced the doors as if this might bring us to the basement sooner. I wasn't far from fancying that all the faces, human and less human, were closing in on me by the time the lift touched bottom.

My car was parked by itself against the wall on the far side of an expanse of empty concrete. As I made for it under the harsh fluorescent lights I grew an unsteady shadow, which was ushered if not urged onwards by two more. All three reared up on the side of the car, and I had an unsettling impression that the shadows of the icons my escorts held had grown disproportionately large, though this wasn't the case with the one I was carrying. As I planted the figurine on the car roof so as to unlock my door, Farr objected "That's a precious item, Mr Sheldrake."

"Take care of him," Black said.

I wasn't sure whether this was addressed to me or to the icon. I would have consigned it to the boot if I hadn't been anxious to leave the men behind. As I ducked into the car, rousing a pain that climbed my spine, I dumped the object on the seat beside my own. The men turned their backs simultaneously, stalking off in unison as I slammed the door. I moved the icon to face away from me before I started the car.

I was heading for the exit when a black Mazda crept out from behind the pillar that housed the lifts. It was close to my rear bumper by the time the barrier deferred to me, and I saw Black behind the wheel, and his and Farr's eyes on me. The barrier detained their car while I swung onto the Strand, where a set of traffic lights brought me to a halt. They hadn't dropped to green when the Mazda sped up the ramp and took up a position at my back.

I was distracted by the icon. Some movement or vibration of the car had inched it around to face me, and I could have thought that despite their lack of pupils the eyes were gazing straight at me. I turned the grinning thin-lipped face away as the lights glared green. I couldn't risk breaking the speed limit on the way home, and whenever I glanced in the mirror I saw Farr and Black. Their eyes looked as dark and blank as the eyes of the icon. More than once I found it had crawled around on the seat again, to present me with the smile its tail and three-pronged tongue were helping to stretch wide.

When I came in sight of home the Mazda was still on my tail. As I parked beside Lesley's abandoned car, which I meant to adopt once I sold mine, Farr and Black watched me through the gateway. The Mazda blocked it until I'd opened my front door, and then Farr raised a palm in an adieu. "Catch you soon," I saw Black mouth.

I was so anxious to check my phone that I divested myself of the icon as soon as I found somewhere to leave it – on Lesley's desk. As I sat at my own I was suddenly convinced that I'd had no reason not to let Black examine the mobile – that it had failed to record because I'd switched the sound off, or had picked up nothing comprehensible.

When I started the playback I heard only silence, and then just a snaky hiss of static. My chest had begun to ache with my held breath when a voice spoke. "Let us reflect on our times."

Christian Noble was distant but perfectly audible. All the Nobles were, and I was thrown by discovering how much of their sermon I seemed to have missed. "Not the ones you know," Toph said at last, which I found no more meaningful than I previously had. The audience made their appreciation heard, and then a variety of vague sounds signified their departure. The Nobles were talking among themselves, and a growing silence gradually isolated their conversation. I craned over the phone to hear better, and then I recoiled, almost touching the wrong button in my haste to replay that section of the recording. I had indeed heard what Toph called Christian. I listened to the end and was immediately afraid that the recording might somehow be erased before I could put it to use. I was hardly able to breathe or swallow until I'd typed as brief a message as made sense and forwarded the recording to Bobby and Jim.

CHAPTER SEVEN

A Family Secret

"The Bible comes closest to lifting its veil at the end," Christian Noble said. "The great truths cannot be contained in language, and so the message that the seven thunders speak is not set down. The sky is rolled up like a scroll, taking back the word the Bible sought to fix in men's minds and revealing the unveiled universe. Land and water flee an earthquake such as men have never seen, and the primal flux is restored. Chaos incarnate stalks the world to revive its secret forms, and one of its embodiments displays tails like serpents. Who can say what the heads of these serpents speak? Not words as men know them, for the great truths are not uttered but experienced. These prodigies the Bible disguises as angels are three in number, which signifies their unity with Daoloth. Their purpose is to unfix men from their bodies so that they may expand towards the truth. In ancient Greece these guardians went by the single name of Cerberus..."

I still had no memory of hearing this at the Church of the Eternal Three. Instead I recalled tracing the shape of the icon in a rhythm reminiscent of the mantra Toby and Claudine had used to send me into a trance. The recollection felt like a threat of retreating into memories that weren't mine, and made me acutely aware of the presence of the icon. Despite the sunshine that filled the front room, I imagined I could sense the figurine resting like a sculpted remnant of the night, if it was no more than that, on Lesley's desk.

"The myth of Cain and Abel tries to hide the truth by admitting part of it." Tina Noble was speaking now. "Cain was jealous not of Abel's sacrifice but of his closeness to what the Bible calls God, which is to say the primal state, and above all to their mother. The worm from the garden was within them all, the larva that's inside the cocoon we call man, but man was already growing fixed and separate. When Adam chose Abel and not Cain to sire the race with Eve, Cain made them three once more. He was cast out from the three to wander, and this has been man's imperfect and incomplete state ever since..."

I understood too much of this, and should have seen the truth sooner. I was even glad to be distracted by Toph's next contribution. "Our bodies still remember paradise," he said. "That's the truth behind all the talk of original sin. Our primal state is dormant in each of us, but the churches have been trying to deny it ever since there was religion. Hell and original sin, they're the ways religion tries to frighten man away from rediscovering the truth within himself, but he who came before you shall come after you..."

I did my best not to interpret this as a threat of pursuit, because I was already nervous of yet again hearing the formula that brought the triple sermon to an end. "In the time of the third birth all shall become one in Daoloth," the trio proclaimed, prompting a large vague response that was the sound of a mass of darkness rising into the air. I remembered elevating my icon, and for a moment my hands felt burdened with an insubstantial chill. "We shall meet again soon," Christian Noble said.

"In your future."

"Not the ones you know," Toph contributed, a prediction I still failed to understand. The audience set about shuffling forth, and the muffled bustling blurred whatever conversation the Nobles had begun to have. I turned the sound up to maximum and held the phone close to my face. This time I was just able to distinguish another mention of a third birth, and Christian Noble's comment was clearer. "Really one," he said.

I remembered hearing the words in the field near Bonchamp. He'd never said that anything was really won. I was no nearer comprehending the phrase now than I had been all those years ago, but I had to concentrate on what he and his family were saying. "To the end of time," Tina said.

"To the ends of the dark," her father said, "and beyond."

"To the end of ourselves," said Toph.

All this sounded like a celebration or a ritual until Tina said "I still remember us."

"No shame in that," Christian said. "We may while we can."

"Soon we'll have gone further," Toph said. "We won't think like that any more."

Some part of his remark produced a silence that felt secretive, and then Tina said "How long do we think it's going to be?"

"It already has been, mother. Can't you keep that in your mind? You're sounding like one of the church."

"Do try to make her some allowance, Christopher. All the wisdom was in you when you were born, but your parents had to learn."

"Then that ought to mean it's in both of you now."

"You've no need to wonder," Christian said – defensively, I thought. "We are the ageless truth, the three. It's just that now and then some of us have to remember."

"Now and then." With equal contempt Toph said "Words, just like remember is."

"They can be feelings too." His mother might have been restraining wistfulness. "Haven't you kept any memories?" she said.

"I've got all of them if I want them." Perhaps in a bid to placate her, Toph said "I remember being born."

"We all do," Christian said.

"And being made. I remember the worm."

"So do I," Tina said with a laugh that made me shudder. "The same one."

"I'm afraid I must bow out at this stage," Christian said. "I've no memory of being fathered. The performer was an understudy, one might say. Not one of us and so unmemorable. No more than a conduit for Gahariet and his essence."

"We said we remember your worm. You've no cause to feel left out, father."

I'd felt threatened with nausea as I listened to the recording once more, and now I had to swallow hard, because it was Toph who'd just spoken. "That's right, you mustn't," Tina said.

"I don't feel remotely separate. We're all as close as anyone could be and still stay as human as we are. Only, Christopher..."

"Father?"

"I was about to suggest you might avoid calling me that here, just in case. Call me Christian by all means. It amuses you as much as it does me."

"I'll call you father for us both," Tina said.

"Let's go up," Toph said. "I want to see how the church is progressing abroad."

There was little more than silence after that until a group of sounds reminded me how the Nobles had opened three doors at once. "Were you waiting for us, Dominic?" Christian Noble said.

After that the phone had picked up nothing of significance by the time I'd retrieved it, and now I switched it off. I was beginning to regret my haste in sending the file to Bobby and Jim. Could I have put them in danger? Suppose my communications were being monitored? As I tried to think how to proceed, I heard footsteps on the front path.

I twisted around so carelessly that pain scrambled up my back. It left me unable to rise to my feet until the doorbell shrilled a second time, and I'd had no chance to see who was outside. I hobbled to open the door and only just managed not to slump with relief at seeing Jim. "This is very serious, Dominic," he said.

His face confirmed it, but I wasn't sure if his greeting did duty as a rebuke. "Come in and tell me," I said, retreating as though we had something to hide.

Once he'd shut the door Jim blinked at the vase that Lesley used to replenish with flowers from the garden. It displayed only dust now, and I thought he meant to remark on it until he said "So you've tracked down your old enemies again."

"That isn't quite what happened, Jim."

"Then what did? Your email didn't say much."

How often had I tried to persuade him of the truth about the Nobles? The prospect of another struggle felt exhausting in advance – and then I had an inspiration. "I'll show you something that will," I said.

As he followed me into the workroom he didn't bring much eagerness with him. He glanced at the dark screens of the computers and stared around the inert room. "So what—" he said, and then his gaze returned to Lesley's desk – to the object beside her computer. "Isn't that the thing they left in the house near Ormskirk?" he said. "Did you go back?"

He picked up the icon but relinquished it so quickly that there was no mistaking his dislike. "This can't be the same one," he said. "It was broken."

"That's from the church my son and his family are involved with, except you wouldn't call it a church. I wouldn't either. You heard one sort of ritual they use that in. At the end everybody holds theirs up, when the Nobles talk about the third birth."

"I heard a lot of mumbo-jumbo we needn't waste our time on. Do I have to take it you were there?"

"It was the only way I could find out what was going on."

"And do you honestly believe none of them could have recognised you?"

"They all did." As I saw this rouse Jim's skepticism – no doubt he was recalling how young Toph had been at the time of Safe To Sleep – I said "You ought to know by now they don't care. They think none of us matter."

"I wonder how true that can be if it's put to the test. When did you find out they were involved?"

"After my son and his wife convinced me to join. The Nobles aren't just involved, they run the church."

"It's odd we didn't know. The organisation is pretty open, you'd think."

"It has secrets, believe me. For a start they're calling themselves Le Bon now. That must be one reason Toby didn't recognise their, the youngest one when he recruited Toby and Claudine."

"Say son if you like, Dominic. I'm still not clear how you obtained that recording."

"I really set out to record the sermon. I wanted to compare it with Noble's journal, and I thought it might be evidence of what the church stood for. Then I realised I could see what the phone might pick up when the Nobles thought nobody would hear them."

"Where did you have the phone while all that was going on?"

"Here for the sermon." Having touched the pocket over my heart, I said "And then I left it on my seat."

"Describe the place to me, Dom."

"One whole floor of Starview Tower full of folding chairs."

"You left your phone on one of those."

"I said so. Are you seeing some problem?"

"You didn't think it might be too obvious."

"If anyone had noticed I'd have said I'd left it by mistake. They wouldn't have been able to see it was recording when they didn't know my password."

"Suppose someone spotted it and the Nobles decided to play up to it? You said yourself they didn't care what anybody thought of them."

I felt close to betrayed. "Are you really suggesting they made all that up for fun?"

"I'm saying their defenders might claim that if it came into the open."

"If." When this and my stare didn't earn an answer I protested "Only if."

"I've told you how serious I think it is. It would be worse than a scandal. God knows what it would do to this church of theirs."

"You're not proposing we should keep it to ourselves."

"Too late for that. Have you heard from Bobby? I saw you emailed her as well."

"I haven't yet. I'm not sure how she may have taken it when she used to be so impressed by Tina Noble."

"She's had days to get in touch. Do you think you ought to call her? I'll speak to her if you like."

"We both can," I said, "if we need to."

Bobby's phone could barely have had time to identify mine before she spoke. "Dom, I was going to ring you. I've been dealing with what you sent us."

"I have as well," Jim said.

"Jim, good, talk later. Dom, is Christian Noble behind this church?"

"All the Nobles are."

"And you can absolutely guarantee that's the three of them we hear talking at the end."

"No question whatsoever. They were the only people in the room."

"All I wanted to know. Writing now. Speak to you later too."

"Hang on, Bobby," Jim said. "Bob, I should say. Just—"

"Bobby's always fine from both of you. Can't talk right now. Ring you back."

When Jim extended a hand to the deserted phone I thought he was about to ask for it, but he said "You'd better call her again."

"She doesn't want anyone disturbing her at work, Jim."

"If she's writing about the Nobles, and it sounded like she was, we ought to find out what she's said before it goes any further."

Rather than argue I made the call, only to see it fail. A second call brought up the same message. "She must be blocking calls," I said.

"Let's hope she rings back as soon as she's finished her work."

I would very much have liked not to need to say "What are you scared of, Jim?"

"What makes you think I am?"

This sounded like an adult version of our old bravado, and not too mature either. "I'm wondering if you want to keep it quiet," I said, "what we've found out about the Nobles."

"You did the finding." Before I could decide whether this was praise Jim said "I just want you to realise they've got everything to fight for and we've got very little on our side."

I could imagine Jack using much the same words in a tale of the Tremendous Three. "We've got their own admission," I protested.

"Which might very well be ruled inadmissible in court with the legal contacts I suspect they have."

I tried to find some hope in this. "You're saying it should come to court."

"I'm saying we'd have to proceed extremely carefully."

"But you mean we're going to."

"Not you, Dom. Not even me. The boys heard what you sent and they're very strong on investigation."

"You're talking about the police." As Jim blinked slowly at me I realised "You mean your sons. They're on the force. They'll be investigating."

"We won't know yet if either of them are. Robert's put in a report. Someone will want to interview you. I hope you're ready for this, Dom."

"I feel as if I have been since we were at school."

"Let's hope we can finally put it to rest. I need to head off, but do you want to try calling Bobby again?" When her phone still proved unreceptive he said "When you speak to her, ask her to let me see what she's written before she sends it anywhere. You could have a look as well."

"I'll see about persuading her, but remember we're talking about Bobby. I can't imagine her letting anybody tell her what to write."

"I just don't want any of us taking risks when there's no need," Jim said, a concern that lingered once he'd gone. While I suspected he had only mundane dangers in mind, I wondered what revenge the Nobles might take. So long as it was aimed at me, I told myself, I had nothing to lose any more. Rescuing my son and his family from the influence of the Nobles had to be worth any risk, so long as it didn't rebound on them. Just the same, I'd grown nervous enough that I clutched at my chest when my phone sounded its old-fashioned bell.

"Dom, I'm sorry I was so abrupt before. I'll blame you, though."

I was glad to hear Bobby, but not her last remark. "Why do I deserve that?"

"You made me want to write, and that's the way I do it."

"In that case I'll be a bit proud of myself. I take it you've finished your piece? Jim was saying—"

"It's finished and sent to my editor."

"Ah." In a way this made it easier to tell her "Jim rather wanted to vet it first, I think."

"She's refused to publish it. Says it's too risky without better evidence."

I felt slighted and yet relieved. "Might you like Jim to look it over before you send it somewhere else, if that's your plan?"

"He can read it whenever he likes, and so can you. The world can." With a defiance I remembered from our childhood Bobby said "I've put it online on my blog, and nobody can kill it now."

CHAPTER EIGHT

The Second Way

This is the hardest piece I've ever had to write. It tells some truths I'd rather not be telling, and some of them are about me. It was meant to be my latest column in the paper, but the editor wouldn't let it go in. I can understand why she disliked it so much. I don't like it myself.

Quite a few people have been inspirations to me over all these years. My parents were for telling me to always be myself, even if they didn't care much for the self I turned out to be. Mrs Day at secondary school and Brian Stroud at university taught me how to look at history and bypass seeing what I wanted to see. My partner Carole of nearly forty years has always supported me in putting out the truth, and that means writing this. Two old friends from my childhood still inspire me – Dominic Sheldrake, who became a lecturer after he made me want to write like him, and Jim Bailey, who followed his father into the police and showed me how to stand up for the right (not the same as "rights") even if it's unpopular. But my biggest inspiration was my biggest disappointment, and made me realise how naïve I am.

I first met Tina Noble when I was at school and she was hardly out of her pram. Even at that age she knew her own mind, and I've never been so impressed by someone I've just met. Now I wonder how I could have missed so many signs that day, even if I wasn't old enough to understand them. Admittedly, back then most people missed them too. Tina's mother was obviously uncomfortable around her, and you could tell there were problems the woman was keeping to herself. It's only now I wonder if Tina was already being abused by her father. That would explain how he gained such a hold over her.

Christian Noble taught history at a Catholic grammar school until he set up the Trinity Church of the Spirit, a front for a cult which ate plants grown on graves as part of the ritual. In 1954 Eric Wharton, a Liverpool journalist, exposed the cult, as a result of which the church was destroyed and the Nobles went into hiding. In the 1980s they showed up near Liverpool under an assumed name, running a project called Safe To Sleep. This claimed to help children with sleeping disorders, when the real purpose was to give them occult visions similar to those the church had offered to its members. I investigated Safe To Sleep but was won over, which shows how persuasive the father could be. The visions I experienced blinded me to signs of the truth. Tina's small son Christopher (then known as Toph) couldn't hide his amusement when his family was referred to as normal. Tina mentioned the family was unusually close but avoided identifying the boy's father, and now I know why. He was her own father.

I was too much of a coward to say this at the time, but I will now: the treatment of the children at Safe To Sleep was a form of child abuse, and I'm certain all their parents would have put a stop to it if they had known. I have no proof that any other form of abuse went on, but I have compelling evidence that Christian Noble had sex with his daughter. All three of the family have said as much. Under yet another name – Le Bon – they are behind the Church of the Eternal Three. Christian Noble may believe it can protect him, but we shall see if it's able to hide him. Call me disillusioned, but sometimes that's how the truth has to work. I simply want to see the truth fully addressed now it is in the open. I'll say only one more thing.

To have managed to exploit somebody as strong as Tina Noble in that way, her father must have more power than any man should have over a woman.

In the days since Bobby had posted all this in her blog, the Nobles seemed to be everywhere online. Some of their enemies were virtually incoherent, and some invented new obscenities to call them. Many of the most impassioned had suffered child abuse, and quite a few were so enraged that they attacked not just Christian and Tina but Toph as well. Defenders of the family pointed out that other religions encouraged unconventional relationships – polygamy, for instance – that were by no means universally approved of. Numerous supporters dismissed Bobby's claims because they saw no evidence, while others maintained there was no reason to believe that Tina and her father had consummated their relationship before she was old enough to consent. A related controversy erupted about Islamic child abuse, though some internet providers tried to suppress the discussion, and over similar behaviour in the Catholic church. Paedophilic politicians and celebrities were savagely resurrected, not least to suggest that too many of their kind remained unprosecuted. Quite a few comments implied or simply said outright that some perpetrators yet to be identified might belong to the Nobles' church.

Most of the media were a good deal less forthright. While a few of the tabloids ran blunt headlines – **NOT SO NOBLE, CHURCH LEADER'S SEX SECRET, NOBBLE NOBLE NOW** – the stories beneath them came nowhere near risking libel. Other newspapers appeared to be waiting for some official involvement in the case, while the television channels that acknowledged the story contented themselves with footage of the Nobles emerging from Venus, an Italian restaurant near Starview Tower. Christian led the way, followed by Tina and then Toph, each of them presenting the reporters with the identical blank look and not a word. Every time I saw the clip I thought each member of the family was gazing straight at me. I wanted to see nothing but indifference, but it was hard to judge when their eyes were so dark.

I hadn't slept much since reading Bobby's piece. I was afraid Toph might decide to take me away in the night for revenge, unless one of his parents did. Even if there was no sign of anybody homing on me, might this mean they planned some reprisal against Toby and his family instead? Too often when I lurched out of yet another fitful doze I seemed to sense an intruder in the house. Perhaps it was at large downstairs, having uncoiled itself from Lesley's desk, or sneaking snakily to find me, extending its split tongue that would be the first touch I'd feel in the dark. More than once I fell to wondering how to get rid of the icon, but I thought it might be needed as some kind of evidence.

I hadn't shown it to the policeman who'd come unannounced to the house. He was a greying fellow decades younger than me, whose black hair dye fell short of the parting, and whose tone was rather too suggestive of a male nurse. His questions felt slowed down and painstakingly enunciated to make sure I understood, though he seemed just to need confirmation that I'd recorded the Nobles and could identify them beyond any doubt. I thought of asking whether Jim's sons were involved in the investigation, but in case they weren't I refrained from mentioning them. The official visit left me feeling more responsible than ever for exposing Christian Noble – more in danger, however undefined. It was one more reason why I didn't sleep much, at least not while I was in bed.

When I awoke I didn't always know where I was or even who. The deserted section of the bed reminded me of lying beside Lesley, and sometimes this brought me memories that should have been only dreams – of visiting another self's wife in her four-postered chamber, for instance, or huddling against my woman on the floor of a room crowded with our sleeping children, where you could hardly distinguish our breaths from the smoke a gale was blowing out of the hearth. The recollections felt unfaithful to Lesley's memory, especially if I had to struggle to grasp whose husband I had actually been. I'd begun to feel safer falling asleep in a chair, which made my mind not quite so desperate to reach back for companionship.

I was doggedly reading some of the latest posts about the Nobles – one commentator speculated about the incidence of incest in the

Church of the Eternal Three, and another argued that the practice should be legal if consensual – when I began to nod as if my body were agreeing with whatever was on the screen. I felt too exhausted to deal with any unfamiliar memories, and so I tried not to think of Lesley in case this led me too far back. Perhaps the attempt to fend it off elicited the reminiscence, and as I settled into sleep I imagined we were in bed. Before I could leave the illusion behind I was unconscious, and then I was lying close to a fire with my mate in a cave. Beyond the dim embers, which looked drained of energy by the vicious cold and the restless night, a blizzard was billowing through the jagged stony entrance. That wasn't why my flat-faced big-eyed partner and I clutched fiercely at each other. We were on the edge of making out the shape that moved behind the storm, a presence vaster than the blizzard and yet able to lurk behind every single swollen flake. Perhaps it lent them some form of illumination, because their faint lurid glow was brightening as the snow crept further into the cave, and even though we had no words for the phenomenon we saw how unnatural it was. The snow wasn't melting, even when it reached the remnants of the fire. As the last ember went out, a vast whisper invaded the cave – the mouthless voice of the shining swarm that raced across the floor to feast on us. I felt as though every inch of my body had been pierced by the icy night, which was freezing us in place so that we couldn't even scream.

I managed to cry out at last, or someone did. I floundered awake to feel I'd left that memory behind but not the self. A noise helped me scramble back into my own identity – a car engine closer than the road. When I heard it stop I knew it was blocking my way out of the drive. Was Christian Noble paying me a visit, or had he sent the police? I did my best to grow more furious than nervous as I propped my fists on the desk to raise myself and hobbled to the front door. As I grasped the latch the doorbell shrilled, and I felt as if the metal had tried to deliver a shock. I snatched the door open and came face to face with my son. "Dad, what did you think you were doing?" he said at once.

The sight of him threw me as much as the question did. "I'll have to ask you to be more specific."

"Christian's had the police at the tower and your friend Roberta Parkin wrote all that about him online." With a hint of hope that I found worse than dismaying Toby said "Didn't they get it from you?"

"If you read Bobby's piece you'll have seen she talks a good deal about her own experience."

"You know what I mean, dad. Did you tell them the thing that's causing all the row? We've even had people leaving the church."

While his anger didn't shake me, the reason for it did. "Why should you think I'm responsible?"

"Because the police say there's a recording, and you left your phone where Christian and his family were talking."

"If you suspect me you have to suspect them."

"I don't see how that follows."

"You're saying I recorded what they said, which I did." As his stare grew disappointed, perhaps even betrayed, I said "Come and hear for yourself."

He closed the door firmly enough to be trying to shut out the world and tramped after me into the front room, so fast that he might have wanted to shove me aside in his haste to be done. He sat fiercely upright on the chair opposite mine and planted his fists on his knees while I lowered myself and groped for my phone. He didn't move or speak while he listened to the playback, but I could have thought the darkness in his eyes grew deeper. As soon as the recording ended he said "Who have you sent that to?"

"Just my friends you met at your mother's funeral."

"Roberta and the one who was in the police, Jim. Mum said you used to play at detectives. The Terrific Three, did you call yourselves? The Terrible Three?"

I couldn't tell if this was sarcasm. "We called ourselves tremendous. We weren't even half your age."

"But you're still playing at it now."

"It's no kind of game, Toby. Maybe for the Nobles but not for us."

"You still haven't said what you thought you were achieving."

"I'm keeping the promise I made to your mother the last time I saw her."

He ducked his head towards the phone, a gesture suggestive of the Noble trait. "What's that going to achieve?"

"I'm waiting to see what it does."

"I'll tell you," he said, and his stare glinted like a cinder. "I don't know how much Christopher and his family trust me any more."

"You think more of their trust than mine, then."

"I don't see why I couldn't have had both."

I had a sense of talking to someone I hardly knew. "You still want to be involved with people who behaved the way they did."

"Christopher hasn't behaved like anything, and is it really anybody's business what the others did? As Christian says, it's in your Bible. It's how we all began."

"It hasn't been mine for a very long time," I protested and was ashamed that this should be my initial reaction. "Toby, what they did is completely against the law."

"Maybe it shouldn't be for some people. Your friend Roberta's right about one thing. Nobody could make Tina do anything she didn't want to do."

I was repelled by my own question. "At what age?"

"If you've any evidence she was involved with Christian while she was too young you should take it to the police. If you haven't I'd be careful what you're saying."

I tried to see into his eyes, but they were unreadably dark. "Who's threatening me, Toby? Not just you."

"Nobody is, dad. I'm giving you some good advice."

"I'm the one who needs it, am I?" Less bitterly I said "If you aren't speaking for Christian, perhaps I should go and talk to him myself."

"You wouldn't get past Joe. You wouldn't even be let into the car park."

"I've been excommunicated, have I? Or does Christian have a different word?"

"I'm saying you can't use the church any more."

I couldn't let myself be touched by Toby's unconcealed distress. "I've done everything I needed to do there, I think."

"You haven't, dad. You don't understand at all. We haven't finished guiding you. It's no use stopping halfway there."

He was acting out so much concern that I didn't know whether to believe in it. "What are you saying I'm deprived of?"

"You won't be prepared like us. That's why we invited you into the church, to make certain you would be."

"Prepared for what?"

"You have to find out for yourself. As Christian says, there aren't words."

"Then I'll just have to be unready, if that's the price of telling some of the truth the Nobles are supposed to be so fond of."

Toby's eyes glistened until he blinked. "We mustn't leave it like that, dad."

"I'll still see you and the family, won't I? Where are they, by the way?"

"Where they should be. At the church." Before I could react he said "I mean we mustn't leave you just able to go where you've been. You don't need to be at the church to be guided. Let's do it while I'm here. Let's do it now."

I would much have preferred not to say "Tell me this isn't Christian Noble's idea."

"It's just mine, dad. I shouldn't think he even cares. I'll swear it if you like."

Though this made me uneasy, I had to ask "On what?"

"On whatever you believe in."

I felt desperate to answer. "That your mother's safe somewhere."

"I'll swear on that and to it as well. I'm doing this for you because of the promises we made her."

Surely he would never use his mother's memory to deceive me, and so I said "Where should I go?"

"Here is fine. Anywhere will be. Where are you keeping your icon?"

"It's on your mother's desk."

"I'll bring it." He darted out of the room, returning faster than I could have reached the door. "I wish we could have guided her as well," he said.

"Why," I said and couldn't hold back from adding "Where would she be now?"

"Only she would know, dad."

I was nervous of enquiring further. Toby leaned down to hand me the icon, and I couldn't help welcoming his awkwardness – his lack of the reptilian grace any of the Nobles would have shown. As he delivered the icon like a newborn child into my hands, the circuitous body seemed to hint at changing shape. Perhaps it was the way the light through the window had caught it, only to appear to be absorbed, but I was unable to judge how the image felt – its endlessly self-consuming form, its unnaturally smooth substance, even its temperature. "What am I meant to do with this?" I said.

"The same as you did at the church," Toby said and sat facing me again. "It helps loosen your mind."

His turn of phrase failed to lend the prospect much appeal, and I delayed it by saying "Who makes these things?"

"Christian has them sent. You'd need to ask him." When I kept my thoughts quiet Toby said "Start relaxing now, dad. I'll help you migrate."

"Doesn't it have to be dark?"

"You shouldn't need that any more. It gets easier each time you go. Before you set off, always think of a way to remember yourself."

This sounded like a warning. "Such as what?" I had to ask.

"We all use how we look."

"I'm not likely to forget that in my case. Sometimes I wish I could." I was still anxious to learn "What did you mean when you said I was halfway?"

"There's another journey you have to take. You need to experience it, not hear anything about it. I'll be here. You'll be safe."

He sat forward, holding me with his dark gaze. "Am I supposed to shut my eyes?" I said.

"Just do whatever feels right. Whatever helps you let go."

His ensuing silence made it plain that he was more than ready to begin. When I saw his lips shift I heard the meditative mantra in my head. As his lips released a whisper almost too faint to be heard, the icon shifted wakefully between my hands. No, my fingers had started to retrace its outline, seeking to define its shape. It felt like learning how boundlessly ambiguous that was – like trying to grasp a void and fix its limits – and distracted me from noticing how the mantra Toby and my mind were intoning had changed. Each set of syllables and their inversion reversed the formula that had sent me into memory. I couldn't concentrate on them, because I needed a mnemonic. I had to recall how I looked in the mirror.

I saw my face at once, as I'd seen it that morning in the bathroom: tousled hair the colour of dust, sticky eyes that appeared to be resting on wrinkled bags, cheeks undecided whether to sag outwards or inwards, nostrils a lair for hairs as grey as the stubble framing the wizened lips. I had a disconcerting sense of fingering its lines and pouches and the prickly pelt of the chin, not the icon in my hands. Its presence was so vivid that it took away all my awareness of the room, and I didn't see how I could leave it behind. Then the mantra someone was repeating broke the hold, and I wondered whose face I was confronting now. I would rather not have realised it was my own.

Not just the unkempt shaggy hair but the loose skin and eyes looked virtually drained of colour, while the head was propped up on a fleshy concertina that might have been producing the unmusical wheeze I heard. I'd hardly clutched at the edge of the bathroom sink, bruising my slow skinny fingers in a bid to support myself, when I discovered I was lying on a bed. A mirror that a nurse was holding showed me how dim my eyes were, not to mention pinched between drooping eyelids and lumps of shrivelled flesh. My face looked ready to expose its bones, a thought I wished at once I hadn't had, leading to another view of the face. Although its eyes were closed, I was gazing down at it, and I saw its regained colour was cosmetic. Experts had rendered it and the rest of the body presentable, dressing it up in a suit I'd never seen before, so that it would stay genteel for visitors until the lid was screwed down on its box.

I didn't know who was having these thoughts or even how many of us were. I was appalled to think that the spectacle of my own corpse was some kind of revenge the Nobles had taken, unless Toby had on their behalf. If I was dead, how could I return to myself? My disorientation felt as though the blackness that the icon seemed to represent had closed around me, trapping me in the eternal void. The sight of my lifeless made-up face had fastened on my consciousness, imprisoning me in the moment, but surely the corpse was separate from me, since I could still think. I could remember as well: how I'd grown too weak to hold a mirror as I lay in bed, and the ache spreading through my hands as I gripped the sink, and then the sight of my reflection – of today's face. The dilapidated object had never felt remotely as welcome, and it embraced my consciousness as though desperate to have me back. "Still here," I gasped or at any rate tried to pronounce. "Not gone."

As my mind regained its grasp of my surroundings I saw Toby stoop to take the icon. I supposed he was removing its influence, though I could have fancied he was protecting the icon more than me. In a bid to bring my thoughts under control – they felt like a swarming mass of panic – I blurted "Who saw that? Was it you?"

"I wasn't there, dad." In a tone I imagined a counsellor might use he said "Tell me what you saw."

"Me." With more of an effort I managed to say "Dead."

"We all see that. Ourselves, I mean, not you. It's the other gate from being born. Now you've found it you shouldn't need to see it again."

I tried to find his attitude comforting rather than additionally unsettling, but had to ask "Have you ever seen me like that?"

"Not yet. Not till it happens."

I thought he was expressing resignation rather than indifference, and what else could I expect from such a question? "If you weren't seeing," I persisted, "who was?"

"It doesn't work like that. It's your future that's remembering."

"Mustn't that involve you?" A surge of panic made me demand "Was it Macy who saw?"

"Not her either, and nobody who comes after her. It's all within you."

"I'm understanding less and less of this."

"It's the start of your future. As Christian says, words don't help much. They just get in the way. You need to go through it for yourself."

"If you have, I can." However much bravado this involved, I crouched forward to reach for the icon that lay like a sleeping pet on the floor between us. "Let's see where I end up next," I said.

"I have to be back at the church now. I'll guide you again soon." Toby leaned forward twice as fast as I had and retrieved the icon. "Shall I put this back where it was?" he said.

"If you have to go," I said too much like a reproachful parent, "just leave it on your chair."

"I'll help you again, I promise. Maybe when you come to ours on Sunday."

The notion of rendering the ritual so domestic and mundane came nowhere near appealing to me. As I limped after Toby to the front door I felt compelled to say "So will you be reporting back to anyone?"

"I'll be hoping Christian isn't thinking about you, dad. And I don't know what he could ask me that he won't already know." Toby turned as he stepped on the path, and I saw a warning in his eyes before he spoke. "Try not to provoke him any further," he said.

"Is that all the advice my son has for his old dad?"

"Almost." My feeble bid for jauntiness had only made him graver. "Wait for us to guide you," he said. "Don't risk going too far by yourself."

CHAPTER NINE

A Desperate Gesture

For most of that week I did as I'd been told, although my doubts were growing. Could Toby's advice have been a means of controlling me – of ensuring I didn't discover too much by myself? However daunting the vision of my death had been, I was tempted to see more of the future, before that event and perhaps after it as well. If my son and Claudine were capable of coping with the future memories our bodies somehow contained or engaged with – if even Macy was able to cope – what business did I have taking flight? If I waited until Sunday so as to be guided, Macy might well be involved in the ritual. By Saturday I'd begun to feel like the solitary coward in the family, so weak that I was liable to put Macy more at risk, and I resolved to take a mental journey by myself.

Lying on the bed was sure to draw me back into my past with Lesley, and sitting in the workroom would. I chose the front room as my base, opening the curtains wider to let in all the light I could. The mid-afternoon suburb was providing a soundtrack: birds in the trees, distant shouts on a sports field, the ruminations of a lawnmower. In case all this wasn't enough to restore my awareness when I needed to return, I looked for a suitably rowdy show on television and found a transmission of the second *Die Hard* film.

I left the wormy icon in the workroom and hoped the mantra was enough to send me onwards. I sat facing the window and the thin outspread television, where Bonnie Bedelia was trapped on a hovering airliner while Bruce Willis battled hordes of villains down below, reflecting that he'd experienced much the same situation in the past.

The airliner reminded me how Lesley had looked forward to a trip with Toby's family once she was able to travel. She'd reminisced about our trip to Disney World, and now I remembered it too. This wasn't the direction I wanted to take, and I began to repeat the formula Toby had used to send me forward.

I kept my voice so low that I wasn't even sure of pronouncing the syllables out loud. I had an absurd sense of trying not to disturb the neighbours or make them wonder what the old man next door was up to on his own. I did my best to fix the situation in my mind – the film that had grown suspensefully hushed, the sunlit room, the faintly creaky armchair – so that it would bring me back the instant I wanted to return. The chair recalled another one, or the flight in the film did, or both. I was tightly strapped into a seat next to a small window crystalline with ice. Below the window an unbroken field of white cloud was racing by so fast that the sight snatched away my breath. At first I thought the further ride to which this led my mind was travelling much slower, and then I noticed that the clouds were streaming vertically past the craft. Before I could adjust to the disorientation, they were left behind as the passenger flight rose towards the dark. Intricate miniature patterns of ice blossomed on the outside of the glass, only to shrink and vanish when the craft passed beyond the atmosphere. I tried to fight vertigo, which felt as if the inside of my skull had grown weightless and unstable, while I gazed down at the dwindling world.

I'd scarcely begun to share the experience when I was drawn elsewhere in space and time. I was contemplating the earth again, but from such a distance that I would never have identified it had I not known. I seemed hungry to be there, and yet some instinct warned me to stay clear by any means I could find. Was the premonition bound up with the vision that had intermittently troubled me ever since my adolescence, of a monstrous hunt across a devastated world? I was sailing towards the planet almost too swiftly to think, but I had a sense of heading for an encounter far worse than my adolescent nightmare – too dreadful even to anticipate. The impression left me feeling like a tiny child at the mercy of the boundless dark, and I was unable to think myself back to my chair, because I wasn't riding in one; I was being carried by the dark. "No," I pleaded, apparently without a mouth, "I'm sitting there, I am," and felt the airless blackness close around me like a trap, all the more inescapable because insubstantial. My mind found room for just one thought: those weren't the words I needed to use. The mantra, yes, the reiterated syllables and their inversion – and just in time, if time had any meaning where I was, I realised that I had to turn the formula around. Then I was battling nausea on the craft above the atmosphere, and watching clouds stream like a milky flood below a window, and with a shudder that felt like a break in an electronic transmission I was back in my own front room.

The film on television had yet to reach the end of the scene I'd last watched. This disconcerted me so much that I wasn't immediately aware of tracing the icon in my hands. No, they were empty, but they'd felt as if they were shaping its outline – as if the syllables I'd been repeating invoked or symbolised its form. I could easily have fancied that it had crept into my hands and then departed while I was elsewhere. As soon as I felt safe to walk without staggering too badly, I made for the workroom. The icon was on Lesley's desk, but had it moved? Even if Toby hadn't replaced it quite where I'd left it, I wasn't slow to lock the smiling object in my desk.

I was acutely aware of its presence in the house. That night in bed, whenever I began to drift towards sleep I felt as though my hands were poised to shape the icon. Recalling the rhythm of tracing its endless ambiguous outline brought the mantra into my head. I couldn't tell which way that might lead me, and I had a fearful notion that it didn't matter – that the same appalling confrontation lay in wait for me in either case. I tried only to know I was alone in bed, but this brought back memories of Lesley. At least they were mine and helped to fix me within myself. The pillow was wet against my cheek before I fell asleep and whenever I awoke.

I might have been keener to visit my son and his family if I hadn't realised there would be several of the icons in their house. Every time

I drove to our Sunday get-together I felt I was going home. They lived midway between my old house and the Nobles' first one, though at least out of sight of the graveyard. Toby maintained that he'd immediately liked the area – the suburban discreetness between the main roads, the trees along the streets, the defiantly independent neighbourhood shops – when I'd brought him home, having rescued him from Safe To Sleep. Their house was more than twice the size of my childhood dwelling, and modernised throughout by the previous owner. If this satisfied them I could hardly object, but it troubled me that they'd imposed no personality of their own. I couldn't help remembering the room in the house near Ormskirk, where I'd first met Toph – the room that had made me think the Nobles' minds must be elsewhere, given how anonymous it was.

As I parked between Toby's and Claudine's cars on the concrete flags that had flattened the front garden, Macy looked down from her bedroom window. At least I knew that room contained favourite toys, not least a dolls' house that lit up at night, and games, mostly on a computer. There were books as well, and I'd tried not to feel perturbed by learning her favourite was *Peter Pan*, no doubt revived by Toby from his childhood. By the time I finished clambering forth she had opened the front door. "Grandad," she cried, and then her eagerness wavered. "Where's your worm?"

I had to fend off any similarity to the secret conversation I'd recorded. "At home, Macy," I said.

Inspiration brightened her eyes. "Is it looking after your house?"

I couldn't see how to avoid asking "Does it look after yours?"

"Our three look after me and mum and dad when we're asleep. Never mind, grandad," she said in case I felt excluded. "You can borrow mine."

"Why, do you think I need looking after? You mustn't worry about me."

"You'll be safe in our house," she said with a gravity I tried to find no more than childlike. "You can have mine to help you migrate."

Even if she'd learned the word from her parents, I was daunted by her use of it. "I won't be doing that today," I said.

"Don't worry, dad." Toby came out of the clinical kitchen past the bare blond staircase. "As Macy says, you'll be absolutely safe with us."

I didn't speak until I'd shut the door behind me. "I know you think you're doing your best for me, but I've had enough."

I heard discreet metallic sounds as Claudine planted utensils on the dining-table, and then she looked into the hall. "You really shouldn't stop yet, Dominic. Toby says you've hardly started."

"I've seen as much as I'd like to see, thanks."

"You've only seen the body, haven't you? You mustn't let that put you off. It's just a way of setting you free to go further."

Dismay prompted me to blurt "Has everyone seen theirs?"

"I have," Macy said with pride. "It was like being a grandma."

"There now, Dominic," Claudine said. "You've no reason to be nervous when she isn't."

I was appalled by Claudine's nonchalance and saw that Toby shared it. Rather than respond to it – I might have lost all control – I said "I've been further. That's what I'm saying was enough."

"Dad," Toby protested, "I asked you to wait till we could make sure you came back."

"As you see, I managed all by myself."

I had a grotesque sense of reducing the situation to decrepit peevishness. "Where did you go, grandad?" Macy said with renewed enthusiasm.

"Perhaps I'll tell you when you're older." I couldn't bear to think she might know from her own experience, or even know more and worse. "I was only trying to see my future," I told her parents.

"It doesn't work that way, dad. Once you've seen your end you see beyond yourself."

"The future's remembering us," Macy said as if she were teaching a younger child.

"But the line isn't the same for anybody else, Dominic. Not even for you and Toby, for instance."

No doubt I looked bemused, and Toby said "Don't wear

yourself out trying to understand. I've told you Christian says there aren't words."

"He's got plenty for some things."

Claudine nodded hard to indicate Macy. "We won't discuss that now if you don't mind."

I thought she was rebuking more than my indiscretion. "If you don't feel comfortable having me here…"

"You've done what you've done, Dominic. Toby's your family and you should be able to rely on our support. The truth will have to be sorted out now. I only hope all this won't harm the church. Now I've already said this isn't the time or the place for a discussion."

As though to make up for her extended reproof Toby said "If you can't trust Christopher and his family, dad, you know you can always trust us."

"Over anything in particular?"

"Guiding you further. Not necessarily today if you haven't come prepared, but soon."

"Can anybody tell me what the point is?"

"Getting ready for the future we're all going to see," Macy said.

I hadn't meant the question for her. I wanted to believe she'd borrowed the idea, but I had to say "That isn't what your mum and dad just said."

"Some futures are stronger than others, Dominic. The strongest one draws everyone together."

Macy was eager to assure me "It won't be like anything we've ever seen."

"That's what you're trying to prepare for, is it?" This was addressed to her parents, and when they nodded in unison I said "It can't be that soon."

"Sooner than you know, dad."

"Not in anybody's lifetime here." I was recalling the passenger flights I'd foreseen. "There are people who come after us," I said.

"The future could be stronger than they are, Dominic. We don't know how far it may reach back."

As I was almost reminded of something one of the Nobles had said, Toby insisted "That's why we oughtn't to lose time. Even the Bible recognises that."

"I'm still not grasping the necessity. Do you think Christian or one of, one of his could make it clearer?"

"If you hadn't gone for him again," Claudine said, "you could have asked him."

"You aren't suggesting I should have kept quiet about them."

"Go and fetch your drink for dinner, Macy. Just stay in the kitchen till we call you. Close the door." Claudine watched it shut and turned to me, lowering her voice. "Why do you keep attacking Christian and his family?"

"You don't think what I found out matters."

"All the trouble you're making could hinder their work."

"Doesn't it matter to you?" I protested, to Toby as well.

"Not like the church does," Toby said. "Nowhere near."

"If it was a choice Christian and Tina made as adults," Claudine said, "quite a few of us don't see why it's anybody else's business. It certainly doesn't seem to have harmed Christopher."

"I should just have let them keep it in the family, you mean." When Claudine grimaced, perhaps at my tasteless turn of phrase, I said "I must be showing my age. Some things still need to be against the law."

"Dad, in time you'll come to see how irrelevant that is."

When I stayed quiet, more from despair than acquiescence, Claudine said "Will it be safe to let Macy join us now?"

"She'll always be safe from me," I retorted and was appalled by my own clumsy language. "With me, I don't need to tell you I mean."

"You don't, Dominic. Now let's forget all about that kind of thing and have a nice family dinner."

I felt patronised, and might have protested that she seemed to find some mundane issues more important than she'd claimed, at least as a means of silencing unwelcome views. As soon as she let Macy into the hall the little girl said "Grandad, are you going to borrow my image?"

I was starting to find everyone's assistance close to unbearable. "As your mum says, let's just enjoy our dinner."

I did my best and tried to feel I was setting her an example, although the Sunday roast resembled inhibition on a plate, an excuse to stop our mouths with food and avoid any number of difficult subjects. Perhaps that was why I overdid my gratitude during the meal and at the end as well. Once I'd added a last thank you on my way out of the house Macy said "Are you coming next week, grandad?"

"Of course he is," Claudine said more fiercely than I thought the question warranted. "That's what Sundays are for."

"I ought to come and see you in the meantime, dad."

"Call me first," I said as if I were far busier than I'd been for months.

He was proposing to guide me again, of course, but I had no desire to venture further when it threatened to revive the nightmare vision I'd suffered in my adolescence – the nightmare I suspected had been no dream. If I didn't mean to voyage any more, I had no use for the icon, and would rather not have it in my house. Better still if it were nowhere in the world.

As soon as I was home I made for my desk and unlocked the drawer. Perhaps my shadow made the interior look darker than it ought to be. I'd forgotten that the drawer contained the copy of Christian Noble's journal. The coiled shape lay on top of the stack of exercise books, gazing up at me with eyes like globes of congealed night. Its wide smile could have been greeting if not mocking me, and I imagined Macy waking up to see the jovial inhuman face beside her bed. A surge of loathing made me grab the icon, which was so cold that my fingers twitched, and limp fast into the back garden to destroy the thing for good.

Rocks protruded from the borders on both sides of the lawn. Lesley had covered them with tiny flowers, but they were bald in patches now. I found the largest section of bare rock and sank to my knees on the damp grass. I meant to smash the icon on the sharp edge of the rock. Its shape made it hard to wield or even aim, so that I could have fancied it was writhing in my grasp. More than a dozen blows left my hands shivering but failed even to chip the icon. Either I was feebler than I had been when I'd broken into the crypt of the Trinity Church of the Spirit or the icon was less fragile than the broken one I'd found at Safe To Sleep. I kept changing hands and tried using both, which was just as ineffective. Splinters flew off the rock while the icon remained stubbornly undamaged. When neighbours started peering out of their windows to see what was making the noise, I desisted. I almost brandished the icon to demonstrate what I'd been trying to break, a gesture that would have conveyed nothing to anyone unless they knew far too much about the church. I staggered to my feet and stumbled into the house, struggling to clutch the icon to my chest with my spasmic hands. In the workroom I slammed the gleeful face against the back of the drawer and locked the icon in my desk.

My failure to destroy it left its presence more pervasive than ever. In the depths of the night I awoke to find it had crawled upstairs and crept into my hands, unless it had summoned me to fetch it in my sleep. No, my hands were empty, although they were describing its shape. Their obsessively repetitive movements revived the mantra in my brain, or else its rhythm prompted the compulsion to outline the icon. The shape was growing more elaborate, not merely concave where it ought to be convex but infinitely hollow yet immeasurably minute. The complexity infected the mantra, which began to hatch a multitude of syllables while retaining the length of each reiterated phrase, and my mind had to grow in order to contain them all. The expansion felt like reaching for the boundless night or whatever lay beyond it, a process that distracted me from noticing how my fingers had to mutate in order to encompass the form they were moulding. The impression dislodged me from my trance, and I clasped my hands together so hard that they shook. When at last I was convinced they hadn't changed I set about trying to relax, but I didn't sleep for some time, and even then not much.

By dawn I was desperate to see the last of the icon. I stayed in the shower until I felt sufficiently awake to be safe to drive, and downed a second mug of fierce black coffee with half a bowl of cereal. Once

I'd binned the remains of my dully healthful breakfast I strode into the workroom, only to falter when I opened the drawer. The icon was still squatting on top of the exercise books, but now it was smiling up at me, and I could have thought its blank black eyes were wide with triumph.

Could I have mistaken how I'd placed it in the drawer? The possibility that my memory had grown more unreliable than I recognised didn't reassure me much. I seized the icon, gripping it harder as its unnatural chill spread through my hands, and hurried out to the car. Once I'd dumped my burden on the seat next to mine I locked the house and climbed into the car to find the icon smiling up at me. It hadn't moved – surely I'd left it like that – but I turned its face away before starting the car.

Birds flew up from hedges and trees as I drove out of the suburb, and a wind swayed branches away from the car. I couldn't feel the wind until I came to a roundabout on the main road, where I had to believe the gust was why the car lurched out of control as though eager to return home. I recaptured my hold on the steering and swerved into the correct lane as horns blared at my back. The manoeuvre twisted the icon around to face me, and I felt anxious to turn the exultant countenance away, but every time I took one hand off the wheel the car began to stray out of the lane. At last I found a layby alongside a bus stop, past which two women were walking twice as many dogs. As I pulled over, all the dogs started to bark, baring their teeth at the car while I adjusted the icon. The women were staring hard at me by the time the traffic let me onto the road. I gripped the wheel and avoided looking at the icon all the way to the rubbish dump.

I hadn't visited one for years. I remembered hurling household items into an enormous pit in an open shed. I was so preoccupied with ridding myself of the icon that I hadn't considered how such places might have changed. A sign beside a narrow one-way track beyond a wire mesh fence identified the dump as a waste recycling site. The track led past anonymous boxy shuttered buildings, a route so nondescript it might have been designed to signify abandonment. At the end, ahead of several battered hoppers big as trucks, men in yellow plastic waistcoats were interrogating drivers at an impromptu checkpoint. One guardian of garbage, a slow stocky fellow with a round flat face that looked determined to be unsurprised, stopped my car. "What are you bringing us today, squire?"

As I pointed at the icon I saw that it had crept around to face me once more. "Just an old trinket," I said.

"Hope that hasn't brought you far."

I'd grown nervous enough to demand "What do you mean?"

"Only saying it's not much to make a trip for." He stooped to peer at it. "Second thought," he said, "some might say different."

"I was passing, that was all." In an attempt to leave unease behind I said "Where shall I dispose of it?"

"Give us a squint first." Having screwed up his face in a mime of concentration, he said "Could mean a lot to someone even if it's not my thing."

"I promise you it's worthless. Would you mind directing me now? I really need to be somewhere else."

Perhaps my urgency made me appear suspect, or the second lie did. The man took time to relinquish his grimace before extending a large hand gloved like a surgeon's. "I'll take it for you, squire."

"That's perfectly all right. I can drop it on my way out. Just tell me where."

"Some of us don't like to see stuff go to waste. Too much of that in the world." As I wondered if I was about to suffer an ecological lecture he said "So long as you're done with it you won't mind where it ends up."

"I might. Where is that likely to be?"

He thrust out his hand, and his blunt fingertips thumped the window, smearing the glass. "Someone here who knows can have a proper look."

I took this to mean they knew about antiques, but I had to put the icon out of anybody's reach, not spread its malevolent influence.

"Maybe you're right and I don't appreciate its value," I said. "I'll take it to an expert myself."

His face was closing around a scowl, whether suspicious or frustrated, as I trod on the accelerator. I'd travelled just a few feet when he shouted "Steve" and jabbed both forefingers at the car. A man as wide as the average door, his torso tightly encased like frozen meat in plastic, stepped into my path. "There's a limit, grandad."

I did my best to fight off apprehension with verbiage. "Where am I supposed to have transgressed?"

"There's the signs."

I was ready to demand which until I glanced away from his unblinking reddish eyes and saw that traffic was restricted to five miles an hour. "Sorry. Distracted," I said, and when this earned not so much as a blink "Age."

He moved aside at considerably less than the posted speed, and I could have fancied he was indicating I should drive no faster than his pace. At least coasting along the virtually featureless exit road gave me time to plan. I turned the icon to face the door, and then I headed for the motorway out of town.

The main road had broken out in potholes left by lorries. Each swerve and bump inched the icon around on the seat until it graced me once more with its grin. Before I could find anywhere to risk taking a hand off the wheel, I was on the motorway. Cones closed off the inner lane and then the middle, reducing traffic to a speed that wouldn't have shamed a funeral. My car was trapped between two juggernauts several times its height, and I could have imagined the icon was amused not just by the hindrance but by the wake of fumes that had started to stifle my breath. They seemed capable of blurring my vision as well, unless that was a symptom of the panic I was struggling to suppress. The cones went on for miles without revealing any purpose, and when at last they came to an end the lorry at my back gathered speed before the one I was following did. For a distracted moment I lost all sense of which way to steer, and then the leading lorry veered into the left-hand lane, swinging its ponderous tail at my car. I raced past with my pursuer still close behind, and left the motorway as soon as I could.

I wasn't just escaping. The bridge ahead was where I'd planned to go. I sped fast around the roundabout at the top of the exit ramp, a manoeuvre that failed to shift the icon. As I drove along a wide dual carriageway, a cat ran out of a large garden and into the path of my car, only to freeze like a stricken rabbit. I trod hard on the brakes, and the icon performed a jubilant hop on the seat as though celebrating the prospect of a sacrifice. The cat dodged, by no means far enough, and then lurched in the opposite direction before twisting around to flee into the garden with a snarling howl that hardly even sounded feline. "That's one you didn't get," I muttered as I headed for the bridge.

It was almost clear of traffic. I parked in the middle and took the icon out of the car, restraining a shudder at how unctuously smooth it felt. I held it on the parapet above the concrete strip that divided the motorway and waited for a chance to let it drop. Whenever a gap developed in the outer lanes, a stream of vehicles immediately raced to fill it, and I couldn't risk causing an accident – suppose a fragment of the icon shattered someone's windscreen? I was still clutching the figurine when a police car appeared on the motorway, and I mimed interest in the distant Liverpool skyline. Perhaps my performance lacked conviction, because I hadn't seen an opportunity to drop the icon when the police came onto the bridge.

Their car stopped behind mine, nearly close enough to touch the bumper, and the driver and her colleague moved to stand on either side of me. They didn't look even as old as my son, and I had to resist thinking they were youngsters determined to act older. "What are you doing there, sir?" the policewoman said.

I couldn't hide the icon, since that would have been obvious, not to say suspicious. "Just sightseeing," I said.

"Which sights are those?"

"The famous skyline." With this inspiration came another. "I've been taking photographs," I said.

"With that."

"With this, that's right." When she and her partner continued to gaze at the icon I said "With it in."

"May we see?" the policeman said.

I did my best to produce a laugh. "I wouldn't claim they're any good."

"We'd like to all the same," the policewoman said.

I fumbled in my pocket while I tried to think. The solitary idea I had was wild, and I could only hope it worked. Before I produced the phone I managed to locate the switch to mute it. As I pretended to search for photographs I took a rapid surreptitious burst with no time to focus or even to check them in advance of showing them to the police. "I told you they weren't much," I thought it advisable to say.

"I wouldn't quite say that, sir."

Her tone went with her colleague's resolutely neutral look. The cluster of images depicted the icon and very little else. The figurine was considerably closer than I'd held the camera, and another caprice made the bulging black eyes and joyful mouth swell larger still. "You've left your skyline out," the policeman said.

"The sun was in my eyes. I didn't know."

Both my interrogators glanced at the sun, which was only faintly visible behind an extensive leisurely cloud. "Can you tell us what that is, sir?" the policewoman said.

"This?" I shoved the icon towards her along the parapet, realising too late that the question had distracted me from a prolonged break in the motorway traffic. I could have dislodged the object while feigning to give her a better look, but now the lanes were busy once more. The only answer I could find was "What it looks like. Just a sculpture."

They must be aware of the Noble scandal and presumably the church. If they made any connections, where would that leave me? The roar of the motorway rose to fill my ears, so that I barely heard the policeman ask "Where is it from?"

"From my house. From my family."

"And where do you live, sir?"

"Liverpool." When the policewoman's gaze appeared to find no purchase on that I said "Allerton."

"You're quite a way from home."

"If you want your skyline," the policeman said, "maybe you ought to go back."

Perhaps I was unwelcome on their territory – little more than an annoyance they wanted to move on – but he'd given me an idea I ought already to have had. "That's what I'll do," I declared and was turning to my car when the policewoman said "What is that actually meant to be?"

"Something diabolical," her colleague said.

"That's how I'd put it," I said.

Both of them gazed at me as though I might be tainted by its nature. "You say it's in your family," the policewoman said.

I was tempted to tell them a great deal, but how could they help? "It's been handed down," I said and made for my car.

I consigned the idol to the boot before I drove off. The police watched me leave the bridge, and I wasn't sure if they meant to follow until I reached the motorway unpursued, at least by them. I'd had enough of my unblinking exultant companion, but now that it was hiding behind me I felt chased by a presence I couldn't outrun. Beyond the motorway the road into Liverpool grew rougher, and whenever the car jerked I heard the icon growing restless. I forced myself to concentrate on the road, because I'd begun to feel the icon was about to revive the mantra in my brain, which would compel my hands to replicate the shape. "No chance," I said over and over to keep the formula out of my mind. "No chance."

I was nearly at the waterfront when I realised that all the parking for the ferry terminal was visible from Starview Tower, and so was the river. Surely even the Nobles couldn't see through bricks, and if any of them saw me from an office window, what were they likely to do? I was supposed to be too insignificant to bother with, although I'd no idea how much my latest intervention might have antagonised them. I mustn't let myself be daunted, even if lifting the lid of the boot resembled opening a coffin where the stiffly gleeful occupant lay in wait. The icon was worse than that, and I jammed it under my arm so that I wouldn't have to look at it while I made for the ferry terminal.

A tethered ship was nodding somnolently beyond the pedestrian ramp. Speakers were emitting *Ferry Cross the Mersey* as if to fix the identity of the vessel, and I remembered that the singers of the sixties ditty were the Pacemakers. No doubt the name referred to the leaders in a race, but now it felt like an allusion to age. As I limped across the gangplank, which gave a lurch as I set foot on it, a crewman stared at the object under my arm. Perhaps he had taken it at first glance for a pet, and I had to tell myself I didn't feel it squirm.

I clambered one-handed up the steps to the top deck and leaned on the rail with my back to the waterfront. While I was tempted to dispose of my burden at once, it seemed best to wait until the ferry was on its way across the river. I tried to put out of my mind Eric Wharton's fate on a ferry – perhaps even this one – most of my lifetime ago, and focused my attention on the ripples spreading across the water directly below me. Their intricate patterns were close to hypnotic, and the rhythm of their progress suggested syllables I could almost hear in my head.

I had no idea how long the ripples held my mind before the captain blasted the horn, wrenching me back to awareness. The engine began to thump as my heart audibly did, and I couldn't have said which was louder or harder. The boat swung out from the landing-stage in a stately arc and brought me face to face with Starview Tower. Above ranks of windows sparkling with sunlight the offices of the Church of the Eternal Three were as black as the icon I was carrying. If Toby and his family were up there, I was dismayed to think they were hidden. It made me realise how little of the dark power of the church I would be overcoming when I threw away the icon.

Surely at least I would be breaking its hold over me. I made myself wait while the ferry sailed into the middle of the river. A seagull swooped towards the rail and then, although I was alone on this side of the deck, veered away screeching a protest. I poised the icon between my hands on the rail, and thought the ripples spreading from the ferry had grown dauntingly elaborate. I avoided looking at them, but needed to find out who had crept up to breathe on the back of my neck — at least, they would have if they'd had any breath. Nobody was anywhere near, and I turned furiously to face the river. The boat was already heading for the opposite bank less than a quarter of a mile away, and I flung the icon with all my strength across the water.

As it fell it turned over in the air to smile upside down at me. It shattered a pattern of ripples with an explosion of foam, and dozens of birds flew up in unison along the miles of river. The icon sank under the surface, but only just, and I felt as though it had paralysed time. Was it about to wriggle into life and swim back to me? Until my chest began to throb, I was unaware of holding my breath. All at once the coiled black shape began to sink — I could have imagined it had changed whatever it might have for a mind — but it was dismayingly hard to be certain, because the further the icon descended, the more it appeared to expand. Some optical effect of the water didn't merely magnify the icon, not least its eyes and its unalterable smile, but distorted it into a writhing shape that I was glad the ripples obscured. It took far too long to vanish into the depths, which it might have been infecting with its blackness. When the ripples faded from the surface I saw them following the shape down into the dark.

Screaming birds flocked above the miles of river, and when they eventually settled I was afraid to see them dragged beneath the surface by whatever presence I'd imagined I could drown. They stayed afloat while the ferry swung towards the terminal, renewing my view of Noble's tower across the water. I could have fancied its reflection was reaching for me like a stubby snake with a swollen head. Certainly the reflection looked more immediate than its neighbours, unnaturally so. The impression faded, perhaps as the angle of the sunlight changed, but didn't leave my mind. My last sight of the icon was lodged in there too, and I did my utmost not to think about the reality of which the icon might be the merest symbol.

CHAPTER TEN

Trials

In the middle of the night an old phone wakened me. As I groped for consciousness I came close to dreaming that someone had rung me up from the past – that Lesley was calling to protect me from the vast gleeful dark. I couldn't see its lipless smile, and managed to fend off any other sense of it as I groped for my mobile by the bed. The caller was unnamed, which felt like an unspecified threat. "Lo," I mumbled before shutting off the vintage ringtone, and then "Hello."

"I was his father before she was born."

At once I was fully awake, and my head was throbbing hard enough to interrupt my thoughts. I flailed my free hand at the light-cord above the pillow and yanked it as if this might trigger more alertness. "S queues me," I said and more distinctly "What did you say?"

"Weren't you sufficiently awake to record us this time, Dominic? Shall we give you time to set us up?"

I was tempted to claim I'd done so, but couldn't see how this would be useful. Despite the pounding in my skull and the nervous dryness of my mouth, I wanted to hear what might be said. "The phone doesn't let me record calls."

"So we can speak freely, can we? We would have in any case. Have you been congratulating yourself on your latest victory, Mr Sheldrake?"

However much I felt surrounded by a darkness that was at the very best unhelpful, I wasn't about to be daunted by a phone call. "Let's say I'm biding my time until I see what happens."

"You have no idea, and that's our promise."

The whispers were intended to be menacing, I told myself. Every sibilance put me in mind of a snake, but I was more troubled by my inability to tell who was speaking, as if the Nobles had developed a single voice. "You continue to disappoint us," it said, "you and your pair of friends."

"They only did as I suggested." With more bravado than I'd shown since my childhood I declared "I'm the man you should be after."

"How important you must need to believe you are, Dominic. Have you made your life so empty that you can think of nobody but us?"

"I'm thinking of my family. They're always in my mind."

"We'd have hoped it would have grown beyond such things by now."

"You seem pretty thoroughly bound up with yours."

"We aren't your kind of family. We aren't your kind at all."

"That's the truth, thank God."

I was hoping to provoke more confessions – although I was unable to record them, I could swear to them – but the voice whispered "So much contempt, and yet you've devoted your life to us."

"You haven't much time for me either, have you? So why are you making this call?"

"You're a distraction, Dominic, and it amuses us to deal with you while we're waiting."

I wasn't going to ask for what. I was more unsure than ever who was speaking, and imagined three faces clustered around a phone in the dark, so close together that their flesh was near to merging. I hadn't spoken when the voice said "And we're interested in the progress of every member of our church."

"I was never one, and I've been told I'm not welcome any more."

"Why, Dominic, you sound as if you feel cast out. There's no need to distress yourself. Once you've participated you're ours for life."

"That's what Toph told me after I joined in at Safe To Sleep. Maybe he's talking to me now." When this brought no admission I said "I don't think you can make anyone belong to anything they don't trust. You certainly can't force them to believe."

"You belong, Dominic. You have its emblem."

"I'm afraid that's at the bottom of the river."

I heard a whispery giggle or else a chorus of them, sounding more childish or more senile than any of the Nobles ought to be. "We thought you might try something of the sort. Did you fancy you were lessening its influence?"

"There's one less to do mischief, at any rate."

"That's not the way of it at all. It's in your head to stay. It was only ever a symbol, a means of shaping your mind. How much longer are you likely to resist? Is it age that's making you so stubborn?"

"If it is I'm glad to be old, and I've no idea what I'm supposed to be resisting."

"Soon you will have. Meanwhile we look forward to seeing you again."

I tried not to let this seem too threatening. "The next time you feel you have to phone me," I said in the hope of finding out how to record, "I'd appreciate a more reasonable hour."

This apparently merited another giggle. "Time you weren't so concerned about time," someone said, and then only static hissed in my ear.

I felt alone and desperate to talk to someone, not least because the Nobles had left me afraid of my own mind. Trying not to think about the icon or the mantra felt like having been compelled to do so, and I dreaded what this might be able to invoke. It wasn't much past three in the morning, far too early to call anyone, and I could only search for memories sufficiently vivid to displace any other thoughts. I recalled letting my father believe I'd stolen Noble's journal, and catching Jim and Bobby in the cinema, and missing Lesley on the night of our Shakespearian mistake. The emotions these and other painful recollections summoned did their best to occupy my mind, leaving little space for fear. At times I even managed to sleep.

I didn't phone until I'd had a shower and then a coffee, all the breakfast I felt like swallowing. Jim's number rang at such length that I was preparing to ask if not beg him to call me back when a voice said "Dominic."

My name was presumably displayed onscreen, but the speaker wasn't Jim. I tried not to feel too nervous as I said "Yes."

"Yes."

"Yes, who is this?"

"Dominic."

For a moment I imagined that the conversation would continue multiplying echoes until it turned nightmarish – as if I were in more than one place, having been dislocated by the Nobles' formula – and then I understood. "You're Jim's son."

"And you're meant to be his friend."

"I hope I'm more than meant." When silence met this I said "Can I speak to him?"

"He's in the bath. He'll be a while." No more encouragingly Jim's son said "What was it about?"

"Our friends the Nobles."

"They're no friends of his." As I regretted using the word he said "Dominic Sheldrake about the Nobles."

I could have thought he was dictating the information – some new system the police were using – until another man said "What about them now?"

"I'm finding out, Rob." Instead of doing so his brother said "Why did you have to involve our father, Mr Sheldrake?"

"I wanted somebody's advice who knew about the law." I would have preferred not to need to ask "Why, do you think I should have kept their secret?"

"No, we think you should have brought it straight to the police."

"The Nobles won't know I didn't, surely."

"I'm afraid the truth may have got back to them. Some of our colleagues belong to their so-called church."

In that case they must have learned the truth from one of Jim's sons, which I might have pointed out if Dominic Bailey hadn't added "So what did you want to say now?"

"They rang me at an ungodly hour this morning."

"Who did?"

"The Nobles. The whole lot of them."

"Did they call the phone you're using now? Have you had the number listed, Mr Sheldrake?"

"Call me Dominic, Dominic. Tell your brother he can too." When my bid to render our talk less official brought no audible response I said "I'm not in the directory, but the Nobles have their methods."

"Which do you think those are?"

"Maybe just asking my son. Or perhaps he put it on the database when I joined their church."

"When did you do that, Dominic? And Rob's asking why."

"Just a few weeks back, to find out what they get up to. My son and his wife have involved my granddaughter. Maybe their beliefs have to be their choice, but they shouldn't feed a child that kind of thing."

"She'll be taught our kind of faith at school, though, won't she? I'd hope and pray she'd see that's the truth."

Jim's sons must know even less about the workings of the Church of the Eternal Three than he did. Before I could enlighten them, if I had the energy for yet another try, Dominic said "Can you say why you're saying they called you?"

"Their reasons, you mean." When he let his question stay ambiguous I said "To taunt me."

"With what exactly?"

"With how ineffective they think I am, or maybe they want me to think it. They were mocking me for not being able to record what they said."

"Was that anything that could be used as evidence?"

"It most emphatically was. He admitted planning to abuse his daughter before she was even born."

"You'd swear to that in court. Be aware you might have to, Dominic."

His use of my name had begun to sound too much like a carer addressing a dotard. "I'll swear to all the truth," I declared.

"What did the others have to say about it? You said they were on the phone too."

"Just more of their harassment, trying to remind me how powerful they're supposed to be. The confession was part of that, and I'm certain Noble made it."

"Why do you need to say that, Dominic? Why wouldn't you be certain?"

"They were all keeping their voices down, but you can see it wouldn't make any sense for anyone else to say what he did."

"We shouldn't really comment, but what are your thoughts, Rob?"

Across a room his brother said "I'd say Mr Sheldrake should think carefully about how he introduces that in court."

"Or even whether he should."

Not least to feel less like an eavesdropper I said "Do we know when the case goes to court?"

"Today," Dominic Bailey said. "About now."

"That's why they called me," I realised aloud. "To intimidate me when they know I'll be giving evidence."

"It doesn't work like that, Dominic. Today will be a hearing by a magistrate. They'll decide if the case will go to jury trial."

"Otherwise they'll send the Nobles to prison themselves, you mean."

"We can't speak for the judiciary," Rob Bailey said.

"But there's no question the Nobles will end up behind bars."

As I spoke I wondered how a prison could restrict their power – if it could do so at all. "The media will be reporting the decision," Dominic said.

This sounded like a dismissal, which provoked me to ask "Has your father finished bathing yet?"

"He'd only just gone in when you called."

"We'll let him know you were in touch," Rob said.

I gave them a goodbye to share and switched on the television in the front room, tuning to a news channel. A human bomb in a marketplace, an aggrieved father mowing down teachers and children with a machinegun, today's threat of war, the latest species of primate to become extinct... Without any warning that I'd noticed, all three

Nobles stared at me with defiance indistinguishable from contempt. They appeared to be posing for a battery of cameras on the steps outside a law court. A newsreader crowded their image aside and made it dwindle, but they gazed over her shoulder while she reported that Christian and Tina Noble had pleaded not guilty of any crime. A judge with a jury would try the case.

I should let Bobby know in case she hadn't heard. As her phone rang I hoped it wouldn't bring me Carole, since calling Jim's had brought his son. It was Bobby who greeted me, adding "Are you in town?"

"Sadly I'm at home."

"Be sure to let me know next time you're down and we'll celebrate old times. How are you faring on your own? No, I shouldn't say that when you aren't."

I was dismayed to find that the Nobles and their interference with the dead had left me unsure of her meaning. "Who are you thinking of?"

"You still have your family, haven't you? They seemed anxious to look after you. I hope they are, Dom."

"They're doing their best." Rather than say how, I said "We may be meeting sooner than we realise. The Nobles are going to be tried by jury. I don't know the date yet or the place."

"So we'll be called as witnesses." With enough of a pause for a substantial thought Bobby said "Were you wanting to discuss what we should say?"

"I think we should just tell all the truth we know about the Nobles and their secrets."

"I'm glad you said that, Dom. That's what I was planning to do."

"I hope Carole doesn't blame me too much for involving you."

"Carole, Dom wants to know if you're holding him responsible for how I outed Christian Noble."

"I'll tell him myself." Before I could take much of a breath, Carole's voice ousted Bobby's. "It isn't your responsibility at all, Dominic. Bob and I take full responsibility for everything we write."

"You don't mind that I sent her the recording in the first place."

"It isn't up to me to mind, but no, I don't. I don't mind anything that helps her deal with the only people who ever duped her to my knowledge." As I hoped none of Carole's fierceness was directed at me she said "Just make sure you give them as good in court as she will."

In a moment Bobby was back. "I expect you're reassured now, Dom."

I couldn't judge whether she was being ironic — whether she grasped how much more reassurance I would need. "I'll let you know as soon as I hear anything we'll want to know," I said. "Here's to our next meeting even if it has to be that one."

We said goodbye, and Carole called one out. I'd muted the television while I was on the phone, but I saw the Nobles once again aiming contempt at the world. When I turned up the volume the newsreader was repeating the report I'd already heard. I switched off the set — I didn't care to watch the Nobles gazing at me over her shoulder, even though of course they couldn't see me — and the phone rang at once.

I could easily have fancied that the Nobles were calling to establish that I couldn't rid myself of them so easily, and then I saw Jim's name. "Sorry I was wallowing," he said.

"Did my namesake tell you about the call I had this morning?"

"Rob did. You should mention it to the prosecution. They'll decide if it's significant."

"Surely you think it is."

"It doesn't matter what we think, Dom. I just wanted to update you on the trial."

"I saw the news. They'll be tried in the crown court."

"We've just heard it's going to be expedited with all speed. Christian Noble's age is being given as the reason, but I wonder who's pulling the strings. I'll let you know as soon as we hear the date," he said, and I could have thought the mantra of the Church of the Eternal Three had undermined my sense of time, because I was disconcerted by how soon he called again to say that the trial was set for next month.

CHAPTER ELEVEN

Versions of the Truth

"I swear that the evidence I shall give shall be the truth, the whole truth and nothing but the truth, so help me God."

Light shone through all the high wide windows of the courtroom, rebounding from the pale walls as though to leave untruth nowhere to hide. Bobby stood rigidly straight in the witness box with her hand resting on a Bible, and when I watched the video Carole had recorded on her partner's behalf with the phone peeping out of her breast pocket, I wondered how much Bobby was putting on an act for the sake of conviction. "Please be seated," Raymond Garland said for the prosecution, "and state your name for the record."

"Roberta Bernadette Parkin."

I'd never realised Bobby had a middle name. As a religious reference it might almost have been designed to lend strength to her oath. Certainly she pronounced her entire name with pride that could have been mistaken for defiance. "And what is your profession, Ms Parkin?" Raymond Garland said.

"I'm a journalist and writer."

"How long has that been the case?"

"More than forty years."

The tall grey man – suit, shirt, hair and moustache – clasped his hands in front of him and gave her a nod that looked not too far from smug, at least to me. "You've been a columnist for all that time."

"Nearly all."

"Just take a moment to mention the titles of some of your books."

"*We Are All Victims* and *The Apology Obligation*, they're the latest."

"How would you sum them up?"

"I'm saying society has become a victim of the victim status too many people are encouraged to feel entitled to, and I'm examining the trend that demands apologies for anything anybody disapproves of."

By now I was wondering how soon Regina Dane might intervene for the defence, if Inigo Arnold – the judge – didn't speak up. Presumably they were giving Raymond Garland time to establish Bobby's credentials, and he said "What would you say is the purpose of your writing?"

"To tell all the truth I can." As if sensing an objection Bobby added "Once I'm satisfied with my research."

"Was there anything in particular that set you on this path?"

"A friend I've had since we were at school used to be a writer, and we were into investigating as well."

"Can you say which of your publications has the largest readership?"

"That would have to be my online blog."

"That's how publishing has developed," the lawyer said as if somebody – perhaps the judge – might need the explanation. "Ms Parkin, how is your blog related to your journalism?"

"They're very much the same. Most of the time they literally are. The blog reprints my columns once they've appeared."

"So the blog upholds the standards you've established."

"Most emphatically, yes."

Perhaps her vehemence roused the judge, who poked his sharp concise pallid face forward under his imposing wig. "I fear we've strayed into areas of opinion, Mr Garland."

"Your pardon, your honour. Ms Parkin, please tell us what led to your publishing an instalment of your online column about the defendants."

"I heard them admit what they did."

"How were you able to do that?"

"I was sent a recording, and I trusted the source."

"Is there any possibility in your mind that the recording could have been altered in some way?"

"None whatsoever, and the Nobles haven't tried to say it was, have they?"

"Ms Parkin," the judge said with a frown that looked weighted by his wig, "please confine yourself to your own testimony."

"Sorry," Bobby said, adding "your honour. I'll just say all three of them couldn't have known they were being recorded."

"Will you tell the court what your motive was in publishing the information?" Raymond Garland said.

"The public interest. That's always what it ought to be."

"Could there have been an element of revenge?"

I supposed Raymond Garland meant to head off the suggestion before it could be used by the defence. "Revenge on whom for what?" Bobby said.

"You wrote that you'd allowed yourself to be swayed in some way by the defendants. Might you have been harbouring resentment about that?"

"No, it just showed me how persuasive Christian in particular could be. I wanted to put the record straight after I'd failed to report on them back then."

"How are you saying you were persuaded?"

"The Nobles used some form of hypnotism at the children's facility they ran in the eighties. I believe they could be using it at the church they're running now."

Inigo Arnold raised his head with a gravity that might have been exerted by the wig. "Is that observation based on experience, Ms Parkin?"

"Not on mine, no. I'll withdraw it if you think I should."

The judge had already looked away from her and past the lawyer. "Please continue, Mr Garland."

"No further questions, your honour."

"Your witness, Ms Dane."

Regina Dane was a slight woman with a disproportionately broad face enlivened by large eyes. Her hair and her suit were dark enough for a funeral. While she looked no older than my son, I suspected she had several years on him. She approached the witness box as tentatively as someone hesitating to ask for directions in the street, and I saw this was part of a performance. "Ms Parkin," she said and extended her hands, though not far. "Please allow me to thank you for taking so much time away from your work to travel to the court."

"You needn't thank me." I gathered Bobby didn't mean this to sound hostile, since she added "It travels with me."

"Is that to say you're working as we speak?"

"No, I'm just telling the truth."

"You don't plan to write about your experience in court."

"I might if I think it's worth writing."

"I'm sure you're always careful with your words." Before I could decide if this was any kind of warning Regina Dane said "You told the court your blog reprints your columns. Does that include the one you wrote about the defendants?"

"No, that's only online."

"Why is that, Ms Parkin? Surely the controversy would have helped to sell the publication you write for."

"The editor thought it was too controversial and wouldn't take the risk."

"Was the decision based on legal advice?"

"Maybe, but I thought it was too important not to publish."

"And may I ask what you earned from publishing it yourself?"

"Not a penny. Anyone can read my blog for nothing."

"You don't think it has earned you publicity."

"If it has that wasn't my intention."

"Would it have made a difference to your editor if you'd named the source of your information?"

"I honestly don't think so."

"Indeed, Ms Parkin, you've taken an oath to be honest. Did your source ask to remain anonymous?"

"No, not at all. I shouldn't think he'd ever do that."

"Then may we know why you failed to name him?"

"Because his family belongs to, let's say the church the Nobles run, and I didn't want to cause them any unnecessary trouble."

"What sort of trouble were you afraid to cause?"

"Ostracising, maybe, or worse."

"That's very vague and speculative, Ms Parkin. Has anything of the kind taken place?"

"Not to my knowledge, but that's not to say it couldn't."

"You'll be aware that the defendants have identified the source. I'll ask you to name him to the court now."

I saw Bobby realise there was no point in secrecy, but she was plainly reluctant to say "Dominic Sheldrake."

"Is he the person you told my learned friend was a writer and investigator?"

"He was when we were at school." A pause appeared to prompt Bobby to add "Maybe later too."

"If he's all you say, why did he send you the material instead of disseminating it himself?"

"He gave up writing a long time ago. I expect he thought I was the best person to publicise what he'd found out."

"Wouldn't putting it online himself have done that?"

"I suppose he preferred me to put it into words." Bobby lifted her head higher, presenting her chin like an emblem of defiance. "And of course he'd passed it to the police," she said.

Regina Dane paused as if a question that she'd had in mind had been anticipated. "Let me remind you of some of the comments you wrote," she said. "You mentioned that Christina Le Bon influenced you even when she was a toddler."

"I don't believe I said influenced."

"You described her as your biggest inspiration, and you set her alongside a number of people you cite as having made you who you are. But you also single her out as the biggest disappointment in your life."

"I'm afraid that's what she turned out to be."

"And you say you're disappointed in yourself for having been so influenced. Would you agree you must be quite easily swayed if you can be so won over by a child as young as she was?"

Bobby jerked her chin higher. "I said I was impressed by her, and I wasn't that much older myself."

"How old were you at the time, Ms Parkin?"

"Twelve. Just twelve."

"Weren't you quite sure of yourself even then?" Regina Dane gave her little time to answer. "You're understandably resentful," the lawyer said. "Is that why you claimed she was being abused at that age?"

"I simply wondered how early it started. These things generally begin when the victim is young."

"When she's vulnerable, you mean." Once Bobby indicated agreement, Regina Dane said "But in your blog you contend that Christina Noble already knew her own mind. Are you accusing her of being implicated even at that age?"

For the first time Bobby looked uncertain. "No, I'm saying when it happened her father must have made her."

"You're accusing him of abusing an infant."

"No," Bobby said with more defiance than I thought was helpful, "suggesting it might bear investigating."

"It's been investigated, Ms Parkin. You're maintaining it was no more than a suggestion on your part."

"If you check you'll see I just said I wondered."

"That was very skilful of you. Quite professional." Regina Dane began to turn away from Bobby and then seemed to find a reason to confront her again, however tentatively. "But you did say you might have been blinded by visions," she said.

"Distracted from what was really going on, you mean."

"I believe you'll find blinded was the word you used. Perhaps you aren't so careful with your language after all." When Bobby let a stare do duty as an answer, Regina Dane said "How did you come to experience these visions?"

"I was investigating the setup the Nobles ran back in the eighties."

"Christian Le Bon and his daughter ran it. You aren't saying Christopher did."

Bobby might have been choosing her words before saying "Just them."

"And you were investigating it at whose behest?"

"My own. It was my idea to find out the truth."

"Hadn't the organisation been brought to your notice?"

I saw Bobby decide there was no point in holding back. "Yes, by Dom Sheldrake."

"What did he tell you about it?"

"I really can't remember after all these years. It was supposed to treat children who suffered from nocturnal seizures. They called it Safe To Sleep."

"Treat them how?"

"By hypnotising them or something like it till they were able to sleep normally, but in fact it was giving them visions based on the beliefs Christian Noble has held all his life. I'd say it was indoctrinating the children."

"All his life." The lawyer seemed poised to pursue this, but said "Please tell the court about the visions you experienced."

"I participated in some of the sleep sessions. I was hypnotised along with the children."

"No, Ms Parkin," Regina Dane said, laying both hands on the ledge of the witness box. "Tell the court what you saw."

When Bobby closed her eyes I was afraid the question had revived the experience. "Beyond the world," she said. "What lives out there."

"Please be specific."

Bobby squeezed her eyes so tight that her face appeared to shrink. "I'd really rather not remember."

The lawyer's fingers shifted on the ledge like a mime of patting someone's head. "Did you publish your observations at the time or since?"

"Back then I was persuaded they were beneficial."

"You do seem easily persuaded." As I willed the prosecution to object, not that doing so could expunge the comment from anybody's mind, Regina Dane said "You're asking the court to accept that visions of a kind you would rather not describe were meant to help children sleep."

Bobby opened her eyes with some force. "That isn't what I said."

"Is that the effect they had on the children?" When Bobby didn't speak the lawyer said "Ms Parkin, wasn't it your observation that the treatment did indeed cure the children of their nocturnal problems?"

"It seemed to."

"And because that contradicted your purpose in investigating, you didn't publish your findings." Before Bobby could respond the lawyer said "Have you met any of those children since?"

"Some."

"And did they appear to be damaged or say that they were?"

"No, but that's how indoctrination can work."

"Indoctrination." Regina Dane turned her back on Bobby, and her gaze passed over me – over the surreptitious lens, at any rate. "I believe," she said, "that many if not all of the people who benefited from Safe To Sleep are positively involved in the church that Mr Le Bon and his family founded."

She scrutinised the spectators at such length that Bobby began to grow restless. As if she'd had an afterthought Regina Dane said "Ms Parkin, you told my learned friend that none of the family knew they were being recorded. Why is that significant?"

"It's why they owned up to what they did."

"How could Christopher Le Bon own up to anything that happened before he was born?"

Bobby made to speak and failed. "No more questions, your honour," Regina Dane said without even glancing at the witness. Presumably Raymond Garland felt the same, since he wasn't heard from. Bobby stepped down from the box, looking frustrated and close to bewildered, but I'd seen and heard none of this when I was summoned as the next witness.

CHAPTER TWELVE

On Every Side

As the doors closed behind me so discreetly that they might have been designed to hush my arrival, the eyes of all the Nobles fastened on me from the far end of the courtroom. Christian and Tina were seated in the pen reserved for defendants, but they conveyed the impression that they were enthroned, gazing down from a high place at the world. So did Toph from directly behind them. Not just the faces – three variations on a single introverted theme – but their eyes might have belonged to a solitary entity that was watching my approach. I couldn't help reflecting that some spiders had six eyes, though the way the Nobles inclined their heads almost imperceptibly in my direction was as reptilian as ever. I thought they looked poised to strike.

I felt their scrutiny gathering on me as I limped along the aisle, not merely weighing on me like a mass of cobwebs but surrounding me, closing in. It seemed to have infected most of the courtroom, where the same contemptuous indifference was trained on me from every side. The room was full of faces I recognised from the Church of the Eternal Three, and quite a few of those that weren't familiar bore the identical expression. Their attention felt like an unnatural darkness that was growing concentrated in the sunlit room. When I caught sight of Toby, seated nearly at the front, I failed to glimpse the look that gave way to concern shadowed by regret. At least Claudine wasn't with him – at least Macy wasn't, thank God.

I did my best to hide my limp – I didn't want to appear vulnerable, let alone as if I were inviting sympathy or condescension – but the stride I attempted to keep up stumbled more than once. Fixing my attention on the witness box felt like avoiding the eyes of the judge as he observed my progress. Although he was seated higher than anyone else in the court, I was sure the Nobles viewed him as lower than them. By the time I reached the witness box my legs had grown shaky, and I gripped both handrails as I climbed the steps. A clerk waited for me to conquer the ascent and handed me a laminated card that bore the oath. "Please take the book in your right hand," she said.

I planted my hand on the Bible instead and felt I was using it for support, though it didn't provide much. Ought I to have declared my unbelief? I imagined it was too late now, and demurring might have weakened my case from the outset. I vowed three times to tell the truth and invoked God's help with doing so, or rather called on God to witness my truthfulness. "Please be seated," the clerk said.

As Raymond Garland stepped forward I made another vow, though silently – to focus my attention on him and shut out all sense of the Nobles, at least all I could. "Please state your name for the record," he said.

"Dominic Sebastian Sheldrake."

"And your profession, Mr Sheldrake."

"I'm afraid I'm retired."

"No shame in that," the lawyer said and interlaced his fingers in front of his stomach, protruding his thumbs. "What have you retired from?"

"I used to teach film."

"You lectured on the cinema at Liverpool University for more than forty years." Having translated my statement, Raymond Garland said "Did you also write about the subject?"

"I published the odd piece."

"Your essays appeared in a number of academic journals, presumably after your work was reviewed by your peers. Your analysis of religion in the cinema attracted a good deal of favourable comment by your fellows in the discipline. Quite a few found your thoughts stimulating."

I might have welcomed all this if I hadn't felt expected to impress the Nobles and their equally indifferent followers. "I'm glad if they did."

"Have you written about any other matters?"

I was reminded of my tales of the Tremendous Three. "Really nothing worth mentioning," I said at once.

"You haven't published anything investigative."

At last I saw what he meant to establish, and tried not to show I did. "Only criticism."

"Let us move on to the issue before the court," the lawyer said, bending his thumbs outwards like a secret sign. "How did you come to record a conversation between the defendants?"

For an instant I was tempted to pretend it had been accidental, but I wasn't such a coward. "I'd been recording a sermon they gave."

"What was your purpose, Mr Sheldrake?"

"I wanted a record of the kind of thing they said."

"Why did you feel you needed that?"

"Because my son is a member of their church."

I saw no point in admitting I'd had a larger aim. I glanced at Toby, only to wish I'd refrained. If his eyes contained anything apart from darkness, it didn't favour me or my testimony. Every eye around him was just as pitilessly dark, as though a contagion had spread from the watchers in the dock and from their son. I felt dismayingly grateful to return my attention to Raymond Garland, who was saying "What did you intend your recording to achieve?"

"I was going to confront my son with it. I might have let some experts hear it too," I said and felt compelled to add "It isn't just my son. His wife and their small daughter are in the church as well."

"But you recorded more than the sermon."

"I thought I could catch what they might say when nobody else was present."

"Had you any preconception what that would be?"

"None at all. I was as shocked as everybody else."

A glance at the spectators showed me not the faintest trace of shock, just dull hostility trained on me. "Please tell the court what you did with the recording," Raymond Garland said.

"I got it to the police and sent it to a journalist. Bobby, that's to say Roberta Parkin."

"The court has heard from her." As I wondered if I was about to learn any of her testimony, the lawyer said "Why did you send it to her?"

"In case she thought it should be written up."

"We have seen she did. I remind you that you're under oath, Mr Sheldrake." Before I could find this too ominous he said "Can you assure the court that the recording wasn't edited or tampered with in any way?"

"It certainly wasn't by me. The only people who could have had access to it besides me were the Nobles, and it makes no sense that they would."

Speaking their name let me meet their eyes – in fact, it made me have to do so. They gazed expressionlessly at me, or darkness wearing three variations of a face as masks did. I felt close to frozen by the confrontation until the judge said "Mr Sheldrake, will you swear that there was no doctoring?"

I groped for the Bible and laid my hand on it. "I absolutely will."

"Please do not touch the holy book."

I supposed this meant it was to be used solely for the initial oath, but I felt as if my disbelief had been exposed, casting me out from any faith. When I lifted my hand from the book a leathery suction seemed to resound throughout the courtroom. As I watched my sweaty handprint dwindle on the cover before vanishing, Raymond Garland moved away from me. I could have thought he was ensuring nobody associated him with me or my behaviour until he turned to the defence lawyer. "Your witness."

Regina Dane's thoughts appeared to be slowing her down as she came to stand by the witness box. She blinked at me, looking unsure how high to raise her eyebrows if at all. "Mr Sheldrake, will you tell us a little more about your published work?"

"What would you like to know?"

"Some of the titles, if you remember them."

"Of course I remember. I'll tell you them all if you like." Perhaps I was wrong to find her request patronising, since her tone was impeccably neutral. "*Watching the Audience: Eyes in Hitchcock's Films*," I said.

"What was your concern in that?"

"How his films often turn the audience's gaze back on itself, *Psycho* in particular."

"*Psycho*, yes." She might have been judging the word rather than repeating the title. "Could you give us another?"

"*Between Laurel and Hardy*." When her inviting look didn't falter I felt prompted to add the rest of the title. "*H. M. Walker's Intertitles as Sufficient Narrative*."

"I think you'd have to explain that to the court."

"Harley Walker wrote the onscreen dialogue for Hal Roach's silent comedies." Though I'd begun to wonder how relevant any of this was to the trial, I said "The continuity titles too. They're famous for their wit, visual as well as verbal. I showed that in many of the films they can be read as separate narratives or at any rate additional."

"Would you say your aim was to find meanings everybody else has overlooked?"

"I'd like to think some of my essays have achieved that. It's certainly one of the functions of criticism."

"My learned friend singled out your thoughts on religion in films. May I remind you of a title?"

"Any you like."

"*A Child Shall Lead Them*," the lawyer said, and I thought she'd finished until she supplied the second half. "*ET as the Second Coming*. I understand it was quite controversial."

"It did generate a correspondence in the journal."

"And rather more when it appeared online."

"I didn't realise it had. Appeared, I mean."

"Or caused a stir, presumably." When I agreed Regina Dane said "Some of your ex-students were reminded of your teachings on religion."

"I didn't see that."

"Here are some of their comments. I wonder if you recognise their names." She strode to her desk, revealing a good deal of concealed purposefulness, and brought sheets of a printout over to me. "Alysha Martin says you treated religion as a joke," she said, "and Brendan

Dowd remembers you as constantly questioning other people's faiths. Katy Davies thinks all this forced your students never to take their beliefs for granted, but the others say that wasn't what they signed up for."

I felt as if the darkness I'd been trying to ignore had crept up to take me off guard. "I think making students examine views they've taken for granted is a crucial element of teaching," I said.

Regina Dane gave me an unhurried blink before she said "Was that your purpose in your poetry as well?"

"Poetry," I said and understood too late.

"Will you confirm this is your work?"

She leafed through the printout and handed me two sheets – a copy of the verses that had brought me and Lesley together. "I wrote those when I was a student," I said.

"Please read them to the court."

"Your honour," Raymond Garland protested at last, "surely this is irrelevant to the proceedings."

"I believe I may see some relevance, Mr Garland," Inigo Arnold said and tilted his bewigged head towards me. "Please read to us, Mr Sheldrake."

The Nobles leaned forward in unison, which put me in mind of the three-headed snake so prevalent in myth. The spectacle couldn't entirely distract me from the lines I was being made to recite to an utterly unresponsive audience. I kept my head down and had pronounced several verses as neutrally as possible when the judge spoke. "I think you have made your point," he said, perhaps to me.

I'd just exhorted worshippers to supplicate the third person of God for a bung. Regina Dane retrieved the pages and handed them to the clerk. "The jury might like to examine these, your honour."

"Let them be passed. Pray continue, Ms Dane."

"Mr Sheldrake, how would you describe your view of religion?"

"Undecided." This hardly helped, and I fumbled for the truth. "As I grow older," I said, "I'm more anxious to find something to believe in."

"Does that mean you believe in nothing at the moment?"

"No, it means I'm searching. It means I hope there's something to believe."

I'd barely finished speaking when I felt as though darkness had craned up to loom over me. Three heads had inched forwards, perhaps to remind me how much they'd given me that I yearned to disbelieve. As I tried to fend off memories of those experiences, Regina Dane said "Was that a reason why you joined the Church of the Eternal Three?"

"I suppose you could say that." I met Toby's eyes while I said "My wife had just died and my son invited me to join."

"Did he believe it would benefit you?"

"I can't speak for his beliefs. I shouldn't think the court would want me to." When nobody responded, not least Toby, I said "But yes, I'm sure he did."

"And did it do so?"

I regretted letting her lead me down this path, and could only say "It helped me deal with my grief."

"Can you say how?"

"It gave me more to think about."

I should have known this wouldn't satisfy the lawyer. "I understand the church offers to bring your past alive," she said. "Was that the case for you?"

"I think it uses some kind of hypnotic regression and that's what I went through."

While this wasn't even close to what I thought, I couldn't imagine telling that truth in a courtroom. I'd begun to grow acutely frustrated with the dogged commonplaceness of the questions, with how far short they fell of everything the Nobles represented. Toby's eyes were dark beyond interpretation, like all the eyes around him, and I looked away as Regina Dane said "What can you tell us about the sermon the defendants gave?"

"I think it showed how far their organisation is from anything most of us would call a church."

"Why would that concern you, given your views?" Before I could object to this she said "Forgive my not asking you earlier why you've ceased to be published."

"The journals I wrote for have been, and so I don't write any more." Not much less defensively I said "I'm concerned for the people who are being fed these beliefs by the church."

"Is that why you set out to discredit its founders?"

"I'd say they discredited themselves."

While I hadn't answered the question directly, the lawyer's responses seemed increasingly haphazard. "You could have published online," she said.

"I'd run out of thoughts, I'm afraid."

"Quite an admission, Mr Sheldrake." Her eyes had grown as unfathomable as my son's. "We aren't talking about your film reviews," she said. "I'm saying that you could have put your recording out yourself."

"As I said before, I sent it to a journalist for her to judge if it should be published."

"A childhood friend you'd influenced in the past."

"She's certainly a friend, but I don't know about influenced."

"In her online piece concerning the defendants she says she was duped."

"Not by me," I said and stared past her at the dock. "By Tina Noble."

The triple gaze met mine, and at once I was unable to make out the faces. They appeared to merge into a single visage that was close to abandoning any pretence of the human. The darkness that was using them to watch me filled the courtroom and loomed at the windows, blotting out the world. I managed to fend off the illusion, if this was all it was, by wrenching my attention back to Regina Dane in time to hear her say "Your friend seems to have been easier to influence than she would like to think."

"That's how the Nobles work on their victims. It must be how Christian worked on his daughter."

"You're asking the court to believe that Christina Le Bon was able to exert control over adults of more than average intelligence and yet under control herself."

"Yes, because the Nobles, they're all—" The composite face seemed to dart at the edge of my vision like the swollen head of a snake, and I searched for words the jury might accept. "Her thoughts and her son's, they're all the father's," I said, an inadequate approximation.

Regina Dane scrutinised this or my face. "Did you hope Roberta Parkin would publish the information you sent?"

"If she thought it should be published, yes."

"Or were you afraid to put it out yourself and used your friend to do so? What were you afraid of, Mr Sheldrake?"

I was seized by guilt that felt as if it had been lying in wait for me. I wanted to think the accusation was unfair, but I was certainly too inclined to put Bobby in danger, at Safe To Sleep and now in disseminating the truth about the Nobles. It was partly anger with myself that made me blurt "What would you say I ought to be afraid of?"

"Perhaps an action for defamation."

"I haven't defamed anyone, and Bobby Parkin hasn't either. We've just told some of the truth the Nobles claim they're committed to."

This fell so far short of the reality the Nobles represented that it might as well have been false testimony. I felt bereft of words I could risk uttering, and afraid of having trapped myself into silence or else recklessness. I could only wait for Regina Dane to respond, and she said "When did you first become suspicious of the defendants' relationship?"

"I know when I should have been."

"When was that, Mr Sheldrake?"

"The first time I saw Tina Noble. Her father was calling her a mother even then."

"When and where was that?"

"When she was still in her pram. I overheard him talking outside my house, when he must have thought nobody else could hear."

"You say you should have been suspicious. Do you recall any other occasions of the kind?"

"Yes, when I met them all at Safe To Sleep. That's the facility they used to run that was supposed to help children like my son. They were very secretive about the identity of Christopher's father, but they didn't mind boasting how unusual their family was."

"So you would say you've had reasons for suspicion almost as long as you've known any of the defendants."

"Earlier than that. Before I even knew Christian Noble was a teacher at my school."

Could I really have had so little sense of my own words and how they might be interpreted? Perhaps the relentless presence of the Nobles – loitering at the limit of my vision without owning up to a shape or indeed a size – had driven me to say too much. Regina Dane looked regretful or at any rate saddened as she said "So your preoccupation with the defendants dates from childhood."

"That's when I first met them." I felt indefinably uneasy to have to add "At least the ones who were alive then."

"And you've tried to undermine their reputation ever since."

"I've told nothing but the truth about them, and I still am. I don't think anyone can disprove that."

"Did you not steal a journal belonging to your teacher when you were at school?"

"I've never stolen from anyone." This was a truth I should have told my father on his deathbed. The memory threatened to overwhelm me – to entice me out of the present – and my voice grew fiercer to compensate. "His father took it," I said, "if you call that stealing. He hid it at the school for somebody to find."

"Why would he have done such a thing?"

"Because he was scared of his son and what he was teaching the granddaughter."

"So you were the child who found the journal."

"Yes, and I took it to the headmaster."

"What did he make of it?"

"He didn't read it. Christian Noble came for it and the head gave it back."

"You're saying the headmaster had no chance to read the journal. Had you?"

"No, I'm saying he chose not to, but I did."

"And what did you find in it?"

"The same kind of occult stuff the Church of the Eternal Three is selling now."

"I gather you were educated as a Catholic." When I agreed as neutrally as I could, Regina Dane said "Are you aware how Christian Le Bon's father died?"

"I saw it, and my friends did. He fell under a tram."

"Are you able to tell the court how this happened?"

"He was chasing us to find out where we lived so he could ask our parents to help him deal with his son."

Once again I was menaced by a recollection – by a dauntingly immediate vision of the unstable monstrous shape Christian Noble's father had borrowed from the fog. "Have you anything more you would like to tell the court?" Regina Dane said.

"Not that I can say."

"Then let me sum up your testimony. I suggest, Mr Sheldrake, that you have been obsessed with the defendants for most of your life."

"So people keep telling me, but you ought to see it makes no sense." I was regarding the jury, who returned my stare, having denuded it of all expression. "Some of them weren't even born," I said.

"I put it to you that your fixation was born the first time you saw Christian Le Bon. When you learned that he didn't share your religion, you tried to cast him as a heretic. You did your best to turn his employers against him, but your headmaster proved to be more tolerant than you."

"That isn't how it happened. I told you the head didn't look at Noble's journal."

"You're asking the court to believe that a headmaster wouldn't examine an item that had been presented to him as evidence of wrongdoing. A Catholic principal at that, and in the nineteen-fifties." With too little of a pause to let me speak Regina Dane said "I understand that Mr Le Bon's father was of unsound mind when he stole his son's journal, which may very well explain the manner of his death. I take it you and your school friends claim no responsibility for that."

"We weren't responsible, but anything wrong with his mind was his son's fault."

"Mr Sheldrake, you seem bent on blaming Mr Le Bon for everything you can. Even losing your religion only made you more determined to defame his."

"It's not just his religion, if you insist on calling it that. It's what he and his family did to my son."

As I gazed across the courtroom at Toby, finding no hint of a response, the lawyer said "What did your late wife think of the treatment they gave him?"

"She was taken in by them like nearly everybody else."

"Whereas you're convinced you alone can see the truth."

"I said nearly everybody. For a start—"

"Of course, your lifelong friend Roberta Parkin. I suggest to you that you sent her the recording of the defendants because you weren't quite as sure of its significance as you led her to believe. You used her to publish what you wanted to be the case because you knew better than to publish it yourself."

"That absolutely isn't true. If I thought anything I thought her name would attach more credibility."

"So you admit it lacked credibility."

"That's not what I meant and you know it." I found that during her interrogation I'd slumped into a posture that suggested the questions or their dogged mundanity had settled on me like a burden. I straightened up fiercely enough to shoot pain through my spine, and remembered barely in time not to touch the Bible, gripping the rail of the witness box for support instead. "I sent it to her because she'd reach a wider audience than me," I said.

"Perhaps you can explain why she simply wrote about it rather than posting the recording online."

"Because she's a journalist, I should think. Did you ask her? If not, why are you expecting me to know?" I imagined I glimpsed doubt on the lawyer's face, and it drove me to continue. "Haven't the police examined the recording and made sure it wasn't tampered with?"

I fancied I could feel the united gaze of the Nobles taking hold of my skull like three digits of a claw, rendering my mind as cold and empty as a space between worlds. I thought it was trying to quiet me, which made me so determined to speak that I scarcely grasped my own words. "You won't intimidate me," I told the Nobles. "You didn't when you rang up in the night to boast about your secrets, and you aren't succeeding now."

There was silence that felt penned in by the bright room full of darkened eyes, and then Regina Dane said "No further questions, your honour."

I was hoping Raymond Garland would question me about the nocturnal call when Inigo Arnold spoke. "Mr Sheldrake, please leave the court at once and say nothing further, or I shall hold you in contempt."

I had the impression I already was, by everyone in the courtroom. The jury looked no more persuaded by my outburst than the smugly indifferent pair in the dock and their son behind them. As I climbed down from the witness box – my legs felt as if they might prove unequal to the job – I saw the Nobles set about mouthing words in unison. I was afraid that they were murmuring the formula I'd learned at the Church of the Eternal Three – that they meant to send me somewhere else, leaving my body to demonstrate to the court how incapable I was. I fought to keep hold of the moment while I limped towards the aisle, and then I saw that the syllables they were shaping were too numerous for the mantra. Either they were preparing words or communicating in some unnatural fashion. I made for the exit as fast as I could but felt I was struggling through a medium composed of the censure of everyone I had to pass. I'd reached the door, which an usher held open in a last small remnant of respect, when Christian Noble spoke. "Enough playacting," he announced. "Time for the truth."

CHAPTER THIRTEEN

Sentences

"Have you reached a verdict upon which you are all agreed? Please answer yes or no."

"Yes," the foreman of the jury said and looked restricted by the answer.

"What is your verdict in the case of Christian Le Bon?"

I suppose the answer came almost at once, but it felt as though the abyssal gaze of the Nobles had fastened upon time to hold it still. "Guilty," the foreman said.

"In the case of Christina Le Bon, have you reached a verdict upon which you are all agreed?"

The foreman seemed uncertain how to respond, and a nervous breath caught in my throat. Perhaps he was simply waiting to be told once more how to reply, because in a moment he said "Yes."

"What is your verdict?"

Since the foreman had stood up he'd kept his eyes turned away from the Nobles, and they stayed on the judge as if the foreman thought the bewigged figure might accord him some protection. "Guilty," he said.

Inigo Arnold thanked the jury for their time and focused his attention on the dock. While his eyes weren't so dark and deep as the cluster that met his, they were just as unforthcoming with their thoughts. "Has either of the defendants anything to say before sentence is passed?" he said.

Christian Noble leaned forward at once, raising his face to the judge with no pretence of deference, and I had the unpleasant impression that a single body the family shared had thrust out its left-hand head. "I shall," he said.

"Please stand." Once Noble had risen to his feet, an action so lithe it looked effortless, the judge said "You may address the court, Mr Le Bon."

Noble rested his hands on the rail of the dock with all the fingers spread wide, a negligent gesture that might have defined carelessness. I thought he resembled a priest in a pulpit, and deliberately too. As he parted his lips I glimpsed the flicker of a tongue – no, three of them, because his offspring had performed the same act. "We told you we weren't guilty under any law that matters," he said.

His contempt for the trial had been plain throughout his testimony and the cross-examination – above all, when he'd declared that the recording I'd made should be heard by the court and admitted as evidence, a suggestion to which Tina readily agreed. I did my best to think he was making the situation still worse for himself, because I was disturbed by how his daughter and their son kept mouthing his words in unison like a silent chorus. More than ever the family put me in mind of a single presence masked by three versions of a face, and I wished the judge would order Tina and Toph to stop their antics. Surely he must find them distracting, unless he was determined to ignore them. I could only hope they weren't daunting him into silence. I hoped he was letting Noble express all his disdain for the proceedings so as to convict him of that as well.

"The world must return to the ancient laws," Noble was proclaiming. "For a period that is less than a moment of the universe, man has invented his own. His world is an insignificant speck that would attract little notice, but now he has presumed to probe the universe with all the means at his disposal. His collective mind is at large in space, set free by the computer. Nobody may rouse the attention of the universe without acknowledging its laws, and soon the oldest will regain their hold upon the world. This court and all within it are of no consequence to them, but the matter upon which we have stood trial is our way of preparing for their revival, our tribute to them."

I thought his final comment was a bid to reclaim significance for himself and his family. More than ever I had a sense of a sermon, most of which might have been translating Gahariet Le Bon. With a precise reversal of his earlier sinuous movement Noble took his seat again. While the judge hadn't looked away from the dock, I couldn't make out his reaction, even once he spoke. "Do you wish to say anything, Ms Le Bon?"

Tina rose exactly as her father had. "Please," she said.

"Pray do."

"Just to repeat what I said before, all my relationships are purely my choice. Nobody can make me do anything I don't want to do. I was a virgin until it was legal even in this country for me not to be, and I've only ever known one man."

I glanced at Bobby as Carole and Jim did, but her face was no more communicative than the judge's. I was hoping to hear some outrage in the court at Tina's statement, possibly even distrust of her claim that she'd been of age, but the only sound was her voice. Might it be exerting some of the hypnotic power the Nobles had employed at Safe To Sleep and at their churches? I did my utmost to resist everything she said. "My relationship isn't contrary to our principles," she was saying. "We believe it is protected by our church."

I wanted to protest that the church was a device the Nobles had constructed for their own purposes, not a religion at all. I'd been not much less than appalled when she and her father were allowed to take the name of the Eternal Three as the basis of a vow to tell the truth. In a moment she resumed her seat, reversing her previous motion just as her father had, and the judge was adjusting his wig as a preamble to speaking when Toph said "Can I say something too?"

"That isn't how it's done." The judge clasped his hands and slid them apart on the desk before saying "I'm prepared to allow it in the special circumstances."

I should have liked to know what he thought those were. As Toph repeated the movement his parents had performed, I willed him to earn them longer sentences and provoke one for himself, although would prison contain their powers or rouse them? I thought the judge might have directed Toph to the witness box, but he left the youngest Noble where he was. "Without these two I wouldn't be here," Toph said.

"Will anybody dare to say they want that? You'll see I had to be born. I had to even before they were. Deny us and you deny your future. The faithful shall be one, and the unenlightened in their own way too."

Inigo Arnold watched him regain his seat with that motion I could easily have fancied was turning time backwards. For some seconds the judge didn't move or speak, and I couldn't tell whether the silence was expectant or apprehensive, not even my own. "There is a question that ought to have been asked," he said.

This sounded like a proposal to rescind time or at least to call back some of those involved in the trial. It left me unprepared to hear him say "Has the act that led to these proceedings been repeated since Christopher was conceived?"

"No."

The response disconcerted me as much as the question. At least two voices gave it, and I was virtually certain one more had. "There was no need," that voice said.

Inigo Arnold regarded Toph, and I thought he was about to warn him not to speak unless invited. Instead the judge returned his attention to the dock. "I can see no reason to delay sentencing," he said.

I saw Jim was surprised by the speed of the proceedings, and I could tell I wasn't alone in holding my breath until Inigo Arnold continued. "In a recent case which may be found comparable," he said, "the sentence handed down to the accused was ten years each."

Would Christian be dead in a decade? Until now I hadn't confronted the issue of his future. If he died in prison, how much would that aggravate his malevolence? I should have realised death mightn't curb his powers any more than imprisonment could. I was starting to feel I'd trapped myself at least as thoroughly as him when Inigo Arnold said "I believe the public interest would expect the same in this case."

Jim gave a nod that I took for approval, and Bobby reached for Carole's hand. I felt as if I was clenching my lungs as well as my fists while I waited for the judge to speak. "Christian Le Bon, I hereby sentence you to ten years in jail," he said.

Quite a few people let out their breath. It sounded like a concerted gasp, and I might well have been involved. As I hoped I hadn't drawn attention to myself, the judge went on. "Given your standing in the community and in particular your years," he said, "I shall suspend the sentence, and I do not anticipate that it will be served."

Why wasn't anyone expressing shock or outrage now? Even Jim went no further than shaking his head while Carole gripped her partner's hand with both of hers. "I cannot see that any useful purpose would be achieved by varying the tariff," the judge said. "Christina Le Bon, I sentence you to ten years also, hereby suspended. Once again, I do not expect any part of it to be served."

Bobby bowed her head while Jim turned his empty hands up as though he hoped some consolation might be placed in them. Throughout the sentencing the Nobles hadn't stirred, and they were the last to rise when an usher directed everyone to stand. I saw Inigo Arnold rubbing his hands together as if to celebrate the end of the trial, or was he simply passing them over each other? I could have thought they were sketching a shape. I was distracted by a sense that others did as he turned to leave the courtroom.

When the audience began to disperse I wondered what I missed hearing. Perhaps courtroom dramas had led me to expect a noisy exodus of reporters as soon as a case was done, but why were no journalists hurrying out to be first with the news? I could have imagined they'd all known or at any rate foreseen it. Spectators – members of the Church of the Eternal Three, no doubt – were offering the Nobles their congratulations, but Christian waved them away, adding an impatient smile. As their supporters backed away so deferentially that I wouldn't have been surprised to see them perform more of an obeisance, the Nobles marched in step along the aisle towards us.

Jim made to rise and then stayed seated. I didn't know whether he meant to head off a confrontation or just to demonstrate he wasn't threatened, but I followed his lead as Bobby and Carole did. The Nobles kept their multiple gaze on us all the way down the aisle, and I felt as if that darkness was not merely approaching but intensifying, closing in. As they came abreast of us, Tina focused on Bobby. "Roberta," she said, "I just want you to know how disappointed I am."

Carole raised Bobby's hand in hers like a double fist. "You've no reason to be."

Tina didn't glance at her. "I always knew you were planning to give Safe To Sleep a bad press, but I tried to show you how wrong you were," she told Bobby. "I wouldn't have expected you to betray us, especially after all these years."

"I wasn't getting at you," Bobby said more defensively than I'd ever heard her speak. "You'll have seen what I wrote."

"You betrayed us all. We're one and nobody can separate us. We only tried to help you, to make you more equal to what's on its way."

"And if anyone thinks otherwise," Toph said, "they'll live to see their mistake."

"Mr Sheldrake," Christian said as if he'd only just noticed me, though his gaze gave no sign that he had. "You're enjoying your latest achievement, I hope."

I became aware that we were surrounded by members of his church as expressionless as him. I reminded myself that we were in a courtroom – that someone official might soon intervene on my and my friends' behalf. "Have you further plans for us?" Christian Noble said.

I did my best to hold my voice steady and neutral. "I'll have to think."

"If only you would. I fear you are losing that ability. Another disappointment, I'm afraid. Do try to use your mind to the full until we meet again." Not just to me he said "We know where you are. We always have."

Jim looked for an usher, but none were to be seen. "That sounds like a threat, Mr Noble," he said.

"Nothing like it, Mr Bailey. We're simply making you aware of the nature of reality. That has always been our aim, and you won't be able to avoid it much longer."

"You're starting to live in our world." Toph had the last word as the Nobles moved away, gliding in unison. "You will until you die," he said. "And then so much more."

CHAPTER FOURTEEN

Across the Water

A TRAVESTY OF A TRIAL

That was the title of an editorial in a national newspaper, but it was the only observation of its kind. Some newspapers reported the verdict without comment, and quite a few hardly reported it at all. Broadcasts of the news were resolutely neutral, and yet I seemed to sense respect for Christian Noble, for how he'd stood up in and to the court without seeking to conceal the truth. Every report mentioned his age, which I felt was being offered as an excuse if not to justify indulging his behaviour. Even the editorial cited it, although only to point out that it hadn't brought him wisdom or robbed him of vigour. The writer saw it as no reason for hastening the legal process, given that Noble showed no signs of failing health. The swiftness was just one of the irregularities. Letting their recorded talk be played in court simply showed how the Nobles scorned the law, and indeed their words on the recording did. Inigo Arnold's verdict had been a parody of justice, and letting somebody who wasn't even a defendant address the court before sentencing turned the trial into a farce. The case had been so thoroughly mishandled that it led one to suspect the motives of those responsible, the judiciary and the police and whoever else might have been involved. The editorial appeared in the first printing of the issue and online, where I read it. In later editions it was replaced by a piece about disunity in Europe and how countries were reverting to their individual languages as tokens of identity – RETURN TO BABEL. When I looked for it online again it had vanished, and by the end of the day the newspaper had seen a change of editor.

The case and the sentence provoked much online hostility and criticism, all of it swamped by responses. Anyone who spoke against the Nobles might be accused of offences worse than theirs, or of trying to destroy a religion the times required, or of making far too much of Christian's relationship with his daughter if not overlooking its positive qualities. Some of the multitude supporting the Nobles maintained that the Church of the Eternal Three sanctioned – indeed, sanctified – their union, and many of their champions called Toph its greatest vindication. No relationship deserved to be censured that had produced him.

All this reminded me how Toph had said we were living in their world. At least, I hoped this was what he'd meant, and nothing worse. Even so, it left me desperate to search out online comments from opponents of the Nobles and their influence, who hadn't yet been daunted into silence or shouted down by foes who appeared to think wholly in capitals. I was at my desk by Lesley's empty one, where her computer screen resembled an emblem of eternal darkness, and reading yet another dispute about the case when someone rang the doorbell.

It shrilled for just a second, and I wondered if I was about to meet another aspect of the Nobles' world. I didn't intend to feel menaced in my own house when I had so little to lose, and I limped fast to the front door. A pair of police officers stood together on the path. "Have you seen someone, Mr Sheldrake?" the policewoman said.

"Seen them where?" Unease prompted me to add "Doing what?"

Her frown failed to make her look even as old as my son. "Seen someone as you were advised to."

I couldn't help remembering Lesley's suggestion of psychiatric help before I recognised my visitors. They'd lost the fake tan the streetlamps had lent them the night they had brought me home. Their skin was much paler than I would have expected, and their hair wasn't black; hers was red, his a nondescript brown. As I tried not to feel they'd removed a nocturnal disguise, the policeman said "Shall we talk inside?"

"Forgive me, but what about?"

"You claimed you'd been intimidated."

"Not by you, either of you. You were helpful when I may have needed it." This scored no response, and I felt impelled to add "There were a couple of your colleagues, but I should think that was before you were even born."

"Did you put in a complaint?" the policewoman said.

"I was given the impression it wouldn't do me any good. The police weren't as accountable back then as they're meant to be now."

I'd just realised this could be taken as a sly threat to complain when the man said "We aren't talking about police, Mr Sheldrake."

"You made the complaint when you appeared in court," his partner said.

"I'm sorry, but I didn't. I might have if I'd seen anyone to tell."

By now both of them were withholding their expressions. "Are we going inside, sir?" the man said.

Perhaps I shouldn't have let this feel as intimidating as it did. "I'd prefer people to see what happens."

"What are you suggesting that might be?"

"Nothing if you're saying nothing. Nothing except talk."

He and his colleague made their patience plain, and I suspected they wanted me to feel like an unreasonable oldster, which provoked me to demand "Just what are you saying happened in court?"

"You accused someone in the dock of intimidating you," the policewoman said.

"I did, yes. They did, I mean. All of them."

"All of whom, Mr Sheldrake? There were only two defendants."

"Maybe there should have been three. Their son was complicit, wasn't he? He knew their secret and kept it as well."

The silence this brought me felt like not just an answer but a reprimand. As a car passed along the road, slowing beside the police car that blocked the entrance to my drive and then speeding onwards, she said "You maintain you were intimidated by all three members of the family."

"That's what I said, yes. Not that they were all in the dock together."

An impression that they had been felt like a memory implanted in my skull. "How were you intimidated?" the policeman said. "They weren't seen to move or speak."

"You must know you don't need to do any of that to threaten people." This sounded too close to an accusation, perhaps even a complaint of feeling menaced as I spoke, and I hastened to leave it behind. "They rang me in the middle of the night," I said.

"Who did, sir, and when?"

"Christian Noble and his brood, not long before the case went to a magistrate."

"What was said?"

"A lot of the kind of stuff they preach at Starview Tower." This didn't lessen its reality, and I saw it didn't sound like intimidation either. "They wanted me to know how insignificant they think I am," I said. "I think they were trying to undermine the testimony I'd give."

"How could they know you would," the policewoman said, "when the case hadn't gone before a magistrate?"

"I'm sure they were planning to say they weren't guilty, and so they'd have known they'd stand trial."

The police scrutinised my face and shone a light into my eyes, or rather the sun sent a fierce beam through foliage across the road. As I leaned my head aside the policeman said "Did you record the call?"

"My phone won't do that. I believe there's a legal issue."

As I grasped that I might have made it sound as though he'd proposed breaking the law, the policewoman said "If you'd recorded it, would you have tried to introduce it as evidence?"

"If the Nobles didn't object I certainly would have, and I can't imagine they'd have cared."

I sidled out of reach of the relentless sunbeam, only for a breeze to stir the leaves and send it after me. It blinded me to the faces of the questioners as the policeman said "The number will be listed on your phone, will it?"

"They hid it. Maybe they aren't as anxious for the world to know about them as they'd like you to believe. Mind you, if I'd recorded them you wouldn't have known who was saying what."

The sunbeam fastened on my face, or the official gaze did, if not both. "You're saying you couldn't identify the callers," the policewoman said.

"They were the Noble family, all of them. I'd swear to that on anything you like."

"That won't be necessary. Do you wish to take this further?"

I could hear she didn't recommend any such course, and I'd already decided. "I don't suppose there would be much point."

"Then we should advise you, sir," the policeman said, "not to waste police time."

I was a good deal too close to retorting that they'd done so if anybody had, and then the policewoman held up a hand. She surely didn't mean a piercing ray of light to stream between two fingers onto my face. "Something you need to explain, Mr Sheldrake," she said. "What would you have told someone at the court?"

"I don't know what you have in mind."

"You said you had a complaint to make if you'd seen anyone to tell."

"The Nobles came up when the trial was over and surrounded us with their followers. Not just me but my friends who'd been involved in the case."

"James Bailey and Roberta Parkin."

I might have been more immediately disconcerted by her knowing the names if I hadn't needed to say "Christian Noble told us he knew where we lived. Jim thought that was intimidation, and he used to be high up in your job."

"We know all about Mr Bailey. Did he file a complaint?"

"Not that I'm aware of."

"Then we'd suggest you should be guided by him," the policeman went beyond suggesting. "And do keep in mind what we said about time."

"Now we'll leave you alone, Mr Sheldrake."

This could have been a farewell or an admonition to make sure I gave them no reason to visit me again, if not a reminder of my solitary state. They'd turned towards their vehicle when I said "Since you know all our names, shouldn't we know yours?"

They didn't look back, so that I had no chance to judge whether they were giving me their own names or their partner's. "DC Farr," the woman said, and her colleague added "DC Black."

I was unable to move while they marched to their car in unison. I felt as if, far from removing a disguise they'd worn at night, they were wearing one that they presented to the world. I was pathetically grateful to observe that their actions as they climbed into the car weren't entirely synchronised. Once the vehicle was out of earshot I stumbled into the house, groping for my phone. By the time I fell into my chair in the front room, a bell that sounded like an echo of the past was ringing. I'd begun to think Jim found the sight of my name on the screen less than welcome when he said "Dom."

He sounded tired, and I could easily have thought I was the cause. "I'm sorry I involved you and your family in my crusade," I said.

"We involved ourselves. We did what we could and that's the end of it."

"I don't know that it is, Jim."

"Dom," he said, an unmistakable reprimand. "What are you proposing now?"

"I've no plan at the moment. I'm just afraid I may have given you and your boys a problem with the police."

"They're well placed to deal with anything like that, and I should think I am. What problem?"

"I've just had two of them here, taking me to task for accusing Christian Noble of intimidation. They made it pretty clear I shouldn't tell the truth if I haven't got the proof."

"I suppose they'd have to take that position. Was it just a verbal warning?"

"They didn't give me anything to show, if that's what you mean. They take after their masters when it comes to not leaving any evidence."

"I meant they're taking it no further." Jim's weariness was approaching impatience. "If I were you I wouldn't either," he said. "Let's try and get on with whatever's left of our lives."

"It isn't that simple, Jim."

"I know your family are still with the Nobles, but—"

"That isn't all. The police who were here, they're the children of the ones that came after me in the days of Safe To Sleep. Farr and Black. Tell me that isn't significant."

"Do you want my boys to look into the situation if they can?"

"I don't want anybody else getting into trouble on my behalf. Better leave it unless Farr and Black have another go at me."

"Then let's hope we can forget all about them."

"I don't know if we can. I told them you accused Christian Noble of threatening us after the trial. They wanted to know if you'd put in a complaint."

"I didn't, and I won't unless you think I should."

"No, then. No but thanks."

"Let's get together again soon. Bobby too if she can make it." A pause left this resembling a farewell until Jim said "And do make the most of your family, Dom. Maybe try avoiding things you disagree about. I really think they care about you, and Bobby thought so too."

I felt he was counselling me to forget as much about the Nobles as I could. "Soon," I said as an adieu without making the word any clearer. He'd left me more aware of Bobby than of any danger to myself, and I phoned her at once.

"Dom." Her enthusiasm wasn't too distinguishable from concern, especially when she said "How are you dealing with fame?"

"I haven't earned too much of that, thank God. It's mainly you the net is after. I just hope I haven't brought you the wrong kind."

"I've certainly multiplied my followers. I think I've enough supporters to take on the hostile mob, and I've kept my column and my publishers."

"You surely didn't think you'd lose them."

"I've a sense there may have been some talk behind the scenes, but they're holding out for me."

I was dismayed to think I could have put her work in jeopardy, but she was saying "How has the outcome affected you, Dom?"

"At least the Nobles haven't anything to take out on my family." Unable to leave it at that, I said "I had a visit just now from the police."

"You think it has something to do with the Nobles."

Rather than bring Farr and Black up again – I felt exhausted of explanations – I said "They didn't like my saying I'd been intimidated."

"You mean the police intimidated you as well? Are you going to put it online?"

I heard her urging me to rediscover confidence as a writer, but it was far too late. "Even if they tried I won't," I said.

"Do you want me to? If you tell me everything that happened—"

"I've made enough trouble for everyone. Everyone except the Nobles." In case Bobby took this for an invitation I said "I'll make it public if anyone does. I only wanted to warn you the police are at large."

"I shouldn't think I've any reason to be visited."

I had to hope the Nobles thought that of her too. "Jim says we should all meet up again soon," I said.

"I'll definitely let you know next time I'm up your way. In fact, I always will."

I felt close to reviving our adolescent vow, but made my farewell instead. The calls had left me feeling I'd done less than I should. Now that I'd brought my friends to the attention of the Nobles, it was surely up to me to protect them. Since the Nobles had boasted about their ability to find us, oughtn't I to learn where they lived? Perhaps in some way this might give us an advantage.

In less than five minutes I found Christian Noble's address in the electoral register, having realised that he and his family would be listed as Le Bon. All three of them were living in a house across the river. An online map showed a three-storey building perched above a precipitous riverside garden taller than the house. It was close to

Egremont Ferry, where the remains of a landing-stage commemorated an ancient crossing of the water.

The image of the house seemed anonymously innocent, but I wanted to see the real place. The present ferry would let me take a look without venturing too near. Where were the binoculars I'd used to spy on Safe To Sleep? I'd given them to Toby not long after so that he could view the moon. I found them in a corner of his old room, lying on a deflated rubber ball that bore a faded wrinkled grin. They were enmeshed in cobwebs, and the lenses looked senile with dust, but once I cleaned the binoculars they worked well enough.

I drove through the town to the river and parked near the landing-stage. The homeward exodus had begun, and commuters were queuing all the way down the ramp from the Pier Head, leaving me in sight of the secretive black windows at the top of Starview Tower. I was glad when strangers closed in behind me, once I'd decided that their faces showed they had no interest in me. Eventually a rattle of chains and a double thump of gangplanks beyond the ramp released the queue. By the time I clambered to the top deck of the ferry, all the benches were laden with passengers, but there was space to stand at the rail above the prow. Once the ferry swung about I would be able to watch the Noble house.

Thunder thin enough to be accompanying an amateur drama resounded beneath the arch that enclosed the ramp – footsteps of commuters sprinting for the boat. The ferry lurched away from the stage with a creak of hefty rope and returned, thumping rubber. A final passenger clattered across the gangplank moments before it reared up, clanking its chains. A piratically tattooed man lifted the rope from its bollard on the dock and pitched it to a crewman. The engines began pounding like an amplification of my heart, and the ferry wallowed away from the stage. It turned as inexorably as the hand of a clock and brought me face to face with the Noble house.

The house looked reassuringly distant until I lifted the binoculars, and then I had to tell myself its immediacy was artificial. One detail that the online image hadn't shown I saw at once. Every item of vegetation

– flowers and dwarfish bushes – on the six deep steps that formed the garden above the promenade was leaning if not straining away from the house, just like the trees around the field where Gahariet Le Bon had built his church. I was disconcerted by how little I could make out of the house. On each of the three floors an identical pair of windows was embedded in pale stone under a steep grey slate roof crowned with three chimneys, but beyond the windows I could distinguish only darkness at odds with the late afternoon sunlight. I might have fancied that the house contained no rooms – that it was a mask worn by a void.

As the building crawled towards me its approach began to drain my sense of where I was, withdrawing the murmur of conversations behind me, the humid breeze that kept tousling my hair, the faint saline smell of the incoming tide. I had to grip the barrels of the binoculars and press my ribs against the rail to convince myself I was safely remote. Even so, I let the binoculars dangle on their strap before raising them again. I'd glimpsed movement inside the Noble house.

My sensations receded as I made out three figures, one on each floor. They were pacing if not dancing rapidly back and forth, passing out of sight beyond the edge of one window before reappearing to cross to its twin and vanish. While I knew they were the Nobles, I was unable to identify which was which. What sort of house had just one room on each floor? Perhaps there were others beyond the rooms overlooking the river, but the sight renewed my impression that the house was hollowed out, occupied by a void and its inhabitants. The movements in the gloom grew more defined, and I saw that each of the figures was describing an intricate sinuous series of patterns with their entire body, not so much a dance as a mime of a state I preferred not to begin to imagine. I was struggling to break the hold the sight exerted on my mind – I'd lost so much awareness that I couldn't even feel how I was clutching the binoculars – when the identical simultaneous movements took another turn. All three figures swooped towards the left-hand windows to press their faces against the glass.

The binoculars dealt my chest a hearty blow as I recoiled. I couldn't be sure I'd seen the stack of faces like a fleshy totem-pole grow far too large and flat against the panes, their scarcely human eyes swelling huge as though their darkness had distended them. I did my best to think they hadn't seen me, but now I realised that the ferry was in the middle of the river, halfway between the Noble house and Starview Tower. From where I stood, and plainly from the house as well, the tower appeared to be situated midway between the two Liverpool cathedrals, and I wondered what meaning the Nobles might find in the trinity this formed. I wasn't anxious to imagine it myself, and I was reaching none too eagerly for the binoculars when I grasped that the position of the ferry was significant as well. It was where I'd thrown the icon from the Church of the Eternal Three into the river.

Venturing back to the rail, I peered at the water. The ripples that the boat was sending forth appeared sluggish, not to mention thick and black as oil. Perhaps shadows of clouds were darkening the river, except that the sky contained just a few clouds, shrivelling overhead. Was the ferry even moving? I had a nightmarish impression that only the somnolent ripples were – that the boat might be trapped between the house and the tower, arrested in mid-river by some submarine presence that was blackening the water but not yet revealing its shape. Could I hear the engines labouring on the way to failing for good? There was certainly a fierce hot stench of oil. I found I was actually relieved to see the Noble house creeping closer once I understood this meant the ferry was still able to progress. I didn't know if I was seeing activity inside the house, ill-defined shapes darting back and forth. They put me in mind of caged creatures, but could I really make them out at such a distance? I took hold of the binoculars, only to decide that the sight of the house and its stealthy implacable approach were daunting enough.

At last the ferry veered towards Seacombe, where all the other passengers disembarked. I was tempted to find another route back to my car rather than be exposed out on the river. Just as I decided to use some other public transport, the gangplank clattered erect, cutting off my escape. I managed to resist spying on the house until the ferry reached the middle of the river, and then my apprehension enraged me. If the Nobles thought I was insignificant, they could hardly object to my watching the house.

I brought the binoculars to my eyes and let them fall at once, grabbing the rail for support. I was desperate to believe that the sight I'd seemed to glimpse was a trick of light and shadow. A single face could never have filled all the windows of the house, glaring out at me with its six monstrously enlarged eyes, bereft of pupils but alive with darkness. I retreated down the steps, almost falling headlong from haste, and took refuge in the saloon on the lower deck. Even there I felt dreadfully vulnerable, as if I were suspended above an abyss that was eager to swallow me, the infinite depths of space that lay below the river – below the world. I had to keep glancing at the banks of the river, to fend off a persistent notion that the outlines of warehouses and dwellings and the crowded buildings on the waterfront had begun somehow to fray, a portent of collapse. It felt as if some awful future was spreading from the river to corrupt them. When at last I reached my car I felt compelled to keep hold of the present moment in any way available to me, and my skull grew brittle with the effort as I drove nervously home. Even the rush-hour traffic barely kept me conscious of where I was, or when.

CHAPTER FIFTEEN

An Ending

That night I didn't go to bed, because I'd grown afraid of wakening unaware of who I was. The impression that my ferry trip had left – that the buildings on both sides of the river had begun to grow furtively derelict – felt as though a catastrophic future was lying in wait. Even if it mightn't be my own, this didn't let it feel less ominous or less eager to appear. I suspected that the drowned icon had given me the vision; perhaps just the thought of it had. I did my utmost to put it out of my mind, but the very effort threatened to lodge it there, along with the mantra it recalled. I could only search for thoughts as remote from it as possible, and even then I feared that my hands would set about surreptitiously shaping the icon if I didn't find another use for them.

After I'd downed some of a token dinner I sat in the front room, leafing through an album Lesley had put together years ago. It was full of photographs of graduations – not just hers and mine but Toby's and Claudine's – preceded by events from Toby's time at school, sports days and prizegivings. Our graduation robes seemed to recall forgotten rituals, and I found it hard to grasp the past we'd actually inhabited. The sports days brought back the afternoon I'd discovered Christian Noble's journal, and even the pride I experienced at the sight of Toby accepting yet another school prize was undermined by knowing how he'd put his intelligence and skills at the service of the Church of the Eternal Three. This helped to fix me in the present, but not in any sense I welcomed, and I looked for another way to occupy my mind.

Television offered very little I wanted to watch. A vanload of killers had driven into a crowd before knifing more victims, and the airwaves abounded with reports of the event and interviews with witnesses and discussions of the issues it raised. While more than one group had claimed responsibility for the random massacre, I thought the perpetrators incarnated chaos. No doubt Christian Noble would interpret the murders in those terms, and did this mean he'd influenced my thoughts? I set about switching channels, but all the other programmes struck me as avoiding if not denying the truth. I made for the shelves jammed with films and grabbed the first title that came to mind.

It was a restoration of Orson Welles' *Macbeth*, the film that helped Lesley and me miss each other all those years ago. Three witches appeared to form out of a fog, and the sight of figures taking shape that way almost made me stop the disc. They'd perfected the rite since I'd last seen them, when an extravagantly damaged print shown at a cinema had them chanting "When shall we three set of sun." I did my best to appreciate how much Welles had achieved on second-hand sets in just over three weeks, but when I wasn't thinking of the hours with Lesley that I'd lost – a foretaste of losing her for good – I found the play even more ominous than normal: the portrait of an inexorable future, unavoidable once foreseen. The spectacle of unnaturally mobile vegetation swarming towards Dunsinane revived my encounter with the restless objects in the crypt beneath the Trinity Church of the Spirit, and I closed my eyes while I tried to remember Lesley instead.

Vegetation brought to mind laying flowers on a memorial. Our garden was her monument, and her memory had no need of dying flowers while her own continued to grow. I hoped her ashes lent them life, but I was drawn to the notion of a remembrance in some favourite place of ours, where I might have a bench built with a motto on a plaque. The idea seemed to lead naturally to a view of some kind of shrine, a marble slab laid in a wide grassy gap between two houses at the summit of a slope. A kneeling woman had just stood a pot that contained a solitary flower on the slab. As the unrecognisable plant, whose piebald swollen blossom was as variously green and white as the thick convoluted stem, began to writhe like a snake I read the inscription on the pallid slab:

CHRISTIAN
CHRISTINE
CHRISTOPHER
LE BON

Below the names a date was hidden by the pot, in which the mutated flower was performing an intricate sinuous dance. The blossom appeared to be mouthing a formula that I was anxious not to hear – that I feared I knew all too well. I struggled to recoil from the sight, and at once the space was blackened and strewn with rubble, and I recognised the houses that framed it. I'd seen them from the ferry, flanking the Noble house, and the memory snatched me back to myself.

I blinked in bewilderment at the television, where several black actors were declaiming lines from *Macbeth*. The disc had moved to an extra feature, footage of Welles' voodoo version of the play. The occult undercurrent didn't appeal to me, and I stopped the disc, which didn't halt the clamour of my fears. Could seeing the present state of the Noble house hold me back from straying into the future? I suspect this was less a thought than a compulsion, and I never knew how much of that was mine.

I shelved the film and stood in the front doorway, hoping the night would enliven my sense of myself. That it was hours later than I'd drifted away from watching the film didn't help my confidence. How long had I been elsewhere and insufficiently conscious that I was? How much had my involvement with the Church of the Eternal Three undermined my awareness of time? An unseasonable chill felt like a touch of the blackness overhead. At least it went some way towards restoring my senses, and once I felt safe to drive I made for my car.

The suburban streets were deserted, and I saw not a single lit window. The main roads were bereft of traffic, and every shop was dark. Even when I lowered the window to let night air stream in I heard no sounds beyond the whir of the engine and the rubbery murmur of the wheels on tarmac. The only movements to be seen were the routines of traffic lights, totting up their colours like a simplified species of abacus. The lifeless streets felt like an unwelcome omen of the desolation I'd imagined glimpsing from the ferry. Streetlamps peopled the route with elongated shadows not quite like their objects and blotted out the stars, an absence that reminded me too acutely of the void I'd explored from Safe To Sleep.

I was still alone on the road by the time I reached the Wallasey tunnel, the newer of two routes that led beneath the river. I drove down the ramp and was in sight of the arched entrance when a thought jerked me further awake. How close would I have to pass under the spot where I'd thrown the icon in the river? I might have turned back if a concrete ridge hadn't blocked all access to the opposite lanes. I gripped the wheel so hard my fingers ached as I drove beneath the arch.

The tunnel was less than two miles long. I ought to be through it in under three minutes. Overhead lights illuminated twin lanes leading to the far side of the river, strips of light in random groups that resembled a Morse version of words in an unknown language. The empty tunnel gave no sign of where it left the land above the roof behind, but long before I reached the midpoint I seemed to sense the massive burden of the river. The impression wasn't just of water. It felt as though a colossal bloated presence was nesting on the roof, shifting restlessly and sending sluggish ripples through the earth if not the substance of the tunnel. I fancied I could sense its wakefulness, a stealthy rhythmic vibration that made my skin crawl as if the presence had commenced infesting my flesh. Had the lights begun to flicker almost imperceptibly? They made the walls look unstable and brittle, close to collapsing and burying me in the dark.

According to the dashboard clock it took me not much longer than a minute to arrive at the lowest point of the tunnel, but the information seemed meaningless, not remotely reassuring. The car began its climb towards the exit, which was out of sight beyond a distant bend, but the delay felt as protracted as a nightmare before the presence that was crouched or coiled or otherwise poised above the roof started to release my consciousness. At last the car emerged from the tunnel, and the sense of darkness massing overhead gave way to a different dark.

Beyond the exit was a line of tollbooths. At this time of night most lanes were automated, but the sign above the furthest left announced it was **ATTENDED**. Even if I could have found the correct change, I felt anxious to talk to someone. The pay booth was occupied by a short pale man with a wide face that looked oddly undefined, patchy stubble helping the dimness to blur his features under a lopsided oily mass of black hair that resembled a slipped wig. He gazed past me as if he was expecting more than my car to appear from the tunnel or from that direction, and then blinked at me as though I'd wakened him. He slid his window open to stick out a pale stubby hand, and I couldn't think of much to say as I passed him two pound coins. "Quiet," I observed.

"Right."

His soft voice was so toneless that I could have thought the word was enjoining silence. When he reached for change the dimness left me unsure whether he was continuing to gaze beyond me as if he was still in a dream. "Any reason?" I tried asking.

"Night."

This could have been a farewell or an invocation. Certainly it might have contained more than it admitted. As he handed me my change I saw that his fingers were longer and thinner than I'd taken them to be. "Is it always so quiet this late?" I persisted.

He shut the window before speaking, so that I wasn't sure I heard him say "Will be."

I was about to remind him to lift the barrier when it rose. I felt as though he'd tried to delay me, and I had to restrain myself from putting on too much speed. I drove around a roundabout beyond a ramp and pulled into a layby alongside a bus stop. Perhaps I wanted company, however artificial. When I switched on directions, the imperturbable manservant's voice of my phone sent me onwards to turn right at the first junction and then fell silent for miles of twisted road. The devious parade of shops and equally unlit houses with their doorsteps on the pavement made me feel more alone than ever, and increasingly uncertain why I was there at all. A junction with another main road tempted me to head for home, but as a red light dropped its amber ball the phone advised me to turn left at the intersection. What was the point of coming so far if I didn't venture to my destination? The green disc ousted or subsumed the rest of the trio, and I swung left at the crossroads to speed along another lifeless road.

Opposite a park where fattened mossy gravestones leaned companionably towards one another outside a derelict chapel, the phone sent me towards the river. Across a main road on which every shop was shuttered if not boarded up, a street descended steeply to the promenade. Halfway down the slope, a cross street contained the Noble house. While I wasn't about to be daunted, there was no need to park too close. Coasting to the riverside, I parked in front of an unlit pub, where the car was out of sight of the house.

I retrieved the black item from the seat beside mine, standing the binoculars on the roof while I eased the door shut with both hands and locked the car with a blink of the lights. Apart from the multiple click of the locks, I was surrounded by silence. Beyond the bay at the end of the river, a minimised cruise liner pricked with lights sank over the horizon as if the abyss below the world had drawn it down. An incomplete contorted moon lay low at the edge of the sea, outlining scrawny windmills as their restless spikes tried to unpick the inky fabric of the sky. The tide was high, and reflections of hotels on the Liverpool riverside were testing the water, though I could have fancied that the lightless inversion of Starview Tower was probing deeper. Ripples slow and black as tar appeared to spread from the middle of the river, rebounding from the banks to elaborate a pattern. The languid intricate repetition put me in mind of a mantra that was being intoned and then reversed, and I felt far too close to hearing it in my head. I turned away from the river as fully as I could and stole to the corner of the pub, which let me see the Noble house.

Although its neighbours were unlit too, its darkness felt less somnolent than secretive. This close the binoculars showed me how desperate the flowers and shrubs in the high steep garden looked to flee the dwelling perched at the top of the slope. The tall pale house crowned with triple chimneys might have been gazing down from its eminence not just at the river but at a world to which it felt superior. No doubt that was why the six identical windows reminded me of the indifferent gaze its occupants had trained on me so often in my lifetime. I couldn't see them or any sign of life inside the house. Perhaps they weren't even at home, if the term applied in any ordinary way. At least I'd established that the place was still intact, and hoped the knowledge would help me overcome any tendency to drift towards its future, whatever that might be. I was about to lower the binoculars when I saw movement near the house.

I had to press the eyepieces against my face and strain my eyes to grasp what I was seeing. Somebody – more than one of them, indeed several – had just dodged around the building. A figure remained at the outer edge of the garden, and another loitered at the side of the house nearest to me, which contained a ground-floor window. He must be watching whoever was at the front of the house, and I guessed they'd given him a sign, because he turned and raised a vigorous thumb to the man in the garden. Seconds later small lights flared – flames that the men applied to objects they were holding. They shied the flaming items through the windows, and I heard glass smash on the far sides of the house as well.

There was a thump – at least a double one – inside the building, and an explosive concussion of glass. In a moment the ground floor was bright with fire. It showed the perpetrators fleeing almost in silence, but one yelled "That's for anybody you all abused." Before the shout came to an end the men were out of sight, and I heard the roar of a car engine and the screech of tyres. I barely noticed any of this, because three figures had reared up in the midst of the blaze inside the house.

They were Christian Noble and Tina and Toph, and from what I could see I deduced they were naked. They clung together as the fire closed around them. The leaping flames made their flesh look unstable, writhing like a mass of snakes. I saw them mouth at one another as if their lips were eager to meet in a triple kiss. They were repeating words I didn't need to hear to recognise, and I thought the ripples that I couldn't avoid glimpsing on the black water had adopted that rhythm. The flames streamed towards the Nobles and raced up their bodies, and I felt as unable to move as they appeared to be. I thought I saw their bodies start not just to melt but to merge into a single monstrous shape. As the flames reached their heads their mouths gaped to cry a name in unison. However agonised the outburst was, I heard triumph in it too, and when the blazing composite mass sank out of view it looked as sinuous as the Nobles ever had.

By now lights had come on in the surrounding houses, and I heard distant sirens – fire engines and police. It would do me no good to be found near the scene of the crime, and I hurried to my car. As I drove away the front door of the pub opened, and I swerved fast up the slope. At the top traffic lights were sending up an amber ball, but I raced through as they leapt to red. I'd progressed just a few hundred yards when the voice of my phone began to direct me back to the Noble house, and I could easily have thought they had made it speak.

I silenced it as a police car sped towards me, flashing its lights. I pulled over, hoping that the driver only wanted to pass, and was able to breathe once he had. After that I encountered nobody, on the roads or in the tunnel. I kept trying to assure myself that I was leaving the Nobles behind at last, though I couldn't stop seeing the agitated fiery mass they'd become. For the entire length of the tunnel I felt as though a dark mass was squatting on the dim brittle concrete tube and about to close around my mind.

CHAPTER SIXTEEN

Visitors

Tina, space and time are formed of correspondences, and we who grasp them may wield creation. Man's universe is but an atom of the cosmos, just as man's history is but an atom of his universe. Yet a flower may hint how a galaxy is shaped, and a flower grown from a grave may adumbrate a shape unrestrained by flesh. We are made of night and stars, and dark stars have walked the earth. Black holes have opened there, which assume the form of men. We are what came from the sea and from the void before it, and we are what voyaged to the stars and beyond them. Tina, we shall be the only past, and we have been the only future. Great power lies in uniting correspondences, and no union shall be the like of ours...

Was this the passage I'd been trying to remember? I had no idea what I'd expected it to convey to me, if I'd ever known. Apart from implying the relationship Christian Noble would develop with his daughter, most of it struck me as obscure and unhelpful. Why had I felt compelled to seek it out now that the Nobles were no more? I would have liked to think the journal could be safely consigned to the past, represented by my adolescent handwriting and the mathematical tables printed on the backs of the exercise books as a bygone aid to schoolchildren, but I couldn't believe the secrets of the journal had become irrelevant or even that the Nobles had. Whenever I thought of them I saw the writhing mass of flame and flesh and heard the triple voice cry out a name, and I feared the memory could summon whatever they'd become. Might anything

Noble had written help me deal with this? That was my hope, but perhaps I'd mistaken the section of the journal that could. I was leafing through the second book, and feeling that I understood the text no better than I had while I'd transcribed it, when the doorbell emitted a single brusque trill.

I thought Toby might be there, although I hoped for Jim. In either case I should have preferred them to call ahead, in which case the bell mightn't have made me so tense. I was about to say as much when I opened the front door, only to find a uniformed couple blocking my way at less than an arm's length – Farr and Black, the younger generation. "We meet again," I said without taking time to think.

"I'm afraid so, Mr Sheldrake," the policewoman said.

In an attempt to feel less menaced I said "Just to check, you're DC Farr."

With no expression her colleague said "I am."

"So you were swapping names last time we had the pleasure. Little wonder I'm confused."

"Please do remind us," Black said.

"You gave each other's names. You couldn't have expected me to know you were. It isn't as if either of you look like—"

Just in time I saw it might be considerably less than advisable to bring up their parentage. "Like what, sir?" Farr said as tonelessly as ever.

"Like your names. I didn't think it needed saying."

"Is that some kind of racial comment?" Black barely enquired.

"I don't go in for those. My father used to but I don't believe I ever did. That's not to say I learned nothing from him that I've kept, or my mother for that matter." I was aware of babbling in a way that showed my age if not my nervousness. "I hope that will be true for my son," I felt compelled to add. "Anyway, you won't be here to talk about him. You'd better come in."

As I lowered myself by degrees into my armchair they perched on the sofa, separated by a gap that would have accommodated a third visitor, and I was unhelpfully reminded of youngsters not quite comfortable in an adult situation. Farr broke the silence. "Is there something you ought to be telling us, Mr Sheldrake?"

"About Christian Le Bon and his family," Black said.

"I said it all in court. It's on the record."

"Since then."

"I know they died in a fire. I believe you think it was deliberately started."

"How would you know what we think?"

"You as in the police. That's what it said on the news."

"And why else would you say it was?"

"Exactly." When they stared at me I said "Exactly, why else."

I thought Black was reaching the limit of politeness as she said "We're asking whether you were involved, Mr Sheldrake."

"Not at all. I won't deny I think the world might be a better place without them."

Was I inspired by that convention of crime stories where characters demonstrate their innocence by admitting they disliked the victim? My honesty fell short of impressing the police. "You've been placed at the scene of the crime," Farr said.

"Placed." I'd begun to feel snagged by words. "Placed by whom?"

"Mr Sheldrake." Black made my name into a caution before she said "Are you claiming you weren't there?"

"I didn't say that, but I emphatically wasn't responsible." Their mute scrutiny drove me to add "I knew killing them was no solution."

A silence let this lie until Black said "Why is that?"

"It's what their church led me to believe." Her unfathomable look provoked me to blurt "I think you may as well."

"Why would you, Mr Sheldrake?"

I'd ventured too far to hold back. "Don't your parents?"

Her lips moved, but it was Farr who demanded "What do you think you know about them?"

"They were in the police and now they're in that church."

"And your friend Mr Bailey stayed more Catholic than you, like his sons who are on the force."

Black's glance convicted him of saying too much, but her gaze at me was more relentless. "Is there any more you want to say about our parents?"

"Not if they leave me alone."

"You may be left alone if you can show you had no part in the crime. Please explain why you were there."

I saw the truth wouldn't be enough, not least because I scarcely knew what it had been. "I was called," I said.

"By whom?"

"They all sounded the same on the phone. They wanted me to know they knew where I live."

"Do you have the phone you took the call on?" Farr said.

"Here it is, but they withheld the number." Perhaps I shouldn't have added "I expect the phone they used has gone the way they've gone."

As I wondered if this might sound too akin to triumph, Black held out a hand. "May we see?"

I could only pass her the phone. As she brought up the call list my throat clenched, almost stopping my breath. I couldn't remember when I'd last deleted entries. Black peered at the screen and showed it to her fellow officer, whose face stayed blank. She handed me the phone, and I was trying not to look anxious to examine it when Farr said "Why did the call make you act like that?"

"Like what?"

I shouldn't have asked that or sounded so defensive. "Driving all the way across the river at that time of night," Farr said.

"I wanted to see where the Nobles lived so they wouldn't have an advantage."

I hoped honesty might win the police over, but Farr said "What else did you see?"

The fiery mass of melting if not merging flesh writhed into sight in my mind, compelling me to admit "I saw them killed. I couldn't have done anything to stop it. By the time I realised what was happening they were on fire."

"Did you see those responsible?"

"I was all the way down on the promenade. I saw some men smash the windows and run off, but I couldn't even tell you how many there were. I heard a man shout, but I wouldn't be able to identify him."

"You can hardly say that in advance, Mr Sheldrake," Black said. "What did he shout?"

"That it was for the other victims the Nobles had abused, the fire was."

"His actual words."

"That's for everybody you abused."

Surely this was close enough to be convincing. I hoped it might lead to an investigation of the Church of the Eternal Three, but Black said "Why didn't you report all this to the police?"

"Someone already had. I heard them and the fire service on the way when I went home." When she made her dissatisfaction plain I admitted "I thought the police might think I was involved."

"But you say you stayed down by the pub."

"That's what I—" I managed to pause, having realised her mistake. "I didn't say that was where I was," I said.

She frowned as if she was trying to look older, but left Farr to tell me "You and your car were on the security camera."

"Then it must have shown you I never went anywhere near the house."

"That doesn't prove you weren't involved. Did you take any photographs?"

"Good God, no," I said and thrust the phone at him. "Look for yourself."

"Many people would have. They could have been crucial as evidence." He waved the phone away and said "All your behaviour suggests you may have been assisting the offenders."

"I didn't do a thing to help them, whatever I thought of the Nobles."

"You might be assisting them now," Black said and stood up as Farr did. "We may need to interview you further in due course."

I followed them into the hall, where Black halted, staring into the workroom. "Is that something you're at work on, Mr Sheldrake?"

She'd noticed the exercise books on my desk. "It's something someone else wrote," I said.

I'd barely finished speaking when she strode into the workroom to examine the book I'd left open. Farr sauntered after her, and as I limped in pursuit she said "Did you make a child write this?"

"Not quite."

"It's certainly a child's writing. Does it have to do with Mr Le Bon and his church? I thought you took the view that teaching children his beliefs was a form of abuse."

"When are you telling me I said that?"

"In your testimony," Farr said. "Do you wish to take it back?"

Although I'd seen neither of them in court, I wasn't going to ask how they knew what I'd said. "I stand by every word of it."

"So did your grandchild write this," Black persisted, "or someone else?"

"It was nobody but me. Just me, long before you were born."

She frowned as if the lines might help mature her face. "You shared these beliefs when you were a child."

"Not even then. Back then I was something of a Catholic."

"You copied them, didn't you?" Farr said. "Copied them down."

I was about to welcome the explanation when its significance overtook me. "How did you know that?"

"No child could have thought all that up. You must have got it from somewhere else. It doesn't read anything like a child."

I thought he'd said too much too glibly. Perhaps Black thought so as well, because she said "It's our job to interpret the evidence."

"As it happens he's right," I said. "Who do you think wrote the original?"

"Christian Le Bon?" I was sure this was simply posing as a question, and I might have said so if she hadn't added "As I say, it's evidence."

"Evidence of what?"

"Of how" – she let me hear a pause – "concerned you've been with Mr Le Bon and his family for so much of your life."

When she straightened up from leafing through the books I thought she meant to impound them as evidence, but she left them on the desk. Once the police drove away I still felt observed, even when I shut myself in the house. I went back to my desk, but whatever I might have been seeing in Christian Noble's journal continued to elude me. The blank computer screen loomed over my reading like an omen of hostility, until I gave in to temptation. I had to find out what people had said about Bobby and me since the last time I'd looked.

Many of today's posts were more rabid than ever. **If that fucking dyke cunt Parkin hadnt writen about them Christian and his famly would still be here to lead the world**, Feedbrain Freedbrain said. **Her and Turdshit Sheldrake got them killed**, REVELation 33 agreed. **The bible has some true bits in**, Will B. Changed contributed, **like an eye for an eye**. Other death threats or proposals were less veiled, not to say more savage, virtually reverting to primitivism. I wanted to believe that anyone who wrote such things wouldn't put them into practice, even though their identities were hidden, and that nobody else might be prompted to act. I kept being distracted from the latest expressions of hatred, because a shadow in the corner of the garden was snagging the edge of my vision, a dark hunched shape that the branches of an apple tree lent unpleasantly numerous limbs. Whenever I glanced at it, the crouched form didn't look nearly so detailed. I was trying to ignore it and be done with reading when the doorbell shrilled twice.

This was so reminiscent of the old code of the Tremendous Three – its initials in Morse – that I made for the door fast enough to leave all thoughts behind. I snatched the front door open to find Toby on the path. He gave me a long but uncommunicative look before saying "So you've got what you want at last, dad."

"You've left the church, you mean," I said and dared to hope. "You and Macy and Claudine."

"I'm saying you've got rid of Christian and his family."

"You think they've gone," I said with another sort of hope.

"As much as anybody ever is, and they'll have more control than most." As I regretted having fancied he would give me any kind of reassurance he said "Say you weren't involved."

"Only by letting the world know what they were." I lingered over shutting the front door, which gave me time to decide to say "You may as well know I saw them done away with."

Toby halted outside the workroom. "How?"

"I was near the house. I had nothing to do with the fire, and I didn't see who had."

"What were you doing there, then?"

The last word sounded far too much like suspicion, which provoked me to retort "Believe me or don't, but I felt called there."

"I do believe you. The future can summon people like us."

I wasn't sure I wanted to learn "People like who?"

"Ones who've followed Christian's path." Before I could protest that I'd done nothing of the kind, Toby said "So what did you see?"

"Men that I couldn't identify setting fire to the house. And I saw the Nobles trapped in there, but I'd rather not remember if you don't mind. I've told the police all I know."

I saw no point in mentioning Farr and Black. We were in the kitchen now, where Toby poured us both a glass of lemonade. He was heading for the front room when he glanced towards my desk. "Dad, is that the copy you made of Christian's journal?"

At once I felt worse than suspicious. "Don't you know?"

"They look like I remember. How did you get them back?"

"I haven't said that's what they are." I didn't want to think he'd come for them, having been told they were here by my previous visitors. I couldn't bring myself to ask, and so I said "I took them the last time I was at Safe To Sleep."

"When you took me home to your old house?"

At least he didn't know the truth, unless he was pretending. "No, after the place was abandoned. I wanted Jim to see what it was like."

"What else did you find?"

"Whatever was living underneath. We got out just in time."

"That's why they left it. They hadn't realised what our explorations might bring back." As I tried not to be dismayed by his nonchalance my son said "Anyway, good for you and him too if he saw."

"He explained it away." I would have liked to stop short of wondering "Good how?"

"Anything like that helps to prepare us. Can I take a look at the journal?"

"At least this time you're asking." All the same, I was loath to say "Go on."

He sat at my desk at once, planting his glass on a faded piebald coaster. When he noticed the display on the computer he took and expelled a loud breath. "Dad, I'm sorry you've had to see all this."

I sat at Lesley's desk and placed my glass on a coaster less dilapidated than mine. "Do you recognise anybody from your church?"

"I wouldn't, but even if any of them are I'm sure they won't do anything. This will be how they're expressing their grief."

"They won't harm me and Bobby because they're in the church, you mean. I didn't know it had any commandments."

"Expand your mind beyond humanity, that might be one. No," Toby said, "they won't take revenge because they know our founders haven't really left us."

With considerable reluctance I said "Have you seen them?"

"Not yet." As he opened an exercise book he said "You might want to hope you don't either."

Although I took this for advice and not a threat, it distressed me. While he turned pages I found myself gazing at Lesley's computer screen, which was as blank as an uninscribed slab, a dead monitor beside an empty bed, a mind devoid of recollections. At least the Nobles hadn't used her for revenge, and I'd even managed not to dream they had, a nightmare that I would have been afraid was capable of making itself real. I was concentrating on memories of Lesley that didn't involve the Nobles when Toby closed the last book. "Thanks, dad."

"I don't suppose there would have been much point in refusing."

"For looking after these, I mean."

I didn't care to be thanked for that, especially by my son. "If that's how you regard it. I don't myself."

"Then what did you think you were doing? You've kept them in the world."

"I was trying to keep them away from people." In a bid to convince myself they'd never had a hold on me I said "Just like Christian Noble's father."

"They're the only copy now. Christian's must have been at the house." Toby used the edges of his hands to arrange the books in a small neat stack. He couldn't have handled an infant more gently, and I was disconcerted to realise he meant to show respect for them. "Can I have them?" he said.

"I'd really rather you didn't."

"Why would you need them any more?"

He was so intent on them I could have thought he was speaking for them. "I've never needed them," I retorted. "I know the world doesn't, that's all."

"We'll have to disagree on that. You won't mind if I make a copy, since you did."

I minded a good deal, and said "I don't want you taking them away."

"I won't have to. I can photograph them here."

His phone was in his hand before I had a chance to speak. I might have objected but couldn't see the use, assuming all Noble's ideas were already rooted in his head. The repeated whir of the electronic shutter sounded like the operation of a lengthy series of traps. By the time he finished, my computer screen had turned as black as Lesley's, as though he'd leached it of information too. "Thanks again, dad," he said.

This was less welcome than ever, and drove me to say "I take it you won't be bidding goodbye to the church."

His hesitation offered me a moment of hope, but his answer bemused me. "I'm sorry for saying you'd got what you wanted."

"That's certainly no reason to apologise. It's true as far as it goes."

"Dad." He backed up the sad syllable by adding "Now Christian and his family aren't there, we're in charge at Starview Tower."

My throat grew so dry it nearly stopped me asking "Who is?"

"Claudine and me."

At least Macy wasn't involved, then. Toby and his family hadn't quite replaced the Noble trio. Nevertheless I would much rather not have had to ask "What are you doing there?"

"Running the sessions. There's a future we must see." Even more evangelically he said "Now we can share this too."

He was flourishing his phone, which displayed the last entry in the journal – the infant Toph's unfinished observation – but Toby had reminded me how my granddaughter had assisted at my initiation into the Church of the Eternal Three. "Not with Macy," I pleaded.

A pause suggested he was pondering how to respond. "Not till it's time," he said.

"And when is that supposed to be?"

"You ought to be past seeing it in those terms, dad. Try and think more of the worm." As though its absence had just struck him he said "What have you done with your icon?"

I felt too exhausted to tell him the truth. "I'm not using it any more."

"You've reached that stage. Well, good." As I let him believe whatever he'd assumed he said "I wish we could bring you back to the church. We will if we can make the members understand you've done no real harm. Meanwhile at least the teachings are in your head."

I didn't trust myself to answer. His grotesque positiveness seemed even more unnervingly inappropriate when he said "We'll see you for Sunday lunch." It felt like a parody of domesticity if not a desperate attempt to pretend everything was somehow normal. I watched him back his car out of the drive, and as I turned away he flashed his headlights as a farewell. A dim crouched shape swelled up in an unseasonable patch of gloom beside the stairs – the shadow of the vase on the hall table. The car swung backwards onto the road, still sending me its headlamp beams until Toby switched them off, and the dark malformed shape appeared to scurry upstairs on an entirely unreasonable number of limbs. Those would be the shadows of flowers in the vase, I thought, and immediately realised the vase had been empty for weeks. I started forward to call Toby, but he'd gone. I had to force myself to return to the house and search it, and even once I established I was alone I felt fearfully certain this was a pretence.

CHAPTER SEVENTEEN

A Family Question

I'm Toby Sheldrake. My wife and I are the leaders of the Church of the Eternal Three for Merseyside and the Midlands. My father is Dominic Sheldrake, and I want to tell you about him. He first met Christian Le Bon when he, my father, wasn't even in his teens, and I believe my father has been influenced by him ever since. Christian shared some of his knowledge with the boys he taught at school, and my father was among them. When Christian paid a visit to Bonchamp in France, where Gahariet Le Bon raised the original church, my father and his friend James Bailey were with him. When Christian's own father stole his son's testimony and hid the book at the school, my father rescued it and made a copy for himself. Decades later Christian and his daughter set up Safe To Sleep, the first of their attempts to prepare the faithful for the changes the world will see. My father entered me there as a child and participated in the ritual himself. My wife's and my involvement in Safe To Sleep led to our membership in the Church of the Eternal Three, which Christopher Le Bon encouraged us to join. My father took part in our rite, and now I believe he is among the chosen.

I want everyone to understand that he was indoctrinated into Catholicism as a child. I'm told this religion is among the hardest to shake off, even when you think you have. Because of this my father has struggled to resist Christian Le Bon's enlightenment throughout most of his life. His struggle often took the form of opposition, and made him try to catch Christian and his family out whenever he could. This must be why he recorded their conversation that led to the recent court case and ultimately to their death, though he didn't bring the prosecution himself.

He passed the information to a friend connected with the police (James Bailey) and their friend Roberta Parkin, who wrote about it online. I am absolutely certain that my father didn't intend their death, which in any case is anything but final. I believe Christian's influence over him is far greater than he can acknowledge yet, but the world should be as grateful to my father as I am. He is the reason I can post Christian's entire journal online now. He has protected it all these years, and perhaps Christian knew he would and gave the custody his blessing. I believe it shows us how the future can reach back and consolidate itself. Without my father all these thoughts of Christian's might be lost to us, and I hope that is how he will be remembered. However misguided my father may have been at times, I'm confident that he will come to see the truth he has brought to the world.

I stared once again at my own teenage handwriting, hundreds of pages of which were online. I still hadn't called Toby about it, not least because I wanted to speak to him face to face. By the time I'd seen what he'd done it would have been too late to suppress the journal, which people were bound to have copied by then. Now I saw that any number said they had. Toby's action hadn't saved me from the loathing I'd attracted, though some commentators had posted in my defence, and I saw just as much hatred for Bobby and now Jim. I couldn't let myself be troubled by the notion that Christian Noble had influenced me more than I'd known; I was too anxious to establish how much he still influenced my son. Once I'd had enough of the vituperation on the screen I gazed out of the window, which showed me no trace of a shadow in the corner of the garden. I felt compelled to watch one grow as the sun edged behind the apple tree, but the shadow was plainly cast by branches, and looked very little like the one I'd previously seen there. I was peering at it hard enough to make my eyes sting when I realised I was going to be late for Claudine's Sunday lunch.

As I drove through the suburb, shadows of branches scurried over the car and groped through the windows. Afterimages made glimpses of them appear to follow me onto the main road. I felt as if they might be loitering just beyond the edge of my vision when I arrived at the house. I was parking between Toby's car and Claudine's, having felt pitifully heartened to see that my granddaughter was enough of a child to have numbered the stone flags for hopscotch, when she hauled the front door open. "Grandad," she cried and ran to me. "We need you."

I was dismayed to feel reluctant to ask "What for?"

"So we're all together."

I would very much have liked to find her answer reassuring. She seized my hand in both of hers and ushered if not urged me into the house. Toby was heading for the dining-room with a bottle of Merlot while Claudine followed with a rack of lamb on a platter. "Here's the man of the hour," she said.

"Only just if even that. Sorry if I'm late."

"No," Claudine said with a faint but indulgent smile. "I'm saying you're in everybody's thoughts."

"Good ones, I hope." When the smile pinched inwards I said "What are yours?"

"I think Toby made your case. I'm not arguing with him."

The table was already laid, and we all sat down. Macy climbed onto her chair quite like a monkey – at least, not at all like a snake. Uncomfortably conscious of her, I searched for questions I could ask while she was there. "What do the rest of your church think?"

"Some are starting to believe you were meant to be part of us," Toby said.

"Some are saying," Claudine said, "you may always have been."

"Maybe that's why you were born, grandad."

I didn't know if I was more unnerved by the idea or by her having thought it. As Toby and Claudine loaded plates my son said "You mightn't be too welcome there just yet, dad. Give them time and I think the rest of them may see the light."

"But you know you're still welcome here," Claudine said.

"Thanks for standing by me." To Toby I said "Thank you for defending me, but I wish you hadn't published Noble's thoughts."

"The world has to embrace the truth, dad. It's time it came back."

"And nobody would have believed Toby about you otherwise, Dominic."

"Dad's keeping you safe, grandad." Macy looked up from cutting her portion of lamb into delicate segments. "Like the worm does," she said.

She'd roused a question I would have given a great deal not to have to ask. I couldn't voice it in her hearing, and did my best to keep the conversation neutral, but every mouthful felt like a postponement of my unhappy preoccupations. We'd reached the dessert, a gooseberry turnover so tart I had to restrain my mouth from wincing visibly, when Macy said "Grandad, why don't you come and live with us?"

I swallowed a harsh half-chewed spoonful so fast that it threatened to turn my throat sour. "Whatever made you think of that, Macy?"

"I think your house must be sad with only you in."

"Perhaps there isn't only me." This sounded inadvertently ominous, and I rushed to add "Perhaps grandma's still with me."

"Have you seen her?"

"I've seen nobody." Macy's eagerness disconcerted me, however sympathetic it was. "I mean she's here," I said, thumping my breast so hard it throbbed.

Macy sucked her lower lip between her teeth as if I'd unintentionally conveyed pain, and Claudine said "Don't hurt yourself, Dominic."

"I'm not that ramshackle yet." Just as much for Macy's benefit I tapped my forehead twice. "And she's in here," I said.

"Then you could bring her with you, grandad."

"Honestly, I still like living in my own house, and you might get tired of seeing me so often."

"We wouldn't, would we?" When her parents shook their heads Macy said "We want you to come back and follow the worm."

Her insistence was making me uneasy. "There isn't room, Macy," I said.

"There is. There's a bedroom with nobody in."

"Nothing like enough room for all the things I want to keep. Besides, if anybody came to visit for a while you'd need that room."

"Then you could sleep in mine. You could come in my bed."

"Macy, you should never say that to a grownup. In fact, you shouldn't say it to anyone at your age or until you're a lot older." She'd prompted me to ask the question I was struggling not to utter, and I strove to tone it down. "You haven't ever," I said, "have you?"

"Just you, grandad."

"You're very kind, but don't be upset, the answer's a definite no. And you mustn't let anything like that ever happen. Tell someone if it even seems it might. Tell me if you like."

Although I wasn't looking at her parents, I sensed their gaze. "Grandad," Macy said, sounding smaller than usual, "I don't know what you mean."

"We'll speak about it later, Macy," Claudine said. "Have you had all you want? Play in the garden, then, while the grownups talk."

"Will grandad be coming to live with us?"

"We'll talk about that too," Toby said. "Do as your mother tells you."

Neither he nor Claudine spoke while Macy tramped out like a mime of dissatisfaction. Once we heard sandals slapping flagstones while her head bobbed up and down beyond the window, Claudine said "What exactly did you mean by all that, Dominic?"

"Do I really need to put it into words?" In more than one way I very much hoped to have no reason. "I should think we're all concerned these days," I said.

"There was no need to make so much of it. What's on your mind?"

"Don't you think someone at your church might be tempted to follow the Nobles' example?"

"I wish you wouldn't keep using that name, and I don't know what you mean by tempted. We've always followed them."

"I'm talking about their relationship."

"They were special, Dominic."

Was she justifying Christian and his family or expressing admiration? "They haven't set a trend," I said.

"We've no reason to think they have in that sense. What they did was for the church."

"How can it have been? If you're going to defend it like that—"

"They had to become one for us. The one that's three and more than three. Maybe they had to die to become truly one for everyone."

However disturbing I found this, it seemed unrelated to my immediate fears, and I turned to my son. "Just what does taking over from the, from Christian and the rest of them entail?"

"I told you, dad, guiding the voyages. Now we have his writings I'll be reading from them and discussing them."

"We're giving spiritual guidance," Claudine said.

Even if I couldn't feign approval, perhaps I shouldn't have betrayed skepticism. It provoked Claudine to say "Just what are you trying to find out, Dominic?"

In a bid to trust what I was desperate to believe was true I said "I think I've had my answer."

"You mean you hope you have. What haven't you been saying?"

I made my words as neutral as I could. "How is Macy going to be involved?"

"She likes helping people start their voyage," Toby said. "You saw she did."

"That isn't what Dominic means, is it, Dominic?"

When she stared at me without blinking, Toby joined in. I glanced towards the window as Macy's head appeared, but their gaze remained relentlessly unchanged. "She'll never be involved the way Tina Noble was," I said.

"Are you asking us that, Dominic?"

"I wish I didn't have to, but can you understand why I am?"

"We understand you." Claudine's blink wiped all expression from her eyes. "The answer is no," she said, "but I'm glad you spoke up. I won't have thoughts like that in my house."

"There's no need for me to have them, is there, Toby?"

"I should say not, and if there's anything else you're trying not to think—"

"No," Claudine said and shook the table with a slap to which her wedding ring added a clank. "I mean I won't have anyone who thought them."

"Claude, don't you think that's going a bit—"

"I don't, no. Dominic, you're no longer welcome here."

"Claude, he's my father."

"Yes, a father who could suggest that sort of thing about his own son."

She hadn't looked away from me, and her eyes might as well have been dead. "I'll go," I said and rose to my feet with a pretence of steadiness, gripping the back of the chair. "I don't want to cause further trouble."

"Yes," Claudine said, "you've made quite enough for yourself."

She remained seated while Toby followed me into the hall. "Why in the name of I don't know what did you have to ask that?" he murmured fiercely enough to sprinkle my face.

"I wish I hadn't," I muttered for him to take however he would.

"I'll talk to Claude after Macy's in bed," he told me lower still.

Macy's hopping faltered as he opened the front door. "Grandad, are you going?"

"He has to," Toby said. "Something's taken him away."

Macy scampered to deliver a hug sufficiently fierce to be trying to arrest me. "Come earlier next week, grandad, and I'll read you a story I wrote about stars."

As Toby opened his mouth Claudine marched into the hall. "Say goodbye quickly," she called.

"Goodbye quickly," Macy said, but her grin turned uncertain when I didn't echo her joke. She let go of me with some reluctance, and I retreated to my car. As I drove into the road she sent me a wave from the doorway of the house. Each of her parents was resting a hand on one of her shoulders, and I came close to praying that they could be as ordinary a family as they looked. Once they were out of sight I felt as though I no longer had a family, and afraid to wonder how much the Nobles were lingering in the world.

CHAPTER EIGHTEEN

A Revenge

I could still rescue Toby. I could halt the bus. As it reached the stretch of road where I was waiting I flashed the headlights. The bus began to lose speed, and I glanced in the mirror to confirm that the road behind me was clear. I was about to turn off the engine and flag the bus down when the cold gelatinous hand closed over my face. It found my eyes, and the substance of the fingers slithered into them, groping like masses of thin scrawny worms for my brain. At once I was blinded, but I felt the car jerk forward as I inadvertently tramped on the accelerator. Now I was additionally terrified that the windscreen would shatter into my face as soon as the car met an obstacle, and in a moment I heard glass smash.

It wasn't so close to me. As I tried to determine how distant it was I saw the Nobles sink into the fire they'd become, their faces united in crying an ancient name. I hadn't heard their windows break just now, an insight that brought me back to myself, though only to confusion. I was slumped at my desk, resting my cheek on my forearm that lay the length of the computer keyboard. Presumably the burden had made the keys produce groups of symbols on the screen, which appeared to be displaying paragraphs in an unknown language. Pushing myself upright must have deleted them, because the screen turned as blank as a night without stars, but I was concerned to grasp the sequence of events. Had I been remembering my crash before I'd heard glass actually break? Once I managed to recall that the sound had seemed to come from the front of the house, I levered myself shakily off the chair as it pivoted back and forth. Panic sent me stumbling into the hall to limp rapidly into the front room.

A fierce sun glared into my eyes, because there was no longer any glass in the middle window of the bay. I staggered fast across the room until I saw the pane was intact. Only my fears and the blinding light had made it vanish. Had someone broken an upstairs window? I turned so quickly that my head spun faster, and then I caught sight of my car.

I lost all my breath in uttering a word I very seldom used. I felt ridiculous for hoping the neighbours hadn't heard, but mostly I felt hollowed out by rage. I stalked out of the house to see my windscreen had indeed been smashed. A large chunk of stone lay among fragments of glass on the passenger seat, and as I dashed to the gate I saw where it had come from – a broken stretch of kerb across the road, where a builder's van had been parked on the pavement last week.

I flung the gate wide, having scraped my fingers on the latch, and sprinted into the road. It was deserted except for a man and a woman strolling past a tree. Each of them was equipped with a spaniel at the end of a leash on a reel, and the dogs lingered to water the tree. "Excuse me," I shouted and ran across the road.

The couple didn't turn until I'd repeated my plea twice and was almost within arm's length, having dodged around the animals and their extended leads. The man's face might have been drooping in emulation of his dog's, and the woman's was plump and pendulous, though none of this explained their downturned mouths. "Are you in a very tearing hurry, old boy?" the man said.

Presumably he wasn't decrying my age, since he looked it himself. "Don't want get by," I gasped with less breath than I needed for coherence. "You see?"

"If you say so," the woman said.

My question had been too truncated to reach them, and I sucked in air that sounded like a dissatisfied sigh. "No, did," I panted, "you see what, happened?"

"What would that be, old chap?" her partner said.

I tried to find the fewest words that would work. "Someone running."

With exaggerated patience the woman said "We saw you."

"Running away." I struggled to suppress my frustration. "Up to no good."

"I'm sure there can't be anyone like that round here."

Her reassurance fell a good deal short of me, not least because I was growing more frustrated with their answers and my abbreviated contributions. "Must have heard," I protested.

"We're hearing you, old fellow."

"Heard them damage my car." My verbal exertions turned my voice savage. "Just did."

"Then why are you wasting time with us?" the woman said as if I'd almost exhausted her indulgence. "You want the police."

"You're telling me nobody came this way."

I meant this as a question, not an accusation, but their continued unresponsiveness left me suspicious enough to blurt "Do you know who I am?"

"Not the foggiest, old chum."

"And it wouldn't make a scrap of difference if we did."

I wasn't persuaded, since I had to say "And you didn't even hear my car being smashed up."

"I'm afraid," the woman said, "we were raised to mind our own business."

I could easily have taken this as referring to my investigation of the Nobles, but the time I was wasting had caught up with me. I swung around to run in the opposite direction, almost tripping over an elongated lead. "Careful there, old pal," the man said without friendliness. "Everyone's property matters, not just yours."

I had no time for a retort, and no breath to spare. As I stumbled off at speed I snatched out my phone. Nobody was to be seen ahead, and I did my best to keep my pace up, but had to slow to an uneven trot while my finger found the emergency button on the screen. I floundered forward as a female voice asked which service I required. "Please," I gasped, or at any rate heard myself say that instead of what I meant. "Police."

"I heard you, sir."

I'd been reduced to a rapid stagger by the time she asked the reason for my call, unless a different voice did. "Car broken into," I said and was just able to add "Mine."

"Is the robbery in progress?"

"Not Robby." Even the incomplete word left me barely enough breath to add "Vanned lissom."

"When did it happen?"

"Fume innit." As I blundered onwards close to helplessly I gathered enough sense and breath to wheeze "Fiver so."

"Where are you located?"

I felt as if the question had collaborated with my fatigue to bring me to a halt. I'd reached a crossroads, from which I could see nobody at all. I would never catch up with the culprit now, and I concentrated on answering. "Drew," I said before managing to collect more syllables, which my panting interrupted. "Druids tone road."

"And the postcode." Once I'd supplied it she said "May I take your name?"

"Dominic shelled rake."

Perhaps she paused only because I had, but her silence felt longer, not to mention suggestive. "Are you at home, Mr Sheldrake?"

"Not at mow meant," I said and tried to squeeze my syllables together. "Chasing hoover did it."

"You've identified who's responsible."

How slyly was this aimed at me? "Didn't see them. Lost them now."

"What is your address?" When I gave the house number she said "Is the damaged vehicle there?"

"Right in front. Didn't care."

"Someone will be there as soon as possible. Please don't move the vehicle or touch the evidence till it has been examined. And for your future information," she said with desiccated briskness, "your call wasn't an emergency, Mr Sheldrake."

By now I suspected her responses had grown more personal than official, unless they combined both. Who else might she speak for?

What future did she have in mind? "I'll be home in a few minutes," I took enough breath to declare. "Not the runner I once was."

I couldn't help recalling the school sports day that had brought me Noble's journal. I was starting to feel as though he and his family bounded my entire life. The operator read me a crime number with so many digits I might have been at the end of a queue beyond envisioning, and then I trudged home at a pretence of speed, hoping someone might have returned to the scene of the crime. The front garden was deserted except for my car, which gaped at me with its vacant windscreen, and beside it Lesley's, a mute empty reminder. I was pitifully grateful that at least her car had been spared. I was in the front room, waiting for the police, when I wondered if and how the culprit had identified which vehicle to wreck.

At first I stood up whenever I heard a car on the road, but an hour later I was staying in my chair. My mind kept returning to the sound that had alerted me to the damage, a memory that threatened to evoke the Nobles' fate. As I fended off thoughts of them I seemed to recall watching the destruction of a stained-glass window that depicted a trinity of figures, not just entwined but merged, even their gleeful partly human heads. If this was a memory, it wasn't mine, and I fought to lodge myself within my own brain. My efforts must have aggravated my exhaustion, because at some point I lost contact with my surroundings until I was roused by a muffled concussion of glass.

The room was as dim as the inside of my eyelids. Apparently I'd been insensible for hours. I lurched to the window to look for the source of the sound, and saw glass fragments glinting in a patch of liquid near the car. I was fumbling for my phone as I hurried out of the house.

Shards surrounded by a dark stain were scattered beside the left headlight, and when I stooped towards them, clutching at the mudguard, I smelled petrol. I dashed to the gate and onto the road, which was deserted. This time I wasn't about to waste my energy on a search. Jabbing the virtual button brought me a voice that might have been the one I'd previously heard. "Police emergency," I said at once.

How alike did all the voices aim to sound? When another or the same one spoke I read my crime number from the screen. "I've seen no police yet and now there's worse. Someone just tried to firebomb my house. You've got all my details. Dominic Sheldrake."

This time I waited at the gate. I was close to phoning once more when a white car appeared at the end of the road – a police car, though displaying no urgency. It stopped across the entrance to my drive and let out Farr and Black. "Is it always going to be you?" I couldn't help demanding.

"We know about your case," Farr said.

"I'm sure you aren't alone."

"We're the closest to it," Black said. "Tell us what you called for, Mr Sheldrake."

"What I reported," I felt I shouldn't need to say, and gestured at the car.

They took out their phones as they made for it, and I thought I saw three faces clustering behind the icons on the screens before my visitors switched on the flashlights. The beams roamed over the debris on the passenger seat as Black said "You called this in as an emergency."

"If someone had been quick enough they might have caught the culprit."

"Do you know who was responsible?"

She'd straightened up to stare at me, and I could very well have felt accused. "Someone from the Church of the Eternal Three," I said, "or a sympathiser."

"That's quite an allegation," Farr said and turned to show me how the night had gathered in his eyes. "You should be careful who you make it to."

"I'm making it to you. Who else is it likely to be?"

"There's no record of any member of the church committing violence."

"Just behaving as if they're above the law."

Black's eyes appeared to be living up to her name. "Why did you put in a second call?"

"They weren't satisfied with damaging my car. They tried to bomb it or me."

"You're saying the same person did."

"Or a member of the same mob," I said and jerked my hands at the debris by the car. "What's left is there."

She and her colleague aimed their lights at the fragments of glass, which gleamed as the stain on the concrete did. "Where is the damage you say it caused?" she said.

"I didn't say it had. It mustn't have gone off."

Farr was the first to turn and confront me. "There isn't nearly enough here for any bomb."

"Maybe when it didn't work they carried off the evidence."

In a tone he might have used to a simpleton Farr said "I'm telling you there was no bomb."

"Of course there was. Look at all the petrol."

"That's from your car."

"You mean they did that too." I sank to my knees on the prickly concrete, where I forced myself into a painful crouch while I sent the beam from my phone under the car. The stain extended underneath, but not far, and I couldn't tell if that patch was wetter. I used the nearest door handle to haul myself to my feet. "I'm not sure that's it," I said.

"Mr Sheldrake," Black said as if the name alone used up a good deal of her patience, "you'd be well advised not to make complaints without more evidence."

"What would you call the mess in my car if it isn't evidence?"

"Not of an emergency."

"Wait a minute," I said, as much to my thoughts as to the police. "How did all this glass end up by the car?"

"That's from the windscreen."

"I'll swear it wasn't there until I heard it and phoned you again."

"Something made it fall," Farr said. "Use your imagination."

I almost expected him to say, as Christian Noble used to, that he knew I had one. Before I could respond Black said "You may be lucky if this goes no further."

"Who are you speaking for?"

"I'm advising you that you could find yourself back in court for wasting police time."

I raised my voice for anyone nearby to hear. "You're telling me it's wasting your time to call about someone smashing up my car. And I still think there may have been a bomb."

"Neither of your calls was an emergency," Black said. "In future you should wait till you have a reason."

"You mean I'll have one."

Both of them gazed at me long enough to undermine my sense of time, and their silence was broken only by the insectoid whir of shutters while they photographed my car and the debris. I thought they meant to leave me without speaking until Farr said "You may expect another visitor, Mr Sheldrake."

"For fingerprints, you mean."

Only the night in their eyes answered, and I was afraid to enquire further. They turned their backs and drove away without sparing me another glance. Their entire visit felt like an omen, an interlude designed to leave me helpless while I awaited whatever it presaged. I retreated to the front room, where I called the insurance and the car repair firm, both of which were represented by answering machines. I tried watching a number of films – Kurosawa, Renoir, Haneke – all of which fell short of my besieged imagination. Eventually I made for bed.

I did my utmost not to think of breaking glass, which was no doubt why I did. At first I thought my preoccupation had brought on a waking dream when I found myself gazing up at Starview Tower. The blank colourless sky conveyed no time of day, not even a hint of the season. The world felt as still as a stone memorial until the silence admitted a sound, a shrill but muted creak of glass that gave way to a slow protracted splintering. The windows of the buildings all around the tower were imploding from the ground floors upwards, caving in with a sluggishness that appeared to deny time. The structures were very gradually collapsing – more accurately, compacting themselves, growing denser as they turned progressively dwarfish. I had an inkling that the cause was as unnatural as the spectacle – that the buildings were infected by the onset of a future I would be more than unwise to imagine. Even the thought of its imminence made me feel its hunger. It put me in mind of a black hole composed of time, and I fled back to memories I knew were mine. The idea of broken glass refused to leave my brain, and I could only concentrate on the damage to my car, replaying the incident – the crash of glass, the minute I'd spent examining the window of the front room when I might have had a chance to see the culprit on the road – until the repetition shut my mind down, or weariness did.

I wakened in daylight, which felt remote and irrelevant, little more than a pretence. I lingered at the bedroom window for some time before I was convinced the car hadn't suffered any further damage while I was asleep. A mug of vicious coffee and a shower helped to rouse my mind, which was weighed down by yesterday's events. I phoned the insurance company and then arranged for a repair, and wished I didn't feel compelled to search online for the latest mob of comments I'd attracted. By now I'd checked so frequently that just the first two letters of my name brought up the whole of it in the search box. More comments about me had appeared overnight, and the first of them – supposedly posted by B. Leaf – made me feel as if I'd been punched in the stomach. **So now Sheldrake's claiming someone tried to bomb his house**.

I was on the edge of phoning to complain when I realised that the information needn't have come from Farr or Black. Last night I'd made sure that anybody within earshot would hear why I'd called the police. Had a neighbour made the gibe at me? **Should have burnt him up like the Le Bons**, Good Ship Worship responded, and Faith Value added **Him and his squeeze Parkin and chuck Bailey in as well**. Last Daze wondered **Anyone got there address** without bothering to punctuate, and Altered Altar ended the discussion by declaring **No need for any of that, people. Let their victims deal with them. We can call the three to do it. Message me if you want to help**.

The suggestion had been posted while I'd lain awake in bed. It left me fearful of secret machinations in the dark. What might the author of the post and anybody working with them have aroused? When a bell shrilled like an alarm I was so distracted that I didn't immediately grasp it wasn't at the front door. As soon as I answered the phone Bobby said "Dom, have you seen?"

"The stuff people have been saying about us? It's just words. If they say it they won't do it."

"They've found me, Dom."

At once I was as anxious as her voice. "Who has? What have they done?"

"Nothing yet. So you haven't seen."

I wished I didn't have to learn "Seen what?"

"Tina and her father and their son. They're all together." As I hoped the phrase meant no worse than it ought to Bobby said "They're all one."

So it did mean what I'd feared. I could have done without any further details, particularly when a blurred shape passed across the computer screen. While the number of limbs put me in mind of a deformed insect, the head looked more human than it should, though nightmarishly misshapen. I twisted around almost swiftly enough to tip the chair over, but the room was deserted. "Dom," Bobby said, "maybe we can cope."

Her voice seemed to trail off with lack of conviction. "How?" I said, glaring around the room.

"We've seen things like that. You have especially. But Jim never has, and we don't know what it may do to him." As if she were investing all her trust in a childhood vow – a charm against terrors too threatening to name – Bobby said "The three of us need to meet and decide what to do."

CHAPTER NINETEEN

Those Who See

The ceiling of the Crown was as spotlessly white as I'd once believed an unborn soul should be. The florid plaster decorations glinted brighter than my memory of them, so that I wondered if the heavenly gilt had been touched up. Though I hadn't been in the pub for over thirty years, it felt as if the memory had regained life. I wouldn't have suggested meeting there except for its nearness to the railway terminal. Across the road the cinema where I'd caught Jim and Bobby in the dark had been boarded up since I'd retired from lecturing, but it still revived thoughts of the crypt where hordes of mutated objects grew restless with unimaginable dreams. I tried to turn my mind elsewhere while I waited for my friends. A large glass of white wine kept me company as I faced the door, but I could have wished there weren't so many shadows in the pub. Upper decks of buses passing along Lime Street interrupted the sunlight, and when I saw silhouettes of misshapen elongated heads creeping across the floor I had to reassure myself that they belonged to passengers on roofless vehicles, tourists on a tour. Whenever the door opened, shadows sprang in ahead of the newcomers, and it wasn't only in the hope of seeing my friends that I was anxious to make out each face. When the door let in a multiple shadow I peered at the mass of bodies blurred and merged by the light behind them or by my worn-out eyes. I couldn't breathe until the new arrivals separated, by which time they'd given me rather more than a look. No doubt they took me for a lonely oldster lingering over his solitary drink, a civilised version of the alcoholics slumped against the boards outside the abandoned cinema or else an early stage of their condition. I could have retorted with an account of my life, but did it actually represent much? My memories felt not just insignificant but potentially perilous, as if reliving them might lead me too far back, regressing through experiences that were never mine. Wherever they might ultimately lead, I could have fancied it was waiting for me in the future too. I strove not to think of the formula that the Church of the Eternal Three had lodged in my head, but I couldn't avoid recalling how I'd seemed to hear people intoning the name when I'd last met Jim in the pub. I looked for distraction on my phone, where the absence of fresh comments about me and my friends felt oppressively ominous. One of my students from more than a decade ago had emailed a rumour that an uncut print of Orson Welles' second film had been discovered in Brazil, and I imagined retrieving somebody's experience of watching the complete *Ambersons* at the preview that had caused the studio to recut and reshoot and reduce the film. This was a past I could have borne resurrecting, and I was risking the wish, not that it seemed to lead anywhere, as the door opened to admit Jim.

He saw me at once and strode over. He looked as resolute as his firm handshake; even his broad grin did. "Quite like old times," he said.

I wanted to share his enthusiasm. "Which, Jim?"

"Don't you remember? We met here once." As though taking pity on me he said "It was a long time ago."

"Of course I do. Can you recall why we were here?"

"Hey, I'm not forgetful either, and don't let my family tell you any different." Having established what I was drinking, he came back from the bar with a glass for himself as well. "We'd never have foreseen it," he said.

I wished I didn't find this ominous. "Foreseen what?"

"Us sitting here with wine instead of pints." As I tried to hitch up a rueful smile he said "And we were here to figure out how to get your lad away from Christian Noble and his daughter."

I couldn't help wondering if Jim had needed to take time to recollect this. "You'll remember what came of it," I prompted him.

"We went to that dive near Ormskirk."

"How much of it has stayed in your mind?"

"They'd cleared out and taken nearly everything. They left the copy of the book you'd done, that your lad's put online now. And we saw where they made Bobby sleep," he said and paused. "She's not here yet, then."

"She called before. Her train's delayed."

"She's pinched your excuse."

The reminiscence of the night we'd all met in the Chinese restaurant failed to calm my nervousness for her, although surely nothing dreadful could be holding up the train. "What else do you remember about Safe To Sleep?" I said.

"That's right, that's what he called it. The name just slipped my mind." Jim paused again as if to fix the memory. "We went down underneath," he said, "and somebody had dug the cellar far too big. No wonder the whole place collapsed."

"There was more to it than that, Jim."

"I know you said so at the time, but I'll be honest, I never thought there was. I think you were letting the Nobles get to you a bit too much."

I was trying to decide how crucial disagreement might be when Jim said "Anyway, we aren't here to talk about that. Don't let all this online stuff bother you too much either. It looks as if it's stopped."

"Perhaps, but have you seen why?"

"Because they're all leaving it to the Nobles to take their own revenge. Which is superstitious crap, but maybe the rubbish the Nobles used to spout has done some good for once if it shuts that mob up. Mind you, I'm sure most of them would never have done worse than shoot their mouths off."

"Why only most, Jim?"

He grimaced as though he was trying to hold in his words. "I don't suppose it's anything at all."

"Tell me anyway. You know I won't make fun."

"Maybe I'd rather you did. I've just kept feeling there's someone round the house."

"Have you seen them?"

"No, of course not," Jim said with more force than I thought the denial required. "And the lads are there if they're needed, but they're sure it's just me going a bit antique. They don't see how anyone can have been getting in, and I'm not pretending I do either."

With some care I said "Is there any evidence they are?"

"None I could show the lads."

"No, but you could tell me about it, and Bobby too."

"I'll be talking to her if she shows up."

His comment roused my apprehension. "Let me find out where she is," I said.

My phone displayed her message – **On train but I'll be late** – and I called that number. When the bell began to ring it sounded odd: not merely hollow but multiplied, as though echoing in some unnatural space. It kept ringing long enough to aggravate my unease, and then Bobby said "All right, I'm here. I'm here now."

Not just her words seemed somehow wrong. Like the bell, her voice sounded as though it was proliferating across a void. "Where?" I pleaded.

"Here, Dom. Here." As Jim blinked at the drinkers around us while I peered nervously about, she said "I'm just trying to see I'm not followed. I don't expect it'll do any good. I'll let you see me now."

I'd begun to panic, having no idea what she could mean, when the door made way for a glare of sunlight and a silhouette pocketing a phone. Bobby and her voice had been outside the window. Jim and I stood up to receive one-armed hugs, and then Bobby nodded at our glasses. "I'll get a bottle," she said.

Her cheerfulness felt at least as determined as Jim's. He stayed on his feet, peering out of the window while Bobby headed for the bar. When she returned with a bottle and another glass he murmured "Was someone following you, then? Did you see them?"

"I don't have to," Bobby said, raising her chin to fend off any argument. "I feel them behind me."

Jim gazed past her in stubborn disbelief. "You can't be now."

"Not now, but I wasn't thinking when I tried to lose them. They can find us whenever they like."

I was afraid she was expecting Jim to accept too much too soon. "You were going to tell Bobby what you saw at home," I said.

"Nothing at all."

"You said there wasn't enough to show your sons," I protested, "not nothing."

"So I did." With imperfectly suppressed resentment Jim said "I heard whispering, that's all."

Having topped our glasses up, Bobby filled her own. "What did it say, Jim?"

"Not that kind of whisper. I thought it was the pipes at first, but there aren't any where it was." Jim looked frustrated, as if language had begun to desert him. "Like someone creeping round the place," he said. "I don't know how to put it better."

"Like a kind of crawling you can almost feel inside you."

Jim gave a violent shrug that might have been designed to rid him of the idea, though it looked reminiscent of a shudder. "I don't know anything about that," he said.

I did. It threatened to revive experiences I'd done my best to put out of my mind, and I should have preferred Bobby not to ask "What have you seen, Dom?"

"Mostly shadows," I risked saying, only to imagine I saw a dark pendulous shape scuttle overhead.

"I don't think they've bothered to be solid yet. Maybe they're waiting till we're more afraid."

Jim expressed a breath fierce enough for a word. "Am I meant to know what you're talking about?"

"They'd mean you to. The people who've been attacking us online, they've got what I expect they prayed for."

"You're saying they'd mean me to know what you mean."

"No," I said, trying to believe that only the irregularities of the ceiling had lent the shadow limbs. "What they've brought back would."

"Which is what exactly?"

"The founders of the church." Although the name felt too close to an invocation, I seemed unable not to say "The Nobles."

Jim stared at the glass he'd just drunk from and then at each of us in turn. "Shall we talk about something else while we finish this?"

"Why, what do you think that will put off?"

"I'm saying there's no need to talk where people can hear," Jim said and lowered his voice further. "Let's save it till we're back at Dom's or mine if you'd both rather."

"We don't want to invite them home," Bobby cautioned. "We don't want them to get in more than they have."

"You shouldn't put your family at risk, Jim, and Bobby's trying to protect Carole by coming all this way."

Jim took another eloquent breath while he scrutinised us both. "I don't think I know why we're supposed to be here."

"We need to agree what we can do."

"I could try and get the identities of some of the people who've been threatening us online. My lads should be able to do it, and there's certainly some hate speech."

"It's gone far beyond that," Bobby objected. "Weren't you listening to me?"

"I've listened to you both, and do you want to hear what I think?"

"I hope we will."

"I think you both spent too much time with the Nobles. You've let yourselves be influenced too much."

"I was. I said so when I wrote about them online, but I'm not any more."

"Don't take this the wrong way, but maybe you only think you're free of them." Before I could point out that neither of us believed this – quite the reverse – Jim said "You mentioned they gave you, what did you say, occult visons. That'll be like hypnotism, won't it? The suggestion can hang around even if whoever's responsible has gone."

"It was never only hypnotism," I said. "We'd like to believe that, but we've seen too much."

"Dom, maybe you can't let go of the Nobles when you've had them on your mind so long. And some of the people who've put these ideas in your head aren't even gone."

"If you mean Toby and his wife they've cast me out. I let them know I was concerned in case they turned into a family like the one the Nobles had."

"Good God," Jim said, though his outrage might have been aimed at me. "I pray that couldn't happen. They didn't strike me as capable of anything like that."

"They couldn't really, Dom, could they? For a start, your son already has a wife."

I felt as if Jim and Bobby were reminding me how obsessed I was, so preoccupied with the Nobles that they'd distorted my view of my own family. "All I'm saying," I insisted, "is they can't influence me any more. Jim, you saw they gave me an icon like the one you meant to bring away from Safe To Sleep, but I threw it in the river."

"That's a pity. It could have been evidence." Jim shook his head, dismissing my mistake. "The fact remains you got involved with their church," he said. "It could still be affecting your mind more than you realise."

"Jim," Bobby said and waited until she had all his attention. "Tell me you didn't see anything wrong at Safe To Sleep."

"I saw plenty I'd call wrong. I saw how you had to hang on to your bed because they'd worked on your nerves so much."

"Not that kind of wrong. Didn't you see what had grown underneath the house?"

"I don't know about grown. The way they'd dug the cellar out certainly wasn't safe."

"Weren't you there when it dragged the whole place underground?"

"I told Dom at the time, that was subsidence."

"I think you're as affected as you want to believe we are, only the effect it's had on you is making you determined not to see." As Jim opened his mouth with a wordless but vigorous sound Bobby said "I didn't come just to keep all this away from Carole. I wanted to help you see what's happening so you'll be ready for it."

Jim closed his mouth and stayed quiet long enough for me to take a generous drink. I was searching for arguments to add to Bobby's when Jim said "All right, show me and I'll do my best to see. It won't alter my beliefs, but I'll try if it's going to help."

"Remember what we used to say," Bobby said, grasping his hand and mine. "We'd always look out for one another."

"That's what it's like," Jim said as if she'd inspired him. "One of those stories Dom used to write about us."

Bobby let go of our hands before I had time to clasp Jim's. "What do you think we should do, Dom?" she said. "You've seen the most of any of us."

Given her days and nights at Safe To Sleep I wondered how true this could be. Was she trying not to recall her experiences? "We ought to go where the Nobles died," I said.

"And let them do their worst. We're still three and we're together."

I hoped this lent us as much power as she assumed. She poured the last of the wine into the glasses and raised hers. "Drink up and let's be on our way," she said. "Here's to friendship that won't die."

"Friendship," Jim and I said together, though I wondered if he shared my feeling that her final phrase was too extreme a claim. We drained our glasses, having clinked them forcefully enough to attract rather more than a glance from the barman, and marched in a moderately steady line out of the pub.

Bobby halted outside, so abruptly that Jim almost collided with her. I thought she'd detected an intruder in the crowd until I saw she was gazing at the abandoned cinema. "That's where we were the day you went under the church, Dom."

"I wish we'd gone with him instead."

"Forget what you were up to," I said. "We weren't really ourselves yet, were we? We were still finding out who we were."

Jim and Bobby stared at me. "What do you think we were up to?" Bobby said.

My hesitation was more eloquent than I could help. "What do boys and girls generally get up to in the dark?"

"Not a lot," Jim said, "at the age we were."

"Just a snog and I wasn't too good at it," Bobby said.

"Don't say you're obsessed with sex as well, Dom."

Presumably he meant besides the Nobles. I saw his and Bobby's faces move apart in the light from the screen, not as guiltily as they would have if they'd known who was watching, and the mutations I'd chopped into writhing bits in the crypt of the Trinity Church of the Spirit. Jim's comment had revived the fury I'd felt then, so that I might have revealed how I'd caught him with Bobby if she hadn't intervened. "He won't be, Jim," she said. "That's all long past, and as Dom says, we're other people now. Let's focus on the past that won't stay dead."

CHAPTER TWENTY

A United Family

Once we were on the bus we began to reminisce about trips across the river. "Seems as if we were always running for the ferry," Jim said.

"Remember when they almost wouldn't sell us tickets," Bobby said, "because we were too puffed to say please."

"And the day the crewman wouldn't let us up the stairs," I said, "because we were too lively for him."

"We always made it to New Brighton, though," Bobby declared. "Nobody stops us."

"Nobody stopped you on the dodgems," Jim remembered. "I came away with bruises every time."

"Well, you nearly sprained my back that time you came after me down the helter-skelter."

"And we always saved the ghost train for the last ride," I contributed.

"And then it was fish and chips on the prom. Remember when the wind blew half of yours away."

"That was when Dom wanted us to hurry so we wouldn't miss any of a film. Films were your life even then, Dom."

Perhaps riding on the top deck of the bus, as we used to do with scholars' half fare tickets, had reminded us of our adolescence, but I suspected we were trying not to anticipate what lay ahead – perhaps even Jim was. I recalled the ferry dipping gently as a cradle or rearing up from the waves, the wheel vibrating in my grasp as Bobby's dodgem dealt my car yet another hearty thump, the mat prickling against the backs of my legs all the way down the spiral ramp, the mechanical howls and doggedly illuminated goblins that lay in wait for the faltering carriages of the ghost train, the smell of fish and chips an unexpected gale served me before wrenching half the newspaper and its culinary contents out of my hands... This brought back memories of newspaper reports of Eric Wharton's death. I felt adrift in time, unable to judge whether this preceded the memory that had revived it or came after. I tried to fasten on another – the Court in New Brighton, a cinema whose screen had remained practically square, defiantly celebrating the old shape of films. Would speaking help to fix me in my mind? "Not my whole life by any means," I said, only for Jim to blink at me as if I'd answered so belatedly that he had to remind himself of his own remark. I had indeed been elsewhere longer than I'd realised, because the bus had reached the tunnel under the river.

I'd overlooked how sitting upstairs would bring us closer to the tunnel roof. As we passed under the arch I felt as though the roof had closed over my skull. Intermittent blocks of light stretched away overhead into the dimness, and I wondered if more of them had gone out since my last trip through, and how this might change the meaning of the code they seemed to represent. My innards tightened like an aching fist as the bus gathered speed down the underground slope. I wasn't only apprehensive about travelling under the river; I was concerned how my friends might respond. I seemed to sense a change in the enormous weight that rested on the tunnel, but neither of my companions spoke. In a minute we came in sight of the lowest point in the tunnel, and Bobby said "Is anyone else feeling that?"

Jim shook his head before complaining "What?"

"As if there's something over us."

"It's called the Mersey, Bob. You haven't been away that long."

She leaned towards us from the other front seat, looking ready to punch him for old times' sake. "Something alive," she said, "or maybe not alive but like it."

"You've lost me, and I've got to say I'm glad you have."

"It's making me feel like, like an insect in a web," Bobby said and tried again. "As if something up there is waiting to be noticed."

"Nothing like that at all. It's just the tunnel. Maybe you've got a touch of claustrophobia."

Jim seemed faintly offended, perhaps thinking only God could be described as waiting up above to be acknowledged. I found Bobby's words unappealingly suggestive, and did my utmost not to experience anything like them. Jim glanced at me, presumably for a comment, but I gave my head a fierce terse shake. I'd begun to fancy that the presence might be crouched over the mouth of the tunnel, waiting to reach for us, too insubstantially and insidiously for Jim to notice. When at last we emerged beneath a sky that had congealed over the sun, I was barely able to restrain myself from glancing back.

Beyond the toll booths the bus followed the route I'd taken to the Nobles' house, and I felt as if it might be retracing time as well. A road miles long wound between blocks of shops and houses as sinuously as a snake. Eventually we left it for a road leading to the junction where I'd turned towards the river. The skewed mossy headstones in front of the abandoned church, where we alighted from the bus, looked better fed than ever. They put me in mind of vegetation nourished by graves, and I had to grasp the edge of the bus shelter while I fended off memories eager to occupy my brain. "Not far now," I told Bobby and Jim.

The street opposite the church led past groups of rudimentary anonymous dwellings clad with strips of whitish wood or plastic. At the far end, which framed a blackened patch of sky, traffic passed along a road above the river. Haze appeared to have gathered on the road, and the outlines of several figures on the pavement at the junction wavered so unstably that I found it hard to count them. I was about to comment on the sight when the three of them moved away in a blurred confusion of limbs. "Did you see them waiting at the crossroads?" Bobby said as though she couldn't quite control her voice.

"Of course we did," Jim said. "Three of them having a gossip."

Bobby didn't speak again until we reached the junction. "So where are they now?"

"In a shop or in a house or down a side street," Jim said, having peered both ways along the main road. "Were they the sort of thing you're wanting me to see, you and Dom?"

"They're the start of it," Bobby said.

There was no sign of haze on the road. Perhaps we were too close to see it any longer, but the day didn't feel hot enough to have produced it, unless petrol fumes had. Traffic lights let us troop across the road, though not before a bus driver ignored them. I was relieved to see warehouses and windmills across the river, where the threat of a storm had turned the sky not much less black than a space between stars. I took care with every shuffling footstep as I led the way down the steep pavement to the remains of the Noble house.

I sensed the place before it came in sight. It felt like the source of the dark in the sky, unless they were related in some other fashion. I came to an unsteady halt on the corner of the street whose gardens sloped down to the promenade. "That's where they died," I said as if this could have been as final as it should.

The house was a dwarfish ruin. Charred lengths of timber poked out of heaps of rubble, haphazard clumps of bricks no longer identifiable as the walls they'd once formed. Flapping scraps of paper clung to the remains, burned too black to be worthy of salvaging, even if they'd been pages bearing occult thoughts rather than fragments of wallpaper. Shards of glass gleamed like ebony among shattered tiles from the roof. The spectacle reminded me of the streets that had surrounded the Trinity Church of the Spirit, which might have prefigured my recurring vision of the human prey that fled through a devastated city. As I ventured towards the ruin I saw that the side walls of the neighbouring houses were stained black, as though some infection had begun. I halted opposite the spot where the front door would have been, and Jim and Bobby moved to stand on either side of me. "What are we expected to do now?" Jim said.

"I wouldn't do anything just yet," Bobby said at once.

"Let's try waiting," I agreed and saw Jim thought we were being excessively cautious.

If we were under observation, I saw nobody in the surrounding houses. I could have fancied they'd been infected by desertion, if living so close to the Nobles hadn't driven out their neighbours. The derelict site was growing darker, and I wasn't sure this was just because blackness was crossing the river. A charred stench caught in my throat, and I felt as though the dark was invading my eyes if not my brain, gathering inside them. I'd begun to find it hard to breathe when Jim said "Come on then, show yourselves if you're going to. Let's have a good look."

He sounded so conversational that at first I thought he was talking to Bobby or me. "No need for that, Jim," Bobby told him.

"There's some need for something," Jim said hoarsely. "If we stand here much longer I'll be losing my voice."

I feared this might be true for all of us. I was about to suggest retreating across the road, not least because of the summons he'd just issued, when he stepped forward. "Where are you going?" I said louder than I'd intended.

"I want to see if they've left any evidence," Jim said and paced alongside the ruin.

I thought he was trying to revert to rationality after his momentary lapse. I had to stay with him, and Bobby followed me. I hoped it was only a breeze that made the ruin seem to grow alert, scraps of blackened paper pricking up like ears, a mass of fused timber emitting a surreptitious creak. The house was so thoroughly devastated that I couldn't even judge where any inner walls had been, and if anything significant had survived it must be buried under the rubble. A length of snaky tendrils caught my eye, and I was afraid it would reach for us until I recognised it for a bunch of exposed wires. Had some of the ash begun to creep towards us? As I swallowed in order to speak Jim said "What's that down there?"

I joined him at the edge of the garden. The binoculars hadn't shown me how entangled the flowers and bushes on the slope were, a mass that looked impenetrable. All the vegetation was crouching away from the site of the house, stretching out stalks in a gesture not unlike supplication. "Does it remind you of anything, Jim?" I said.

"Such as what?"

"The trees around the field in France we followed Christian Noble to."

"Maybe, but I don't mean that." His voice had grown harsh with impatience or ash. "I meant the writing down there," he said.

I had to lean out to identify what he was seeing. A crumpled piece of paper had lodged among the twigs of a bush near the foot of the slope. Despite its restlessness, I could see it bore words. "Let's find out," Jim said.

As he made for the street I thought a wind must be at large in the ruins of the house – at least, I hoped it had lifted the piece of debris from behind a clump of bricks. I didn't glance at the dark wavering shape as I followed Jim, and I tried to quell an impression that the blackness left by the fire was capable of rising up to grow more solid, reconstituting a version of the house. No doubt this was a symptom of the influences the Nobles had planted in my head, but I was grateful when the three of us reached the street and turned away from the ruin.

By the time we set foot on the promenade my legs were aching, my rickety ankles in particular. A cyclist raced past with a whir of wheels, but otherwise the possibility of a storm seemed to have cleared the wide pavement and the narrow beach. Infrequent benches faced a waist-high railing and the view of three spindly windmills across the river, skeletal white vanes groping at the black sky as if to drag it down. Between the promenade and the steep gardens, trees rose from an elongated strip of lawn, and Jim picked up a fallen branch as he made for the bush that had trapped the crumpled paper. He was just able to snag the page, which he grabbed as a wind set it fluttering like an impaled insect on the branch. He glanced at his find as he let the branch drop, and looked ready to bin the piece of paper. "Well, that was a mistake," he said.

Bobby glanced at it and then peered closer. "I don't know, Jim."

It was a page from a local newspaper, reporting the destruction of the Nobles' house. Bobby took it and unfolded it, and I saw that the edges were scorched. "Look again," she urged.

It wasn't merely scorched, it was charred around the edge. In fact the fire had discoloured it more than I'd seen at first, and some of the print resembled the marks of a brand. As Jim ducked towards it like a mime of patience, the page darkened further. I wasn't sure whether this was because the sky had, even once the paper started crumbling in her hands. It disintegrated into fragments that fell on the grass like black snow.

Bobby gazed at the spectacle as though it had left her without words, and then she said "Do you realise what that means?"

I wanted Jim to answer. "It was in the fire," he said.

"But it couldn't have been, could it?" I felt desperate to remind him. "It was published later."

"Then obviously someone set it on fire afterwards."

"I don't think so, Jim," Bobby said. "It feels as if time went wrong."

"Time should be no more." This sounded like agreement until Jim said "That's what the Bible used to say about the apocalypse. It's nothing like yet, though."

He stepped off the grass before I could give him an argument. I saw he meant to keep an eye on the garden and the ruined house, but then he glanced over the railing. The sight beyond it took him across the promenade. "Dom, have a look at this."

Bobby joined him at the railing before I did. Beyond it a drenched breakwater like a remnant of the ancient jetty extended into the river. An unstable shape leapt up from it – a wave – and I couldn't help hoping he'd seen nothing as lively as that. The sinuous fringe of the river drew back from the sand in front of us, and eyes gleamed at us out of the water. A wave engulfed the hairless head and then retreated, exposing the gleeful face of the object that lay coiled on the beach. "Bob, you ought to recognise that too," Jim said. "It's like the thing Dom and I forgot at Safe To Sleep."

"The Nobles all had them. They gave me one." Bobby shivered, perhaps just with the unseasonable chill that had crept around us. "They used to stroke them like pets," she said.

"We won't be forgetting this one," Jim said and made for a ramp near the breakwater.

I couldn't tell whether the item on the beach was the icon I'd thrown in the river. "I don't know if that's advisable," I said.

"You brought me here to see, Dom. That's the first solid bit of evidence I've seen."

I hoped nothing else of that kind we might encounter would prove to be as solid. I didn't think Jim should be alone on the beach, and I followed him down the slippery stone ramp as Bobby did. Beyond the ramp wet sand closed around our shoes while the massive sandstone blocks of the sea wall towered above us. The river was empty of ships and as black as the sky, and sent waves outlined by dark foam towards us as we trooped abreast along the beach. Now I saw the icon was embedded in the sand and coated with it too, which made it look as though it was decaying into particles, not least the eyes that bulged above the grin stretched wide. A wave coursed over the icon and recoiled, which made the coiled shape appear to raise its watchful head. If Jim noticed the illusion – surely that was all it was – he ignored it, stooping to pick up the icon at once.

As he dug his fingers under the noose of a body I heard a commotion above the sea wall. It sounded as if an object had been dislodged from a garden overlooking the river, and as it slithered down to the promenade I could tell it was substantial. I didn't know whether my friends had heard it, but I was wary of distracting Jim. Before I had a chance to speak he straightened up with a grunt of effort or distaste or both.

He was holding the icon. It looked unpleasantly moist, glistening like a snail just emerged from a shell, and I wondered if this was the cause of his disgust. I heard the object on the slope drop to the grass, a muted surreptitious noise that was succeeded by a confused scurrying. In a moment three heads peered over the railing above us – three faces, at any rate. When I glanced up they'd gone, and Jim was gasping "What the devil."

He didn't mean the watchers I'd glimpsed. Both he and Bobby had their backs to the sea wall and were staring at the icon. He was doing his best to keep hold of it as it sagged in his hands, drooping like a dead reptile. When he tried to take a firmer grasp the icon started to disintegrate as if it was composed of sand. Perhaps the actual figurine was still at the bottom of the river, in which case I had a fearful notion that whatever it represented was infesting its surroundings. Jim's prize was collapsing in his hands, a spectacle that left me all but unaware of some activity receding along the promenade. He jerked his hands apart, and the remnants of the object landed on the beach, where they were indistinguishable from the sand. No doubt Jim's gesture signified defeat, but it reminded me how Christian Noble had sown the field in France with fragments of his ancestor, a symbolic broadcast of his influence. I didn't think Jim was recalling this as he stared at the sand and then at Bobby and me. "Good God," he said in very little of a voice, and I was about to offer any reassurance I could find when my breath faltered, and my heartbeat did. He was staring not at us but beyond us.

If his words hadn't made his dismay plain, his eyes would have. I felt not just reluctant to turn but not much better than incapable of doing so. Bobby turned first, and pressed the back of a hand against her mouth so hard I thought it might draw blood. This seemed to intensify the dreadfulness of whatever waited at my back, but I couldn't let my friends confront it without me. I shook from head to foot with the effort of overcoming my paralysis, and twisted around to look.

A shape was perched on the ramp beneath the black sky. The longest of its outstretched limbs almost spanned the ramp. They and the rest of a cluster of a dozen extravagantly unequal limbs ended in clumps of digits with some ambition to resemble hands. The profusion of limbs was surmounted by a gibbous mass of flesh that glimmered like a moon obscured by clouds. While the swollen roundish lump was largely featureless, it had more than one face.

I tried to be reminded of a totem pole in case this helped to keep the sight at a distance from my mind. Christian Noble's face grinned from the bottom of the fleshy heap, tucked under Tina's chin, while Toph's face overlapped her brows and competed with his parents for elation. It was even harder to tell them apart now, especially once the faces began to crawl over one another like insects in a nest before merging into a single bloated exultant mask. The pairs of tumid lightless eyes split apart to swarm over the composite face, and I was appalled to realise that the Nobles were celebrating their state – their potential for mutation. Some of the eyes migrated onto swellings like enormous blisters on the gathering of flesh, and as faces formed around the eyes the three heads craned towards us on contorted reptilian necks. Throughout the performance all the limbs had been shifting back and forth with an impatience that suggested some unimaginable hunger, and now the shape scuttled crabwise down to the beach.

I didn't know how many of us made a noise. Certainly I made one that had no time to form a word. I stumbled backwards, almost tripping over my own senile feet. I thought I'd lost all sense of direction, because I found myself floundering through water. No, the tide appeared to be coming in, though when we'd reached the promenade it had been receding. It was already splashing against the sea wall a few hundred yards away, and falling back with a sluggishness that looked unnaturally reluctant, not quite like water. As I staggered clear of the waves that were narrowing the beach, Bobby grabbed Jim's arm and mine. "Steps," she urged.

A flight of them, strewn with sodden seaweed and slimy with lichen, led up from the narrowest section of the beach. We'd hardly started for them when the river set about pursuing us with waves that flung ripples across the sand to catch at our feet. I had a nightmare sense that the ripples were passing through the sand, which had begun to quiver underfoot. Bobby was first at the steps, and as she seized the handrail to haul herself upwards I made myself look back.

The trinity of faces had crowded together on the malformed head to watch us. Above a horrid confusion of features the eyes clustered like an insect's. As they met mine, the creature scampered with appalling rapidity onto the beach, splaying all its limbs wide and rearing high as they grew unequally scrawnier. I was afraid to draw my friends' attention to the sight, and managed not to plead with Jim to hurry up, to give me space to follow him and Bobby on the steps. While I forced myself to wait I felt the beach shift under my feet, and sand crawling into my shoes to weigh them down. The moment Jim gained the third step, I clutched the chilly handrail and lurched after him.

The worn steps were even more precarious than they looked. I heard water or some other fluid substance slop against them, and seemed to feel a ripple pass through the step I was trapped on. "Don't stop," I couldn't help telling my friends, "go up." Of course they were already climbing, and no doubt only panic made me think time was slowing down, gathering about us like amber. They stumped quickly upwards, and I followed almost close enough to nudge Jim's spine with my forehead. Whenever my feet slipped, which was distressingly often, I gripped the rail so hard that flakes of paint or rust came off in my hand. I was struggling to concentrate on our ascent, to put out of my mind the cause of our flight. I saw Bobby use the top of the rail to swing herself onto the promenade, and then Jim did. Both of them stared towards the ramp, and their expressions left me terrified to look. I managed not to do so until I was on the top step.

The shape on the beach had split into three. The section that bore Tina's face was swimming past the steps, propelling itself with a boneless motion of its elongated limbs. The others had climbed the ramp, and the lanky mass that Christian Noble had become loitered at the top while the object that was Toph scuttled out of sight towards the main road. The creature below us writhed out of the water to stretch its limbs wide and clamber spider-like up the sea wall to rise taller than any of us on the promenade, its thin tongue outlining Tina's smile of triumph. I heard the river smash against the wall and the steps, and knew the Nobles meant to cut us off in every other direction. I sensed inhuman playfulness, if it wasn't a remnant of their version of humanity – a malevolent game intended to render us meaningless, an interlude of self-indulgence before they moved on to their next unimaginable development. The oppressive notion, and the abnormally black sky that surrounded us with a premature dusk, seemed capable of paralysing me until Jim spoke. "Up there, quick."

He was pointing at the nearest side street, and I had an awful premonition that the route would prove to be a trap. While it led to the main road, it was so precipitous that the pavements were furnished with handrails. The apparition with Tina Noble's face was prancing back and forth across the promenade, and her father's distorted remains were performing a similarly ghastly dance at the top of the ramp, but where was Toph? Staying put wouldn't save us, and I tried not to feel fatally ensnared as I dashed uphill after Bobby and Jim.

Patches of the cobbled roadway exposed older stone beneath, and more than one upright of the handrail was unsteady in its socket. Just a few paces slowed us to a desperate trudge. Before we'd climbed halfway we had to drag ourselves upwards by the rail like senile mountaineers on a rope. Every house we passed was full of the black sky, and I suspected that even if anyone was inside they were somehow blinded to our plight. I glanced downhill to see that the invader of the promenade had extended all its limbs to fence off the junction. At least the slope grew gentler where the handrails ended, beside the street that contained the ruined house. We stumbled past the rail, and I saw the cross street was deserted. At least, it was until the shape with Christian Noble's face sprang along it faster than a spider.

"Keep going," Bobby cried as if this might save us, and I could only comply, however hopeless it seemed. We struggled up the higher stretch, and my heartbeat grew painfully fierce. Though it was close to deafening, I heard my friends' effortful breaths. The pounding of my head appeared to shake the black sky, unless the sky was growing impatiently wakeful. We staggered onto the main road and leaned against the nearest building, a silent pub. The road wasn't quite empty, even if unnaturally so. While it was devoid of traffic and pedestrians, Toph came sauntering towards us on a cluster of skeletal many-jointed legs, nodding his joyful deformed parody of a head.

The monstrous version of his father darted past us to help both the offspring hem us in. When they began to approach in an intricate many-legged dance, I thought we were the victims of a ritual. I was afraid the hypnotic patterns their movements described might be able to reduce us to a single psychic entity, a mocking imitation of the Nobles' own state – a slave they could use for play or worse. I might have closed my eyes to shut out their magical antics, but I was still more afraid not to see. Bobby clutched my arm, and then Jim stepped forward, ignoring or at least feigning to ignore the Nobles' approach. "This isn't right," he said in the strongest voice I thought he could find, and stared both ways along the empty road. "I don't believe in this. It can't be so."

In a moment Bobby seemed to catch his purpose. "I don't either. This can't have happened yet."

I feared all this was a pitifully feeble defence, but I couldn't see a better one. "You're right," I said and cleared my clogged throat. "This isn't our world. We don't belong here."

I had a sense that we hadn't found the correct words and mightn't ever, but Bobby clasped my hand and Jim's as if she was seized by inspiration. Before I knew what she was planning, she urged us into the road. "Not so," she cried. "It's just a trick. I won't have it. No."

"No," Jim shouted, and I tried to summon up all my conviction as I echoed him. I heard a scurrying of many limbs behind us, and then faces reared over us, though only one head. I heard a screech and saw a gout of red. I was wondering dismally which of my friends had been injured if not killed when I realised brakes had made the sound. We were halfway across the road, and the red belonged to a traffic signal that was forbidding us to cross. A car had almost run us down, and its driver had a monologue for us about old idiots, involving rather stronger words. Pedestrians were staring at us in disbelief or contempt, but we ignored them as we made arm in arm for the opposite pavement, our gait wavering between a stagger and a swagger. When we turned there was no sign of the Nobles, and the sky had begun to clear without delivering a storm. Bobby let out a gasping breath that did duty as a bid to laugh. "I don't know what we did," she said, "but it worked."

"I've no idea what happened," Jim declared, "and I'd rather not have. It's done with now. It's gone."

Despite his resolve, he was shaking – we all were – but I couldn't insist he admit any more than he'd said. "Let's hope so," I murmured, and did my best to think we could.

CHAPTER TWENTY-ONE

On Their Own

"Back together again."

"The three of us, just like old times."

My voice was the loudest. "We'll always look out for one another."

We were ready for anything now, I told myself. We'd achieved our greatest triumph, to which our entire lives might have led. I could almost have thought we'd been born for the purpose. I felt as if we had restored the world to its everyday self. The streets through which the bus was bearing us looked as they had on our way to the burned-out house, but time wasn't running in reverse; it was back to normal. Slim clouds were scrawled on a sky rendered pale blue by the sun, and the glinting needle of an airliner passed a thread through a frayed white cushion. As the road wound back and forth towards the tunnel the sunlight showed us occupants of rooms above blocks of shops: a woman sitting at a computer, a girl playing a video game, a man resting his feet on a table strewn with plates while he read an electronic reduction of a book. When the tunnel entrance came in sight I saw Starview Tower beyond it, across the river. If we still faced any kind of threat, I believed we could deal with it together. Perhaps the mature exploits of the Tremendous Three had just begun.

As a queue for the left-hand toll lane halted the bus, the tower slipped out of sight. Just a lorry was ahead of us when I glimpsed movement on the gantry that displayed signs above the toll booths. A hunched lanky shape had run across the metal bar to vanish overhead. The bus advanced to the barrier, and I heard a large object fall on the roof.

Jim stared at me and grimaced. "Not again," he said, though it sounded less like a complaint than a challenge.

"If it is we're equal to it," Bobby said with equal fierceness.

I felt bound to measure up to them. "More than equal," I contributed. "We're the Three."

The bus gathered speed towards the tunnel, and I wondered if the arch might dislodge the unauthorised passenger from the roof. As we entered the tunnel I glanced back. All the seats behind us were unoccupied, and the rear window showed only the receding booths. I was staring at it in the hope of seeing the intruder belatedly swept off the roof, having retreated along it as far as it could, when Bobby said "Dom."

I turned to find neither her nor Jim looking at me. They were gazing at the window directly in front of us, outside which three variously misshapen heads dangled upside down. Despite their inversion, their gleeful smiles were unmistakable. "Go away," Jim said loud enough to be heard throughout the bus. "We got rid of you once."

"And we'll do it again," Bobby vowed.

"Every time you show up," I said, "so don't bother."

Tongues slithered out of the inverted mouths, shaping wider smiles, and objects too varied to be called hands closed over the windows on both sides of us. They might have been preparing to crush us or, I thought, seep into us. "That won't convince us," Jim declared. "We didn't believe last time and we don't now."

"Listen to Jim," Bobby said.

I wasn't sure if she was addressing the faces or me. "That's the truth, you need belief," I said. "You feed on it, but you'll get none from us."

More attempts at hands pressed against the side windows, and I heard the glass creak. The trinity of faces grew flat against the pane in front of us, putting me in mind of the undersides of snails, and Jim leaned forward to deal the glass a thump with the side of his fist. "And I'll tell you what," he said, "God doesn't believe in you either."

The inverted pairs of lips stirred, forming identical sneers, which enraged Jim. "Laugh at this if you can," he said through his teeth.

Before he'd finished speaking he had taken out his phone. He brought up an image of a luminous cross, which he thrust at the faces. I thought I saw them shift uneasily before the pallid lumps that bore them huddled together to merge. "Bobby, Dom," he urged. "You can do it if you want to."

I pulled out my phone as Bobby rummaged in her bag. While the ruse reminded me of my adolescent tale in which students overcame their occultist tutor, did this matter so long as it worked? I'd seen the phrase Jim had used to find the image – **shining cross** – and entered it in the search box. Moments later I had a picture similar to his, and held it close to the faces, which had begun to swarm over one another. As Bobby added her phone to the defence Jim cried "No belief for you. This is the only one we'll ever have."

I supposed that in a sense this might be true, at least as a form of words. The faces were crawling over one another in a growing confusion of features, of misplaced eyes and dislocated mouths. Jim began to follow them with his phone, sliding the lit cross back and forth over the pane, and we copied him. "God doesn't see you," he called. "Nobody does."

At the very least his words or the nearness of the phones seemed to offend our persecutor. Any number of digits slithered over the windows as the composite head reared up, just in front of a hanging sign that warned drivers to stay in lane. We heard a large soft thud that produced an inhuman cry, and an object scraped backwards along the roof. All of us looked back in time to see a partially demolished shape sprawl off the far end of the roof and plummet helplessly to the floor of the tunnel. Now we were on the uphill slope, which let us see a lorry crushing the shape beneath its wheels in an agonised flurry of limbs. The lorry sped after us without slowing, and I wondered how odd the driver of the bus might find our outburst of cheers and applause.

Why couldn't it have ended like that, or at any rate along those lines? Even if that hadn't been the end, we would have demonstrated once again that we weren't to be cowed. We did indeed take the bus to Liverpool, and our route – traffic on the roads, pedestrians on pavements, people glimpsed in shops and flats above them – reinstated the mundane. While I was sure that we oughtn't to take it for granted, I couldn't tell whether my friends thought so too. We hadn't spoken since making for the bus stop, where we would have been overheard by a queue, and we weren't the only passengers upstairs on the bus. Did Jim and Bobby detect anything as we passed beneath the river? Bobby glanced towards the roof and then stared at the floor, while Jim crouched over his clasped hands, quite possibly in silent prayer. I was afraid I sensed a dormant presence at least as wide as the river, and was dismayed to think how much the Nobles and their practices might have left in the world.

The bus brought us to the foot of the road that sloped up to the main railway station in Liverpool. When Jim and I made to escort Bobby to her train she planted her hands on our chests. "I'll be all right by myself, boys. There'll be plenty of people."

The contradiction left me uneasy about leaving her. "You've just missed a train. The next one isn't for nearly an hour."

"I expect I'll find something to read."

Jim cleared his throat as though to rouse himself, and I had the impression that he was determined to fend off the experience we'd gone through. "We could have a farewell drink in the Crown."

"I've never liked farewells, Jim, and anyway this isn't going to be one. Let's just say till next time and head for home. I should think you might want to be with your family."

I suspected she was just as anxious to rejoin Carole. Perhaps she realised that my family wasn't so available to me, because she embraced me even more tightly than she hugged Jim. "That's it for now," she said, turning swiftly away. "Look after yourselves, and next time let's just meet because we're friends."

"We'll look after one another," I called after her, and she lifted a hand without glancing back.

Jim and I watched her trot resolutely uphill, outdistanced by a succession of buses, and then he gave me an apologetic look. "If you don't mind, Dom, I will get back to the lads. Dominic's meant to þe making us all dinner."

"You head off, Jim. Bobby's right, they're what you need."

"Do you fancy coming back with me? He always makes too much for us."

"It's your family evening. Don't worry, I'm off home."

Jim hesitated but spoke anyway. "What's the chance of you getting back together with your lad?"

Was Jim determined to forget not just the Nobles but the Church of the Eternal Three? I could only say "I'm hoping. Best to give it time."

I would have felt like an intruder in his house, and I feared this might be true of Toby's and Claudine's. We trudged up the road Bobby had climbed, and shook hands at length when we reached Jim's stop. His bus came before mine, and as it moved off he gazed down from the top deck, shaking a fist twice in our childhood gesture – the code of the Tremendous Three. Despite odd looks from my companions at the bus stop, I flourished a fist in response.

At first I had company on the bus I caught, but soon I was the solitary passenger, upstairs at any rate. I sat sideways on the end of a front seat to keep an eye on everything behind, but saw no unwelcome activity and sensed none. I let myself fancy the Nobles had gone at last, having lost the little interest in us that they'd had. I know I wasn't wishing them away just from myself.

As I walked home through the suburb the trees stayed as still as the cloudless sky, all of which felt like a hint of peace. If I was going to be alone, at least perhaps this meant I wouldn't encounter any uninvited visitors. I might be assailed by memories of the confrontation at the river, not to mention recollections of other such experiences, and I was trying to think how to fend them off – surely by reminding myself that I'd survived – as I reached home. I was opening the gate when my heart jerked as though my body had realised something before my mind did. No, the phone in my breast pocket had just received a message.

I did my best to hope there was no reason to be apprehensive until

I read it. Bobby had sent it to me and Jim. **It's on the train**, it said. **It's worse**.

I felt so guilty that I was left almost unable to think. What had I caused by taking us all to the ruined house? I was about to call Bobby, having been distracted by the shamefully irrelevant thought that even under duress she was determined to punctuate correctly – no doubt her phone was doing that – when a second message arrived. **Don't phone**, it told us. **Can't talk while nobody else can see it. Can't stand feeling trapped. Getting off next stop.**

I didn't know what her plan could achieve, but I hadn't responded by the time Jim did. **Which?**

In seconds we had our answer – **Crewe** – and Jim replied at once. **See you there. Dom?**

I was already running to my car, and sent the response my phone suggested. **On my way**, I promised.

Driving out of Liverpool as fast as I could risk left me little chance to think. I did wonder how much Jim believed now or even let himself recall of his experience. If we were resolved to protect Bobby, not to say ourselves, that had to be enough. Any other speculation threatened me with panic, and I concentrated on the road.

Driving to Crewe took most of an hour. Towns gave way to villages, and then intermittent groups of houses flanked the road, settlements apparently too small to bear a name. I'd left my phone on the seat beside me, but it showed no further messages, which I tried to find encouraging. Though the road had grown devious, I was making good time when I began to hear distant howls or wails or shrieks. They might have been voicing my suppressed apprehensiveness, since they were sirens. They belonged to ambulances and police cars, and perhaps they weren't so distant after all; they seemed to be converging somewhere ahead from all over the countryside. When a police car flashed its lights and raced past me I swerved onto the verge, scraping one wing on the thorns of a hedge. As I reached for the phone I almost fumbled it onto the floor, because my hand had begun to shake.

While I searched for a live feed from the local police force I came close to praying, but prayer wouldn't have worked unless it could turn time back. All too soon I read **Liverpool to Euston train in crash** and a warning of delays on the road I was following. I dropped the phone on the seat and sent the car forward, barely slowing at bends, however sharp. At least no traffic was approaching in the opposite direction, but I was afraid to see why. Keeping the car out of the ditch occupied most of my mind, so that I wasn't overwhelmed with dread until I came in sight of the train.

A carriage blocked a level crossing, the nearside barrier of which lay splintered beside the line. Ambulances and police cars were parked on both sides of the road, throbbing with lights like heartbeats rendered visible. About a dozen spectators had gathered on a pedestrian bridge above the track. As I parked behind the nearest police vehicle, two attendants with a stretcher marched around the barrier at a pace too reminiscent of a funeral. The contents of the stretcher were covered with a sheet from head to foot. I was both desperate and terrified to learn who they were carrying, but by the time I came abreast of the ambulance they had shut the doors, and the driver was turning onto the road. I found I preferred to hope rather than know – surely I'd no reason to think what I feared – and told myself I oughtn't to delay them. Instead I made for the bridge.

I was halfway up the steps when I faltered, clutching at the clinically chilly handrail. The train had hit a car on the crossing and dragged it for hundreds of yards. The wreckage was partly upturned, propped against the driver's cab like an improvised memorial. The car was as red as the stain on the smashed window of the buckled door. By squinting hard enough to send an ache into my eyes I managed to distinguish the registration number, the last three characters of which were TOT. I'd once told Jim that it sounded like the emblem of an infant version of our childhood gang. The wreck was his car.

I might have been too appalled to move if I hadn't thought of Bobby. As I groped for the phone I'd shoved in my pocket, a hefty bearded man wearing an ensemble that included shorts and muddy hiking boots said "He never had a chance."

Though I was almost too distressed to speak, this provoked me to demand "Did you see what happened?"

"We saw it all," the man's companion said.

She was attired and muscled much like him. Their vitality felt disrespectful to my friend, the opposite of Jim's state. I scrambled up the steps onto the bridge. "What did you see?"

"We only came up here to watch the trains," the woman said as if she was defending the couple against an accusation I hadn't meant to make. "The barriers were closed when he got to them but he didn't even start to slow down."

"We think he was having some kind of a fit."

"You'd have thought he was fighting with someone. He took his hands right off the wheel."

"Fighting with himself," the man said. "He was positively clawing at his face."

I had no doubts about the nature of the adversary they'd failed to see. My solitary pitiful hope was that the tragedy could mean Bobby had been left alone for now. I fumbled my phone out and brought up her number. I very much wanted her phone to start ringing within earshot, but heard only its simulated bell on mine. It continued to shrill while my chest grew painful with holding a breath. At last Bobby said "Dom, I told you not to phone."

She sounded as breathless as I felt, and far too distant. "Where are you?" I pleaded.

"Not on the train." Before I could respond she said "It crashed. I wasn't hurt much. Some people were. I had to get off."

"Why couldn't you have waited? I'm there now."

"It was there as well. It, the Nobles, them. It was dancing on the people who were injured worst. I think it was waiting for them to die, hoping they would." She took a breath so as to add "I tried to stop it but people drove me away instead."

I hoped Bobby had left it behind, although what would this mean for victims of the crash? As I saw some of them being carried to the ambulances I said "So where are you exactly?"

"Dom, I don't want you to find me. That's just more likely to attract it to us. Tell Jim that too."

This silenced me, and I hadn't thought how much to say when Bobby said "Maybe it's best if we all stay apart for a while. If it's not we can all get back together."

"Bobby—"

"And we'll always, you remember our promise. Tell Jim I've always loved you both," she said and was gone.

I might have tried to call her back, but knew she wouldn't answer. In desperation I asked the hikers "Did you see anyone leave the train?"

"An old lady did," the woman said.

"She went off at quite a clip. Here's hoping we're as spry at her age."

"Which way?" I begged before the man had finished.

Both of them stared, having apparently found me rude. "The way you came," the woman said, pointing past my car. "Why, there she is."

I swung around, praying without words that Bobby had returned. At first I saw nobody at all in the empty landscape, not on the road or in the surrounding fields. I had to squint before I located a figure in the middle of a meadow, so distant that I couldn't judge the gender or whether they were fleeing. "Is that who you mean?" I demanded.

"We can't see anybody else," the man said, "can you?"

Was a wind disturbing a patch of grass in a field beside the meadow? I couldn't linger to be sure. I clattered down the steps two at a time as my ankles flared with pain, and limped to my car as fast as they would let me. By now traffic was arriving at the scene of the crash only to turn back, and I had to wait for altogether too many seconds before I could move my own car.

I overtook traffic wherever it was safe to do so, and sometimes where it nearly wasn't. I was growing increasingly concerned about the activity I'd glimpsed in the field by the meadow. At least the road I was following should take me to Bobby, however indirectly, but I wished the hedges wouldn't block my view. Infrequent gaps framed placid views worthy of a photograph, but Bobby wasn't to be seen. She was at least half a mile away when the road climbed a humped bridge, and I saw her.

She'd reached a path across a field, and was nearly abreast of a copse, beyond which a bridge led across a river. This wasn't all I saw, and I seemed to feel my innards wither. A shape had leapt out of the grass at her back and swarmed up a tree to crouch among the branches. Was Bobby determined to ignore it, or had it made too little noise for her to notice? "Bobby," I yelled, and swerved off the bridge onto the verge before dashing across the road.

Perhaps she hadn't heard me either. Her progress looked as resolute as ever – the dogged flight of a tiny figure beneath an irrelevantly sunlit sky. I cupped my hands around my mouth and shouted her name as loud as I could, but she didn't turn. She was past the trees now, and I saw the shape run across the treetops as lightly as a spider and thrust objects towards her that I was all too sure were heads on necks. I was terrified to see it leap on her, and almost frozen by the prospect. I tried a last shout that left my throat raw, and when it had no visible effect I sprinted back to the car.

The road grew more twisted, and the hedges cut my view off. I had no idea where Bobby was when I heard a cry. Although the landscape rendered it microscopic, this seemed to concentrate its terror, and it was dismayingly brief. I trod on the accelerator and tore around the bends, hoping I wouldn't encounter oncoming traffic. I hadn't by the time the trees near the river came in sight. I could see nothing among them, but this brought me no reassurance. I drove across a bridge that spanned the river to park askew on a swampy verge before floundering out of the car.

A shape was prancing with all its limbs on a body that lay face down in the river. It might have been performing a rite or expressing its glee if not both. As I scrambled down a grassy slope to the riverbank, the dancing monstrosity turned all its faces to me. The eyes and mouths widened in a cluster of simultaneous grins that conveyed recognition and a promise I didn't want to begin to imagine, and then it sprang across the river.

In a moment it was lost among the tangled shadows of the trees. I had no idea when it vanished, and I hardly cared. I'd waded into the river to haul Bobby onto the bank. When I turned her face upwards her chin jutted up like a final gesture of defiance, and I saw her eyes were open. They weren't seeing me, and resembled pools of stagnant water. I did what I could, leaning frantically on her chest to expel some of the river from her lungs. I was ashamed to reflect that my adolescent self might have welcomed even this opportunity to touch her breasts. When at last I ran out of breath I still hadn't restored hers, and knew I never would. I closed her eyes and kissed her forehead, and then I phoned the emergency services, even though this was no longer an emergency. Once we were alone again I felt compelled to talk. "We did our best to look after one another, didn't we," I said and found I could no longer speak.

CHAPTER TWENTY-TWO

The Third Call

The police arrived while the attendants were carrying Bobby's shrouded body to the ambulance. The officer who joined me on the riverbank was a middle-aged heavy-set fellow with bristling reddish hair and eyebrows that resembled generous samples of the same. His broad ruddy face might have belonged to the sort of policeman who once gave rise to comic songs, but he scrutinised me so thoroughly I thought I'd been recognised. I had, though not in the way I'd suspected. "Weren't you at the crash?" he said.

"I was on the bridge."

"That's where I saw you." Confirming this appeared to turn him more official. "What are you doing here, sir?" he said.

I hadn't many words I could risk uttering. "She was my friend," I tried saying. "Bobby Parkin."

With a hint of a tone I took for sympathy the policeman said "What can you tell me about her?"

"She was a writer. Books and journalism. Online too. You may have heard of her," I added, not unlike a challenge.

"Was she involved in a court case recently?"

"She was. The Le Bon incest case." Out of loyalty I said "I was as well."

He paused long enough to let me wonder why. "What can you tell me about the situation, Mr…"

"Sheldrake. Dominic Sheldrake." This was easier to say than "She exposed them but too many people supported them. Maybe she shouldn't have bothered."

This time his pause felt heavier. "This situation, Mr Sheldrake."

"She was," I said with increasing difficulty, "drowned."

"Were you a witness?"

"Not quite." My mouth almost got in the way of admitting "I was too late."

"So you've no idea how it happened."

I'd managed to invent a version of events to present to the world. "I have to think she was so upset by the crash she wasn't taking care. I ought to say she was on the train."

"Don't you think that's rather an extreme reaction? Nobody else ran away."

"She wasn't responsible, if that's what you're suggesting."

I might have confessed my own responsibility if that could have helped, but I'd only antagonised him. "I'm asking you why you think your friend would have behaved liked that," he said.

Perhaps the incessantly unfurling patterns of the river had distracted me, since I answered without thinking. "Another friend of ours was involved in the crash."

The policeman's scrutiny was growing keener. "Who was that, Mr Sheldrake?"

"His name was Jim Bailey." My mouth had turned unwieldy again, so that I had to make quite an effort to say "It was his car."

"His car that caused the crash." When I nodded, though it felt like trying to dislodge the truth, the policeman said "And you were at the scene as well. Can you explain why you all were?"

My answer felt unfair to Bobby, but how could I tell the truth? I almost wished my questioner knew as much about the Nobles as other members of the police force did. "She was upset before the crash," I said.

"Please go on."

"She'd been receiving threats online ever since she exposed Christian Noble and his family, and the way the court case went didn't help. There were threats to Jim and me as well. Bobby came to Liverpool to discuss what we could do. Jim used to be in the police and his sons still are, and he thought the threats wouldn't lead to anything." I was ashamed to feel so fluent in all this partial truth. "Bobby seemed happy with that," I said, restraining a convulsion of my mouth. "But then she contacted us on her way home and obviously wasn't, and we all arranged to meet at Crewe. Instead, well, you've seen."

"You say your other friend was with the police. What do you think could have caused an accident like that?"

"I wasn't there. I couldn't say." When the policeman's gaze didn't waver I said "Someone on the bridge told me they thought Jim was having a fit. I'd say that sounds like a stroke."

I was hoping this would divert the policeman to finding the other witnesses, but he said "Did the lady contact you on the phone you used to call us?"

"She did, yes."

"Did she phone or text?"

"She sent a text. She was a writer to the end."

I'd almost finished speaking when I realised how I'd trapped myself. "May I see?" the policeman said.

I was unable to recall Bobby's exact words, and was tempted to say I'd erased them by mistake or even by design. I had no chance to delete them unobserved by the policeman, and could only hand him the phone. "You need to unlock it, sir," he said.

I impressed it with my fingerprint, feeling even more suspected because of the entirely pointless delay, and passed it back to him. While he examined the images, the relentless liquid blather of the river reminded me of its part in Bobby's death. At last he said "What did she mean, it's on the train?"

"She was talking about her state of mind, do you suppose?" When he didn't reject the suggestion I said "Her depression that was getting worse."

He gazed at the phone and then at me before returning it. "Have you some identification, Mr Sheldrake?"

I displayed my driving licence on the screen for him to copy the details. Once he'd taken my phone number he said "We may be in touch with you again."

"Will you be after the hikers I spoke to on the bridge?"

"We've already interviewed them and the other witnesses. You were the only one who made himself scarce."

"That's because they told me they'd seen Bobby run. I wish to God I'd been quicker."

"Unless God meant you not to be."

Perhaps this was his notion of comfort; his face suggested as much. When I was unable to respond he climbed the grassy slope to the road and drove away. I couldn't linger by the river, even if it had offered any sense of peace rather than a mindless babble that sounded far too gleeful. Although I'd dealt with the police, I still had tasks to finish.

I took my time over driving home, not least because I felt dangerously distracted. It was dusk when I reached the house, and imminent darkness seemed to linger within even once I switched the lights on. The mobile phone numbers I'd stored on my phone were redundant now, and I found my old address book in my desk, where it was keeping company with my adolescent transcript of Christian Noble's journal. I felt unheroic for starting with the call that might give me less trouble. I didn't know who I would prefer to answer, and I hadn't been able to prepare what to say by the time the bell was interrupted. "Dominic."

I didn't want to revive our feeble inadvertent comedy routine. "Sheldrake," I said.

"Dominic. Dad isn't here just now." His pause let me imagine how his expression might have changed. "I thought he was meeting you and your friend," Dominic Bailey said.

"He did, and then we, then we parted." I struggled not to hesitate too long before saying "Dominic, he's been in a car crash."

"That doesn't sound like him. Are you absolutely sure?"

"They're saying he had a stroke at the wheel." I detested myself for being so verbally skilful and for delaying what I had to say. "Dominic, forgive me," I said, "but I'm afraid it was fatal."

"What was?" Even more skeptically he said "A stroke?"

"The accident it caused. He was hit by a train."

"I thought you said it was a car crash."

"The car was hit. Please believe me. I give you my word I'm not making this up."

"Dad said you never stopped telling stories." Still without changing his tone Dominic said "Where is this meant to have happened?"

"Near Crewe. We—"

"That makes no sense. He was meeting you two in town."

"As I say, we met." I felt desperate and close to incompetent with language. "Then Bobby called us from her train home," I said. "We were worried about her and went to find her, but Jim went through a barrier and ended up on the line."

"How can you say all this? Were you there?"

"I was, only too late. I swear what I'm telling you is true. You can check with the police."

"Just hold on." This might have prefaced a further objection, but it brought a silence that I couldn't understand until Dominic said "He isn't answering his mobile."

"He won't, Dominic. I'm dreadfully sorry." With some notion of confirming the situation in his mind I said "Bobby's gone as well."

"You'll excuse me if I don't care much about that." As I sensed his disbelief was wavering, a mobile phone rang close to him. "Hello?" he said like a hope if not a prayer, and then "Who is this?"

His voice moved away, but though I couldn't make out his words I guessed who had called him – the police who had Jim's phone. "Thank you," he said eventually as if the phrase was drained of meaning, and came back to me, though not at once. "So you weren't making it up."

"Dominic, I hope you wouldn't think I could."

"Something somebody made up took him away from us." Apparently in case I didn't feel accused he said "I wish to God he'd never known either of you."

"I understand how you feel, but Jim wouldn't have—"

"Don't you dare try and speak for our father."

This left me feeling I couldn't speak for myself either, and I was about to say goodbye when a woman called "What's wrong, Dominic?"

I was so distracted that I almost began to answer. "Maybe you should speak to this, this friend of dad's," Jim's son told his mother, immediately adding "No, you shouldn't. Goodbye, Mr Sheldrake."

I felt expelled into the growing darkness that the lights in my house seemed powerless to fend off. At least Jim's wife and their sons weren't alone, but this only reminded me how painful my second call might be. I held the phone and tried to prepare, which simply left me unable to think. At last I keyed the number, and was striving not to hope my call would go unanswered when the bell was silenced. "Carole Ashcroft," Carole said.

She sounded so breathless she'd left her emotions behind – as if her voice had no room for them, at any rate. "Carole," I said, "it's Dominic Sheldrake."

"Bob's still on her way home. I believe she's on the tube just now. Her phone's not responding." Carole took a breath that might have given me a chance to speak. "Shall I tell her you called," she said, "or is there a message?"

"Carole, she isn't—" This was a uselessly false start, and I could only add "She isn't on her way."

"She's still there with you and your friend."

"No." This only meant I had to say "She isn't coming back."

I could have thought I sounded guilty of stealing Carole's partner, which was variously and grotesquely inappropriate. I might have preferred Carole to say almost anything other than "What do you mean?"

"There's been an accident, Carole, a fatality." Perhaps I imagined this would make it easier to say or hear "I'm truly sorry, but she's gone."

A silence left me fearful that Carole hadn't heard until she said "Gone how?"

"I'm afraid she was drowned."

"Drowned." More fiercely still Carole said "Who drowned her?"

"I don't know that anybody did." I managed to move closer to the truth by saying "She was running away and she fell in the river."

"Bob wouldn't run away from anything. That's why she wrote

about that woman and how she behaved with her father." In a challenge that sounded not too far from threatening Carole said "Did you see her run?"

"I did, and I saw why." For a moment I wanted to tell Carole the truth, but was sure the attempt would be vain. "The train she was on hit our friend Jim's car," I said. "He'd had a stroke, I was told."

I was feeling disloyal to Jim, and wondering how long it would take me to accept my own manufactured tale, when Carole said "What are you asking me to believe? That wouldn't make Bob do away with herself."

"There was more to it, Carole." I had to risk asking "How did she act after she'd exposed the Nobles and been in court?"

"She was nervous but she wouldn't take anything for it. I'm sure the things that Noble girl put in her head were catching up with her. I encouraged her to write about them and that whole family. I supported her." Before I could judge whether Carole was expressing regret she said "You're honestly telling me she's gone. There's no possibility of a mistake."

I sensed how rigid she was holding her emotions. "I only wish there were."

"I should have come with her to see you. I offered but she said it had to be just the three of you." As I searched for a response Carole said "So now you're on your own."

I took this for sympathy and almost told her she was too. I was about to offer all I could when Carole said "Where were you when all that was happening?"

"On my way there. I'd have given anything to be in time. I ought to say I wasn't saying Bobby drowned herself. As I said, she fell in."

"That's right, she was Bobby to you." However Carole meant me to take this, she went on at once. "On your way where?"

"We were supposed to meet Bobby at Crewe. She sent texts from the train."

Carole paused, apparently preparing to ask "Can I have them?"

I could hardly refuse. "I'll forward them now."

There was silence while I did, and after that as well. "Thank you," Carole said at last. "Do you know where Bob is now?"

I'd expected her to question the messages, but wasn't about to prompt it. "They took her away in an ambulance."

"Didn't you give them my details?"

"Of course I did. Your name and address. I didn't have your number with me."

"I should wait to hear, then." With what I suspected was the last of her restraint, to be abandoned as soon as she rang off, Carole said "Will you be attending her funeral?"

"Try and keep me away."

I regretted the form of words before it was finished, but perhaps Carole hadn't time to take offence. "I'll be in touch," she only just said, and ended the call.

Now there was nothing to distract me from how empty the house was or from fearing that I mightn't stay alone much longer. I couldn't wish for Lesley or my friends when recalling them might inflict monstrousness upon them, the revenge of the Nobles. Christian and his progeny were the visitors I dreaded, in whatever hideous form they took. Every moment felt like imminence, all the more acute when no intruder appeared. As the vacant minutes became hours that gathered into days I began to feel almost resigned to the encounter that I fancied was biding its time so as to aggravate my dread. I deserved it, after all, for bringing it upon Bobby and Jim. I even slept, sometimes in bed, despite repeatedly starting awake for fear of drifting into someone else's experience, past or still to come. I had a nightmare notion that if I found myself sharing memories that weren't mine, the Nobles would hunt me down through time while I was helplessly lost. Perhaps they would already be there, waiting somewhere I couldn't even call on my own strength.

I was dozing in the front room as Gene Kelly celebrated a storm when my phone jerked me awake. Previously I'd thought I could never tire of *Singin' in the Rain*, the greatest analysis of cinema on film. I hoped the call might be from Carole, though I suspected it was from the police, but it was neither. "Dad, it's Toby."

"Toby, it's good to hear from you," I said, hoping this would be the case. "What can I do for you?"

He hesitated long enough to let me think he had no answer before saying "Will you come back to the church?"

"I don't think I'd be very welcome, or at all."

"We'll make sure you are, I promise."

"Who will? Certainly not Claudine."

"Yes, dad, Claude too, so that shows you ought to come. She's seen you were only concerned when you said what you said. It's all forgiven."

"That's very Christian of you both." While this felt mean, the name clarified my suspicions. "Whose idea was it to entice me back?" I said.

"Ours, of course. We're in charge."

"Not the ones who used to be."

"If you mean Christian and his family, how can you think that after what happened to them?"

"You share all their ideas, don't you? And you aren't telling me you really think they've gone themselves." I would have liked not to feel provoked to ask "Haven't you seen them since?"

"Dad, we're calling a retreat for members of the church. I'll swear to you on whatever you like it's our idea alone."

I was unexpectedly offended that he should have borrowed the concept of a retreat – a meditative gathering of the kind I recalled from my childhood religion. He hadn't answered my question either, and I couldn't judge how slyly skilful his response had been. "I'm not a member," I said.

"You're as good as one. Dad, this is the most important thing we've ever done and we want you to be there."

"If you believe it's so important I won't argue with you, but you mustn't expect me to join in."

"Dad, it's for your good."

I'd been close to promising to attend if I could simply observe, but this antagonised me beyond bearing. "Just let me decide what is. I'm not past making that decision for myself yet."

"You can't when you don't even know what's involved."

I knew that in a sense the Church of the Eternal Three was responsible for the deaths of my friends, which made me retort "Then let me know."

"Dad, will you trust us? If you come you'll see we were right, I promise."

I couldn't shake off the conviction that I'd endowed him with some of my own deceitfulness, and I wasn't about to be lured into the church. All the same, I said "When's the occasion?"

"As soon as we can get everyone together, and that includes you."

This was one insistence too many for my taste. "Let me know when it's scheduled," I said with dwindling interest or enthusiasm, and asked after the family before bidding him goodbye. I'd sensed none of the desperation that must have made him call. If I'd had an inkling of the reason I would never have let him go – if I'd grasped why he was leaving so much unsaid.

CHAPTER TWENTY-THREE

The Retreat

"Dominic, this is Dominic."

"So is this."

Perhaps he thought the politest response to my rickety quip was silence, after which he said "I want to apologise for some of the comments I made last time we spoke."

"Just some?" I didn't say that, nor "Which ones?" Instead I told him "Honestly, I understand. I understood."

"We appreciate your judgment, and we know our father would."

I was aware of an omission. "How's your mother, Dominic?"

"She spends her time praying for him. You'll be seeing her yourself."

We'd met just once, at the wedding. She was a slight but intense woman who had grasped my hand in hers, renewing her appreciation of my friendship with her husband, whenever I'd encountered her at the reception. "When will that be?" I said.

"At our father's funeral, we hope."

"Of course I'll be there. When and where?"

"On Monday at Holy Trinity Church in our road."

The name and the place were Catholic, so that I was disconcerted how they brought Christian Noble and his brood to mind, but this wasn't why I felt reluctant to speak. "Monday," I said.

"This coming Monday, yes. Next week."

I held back from retorting that I didn't need the clarification. "When on Monday?" I said with little hope.

"Noon, and you're welcome to stay for the wake."

"I'm glad I am. I would, but Dominic, please don't be offended, only Bobby's funeral is that day too."

"That wouldn't have occurred to us." Just as tonelessly he said "What time?"

"In the afternoon, but I have to travel there. It's near London. Not that near."

"So which do you think you'll attend?"

However neutral this was meant to sound, there was no mistaking its intention. "Dominic," I had to say, "I've promised Bobby's partner I'll be there."

"We wouldn't want you to go back on your word to him."

"Her."

"Just as you like." His pause suggested thought, but perhaps he was trying to restrain his next observation. "You may as well know," he said, "Rob and I took some time to persuade our mother you should come."

"I'm awfully sorry," I said, not least from feeling I might deserve to be excluded for my part in Jim's death. "I hope she'll understand. I hope you do."

"You can't expect us to alter the arrangements just for one person."

"I wouldn't. I'm sure you wouldn't expect it of Carole either." When I heard no response I said "At least your family hasn't been left on their own."

This earned a pause I could have thought was hostile. "Can I make a donation at least?" I said.

"A donation."

"Not to the costs." As I realised too late that his repetition hadn't meant that, I said "Or are you having flowers?"

"No flowers," Dominic Bailey said with such distaste that I was reminded of the vegetation in the crypt beneath the Trinity Church of the Spirit. "They're a waste of resources. We're inviting donations to the parish. I don't know how that sits with you, since you've lapsed."

"I'll be happy to make one in Jim's memory."

"Then perhaps some good has come out of all this. Let me give you the information." Having read out the bank details, which my phone helped me type, he said "If your situation changes, you could let us know."

Presumably he meant if I should change my mind. At the weekend I phoned Carole to check the schedule, but as I feared, it hadn't altered. Wishing I could attend Jim's ceremony distracted me from other preoccupations – the monstrous intrusion I fancied was biding its time, the retreat Toby proposed. At least he hadn't called again, which I took to mean he had yet to arrange the event. I didn't hear from him until I was on the train to Bobby's funeral.

The motion of the carriage had rocked me to sleep, and I was somewhere I couldn't see. Though it felt like an absence of light and time, it wasn't dark. I knew Jim and Bobby were nearby, because I could hear them. "They've forgotten us," they were saying in chorus. While I wasn't sure whether this expressed wistfulness or relief, I felt they were waiting for me to join in. I was about to plead with them to be clearer and to show themselves when the phone startled me awake.

Perhaps it had been shrilling for some time, since the man seated opposite me across a table was sending me a frown over the vertical screen of his laptop. "Soy," I mumbled and groped for my phone, cupping it in both hands when I saw Toby's name. I might have retreated to the vestibule of the carriage to avoid being overheard, but I was concerned to learn why he was calling. "Dad," he said, "have you thought again?"

"What do you want me to think?"

"About coming to our retreat."

"I don't know what would change my mind." This sounded so inadvertently ominous that I added "And I don't want anything to get in and change it."

"Here's someone who may, though."

"Grandad, won't you come? We all want you to. It won't be the same if you aren't there."

"Macy…" I was appalled not only by her being used to coax me but by the thought that she would be involved in this latest ritual. "Toby," I said, "isn't she a little young for that?"

"I'm not, grandad. I've been to all the places mum and dad go."

"There'll be younger ones at the retreat than her," Claudine said. "We've managed to call the whole chapel together."

"If you want to see Macy's looked after you should come to the retreat, dad."

While I was dismayed by the methods Toby was using, I'd begun to feel bound to attend. "When is it going to be?"

"Tomorrow noon at Starview Tower," Toby said. "We can send someone to fetch you and then you won't have to drive."

Perhaps I didn't need to find this threatening, but I demanded "Who will you send?"

"I meant we've asked someone who lives near you to pick you up."

"You can tell them not to bother. I won't be at home. I'm on my way to Bobby's funeral."

The silence felt absurdly like a triumph I'd achieved until Claudine said "Toby, maybe it won't matter."

"What won't?"

"Dominic hasn't really been part of the church, has he? He isn't really like any of us. Dominic, have you been voyaging much by yourself?"

"I haven't and I don't intend to."

"There then, Toby. Maybe you needn't worry so much."

"We'd still like you to make the effort, dad. You could get there in time, couldn't you?"

"Perhaps I can." I was growing anxious to protect anyone I could, Macy in particular, but I said "We'll see."

"We'll see you, grandad."

"Let's hope so. Now I'm on the train and I shouldn't disturb people any more," I said, although other passengers were talking on phones too. "And if I miss your gathering I expect there'll be more."

"There won't, dad, no."

If Toby had dared to be more explicit, how would I have responded?

I thought he was simply attempting to exert more pressure on me – to lure me back to his beliefs. "Tomorrow will decide," I told him and said goodbye without going any closer to a promise. As I pocketed the phone my neighbour glanced over his laptop, inquisitively enough to make me say "My son and his family want me in their church."

"Will it keep the peace?"

This was more direct than I'd meant to invite. "I wouldn't say it was that kind of church."

"In your family, I'm asking. Will it stop them worrying about you?"

However intrusive this might be, not to mention patronising, I supposed he could hardly have avoided overhearing my conversation. "I don't know," I said, "and it isn't as simple as that. We're talking about the Church of the Eternal Three."

"That could be what the world needs. Isn't it meant to be the oldest church?"

"What else have you heard about it?"

"Oldest does for me," he said and kept his deep dark gaze on my face.

I was reduced to thinking that he surely couldn't belong to the church, but in some ways this demonstration of its pervasiveness was worse. I looked out of the window until he returned his attention to the laptop, and neither of us spoke again during the hour and a quarter the train had yet to travel.

At Euston I limped to the underground station as fast as I could, clinging to the handle of my four-wheeled suitcase on the escalator. I remembered hurrying to meet Jim and Bobby after her book launch – remembered how much fitter I'd been then. Nobody could smoke on the station now, and yet the subterranean platform that was trapped between two mouths of the dark felt even more oppressive than the memory. A train took me to London Bridge, and another one to Hither Green. However poetic the name sounded – a summons to verdure – I had to tramp through a suburb, having found no bus or taxi to the crematorium. My route took me and the rumble of my luggage through a Victorian cemetery, where stone angels with upraised hands appeared to be directing visitors. At least one angel was accompanied by a sculpted victim of the First World War, and thoughts of Christian Noble's father pursued me all the way across the graveyard.

The crematorium was a wide low block with a peaked porch and a rudimentary tower elevating an aerial, which might have been designed to invite inhabitants of the ether. A pale angel was flattened like a specimen against glass above the entrance. Dozens of mourners, none of whom I knew, had gathered in groups beside the porch. I loitered nearby in the vague hope that someone might ask who I was, but nobody did. Well after I regained the breath I hadn't needed to expend in hastening across the cemetery, a hearse appeared, followed by a solitary limousine. When Carole climbed out, slowed down by age or grief or both, she was on her own. I almost went to her, but several people did at once.

She hadn't even glanced at me by the time she led the procession after the casket into the crematorium. Where as a child I would have expected an altar to be, a plinth for coffins stood in front of a triptych of tall stained-glass windows full of a reiterated circular symbol that meant nothing to me – an all-purpose motif, perhaps. The area was flanked by a low podium and a door beneath a sign composed of a stick figure out for a walk and an arrow like a download icon. Having brought up the rear of the solemn procession, I took my place on an empty pew near the back.

I had very little sense of Bobby's presence at the funeral. Given the horrors I'd seen visited upon the recently dead, I supposed I should be glad for her. The mourners had been greeted by the sound of Frank Sinatra vowing to see us in familiar places, not least a children's carousel. This put me in mind of Bobby's first encounter with Tina Noble at the playground in the park, but otherwise the choice of music seemed to represent an aspect of my friend I'd never known. During the secular service Bobby's colleagues reminisced about her from the podium, and the combative dauntless character they brought to life sounded more like the person I recognised. Carole read from *The Fashion for Offence*, Bobby's unfinished book in progress, where Bobby observed how words forbidden in our childhood were routinely heard in public these days while words and phrases then in common use were censored now. According to Carole she'd planned to question fashionable squeamishness, but we would never have her thoughts.

The ceremony ended with a silence designed to conjure memories, although it reminded me too much of entering a trance in Starview Tower, and then we were treated to *Ferry Cross the Mersey* while curtains drew together to hide the coffin. Had Bobby meant the song to evoke her hometown and her childhood? No doubt all the music was her choice, but I couldn't help recalling the ferry from which I'd thrown the icon into the river.

Carole was waiting fiercely dry-eyed to receive hugs and condolences outside the crematorium. When I delivered a two-handed shake that perhaps I should have halved she said "Won't you be staying? Bobby would want you to stay."

She was inviting me to the wake at a nearby pub, the Greener Woman. An unobtrusive plaque established that the timbered building used to be an inn, long known as the Green Man. The interior was split into small irregular rooms under low oak beams, and Carole had commandeered the largest space, which barely accommodated a buffet and the congregation from the funeral. I'd just finished collecting token items on a paper plate when a towering angular woman with a silvery moustache – an editor who had commissioned books from Bobby and spoken at the podium – handed me the glass of wine I'd planted on the narrow elongated table. "How did you know Bob?" she said.

"Dominic was an old friend of hers." Carole had made her way skilfully and swiftly through the crowd. "Frankie, Dominic Sheldrake," she said. "Dominic, Frankie Borne."

Frankie Borne dealt me a hefty handshake while she scrutinised my face, a process that led me to expect more of a question than "Didn't you want to speak, Dominic?"

"I'm glad to meet Bobby's editor," I tried saying.

"No." As if she might be addressing someone of limited wit she said "At the funeral."

"I wasn't asked."

"I didn't ask anyone," Carole said. "They all asked me, and of course I said yes."

I felt as if the room had grown hot and oppressively cramped. I was trapped in a corner with burdens in both hands, and took rather more than a sip of my drink, which enabled me to say "I mightn't have been up to it. I'm afraid I'd have been too emotional."

"Nothing wrong with feelings," Frankie Borne said. "They're why we're here."

"Dominic may have been the last person to see Bob."

The editor's scrutiny grew keener, though she spoke to Carole. "He saw what happened to her, do you mean?"

"She panicked, Frankie. That cult and its founder I encouraged her to write about, she started thinking they had more power than she'd thought. She'd tried to investigate them years and years ago, remember, but I'm afraid she was indoctrinated even though she didn't realise. Now the people responsible are gone too, and at least that's the end of it."

I might have welcomed this interpretation if Frankie Borne hadn't continued to examine my face. In a kind of reluctant triumph she said "I know your name."

"Bobby dedicated a book to me and Jim, our other friend."

"Was that you? I wonder if she still would." Before I could react she said "Didn't you just try and tempt people to join your cult?"

"It isn't mine and it never will be. I'd like to know what on earth you mean."

"Didn't you post any amount of verbiage about it online? I could have sworn the name was Sheldrake."

I took no pleasure in clearing myself. "That was my son."

"And how did he become involved?"

"He was fed their beliefs from the earliest age they could work on him. A lot of children were, and when they grew up they helped to set up what they call their church."

"I don't understand how you could have allowed that to happen if you knew what Bob knew."

"I didn't just know it, I told her about it. I was why she went after the cult in the first place."

"Well, that's left it unharmed and her dead. What do you intend to do about it now, if anything?"

My rage seemed to darken the room and shrink it as well. "What did you ever do about it? Would you have published a book about it if she'd written one?"

"Most emphatically. We always supported Bob's right to say what she thought. If you wrote a book along those lines we'd give it a good look."

I couldn't judge how serious she was. If her offer was genuine, just now it felt more than grotesque, which made me retort "I'll be visiting the church tomorrow to find out what they're up to now."

"You keep calling it a church. I hope you won't let yourself be taken in just because your family's involved." As she moved away, having loaded a plate in a few deft movements, Frankie Borne said "Be sure to keep us informed, won't you? Carole, you can pass on the developments."

Carole gave me an apologetic look and lowered her voice. "Dominic, do you think I could have helped?"

"I expect I deserved some of that. Perhaps I deserved it all."

"Not with Frankie," Carole said, producing an approximation of a laugh. "Could I have done more to save Bob?"

"I don't see how." Despite feeling unduly eager to vindicate myself I said "I don't think any of us could have stopped her, ever."

"Do your best to save your son instead," Carole urged me, instantly adding "Excuse me if I have to circulate."

I lingered for a while, sharing childhood memories and later ones of Bobby with her friends, and felt as though I was trying to justify attending the wake. I'd booked a room near Euston for the night, since my age had left me unequal to travelling both ways in a day. By the time I reached the hotel off Tottenham Court Road my fingers ached from hoisting and trundling the dwarfish case. I ate at the nearest restaurant, a Turkish where a waiter kept asking me how it was good, which was to say the hearty dips with plump hot bread and hefty kebabs and carafe of dense red wine. I could have thought he was trying to keep me company, this solitary ageing diner with just a phone for a companion. Whenever I glanced at the screen there was no message. There weren't many people left to send me one, but I was making sure I hadn't heard from my son.

The hotel room was efficiently anonymous and mostly white: the walls decorated with sketchy abstracts, the sheets stretched taut on the bed, the furniture, the tiles in the decidedly compact bathroom. I could only hope it had sufficient presence to anchor me in the moment. I hadn't been away since Lesley's death, and felt incomplete for not phoning her to say goodnight. I was tempted to call Toby if that mightn't have wakened my granddaughter. I switched off my phone and set the bedside alarm.

I didn't expect to sleep much. I found myself recalling the dream on the train, unless it had been some kind of vision – Jim and Bobby declaring they had been forgotten. Since they hadn't seemed to be protesting, might it mean the Nobles had lost interest in them? I hoped – indeed, as good as prayed – this was the case. Perhaps the Nobles had even forgotten about me or at any rate no longer found me worthy of attention. Before I knew it, the possibility let me sleep.

A voice wakened me. I wasn't alone in the room. The word my visitor was repeating sounded unpleasantly reptilian, since it seemed to commence with a hiss. My eyes struggled open to see a face leaning close to mine. "Sir," it was whispering. "Sir."

I'd bruised my scalp against the headboard by the time I grasped that I was looking at a chambermaid. "What do you want?" I demanded. "What time is it?"

"Sir, time you are gone."

I was preparing to argue, by no means politely, as I grabbed the clock beside the bed. Either I'd slept through the alarm or inadvertently silenced it while setting it, and the time was just past noon. "Few minutes," I declared, waving her out of the room.

As I stumbled to the bathroom I switched on my phone. Toby had left me a message a few minutes old. **Dad, we have to start now. I think Claude's right and you needn't be here because you weren't involved enough. You'll learn more but not now**. I phoned at once, but he'd turned off his phone during the retreat, of course. **On way**, I typed and did my best to be at once.

The hotel receptionist, an unreasonably burly Russian, tried to charge me yextra for a second nyight. I didn't waste time arguing or paying, since they'd already charged me for one night and the notion of a breakfast. I left him with the card that did duty as a key, and as he continued to demand my credit card I made for the exit. When the glass door remained stubbornly shut I thought he'd locked me in. I was about to pound on it when it slid aside, releasing me and his rant as well.

My fingers were numb with tugging the suitcase by the time I reached Euston, which was rather less close than the hotel alleged. At least a train to Liverpool was waiting by the platform. For two hours and quite a few more minutes I watched fields and houses pass beneath a pale brittle sky that made me feel the train was inside a shell. Beyond Crewe I began to grow tense, but I might have missed where Jim had died, since the barrier had been repaired, if I hadn't glimpsed shattered glass glittering beside the track. The sight renewed my guilt at having failed to attend his funeral.

Throughout the journey I kept checking my phone, but Toby hadn't been in touch. I assumed the retreat would last for hours, and as soon as we arrived at Lime Street I headed for the underground. Two stops brought me to James Street, where I limped down to the waterfront accompanied by constant thunder. It was just the progress of my suitcase, but I could have fancied it was hinting how temporary the bright flat sky was – how vulnerable to a storm or to darkness.

As Starview Tower came in sight among the skyscrapers along the waterfront it reminded me more than ever of an unnatural bloom sprouting beside the river. It looked as if the blackness on the topmost floor had made the concrete stalk swell outwards, blossoming to feed upon the dark beyond the sky as flowers reach for the sun. I tramped fast into the shadow of the tower, which surely wasn't colder than it ought to be, or darker. I was nearly at the glass doors when I realised Joe wasn't to be seen.

Had he locked the doors against intruders? I marched up to them, to be greeted by stillness. Even my suitcase had fallen silent, and the only sound was the passing of traffic on the road, which seemed irrelevantly remote. I was searching for a bell to ring for admission when the doors gave a small impatient shudder and glided apart. I crossed the lobby, accompanied by a prolonged peal of indoor thunder, and thumbed the button between the lifts. There was no response.

I poked the button and kept it pressed, but the light above it stayed unlit, and I heard no sound from the lift shafts. In desperation I made for the reception desk, hoping to see how to activate the lifts. Security monitors surrounded a computer screen, and I clutched at the back of an abandoned swivel chair. While some of the monitors displayed empty levels of the tower, several showed extensive rooms – office floors from which the inner walls had been withdrawn – full of seated people. Every one of them had splayed their limbs in the posture I remembered all too well from Toby's childhood.

The monitor for the floor beneath the offices of the Church of the Eternal Three showed him and Macy and Claudine in the leather chairs at the far end of the vast room. His and his wife's limbs appeared to be reaching for Macy between them, but even though she'd adopted the same pose she was out of range. I felt cut off from them and desperate not to be. Was one of the icons on the computer screen meant to resemble the doors of a lift? I clicked on it and limped back across the lobby to jab the button. The indicator flickered alight, and I heard a lift stir high up in the tower.

As soon as a pair of doors offered enough of a gap I stumbled in, dragging my suitcase. I had to wait for the doors to open wide before I could shut them and send the lift upwards. The mob of my reflections seemed to be avoiding one another's eyes so as not to aggravate their fears, but this failed to assuage mine. Apart from the faint creak of a cable and a repetitive metallic twang as the lift climbed past each floor, the building was utterly silent. Retreats were supposed to be mute, I kept telling myself. At least Toby and his wife and child weren't intoning any of Christian Noble's occult formulas, unless they were doing so inside their heads. On the monitor I hadn't seen their lips move – in fact, I'd seen no movement at all.

At last the doors opened, and I lurched between them. The instant I let go of my suitcase, silence closed in. It reminded me of the sleeping room at Safe To Sleep, or perhaps of the way the house had felt when Jim and I explored it after the Nobles fled. It hushed my breath, or apprehension did. I had to force myself to cross the lobby and ease the nearest door open.

It gave onto the expanded room composed of all the offices. Hundreds of figures were propped in folding chairs with their limbs thrown wide as though to embrace emptiness, yet the room felt as vacant as space between stars. I hadn't time to glance at them as I limped rapidly across the room, but I knew none of them stirred. Nor did my son or his wife or my granddaughter – not when I gave up trying to be silent while I approached, not when I seized his hands and gazed into his emptied eyes, which darkness appeared to have forced wide. I could feel a hectic pulse, but it was only mine. "Toby," I said, quietly at first, but even when I cried it out my voice was the solitary sound in the room, and the only sign of life.

CHAPTER TWENTY-FOUR

The Newcomers

To every last one of our family in the faith:

These will be our final words to you, to everyone attending the retreats we have called across the world and the few members the church was unable to reach. We urge anybody who is left to heed our message and act as we have at once.

Some of these truths you already know. We are all born to the future, and some of us were privileged to be singled out by it, when it took the name of Noble and later of Bloan and then resurrected Le Bon. My wife and I, and many of the early members of the Church of the Eternal Three, were chosen by Christian's trinity at birth if not earlier. They saw our future, which they had already created. They revealed the secret shapes of space and time to us as soon as we had minds, and grew our minds in the process. Few people would have dared even to dream of the experiences we took for granted from our infancy, but we have devoted our lives to sharing them with the faithful.

All these adventures only hinted at the revelations granted to our founders. They came from the creator and the soul of our church, Gahariet Le Bon – not just the revelations but the trinity itself. He was at the heart of our faith when it bore the name he gave it, and when it regained life as the Trinity Church of the Spirit and Safe To Sleep. He was within Christian when he was conceived, and he was the essence of Christian's daughter and son. Perhaps Gahariet was seeking to resume humanity, having been transformed by his encounters with the truth beyond the dark. We believe that, having been extended through time and space to the end that is always the beginning, Gahariet had become an avatar of that whose secrets he sought to learn. Be aware that we should no longer speak or write its name.

We of the faith know that death is a transformation, never an end. The deaths of the bodies of Christian's trinity may have helped them to grow whole, to rediscover their primal core. The form in which they walked among us was merely a stage in their evolution, the larva of their ultimate state. Since they have yet to descend on our church, we conclude that it is carrying out their purpose. We have reluctantly agreed that they failed to make that purpose clear to us, and may have deliberately withheld it from us and from other leaders of the church. "The faithful shall be one in D----th," Christian used to say, but we never fully understood.

Our rites have helped us prepare for a future of which our voyages beyond the world are scarcely even intimations. However, we have been forced to realise that the church has brought that future closer, as it was designed to do. Perhaps the future in the form of an imperfect revelation produced the church. We do not want the world to be consumed as we have foreseen, and we hope no other members of the church have shared the vision, since to foresee is to invite. We do not want that world for ourselves or our loved ones, some of whom may be outside the church, or even for the mass of humanity. Since we have rendered it so imminent, it is the duty of us all to undermine its certainty if not to achieve its cancellation. It would have brought us all together in a form we should not attempt to imagine, and so our solution must be to become unalterably separate.

Every member of the church has learned our journeys back and forth through time belong to that person and nobody else, but the eager future would have united us in its chosen form. Our retreat must be as simultaneous as we can make it, but it will part us for ever. In this final rite we must never use the secret name, but only our sense of ourselves. Let each of us go back to embrace the memory we most profoundly are, and fix ourselves there for eternity. We can achieve this because we are the chosen. Let us do it now for the world.

Toby Sheldrake
Claudine Sheldrake
Macy Sheldrake

I'd imagined that nothing could appal me any further – that my emotions were used up – until I saw Macy's name at the foot of the message. It was on the site of the Church of The ETernal Three, where I'd never previously noticed how closely the emphasised letters resembled headless crosses. How much of the authorship had my granddaughter meant to claim? I could only hope that, as a child might, she'd wanted to be included, and her parents had agreed as a last indulgence. As I interpreted the message, they were forever separated now, secure in their solitary memories – at least, I hoped as fervently as they must have that they were secure. I had no idea what memory my granddaughter might have found to keep her safe. If it involved me, I would never know.

She hadn't been by any means the only child in the lifeless gathering at Starview Tower. Among the adults I'd seen Inigo Arnold, not to mention Farr and Black, both generations of them. I wondered how the police had dealt with their presence, which hadn't been mentioned in the media. I'd reported the situation at the tower once I was able to speak at all coherently. The police had interrogated me like a suspect, despite Toby's text on my phone. No doubt the final online statement helped exonerate me, and once they let me go I heard no more from them.

The multitude of deaths at Starview Tower had been replicated in chapels of the Church of the Eternal Three around the world. In every case the inquests found no trace of poisoning or violence. Anthropologists cited the ability to wish oneself dead that still existed in some cultures, and some commentators suggested that the members of the Church of the Eternal Three had reverted to a primal state. The phrase disturbed me, and I didn't want to examine why I hoped it wasn't so. It was enough to know my son and his family were dead.

I was almost alone at the joint funeral, where Macy's little coffin was flanked by a pair of caskets twice the size. The only other mourner was Claudine's mother Judith, looking depleted no less physically than mentally as she clambered out of her car into a wheelchair. I refrained from observing that we were outnumbered by our dead. The sight of all the empty pews inside the crematorium plainly distressed her, and I felt compelled to say "All their friends must have died with their church."

"Even Macy's?" she protested with a hint of her old vigour.

"We'd have to think so, wouldn't we? Her parents must have chosen all her playmates. I suppose it makes a kind of sense."

Judith stared red-eyed at me. "If you see any sense in this, please share it with me."

"I only meant they met at Safe To Sleep, so they'd be used to having friends with the same whatever you would call it."

"What would you call it, Dominic?"

"Beliefs. Experiences." When her stare maintained its force I gave in to saying "Upbringing."

"I brought Claudine up to know her own mind." As if she was making an allowance Judith said "We ought to have done more to guide them away from those people."

It required some restraint on my part to say only "I tried."

"Could I have been more help?"

I saw no point in worsening her feelings, especially since she would be left alone with them. "I think the Nobles had their minds long before anyone else noticed. We would always have been too late."

We left the eulogies to the secular celebrant, a tall solemn woman in generalised robes. Her pause for silent recollection was preceded by a tape of Macy singing *We Three Kings of Orient Are*, her contribution to the amalgamated play of many faiths her school had staged last year. I was unable to glance across the aisle at Judith, where she was hunched next to her compacted wheelchair. While grief made me avoid her eyes, I was also wondering how Christian Noble would have interpreted the theme of the carol – three mages who'd acknowledged the birth of a new seer, perhaps. At the end of the ceremony the curtains glided shut to the sound of a Richard Strauss fanfare, the opening motif of Toby's and Claudine's favourite film ever since their childhood. No doubt the ending of the film, an interstellar voyage that led to transformation, had meant more to them than I cared to discuss with Judith.

Afterwards I asked if she would like to go for a drink, but felt relieved when she declined. I suspected that we'd said all we should say to each other. I saw her to her car, but she refused to be assisted into it. I drove home to a house that felt as empty as I did — as I thought the funeral had been. At least this let me believe that Toby and his family were safe elsewhere, which ought to be as reassuring as the emptiness of Starview Tower. I had yet to realise how that emptiness invited visitation, unless the tower itself did.

I found out days later. A portable radio was keeping me company in the bathroom while I took a shower that felt like yet another meaningless ritual. I had the local news on, mostly to catch the newsreader's offences against language: grevious, heinious, on behalf of she and her husband... They brought back Lesley's weary resignation at the linguistic standards of the latest student intake. Sometimes she'd thought usage was reverting to a state before it had been shaped by rules. I was trying to recall when she'd said this — I wanted to fix all my memories of her — when a news item made me turn off the shower to listen. A group of activists calling themselves Hearts Released had moved dozens of homeless people into Starview Tower.

"Mustn't," I protested so fiercely that it left coherence behind. By the time I'd finished showering I was resolved to intervene, and as soon as I was dressed I hurried to my car. Was the car park beneath the tower still accessible? The prospect of descending into the subterranean dimness, if indeed it wasn't wholly dark down there, didn't appeal to me, and I parked near the ferry terminal. As I made for Starview Tower I saw the glass doors had acquired notices apparently signifying possession. The swollen top floor loomed over me, and I could have fancied that its shadow felt like an omen if not a hint of its lingering power. It seemed to darken the lobby as I read the handwritten posters taped to the doors, H♥RTS RELE♥SED ARE HERE and PROPERTY RECL♥IMED BY H♥RTS RELE♥SED. I was trying to decide what the inverted symbol suggested to me when a woman strode across the lobby to scrutinise me through the glass. "Help?" she said.

She might have been offering aid or asking if I needed it, unless she wanted to learn whether I represented some. She was a small but brawny person in dungarees and work boots, with a squarish face topped by a grey practically hairless scalp. Her bare arms swarmed with tattoos of hearts, and she was gripping her hipbones with splayed stubby fingers. I'd heard an interviewee on the radio who sounded much like her, and so I risked saying "Denny Muldoon?"

"Me." As I wondered how monosyllabic she might prove to be Denny Muldoon said "On your own?"

While she could have thought I was seeking accommodation, I suspected she was checking if I meant to lead a raid. I gestured around me at the pavement occupied only by shadow. "Here by myself, yes. May I come in?"

"Let us know a bit about you. What's brought you here?"

"Concern. My concern for your people." I wished I didn't need almost to shout to be heard through the glass. "I know you have opponents, but I'm not one of them," I said. "Please believe me when I say this isn't a good place."

An expansively bearded man in a business outfit – striped suit, equally frayed white shirt and tie – emerged from a lift and strode over. "It's good for us," he said.

"Don't you know what happened up there?"

"Certainly we do," Denny Muldoon said. "Hundreds of people wished themselves dead. We feel for every one of them. It's government policy that's driving people to suicide, and we're dedicated to saving them."

"Not by housing them where there was a mass suicide." Desperation raised my voice still further. "How do you think that could affect their minds?"

"We feel wanted," the man said, "for a change."

"By this lady and her friends, I realise that, but I'm certain there are other empty properties around town that could be opened up."

"We're wanted by the Hearts, but not just them. By this place."

Perhaps it was a shadow on the glass that made his and Denny

Muldoon's eyes look unnaturally blank. "Is that honestly all it makes you feel?" I said.

"You sound like you hope there's worse," Denny Muldoon said. "Just who are you anyway?"

"My name's Sheldrake." I was seeing Toby's vacant body next to his departed family as I said "My son died here."

"Then we're genuinely sorry, but surely that's shown you how desperate people can get. Why wouldn't you want to support them all you can?"

"Desperation didn't make him do it, not the kind you mean. He led the whole thing. Didn't you read what he posted online?"

Denny Muldoon let go of her right hip to plant the hand on the door while she squinted more closely at me. "Did you say Sheldrake?"

"That's my son's name and his family's, and—"

"Not him. Didn't you blow a whistle on the people who used to run the church here?"

"I did, and so did—"

"We know, your friend Roberta Parkin. The woman who said every squatter should be housed in jail."

"Bobby said a lot of things. Some of what she said about this church led to her death. Believe me, she was as tough as her writing, but it didn't save her. That ought to show you how much power the church had, and I promise you that hasn't gone away."

As I regretted having characterised this as a promise the man said "Hope you will."

"That's Michael's choice," Denny Muldoon said of him, "and it'll be everyone's."

"I'm trying to help," I protested. "I want to make sure nobody here ends up like my son."

"You can help by leaving us alone. All you're doing is disturbing our peace."

"What kind of peace can you find in there?" I pleaded, though it came out as a yell.

"Seeing all the stars at night," bearded Michael said. "Up top they're everywhere you look. Some of us haven't seen that many ever in our lives or all the patterns they make."

As I searched for an objection it might be worth putting into words, Denny Muldoon said "Now we've got better things to do than listen to you any more, Mr Sheldrake. Hang about there all you like but you won't be getting in. We've kept worse than you out in our time."

"You ought to be afraid what you're keeping in," I shouted, but they were already making for the lifts, and didn't turn. Once they were out of sight I tried walking at the doors in case the mechanism might acknowledge me, but all my lurches didn't even earn a twitch. When I retreated at last I felt as if the shadow of the tower kept hold of me longer than it should. I was anxious to speak to someone about the situation, but not while I was so close. I took refuge in my car and drove home.

I listened to the radio and looked online before making the call, but there were no updates about Starview Tower. At least I had a direct number, and soon I was saying "Can I speak to Inspector Deacon? It's Dominic Sheldrake."

I'd begun to wonder how unwelcome my call was when a brisk voice said "Deacon."

"You'll remember me, won't you? You interviewed me about Starview Tower."

"That case is closed, Mr Sheldrake. I take it you've no fresh evidence."

"Not evidence exactly, but it's starting up again. You'll know about the people who've moved in."

"We do, but I don't know what you mean by starting up."

"I'm saying there shouldn't be anyone in there. It's affecting them how you'd expect."

"How would that be, Mr Sheldrake?"

"Affecting their minds. They're already susceptible, so how couldn't it? It made your colleagues take their own lives, you remember."

"Their beliefs did that, but it's not a matter for discussion."

"Forgive me for intruding, but I could tell you were upset about them. Do you really want people breaking in where they died? I'd say at the very least it's disrespectful."

"Maybe bringing new life there is what it needs." Before I could start to argue, though in a sense her words struck me as unnervingly accurate, she said "In any case it isn't up to us to judge. The situation is being monitored, and it will be dealt with as appropriate."

"It wasn't when I was there less than an hour ago."

Her voice rediscovered briskness. "What were you doing there?"

"Seeing for myself. Seeing what they're up to where my son died."

Perhaps this sounded like a bid for sympathy if not for special consideration, because she said only "What did you see?"

"Denny Muldoon and one of the people she thinks she's taking care of. And I saw how they're both under the spell of that place. They absolutely refused to accept anything was wrong, and that shows how much is."

"Mr Sheldrake…" Inspector Deacon hardly needed to add "I think maybe you're as much affected by the place as anyone."

"How can you say that? Have you been to see yourself?"

"Not yet." With too little of a pause to let me speak she said "I appreciate you're still concerned because of your son. You may like to know the eviction process has been started."

"How long will it take?"

"I'm afraid I couldn't tell you that."

"They ought to destroy the whole place. Not Denny Muldoon and her people, whoever wants to be responsible. There've been cases where crime sites have been demolished, haven't there? Even the rubble was taken away so nobody could steal any souvenirs."

"I hope you aren't planning anything like that, Mr Sheldrake."

"I want nothing to do with it." I was belatedly nervous of reminding her how the Nobles' house had been destroyed, since I might still be a suspect. "I'm saying the authorities should," I said. "Is there any chance you could let me know when the eviction goes ahead?"

"You should follow the media reports." In case this was insufficiently pointed she said "I'd advise staying away from the scene. I'm sure you wouldn't want to obstruct proceedings or risk arrest."

I could have taken this as an excuse to stay well clear, and for a while I did. Over the next few days the radio reported that supporters of Hearts Released were picketing Starview Tower, opposing a police cordon that prevented access. Calls about the situation overwhelmed the lunchtime phone-in show, some encouraging the council to send bailiffs in, owners of nearby businesses complaining that their trade had suffered, local politicians blaming homelessness on the government, even unofficial tenants of the tower, who said they hadn't slept so well since they could remember and who hoped to have more dreams of the sort that were visiting them. They fell short of describing those, and I preferred not to imagine them. Just the same, I felt someone should enquire into the nature of these dreams, and almost rang the station to suggest a reporter should.

I managed to restrain myself from any kind of intervention until the morning when the bathroom radio reported clashes between protestors and police outside Starview Tower. What might violence at the building summon or arouse? I felt compelled to see the worst, and hurried out as soon as I was dressed. I believed I was acting on my instincts, but some influence must have dulled them. Otherwise they might have given me at least a hint that I was heading for the end I'd foreseen ever since my childhood.

CHAPTER TWENTY-FIVE

The Elevation

I was about to use my car when I locked it and headed for the gate. The police knew the registration number from the night the Nobles' house had been destroyed, and I didn't want them to confront me before I reached Starview Tower, let alone cut me off. Perhaps that was unlikely, in which case some instinct that couldn't make itself plain had attempted to delay me. At the gate I thought of taking Lesley's car, but using it for subterfuge felt unworthy of her memory, close to betrayal. I'd already involved her enough in deceit and untruth. On the bus into town I refrained from checking my phone for the latest news, instead gazing out at a sky so colourlessly nondescript it resembled a denial of its own existence. If I'd driven, might I have been in time to do any kind of good? I suspect I would always have been too late, and worse.

As I limped along the main road past the waterfront I heard shouts and breaking glass. Among the skyscrapers the top of Starview Tower stretched wide as though to haul the vacant sky lower still. Before I came in sight of the entrance to the tower I saw police directing traffic away from that stretch of the road. Perhaps I looked too purposeful, since the policeman diverting the traffic gave me a glance sharp enough to suggest he meant to redirect me too. Even when I was well past him I felt watched, although all the visible spectators were intent on developments at Starview Tower.

Beyond the tower a policeman was rerouting traffic at a junction, leaving several hundred yards of the wide road clear. At least a dozen police vehicles – cars and large vans – were parked near the tower. An audience had gathered on the pavement opposite, above which offices were full of watchers. Just now Denny Muldoon was entertaining them. "These are people," I heard her shout. "They're as much people as you are."

The glass doors of Starview Tower had been shattered. Police, some of them in riot gear, were leading pickets and squatters to the vans. Most of those in custody appeared to be miming resignation, but there was the odd flurry of a struggle and a disorganised chant of "Homes not cells." The pavement was strewn with placards, more of which were propped on flimsy shafts against the tower, and as I ventured closer I made out slogans: **GIVE THEM A HOUSE**, **ACELERATE ACOMODATION FOR ALL, DONT LEAVE THEM FLAT WITH NO FLAT**... I couldn't locate Denny Muldoon until she gave another shout. "He started it. That's him."

She was at an open office window just above the entrance, and she was pointing at me. As any number of police and captives turned their heads in my direction I protested "This is nothing to do with me."

My voice sounded smaller than hers, shrunken not just by the looming overcast but by a nervous suspicion that I'd told less than the truth. Did I have my call to Inspector Deacon in mind? I couldn't see her anywhere, and in any case I had an inkling that I was somehow otherwise responsible. "You tried to get rid of our people," Denny Muldoon was shouting. "You wanted us gone."

"Only from up there. I don't mean to deny anyone a home."

I wished I could stop responding, since everything I called out made me feel more watched. Of course there were dozens if not hundreds of observers, but I had a sense of an altogether more unwelcome presence that had yet to be revealed. I was pathetically glad when two policemen wrestled Denny Muldoon away from the window, except that the sight infuriated many of her supporters. "Get your fucking hands off her, you cunts," a woman yelled.

The possibility of violence brought me close to an undefined panic. My mouth grew dry and my breaths faltered while I waited for Denny Muldoon and her captors to appear. When they emerged from a lift, each policeman grasping one of her arms, she looked composed enough. As they stepped out of Starview Tower a glass shard splintered underfoot, but otherwise there was a silence that paralysed my breath. The police were escorting Denny Muldoon towards the vehicles when the woman who had shouted on her behalf wrenched herself free of the officer holding her arm and ran to grab a placard on a pole. Before anyone could intervene she set about bludgeoning Denny Muldoon's captors, and I was terrified, however imprecisely, where this might lead. "Don't," I cried.

All her supporters who weren't already in the vans tried to surge towards her as the police formed a cordon. A pair of riot officers disarmed the woman with the placard, and as they dragged her to a van I made for Denny Muldoon, hoping desperately that I could persuade her to forbid any further mayhem near Starview Tower. I was almost sure its shadow was expanding, not with any movement of the sun, which was hidden by the congealed sky. Was the unnatural gloom why Denny Muldoon's hands looked wrong? She'd clenched her fists, but I could easily have thought her hands had atrophied, reverting to foetal lumps of flesh. I wasn't close enough to address her except by shouting when a policeman barred my way. "If you aren't involved here, sir, please move on."

This sounded like more than one compacted threat, but it wasn't why I recoiled. I had an outlandish impression that he was poised to tower over me – to turn scrawny as he sprouted taller, elongating and narrowing his head. "I've gone," I blurted and backed away, striving to hold the sight of him unchanged. When he extended a hand, presumably to speed me onwards, I fancied that I glimpsed the fingers growing not just longer but of equal length, the thumb as well. I was afraid that I was somehow causing the transformation. If it was illusory, as I fervently hoped it was, this still meant I was the focus. I forced myself to turn away and fled.

I felt as if the shadow of the tower was keeping pace with me. When I glanced back a swollen blemish was taking shape on the sky above the roof. Surely it was just a mass of dark clouds and wholly unrelated to the tower. It might be a sign of an imminent storm, which was another reason to hurry home. Perhaps it explained why there were so few people or vehicles on the wide main road, though I supposed they could have been sent away by the policeman who was diverting traffic. I couldn't recall having passed him on my return, and when I looked back there was no sign of him.

The alteration of the sky didn't much resemble storm clouds, despite its slaty gloom. As it swelled above the tower I could have thought the patch of sky was taking on more substance. I was tempted to point it out to the very few pedestrians I encountered, but they were hastening faster than me, heads bent as if they were determined to ignore the spectacle. The faces looked so downcast that I had to fend off an impression that they were about to dangle lower, and I no longer wanted to speak.

The area around the Pier Head was entirely untypically deserted. The open space enclosed by buildings both old and aggressively new intensified my sense that the sky had been invaded. Hundreds of office windows reflected the expanding mass, which made the buildings look abandoned. Here and there a face peered out, so surreptitiously that I wondered what they were looking for. Across the river I could see where the Nobles' house had been. The gap between the houses looked as dark as the activity overhead, though surely less substantial.

A few people stood in the long glass shelters of the bus station. Presumably they were watching for buses, but I felt inexplicably glad when they didn't turn to me, even if some movement on their part might have been welcome; I was close to concluding they preferred not to be noticed. Nobody was waiting at my stop, and no buses had arrived by the time I grew acutely aware of the sky above the glass roof. I thought it was swelling downwards as it darkened, and when I stepped into the open, hoping to see my mistake, I couldn't help observing that it had begun to writhe as if it contained some element that was about to grow livelier. The sight reminded me far too much of the vision of the devastated city I'd had as a child and in adulthood too. It left me feeling not just vulnerable but potentially responsible, as though my fears could let the future in. I was afraid that staying out beneath the sky might do so. In a sudden panic that gave me little chance to think, I retreated into the shelter, only to rediscover that the roof didn't obscure the view of the sky. I dashed out of the bus station with my head down, no longer caring where I went so long as it provided a refuge.

A deserted shopping plaza brought me to a department store with its glass doors open wide, and I hurried in. Once I recovered from the sight of the unnaturally bloated sky – better still, put it out of my mind – I meant to call a taxi and wait in the entrance until it showed up. I was anxious to shut myself in at home, to leave Starview Tower behind along with the events it had provoked. I could only hope my house was sufficiently distant to free me of its influence – of the threat of invoking the future I'd foreseen.

The ground floor of the shop was an extensive labyrinth of counters and displays. Merchandise surrounded me in no order I could grasp: perfumes, kitchen utensils, crockery, electrical equipment, televisions by the dozen… Some items I could scarcely make out, given the unhelpful dimness. I might have enquired why the place was so poorly lit if I'd seen anyone to ask, or were my eyes or my mind to blame? I headed for the televisions, which ought to lend me some illumination while I waited to feel equal to venturing outside again. All of them were silenced, and every one was showing footage of a film about a war zone if not a city devastated by some other disaster. A subtitle was gliding off the screens, but I caught the single word **WORLDWIDE**. I was growing uneasier than I cared to define when I noticed a man, presumably a sales assistant, in the furthest aisle of screens. "Excuse me," I called, "what's happening there, do you know?"

He was turning towards me when I began to wish he would do nothing of the kind. Far from growing more prominent as it came, his profile appeared to be shrinking, the long sharp nose and outthrust chin dwindling by the instant. On the whole I was glad of the dimness, which prevented me to some extent from seeing his face. If only this had been the solitary reason that I couldn't make it out – but as he confronted me across the screens displaying desolation I saw his face implode, sucked inwards like a rubber mask turned inside out. Before the features disappeared into the bulb of flesh perched on the neck he thrust out a hand, if very little of one. As the fingers swiftly atrophied I realised he was pointing the rudimentary lump at the end of his arm at me.

The sight was just a vision, I tried to tell myself: some kind of obscure omen that my question had called up. If the gesture was an answer, I didn't want to understand. Surely the spectacle was at worst a symptom of the influence the Nobles still exerted over me, a depiction of the primal state they wished upon humanity for their own occult purposes. The virtually featureless shape in a suit began to grope its way along the far aisle, halting in confusion as a screen toppled to the floor and shaking its remnant of a head as though desperate to bring its face back to the surface. I couldn't bear its blind approach, let alone the threat of being touched by those worse than embryonic hands, and I fled.

The nearest exit was on the opposite side of the store from the way I'd come in. As I limped between the screens and their catastrophic vistas, I saw that the gloom wasn't simply dimness. It was crawling up the walls and across the floor like accelerated lichen, coating any lights that it hadn't extinguished. I was nowhere near the exit when the walls began to crumble with an insidious whisper of pulverised concrete. I felt as if the future I'd envisioned was racing to engulf the present, and had a dreadful notion that I'd attracted it somehow. It made me desperate, however irrationally, to be in the open once more. I was terrified that the increasing darkness might leave me no less blind than the follower I heard blundering along an aisle behind me. Even the exit doors had grown so grimy that I couldn't see through them. I had to wrench them apart, bruising my fingers, in order to struggle between them. I was so relieved to be outside, away from the pursuer in the dark, that for a moment I didn't grasp what I was seeing, and then I gave a cry that used up all my breath.

Most of the city was gone. The jagged lower storeys of collapsed buildings as incomplete as tree-stumps huddled under an engorged sky. The streets and the spaces between buildings were strewn with blackened rubble. I was striving to convince myself all this was no more than a vision when the store I'd just left began to sag and groan. As I retreated the walls crumpled, falling away from me but filling my nostrils with brick dust. The screech of tortured metal, peals of glass, huge thumps of chunks of concrete deafened me. The spectacle seemed far too vivid for the vision I yearned to believe it was, and so did the rubble that caught at my feet as I staggered backwards. I was surrounded by desolation with no idea where I could go. It stretched out of sight on every side, and I had no reason to assume it ended at the horizon. As I stared about in utter desperation I caught sight of movement across the river.

The destruction of the city gave me a direct view of the site of the Nobles' house. The gap was no longer all its neighbours framed. A crouching shape reared up as though my attention had brought it to life. At that distance it resembled a malformed spider, which scuttled down the slope to the promenade and leapt over the railings onto the beach. In a moment it was bounding with all its limbs across the river at a speed that suggested a determination to move too fast to sink.

I tried to stand my ground, even if only out of hopelessness. I didn't know what the Nobles could do to me that they hadn't already done, or to the world. The shape vanished before scrambling up the sea wall, and then it sprang onto the ravaged waterfront and rushed towards me as though to overwhelm its enemy if not to greet an old acquaintance. Its three faces swelled wide as they merged, and all its eyes crawled in and out of one another while its mouths combined to produce an enormous parody of a grin. I managed not to waver until it extended a spindly limb that might have been about to caress my head or penetrate my skull. Either prospect was more than I could stand, and I fled towards the only refuge I could see, the solitary intact building: Starview Tower.

No doubt I should have realised that the presence at my back was herding me towards the tower. Perhaps the mouths had separated, since a trio of voices was repeating the occult name I'd originally heard at the Trinity Church of the Spirit. They crowded into my brain, overlapping and transmuting the syllables into a form beyond definition, which drove out of my head the last of my ability to think. I could only concentrate on keeping my balance while I dodged through the rubble that was strewn across the desolate road all the way to Starview Tower.

The entrance was still doorless. As I limped towards it I glanced back. My pursuer was dancing on all its attenuated limbs and thrusting out its heads on a trinity of necks. The features had found their heads, but with an awful haphazardness that distributed the eyes unequally and dislocated the exultant mouths. When the heads snaked at me, weaving patterns in the air, I fled into the tower.

Was there any point in continuing to flee? No doubt the Nobles would follow wherever I went, to my death if not beyond. My dread outdistanced any thoughts of this kind, indeed any thoughts at all, and I stumbled to the lifts. Perhaps only confusion led me to expect them to be functioning, but when I jabbed a button, the indicator light responded. As soon as a lift opened I lurched in. I was prodding the topmost button when the misshapen mass of flesh scampered across the lobby, waving its heads in glee while the mismatched sets of eyes bulged unequally wide to feast on my plight. I was glad that the doors shut out its approach, but I should have known nothing in their world would hinder the Nobles. The lift had scarcely begun its ascent when I heard a large object land on the cable and clamber upwards, making the lift quiver. I saw all my reflections hug themselves as if they were trying to shrink into invisibility, and then I heard the voices of my shepherds. "Go and see."

If even worse was to be seen, I didn't want to know. I poked frantically at the buttons for every floor I had yet to reach and the ones I'd passed, but the lift didn't hesitate. It didn't even halt at the highest floor, instead continuing to rise until it came to rest in an enclosure on the roof. I retreated from the doors as they crept open, and attempted to hide among my unhelpful reflections in a corner. Beyond the doors

I saw only the unnaturally active sky, and I was hoping to see no worse when I heard an object squeeze against the wall behind me and extend its limbs on every side. It felt as if a flattened but hideously vital spider was about to close itself around me. However senseless my panic was, it drove me out onto the roof.

The high place showed me everything I'd feared. As far as I could see in all directions, the world was a ruin. No building stood more than a few floors high, and very few had roofs. Whatever event had demolished them appeared to have erased most of the vegetation. Here and there I saw a withered drooping clump of trees, and had a sense that they were composed of little more than ash or dust, clinging together to sketch a recollection of their outlines – that they might collapse if this dead world weren't so breathlessly devoid of wind. The change that had begun above the tower was at least as wide as the horizon now. The entire sky had grown as lurid as the preamble to a storm, and was swelling like a mass of eggs about to hatch. I felt my skin start to crawl and twitch in sympathy, and I might have sought refuge in the lift if my monstrous guide hadn't squeezed out of the concrete box to sprawl on the roof of the tower, bloating plump in instants and rearing up to gesture at me with its trinity of heads. "Ready," said all the mouths in unison.

I didn't know whether it was referring to itself or me, but the word sounded like an invitation to a dreadful game. The composite monstrosity was blocking my way to the lift, which in any case was no more than an illusion of escape. Just the same, my only way out was down, and perhaps I knew what that had to mean. I stumbled across the roof to the parapet, which was no higher than my waist. I would fall on some of the jagged rubble that was scattered all around the tower, which made the prospect seem more painful. Even if this was as craven as it was ridiculous – it only mattered that the fall should be fatal – did I really believe my bid to end the nightmare would be final? Perhaps the shape towering at my back was the triple-headed guardian of the afterlife, eager to conduct me into its version of the underworld. If I could never escape it, what reason did I have to hesitate? I was about to climb onto the parapet if my worn-out body would let me, though it might be more efficient to lean out too far, when I glimpsed movement at the edge of the world.

Had a remnant of the mundane survived after all? At the far edge of the bay lanky windmills were still active, though the sky hung so close to them that the motion of their vanes was apparent only as a disturbance within the gloomily luminous clouds. I was about to embrace this inconsequential shred of reassurance that the world hadn't entirely changed when I saw my mistake. The clouds weren't obscuring any vanes, and the activity above the rim of the bay belonged to none. It was just an aspect of the restlessness that had infected the whole of the sky, and the thin shafts buried in its substance weren't windmills. I was struggling to cling to misperception – at any rate to believe that I was only suffering another vision – when the presence that had usurped the sky lifted itself on the shafts and the rest of its myriad limbs that rose all around the horizon. At least they were in the distance, which might have left me some pathetic comfort if they hadn't set about groping towards me from every side of the dead landscape.

When I dodged around my hideous companion on the roof it made no move to hinder me. I should have recognised how ominous this was, but I was desperate for refuge. I had a wild hope that the one-way windows at the top of Starview Tower could hide me. I sprinted into the lift and poked the button for that floor, but the door stayed wide. However much I bruised my finger, the door didn't stir. I retreated to a corner, where I was surrounded by a mob with my face, each emitting a scream as silent as mine. I was trying to crouch lower and smaller despite all the pains this entailed when two appallingly elongated limbs reached into the lift for me.

They were translucent and gelatinous, grey as slugs and no thicker than a baby's arm. Their substance looked restless with eagerness, twitching with a rapid intermittent pulse. The conical tips crawled along the side walls of the lift, slithering over innumerable multiplications of my petrified face, and I was wondering how long I could avoid them – I was preparing with an awful weariness to try – when they sprang off the mirrors with a sound like a moist kiss and came straight for me. I wanted both to dodge and close my eyes, but had no time. In a moment the thin tips plunged into my eyes and fumbled deep into my brain.

I felt them swell and merge with it. I had a sense that they were transmuting the whole of me into their substance or else draining me into themselves – not my body but my essence. The sensation of hatching that had almost overcome me when I'd last visited Safe To Sleep had caught up with me at last. Before I could struggle, however I might have, I felt myself drawn out of my body as if it were an egg if not a chrysalis. In a moment, though time seemed to have lost all significance, I was elevated high above the world.

I was no longer Dominic Sheldrake. I was an insignificant aspect of the entity that had encircled the world to feed upon every scrap of life it still harboured – to aid the planet in taking its minuscule role in the reversion of the universe. Even that entity was no more than a minor participant in the eternal cycle, the cosmos returning to its primal state in order to give birth to new and unimaginable kinds of life beside forms recalled only in myth, perhaps together with a recurrence of humanity on their little globe. Perhaps the entity in all its vastness was only a function of the process. All this knowledge and a great deal more came to me in an instant, and I was further overwhelmed by using the entire sky to perceive the world, less like a gigantic eye than as the organ of an amalgam of inhuman senses. It was very nearly too much for my consciousness, which felt simultaneously dwarfed and expanded by the colossal intelligence of which I was an atom. I'd passed beyond terror and awe – I seemed to have no option other than to shrink into acceptance – but some residue of my personality made my awareness loiter near Starview Tower, clinging to that last trace of familiarity. I was wondering if I might be afforded a sight of whatever remained of me on the roof, if anything did, when I sensed movement near the tower. Someone was trying to hide.

Perhaps my perceptions were so acute because they had only just been fully wakened. If adding them to the monstrous consciousness had helped it locate its prey, I felt shamefully proud. Tendrils of which I had become a part stalked across the dead city to close around a house in the middle of a terrace that had retained some of its roofs. All the windows of the house had been blocked up from within, a betraying detail. Our tendrils dislodged rubble from the frames and stretched into the house, where they showed us a ragged grimy man cowering in a corner of a derelict room. Before they reached him he bolted out of the house, almost sprawling over wreckage as he fled. We had many tendrils ready for him, but we let him dodge like a rat through the maze of desolation while we relished his invigorating terror. For a time we kept a tendril poised above him, and at last extended it to pierce his skull.

I was only distantly reminded how tendrils had entered Dominic Sheldrake's head, whoever that had been. We feasted on the man's terror and his essence, leaving just enough of a mind within the withered remnant to send it jigging through the ruined city in a helpless convulsion of panic. A frisson of pleasure at the spectacle and at consuming a life passed through our body that cocooned the world. Eventually the shrivelled victim fell to crawling on all fours and then to writhing on its emaciated belly until it found a patch of mud. As it wormed out of sight the transformed earth grew visibly eager to help it on its way – hungry to revert to the primordial state that would redefine life.

My senses were continuing to expand. I embraced other hunts that were taking place, countries and continents apart. The elation I'd experienced at helping track down and pursue the first victim felt like attaining a height, a vantage Sheldrake could never have begun to imagine. It must relate to being elevated above the prey as the alternative to becoming one, but why should that matter? Lesley was gone, and Toby too, taking his wife and daughter with him. The Nobles had done away with Bobby and Jim, and so the searching tendrils could find nobody I cared about. If the prey were anything more than infinitesimal elements in the progress of the cosmos, they were simply objects of sport, robbed of individuality by the terror that was all their little minds could hold.

The dismissal didn't quite convince me. It belonged to the entity that had reduced me to an aspect of itself; it wasn't mine. Even if the victims were utter strangers to me, whatever race they were and of whatever creed, they were human. My memories of family and friends had restored a sense of myself that hadn't quite been engulfed, and I grew conscious of Starview Tower. My awareness focused on it – on the deformed mass the Nobles had become, roaming back and forth on the roof. All their eyes were turned up to me, and a single grin stretched across the entire width of the bunched heads. Perhaps it expressed triumph, or even satisfaction that they'd brought me at last to my appointed place.

They'd appointed it, I thought. In some way they'd used me to help bring about the future they were bound for. Loathing overwhelmed me, not just of them and all that they incarnated but of myself. I'd agreed to a bargain I had lacked the courage even to define – to join the predator so as not to be a victim, to deny my humanity in order to scapegoat the human. I began to struggle to wield a tendril, to skewer whatever was left of me on the roof and drain it of everything but terror. I had to think this would return me to my body, and however dreadful my fate would be, remaining complicit with the feaster on the world was infinitely worse.

I'd gained no physical control when I was flung into a void. I felt as if my thoughts had caused me to be cast out, unless I'd been ejected just for staying stubbornly human. I sensed something like contempt, although by no means as definable, so enormous it seemed cosmic. In addition somebody, if that term was even remotely appropriate, was disappointed in me – the Nobles, as though a prize pupil or an item they'd chosen to display had let them down. For a moment all this helped define how human I'd managed to remain, and then I knew nothing at all.

CHAPTER TWENTY-SIX

Gone Back

"Watch out, you old twat."

"Try looking where you're going."

"Does he know where he is?"

A loud loose thunder had produced three voices. My head was as wet as a baptised infant's, and once I grew aware of this I grasped that I could see. I was one of an indeterminate number of people who had been herded into an enclosure whose translucent walls writhed like restless flesh. No, we were in a bus shelter that was blurred like my vision by the downpour drumming on the roof. I must have stumbled out into the rain, perhaps almost in front of a bus as it arrived at the shelter. Presumably someone had rescued me or at least pushed me out of their way to let them board, and as I blinked about me in bewilderment, passengers crowded onto the bus. The last of them was finding a seat when the driver stared at me. "Do you want this?"

His was the last of the voices I'd heard. I rubbed my eyes clear of water with a hand that felt as though it was rediscovering its use. A narrow screen above the entrance to the bus displayed a number, and I struggled to understand its significance. Once I succeeded in recognising it I found words. "That's me."

"Don't keep us waiting, pal."

I did while I recalled the need for a travel pass and found mine. Having fumbled the card onto the reader in his cabin, I lurched along the aisle as the driver sent the single-decker forward. I had to quell my progress by grabbing a metal pole, which let me collapse on a seat beside a woman with an obtrusively outspread handbag. I might have welcomed her presence if it had helped me return to myself. More rain met the bus as it emerged from the terminal, but the world looked no more distorted and unstable than I felt. I hoped any difficulties I was experiencing with my eyes could be blamed on the downpour, but I had an awful notion that they might consist of more than their own substance – that I could. Even if I was able to believe where I was now, I had no idea of when. I groped for my phone and peered uneasily at the screen.

It was still the same day, and apparently not much later in the afternoon than I'd retreated from the confrontation at Starview Tower, Hearts Released and their supporters opposing the police. All this felt hardly real, any more than the local news feed I brought up. The last of the squatters had been evicted from Starview Tower, and police were ensuring nobody could enter. I was trying to judge what if any difference this made when I realised my seatmate was reading the screen. "Got them out, have they?" she said. "Good riddance and hope we don't see any more of them."

"I wonder if something else will take their place."

"Shouldn't leave places empty, then." As I tried not to feel personally accused she said "Maybe it can still be a church."

I wondered how much knowledge her comment involved, or what proportion of ignorance. She wasn't helping to anchor me in the present, and I tried to concentrate on the journey, the abrupt stops and jerky recommencements of the bus, the passengers inhabiting the worlds of their own phones, even the smeary view the windows admitted, veiled by breaths on the panes as well as rain. None of this convinced me much, and by the time I reached my stop I could have concluded the world was so temporary and vulnerable it wasn't worth calling it real.

Trees anointed me with raindrops as I trudged through the suburb. The storm had moved on, but I felt as if its residue were tapping for admission to my skull. Although I'd had far worse invade my brain, this was an unwelcome reminder of how exposed it was. The sensation pursued me all the way home. In the drive Lesley's car rested next to mine, both glittering with beads of rain. As I let myself into the house I wondered who would dispose of them and so much else, a concern

I found irrelevantly banal. Perhaps it was a last bid to engage with the mundane, to hold myself back.

The house felt no more substantial than I did, nor any less impermanent. I limped straight to my desk and began to record the most recent events of my life. I could only be thankful that I'd already set most of this down. For a long time I'd imagined I would be addressing my descendants, helping them understand whatever they needed to grasp and warning them, but Macy was gone with her parents, leaving nobody to follow me. Subsequently I'd been trying to secure myself, to fend off the pull of the past and the future and where they both led, a ruse that hadn't worked. Even if my genes led nowhere after me, the Nobles had already shaped my future. No wonder Toph had told me I was theirs when they wanted. Starview Tower was cleared, but that had never been the focus of the future the Nobles were born to herald and to cultivate. The name of the focus was Dominic Sheldrake.

Had Toby suspected this at the last? Perhaps that was one reason why he'd tried so hard to persuade me to join the retreat before Claudine had reassured him, but I would never know. Deep within myself I felt a stirring of nostalgia for the hunt I'd taken part in – for being elevated above humanity and the world, no doubt as a preamble to viewing greater secrets of the universe. The longing appalled me more than the hunt itself had, and I was afraid to delay any further. I felt sure the Nobles would come for me again. However much they'd found me wanting, that wouldn't be their only bid to lodge me in the future they lived to achieve. Returning me to it might even be their notion of an honour rather than a revenge, a grotesque celebration of how intertwined our lives had been.

Death in the ordinary sense wouldn't rescue me from them. I would be more at their mercy than ever. I had to follow Toby's lead, though not my son himself. I mustn't invade his eternal refuge or anybody else's, in case this put them at risk. Suppose my experiences at Safe To Sleep and at the Church of the Eternal Three had left me capable of finding him? There was far too much I didn't understand, and I couldn't take the chance. Even thinking about him or anyone I'd lost might take me dangerously close to joining them – dangerous because of what I might bring to them.

I was unable to refrain from looking in my desk for a last reminder. The stack of tales of the Tremendous Three had grown precarious, and I lined up the volumes, feeling as if I was tidying the past into a preferable shape. "We always did," I murmured when the sight recalled the vow I'd made with Bobby and Jim. The transcription of Christian Noble's journal was piled beside the stories, scarcely distinguishable from them. However innocent it looked, it felt eager to call up the author and his brood, and I shut the drawer at once.

I had no reason to delay any longer. I strove to put the Nobles out of my mind before they could head me off. Even saying now that I did so feels capable of bringing them. I can only hope — yes, pray — that I'm able to accomplish what Toby and the others did without having seen exactly how. The night of *Macbeth* has to be my destination, my most vivid memory that need involve nobody else, because we were waiting for each other miles apart across a town I might no longer recognise. "When shall we three meet again..." I mustn't let that recall my friends, and I mustn't summon Lesley into my refuge either. "If you can look into the seeds of time..." That was one of her favourite quotations, but in my case the trick would be to avoid seeing the future — any of the futures I've seen. Waiting for her will be enough, even if I know she mustn't come. Eternal anticipation will be its own kind of paradise when I know I'm keeping her safe, and protecting who can say how many others too. Everlasting hope is my reward, and for that I have to be alone. May that keep me out of reach of the Nobles and their eager future — even hinder it, perhaps. May anyone who reads this find it of some use. Perhaps I am after all.

Material retrieved during search for content about Gahariet Le Bon
Fiction content undetermined
Relevance to be established
Archived 21 March, Third Year of the Transformation

ACKNOWLEDGEMENTS

Jenny was there first, as ever. Perhaps in the case of this trilogy I should say almost first (though anything but second best), since without our good friend Pete Crowther the books would never have been conceived. Paul Finch must not be held responsible for any of my inventions in this volume, based upon advice and information he kindly gave.

Like most of my books, this went on its travels. It was worked on at the Myeongdong Ibis Style hotel in Seoul, our well-loved favourite the Deep Blue Sea apartments in Georgioupolis on Crete, and over Fantasycon in Peterborough.

Once again Keith Ravenscroft kept me supplied with recherché films on disc – some of my well-nigh daily rewards for finishing work.

FLAME TREE PRESS
FICTION WITHOUT FRONTIERS
Award-Winning Authors & Original Voices

Flame Tree Press is the trade fiction imprint of Flame Tree Publishing, focusing on excellent writing in horror and the supernatural, crime and mystery, science fiction and fantasy. Our aim is to explore beyond the boundaries of the everyday, with tales from both award-winning authors and original voices.

•

The First Two Books of the *Three Births of Daoloth* series:
The Searching Dead
Born to the Dark

Other titles available by Ramsey Campbell:
Thirteen Days by Sunset Beach
Think Yourself Lucky
The Hungry Moon
The Influence
The Wise Friend
Somebody's Voice

Other horror and suspense titles available include:
Snowball by Gregory Bastianelli
The Haunting of Henderson Close by Catherine Cavendish
The Garden of Bewitchment by Catherine Cavendish
The House by the Cemetery by John Everson
The Devil's Equinox by John Everson
Hellrider by JG Faherty
The Toy Thief by D.W. Gillespie
One By One by D.W. Gillespie
Black Wings by Megan Hart
The Playing Card Killer by Russell James
The Sorrows by Jonathan Janz
Will Haunt You by Brian Kirk
We Are Monsters by Brian Kirk
Hearthstone Cottage by Frazer Lee
Those Who Came Before by J.H. Moncrieff
Stoker's Wilde by Steven Hopstaken & Melissa Prusi
Creature by Hunter Shea
Ghost Mine by Hunter Shea
Slash by Hunter Shea

•

Join our mailing list for free short stories, new release details, news about our authors and special promotions:

flametreepress.com